Praise for *Fellowship Point*

"Longing for an old-fashioned nineteenth-century novel—but without the time travel? *Fellowship Point* earns its nearly 600 pages with a quietly complex structure, starring two octogenarian women whose long friendship is entangled with their families' landholdings in coastal Maine. As they seek to save the acreage from development, Agnes Lee and Polly Wister must also confront their past choices and find some peace in the present."

—*Los Angeles Times*, 10 Books for July

"An engrossing, relatable tale about female friendship and the growing pains of long relationships."

—*Real Simple*

"Marvelous. . . . Reading this novel is a transportive experience, similar to spending a long, luxurious summer on the shores of a picturesque Maine peninsula."

—Alice Cary, *BookPage* (starred review)

"A sweeping story of lifelong best friends . . . you will surely want to read this book. Elegantly structured, beautifully written, and altogether diverting, with a powerful message about land ownership in America."

—*Kirkus Reviews* (starred review)

"Each of Dark's captivating narrators is even more than she seems, while the history of *Fellowship Point* is a microcosm of the conflict between human desires versus ecological viability. Capacious, psychologically fluent, funny, and intricately and meaningfully plotted, Dark's novel of love, trauma, guilt, and justice explores women's struggles, the devaluing of nature, and how stories are told and by whom."

—Donna Seaman, *Booklist* (starred review)

"Dark celebrates women's friendships and artistic mentorship in this expansive yet intimate novel. The families and their grudges and grievances fill a broad canvas, and within it Dark delves deeply into the relationships between Agnes and her work, humans and the land, mothers and children, and, most indelibly, the sustenance and joy provided by a long-held female friendship. It's a remarkable achievement."

—*Publishers Weekly* (starred review)

"In this long-awaited novel, Alice Elliott Dark brilliantly contemplates aging, the environment, and feminism, as well as the deep, lifelong friendship between two women: a children's author who stayed single, and a well-off married woman with children."

—*New Jersey Monthly*

"[*Fellowship Point*] is very much an epic read, a book for readers who want to settle in for a story at a near whopping 600 pages by the author of one of my favorite short stories ever, 'In the Gloaming.'"

—John Searles, *New York Times* bestselling author of
Strange but True

"*Fellowship Point* is a miraculous generational saga. Alice Elliott Dark has drawn the desire lines between men and women, privilege and historical imperative, fated consequence and tragic accident. Her surprising, consummate novel goes to the heart of relationship and redefines the term 'soul mate' for these our confused, estranged times. Literature insists on hope: *Fellowship Point* will endure."

—Jayne Anne Phillips, author of *Black Tickets*,
Machine Dreams, and *Lark and Termite*

"I can't remember the last time I've fallen so hard for a book. *Fellowship Point* is about many things: friendship, secrets, legacy, love, family—but the true magic here is in the writing. Alice Elliott Dark has conjured a world so immersive I can still feel it in my bones. I mourned the finish, when I would have to leave behind the characters I grew to love. This captivating, unforgettable novel is thrillingly good."

—Cynthia D'Aprix Sweeney, *New York Times* bestselling
author of *The Nest* and *Good Company*

"*Fellowship Point* is a marvel. Intricately constructed, utterly unique, this novel set on the coast of Maine is filled with insights about writing, about the perils and freedoms of aging, about the great mysteries, as well as the pleasures, of life. The story about the relationships between three women unfolds, as life does, through joys and losses, confrontations and confessions, with twists along the way that change your perception of all that came before. This is a world is so closely and acutely observed that I felt I lived in it. I was sorry to leave."

—Christina Baker Kline, #1 *New York Times*
bestselling author

"I positively inhaled this novel—and then stingily meted out the last few pages, not wanting it to end. *Fellowship Point* is a marvel—masterfully executed, beautifully layered, huge-hearted, and sharp-witted—and Alice Elliott Dark is a writer of great empathy and incredible skill."

—Claire Lombardo, *New York Times* bestselling
author of *The Most Fun We Ever Had*

"I fell into *Fellowship Point*—fell in step and in love with its characters, with its landscape, with its ideas about art and marriage and, above all, friendship. It's a beautifully passionate book about what it means to love a place and to love all the people of your life, and how life itself is a riveting plot and deep mystery."

—Elizabeth McCracken, *New York Times* bestselling
author of *Bowlaway* and *The Giant's House*

"*Fellowship Point* is deeply relevant in its concerns—about the land, the creatures who inhabit it, and the legacies of ownership, stewardship, and friendship—but it's also just a great, absorbing, and transformative read. Like a Maine glade, Dark's book is filled with light."

—Jo Ann Beard, author of *Festival Days* and
In Zanesville

"Alice Elliott Dark is a writer I've long admired. With the splendid, engrossing *Fellowship Point* she has written a novel that is both sweeping and intimate as it deftly explores friendship, class, and the tricky nature of time."

—Meg Wolitzer, *New York Times* bestselling author of
The Female Persuasion and *The Interestings*

"This is a virtuosic performance, indisputably a work of genius, but even fervent adjectives can't capture the almost numinous effect of reading these pages. In *Fellowship Point*, one feels oneself in the rare presence of the truly sublime. Every exactly described gesture, every bit of inspired characterization, every gorgeous sentence is run through an obsessive mind grappling indefatigably with the weightiest materials: the powerful gravity of enduring relationships and the psychic costs of managing them; the sometimes-crushing conflict between duty to self and responsibility to others; and the desperate urge to conserve a small corner of a stressed-out planet and defend a worthy way of life from extinction. The equal manner in which the past and present, like overlaid supersaturated transparencies, come so vividly to bloom in one book recalls the bottomless ambitions of the timeless greats—which is fitting, as Alice Elliott Dark is one of the best writers working in English today."

—Matthew Thomas, *New York Times* bestselling
author of *We Are Not Ourselves*

"I loved *Fellowship Point* so intensely and so tremendously, I'm struggling to find words that capture its brilliance. At once a rich, deeply felt investigation of female friendship and a bold novel of ideas, *Fellowship Point* offers the most profound pleasures. It reminded me of my favorite novels—those I return to, over and over—*Great Expectations, Howards End, Middlemarch.* I wanted to live inside it forever."

—Joanna Rakoff, author of *My Salinger Year*

"I've just sat up nearly all night finishing Alice Elliott Dark's *Fellowship Point.* Dark took a decade to craft this magnificent novel, and the result is an instant classic: an epic tale of love, family, friendship, literature, and the American landscape, laid out on the capacious scale of a nineteenth-century classic, yet effortlessly contemporary in its voice. Tracing her story over decades and generations, Dark offers a portrayal of the complex inner worlds of three extraordinary women with an unerring insight that rivals that of Edith Wharton or Elena Ferrante. Replete with humor, irony, gimlet-eyed observation of social mores, and a deep underlying spirituality, it's a novel so immersive you don't just read it, but practically move into it, like one of the rambling, shingled summer 'cottages' that come to life in its pages. We readers emerge at the end with a deep nostalgia for the wind-battered pines, lingering ghosts, and imperiled eagles' nests of Dark's unforgettable Maine coast."

—Andrea Lee, author of *Red Island House*

Praise for *In the Gloaming*

"The stories achieve, in their style and beautiful detail, a wonderful clarity."

—George Saunders, author of
The Tenth of December and *Lincoln in the Bardo*

"Beautifully composed . . . each story exudes the gravitas of a radically distilled novel."

—Joyce Carol Oates, *New York Times*
bestselling author

"Dark writes with great sympathy for the complexity of ordinary lives. Her stories are like the proverbial iceberg: We look at the tip but are compelled to think about all that's hidden below."

—Anne Stephenson, author of
Making Up Is Hard to Do and *Revenge with a Twist*

MARYSUE
RUCCI
BOOKS

FELLOWSHIP

POINT

ALSO BY ALICE ELLIOTT DARK

Think of England

In the Gloaming

Naked to the Waist

FELLOWSHIP
POINT

a novel

ALICE ELLIOTT DARK

MARYSUE
RUCCI
BOOKS

New York   London   Toronto   Sydney   New Delhi

MARYSUE
RUCCI
BOOKS

An Imprint of Simon & Schuster, Inc.
1230 Avenue of the Americas
New York, NY 10020

First Marysue Rucci Books trade paperback edition May 2023

MARYSUE RUCCI BOOKS and colophon are trademarks of Simon & Schuster, Inc.

For information about special discounts for bulk purchases, please contact Simon &
Schuster Special Sales at 1-866-506-1949 or business@simonandschuster.com.

The Simon & Schuster Speakers Bureau can bring authors to your live event. For
more information or to book an event, contact the Simon & Schuster Speakers
Bureau at 1-866-248-3049 or visit our website at www.simonspeakers.com.

Interior design by Carly Loman

Manufactured in the United States of America

1 3 5 7 9 10 8 6 4 2

Library of Congress Control Number: 2020952547

ISBN 978-1-9821-3181-4
ISBN 978-1-9821-3182-1 (pbk)
ISBN 978-1-9821-3186-9 (ebook)

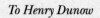

To Henry Dunow

"What is this you call property? It cannot be the earth. For the land is our mother, nourishing all her children, beasts, birds, fish, and all men. The woods, the streams, everything on it belongs to everybody and is for the use of all. How can one man say it belongs to him only?"

MASSASOIT

"The best mirror is an old friend."

GEORGE HERBERT

Cape Deel

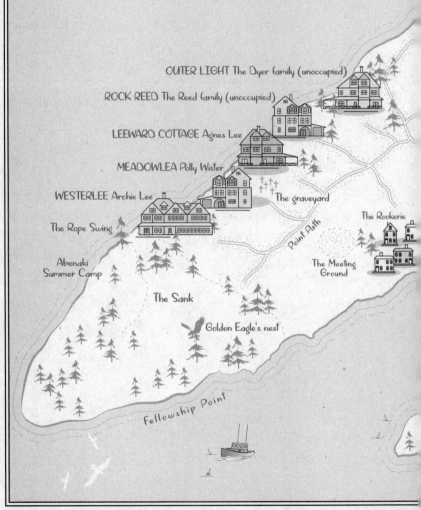

OUTER LIGHT The Dyer family (unoccupied)

ROCK REED The Reed family (unoccupied)

LEEWARD COTTAGE Agnes Lee

MEADOWLEA Polly Wister

WESTERLEE Archie Lee

The graveyard

The Rope Swing

The Rookerie

Point Path

The Meeting
Ground

Abenaki
Summer Camp

The Sank

Golden Eagle's nest

Fellowship Point

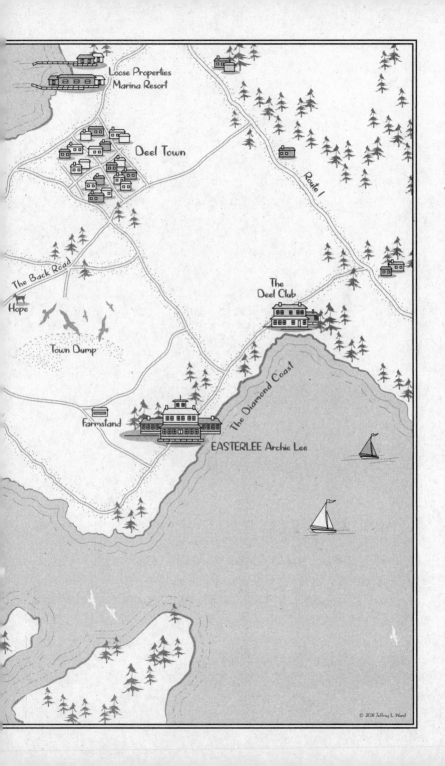

FELLOWSHIP
POINT

A Leading

CHAPTER 1

Agnes, Philadelphia, March 2000

SUCH A PERFECT DAY FOR WRITING, GRAY AND QUIET. BUT nothing came to her. Not a sentence, not a phrase, not a word worth keeping. Her wastebasket was full. Her pile of index cards was robust. Graph paper covered with diagrams was neatly pinned to a sheet of felt on the wall. But the spot where her stack of usable pages usually accumulated was an empty nest.

This had never happened to her before. Agnes Lee had written six novels and dozens of books for children without hesitation, composing and rewriting and tossing, fearlessly killing her darlings, trusting many more would come along—not to mention volumes of journals and logs secreted in a captain's trunk in an attic room at the cottage, and lots of articles and essays under various witty pseudonyms. She might rewrite an entire manuscript, but she'd never before been at a loss at this juncture, after her research had produced new material and the time had come to sit down and draft the book. The words had always arrived. Her writing was on tap. All she had to do was pull down on the handle and out it flowed. That fact was at the center of her self-conception. She wrote. If she couldn't, if the tap was dry, then what?

This sorry state—that was what. She was racing through barrels of Rapidograph ink, and wearing down a new pencil sharpener. Yet her book, her *novel*, the work that would round out a series written over decades, had garnered a usable word count of zero. All winter, she'd gotten nothing done.

Agnes had lost hope for today, too, but her allotted writing time wasn't up yet. So she sat. Her rule was five hours, and dammit she'd put in five hours. Habits filled in the fissures of an aging body and mind, and she couldn't afford to let them go. She'd seen her mother attempt to do a few sit-ups on her deathbed, and though Agnes felt little but a generic filial regard for that soulless snob, in that moment she hoped she'd be as disciplined at the last. She kept an inviolable schedule, afforded by some inheritance and abetted by having had the vocation of writing for the last nearly sixty years. Rarely did she have to compromise for anyone, a privilege she did not take for granted and refused to squander. She was eighty, but she had not slowed down. Just the opposite. Her remaining work was urgent, and she was well aware of working alongside the specter of the unknown moment of her last breath.

Since Mrs. Blundt had placed the mail by Agnes's place at lunch, and her perusal of several of the items had brought agitation into her controlled small world, she'd been particularly distracted. She paced her room and looked out the window and paced again. She allowed herself to pace into the living room, too, as long as she kept her mind in her work. Mrs. Blundt had bought fragrant lilies and Agnes dropped her nose into their midst, inhaling heaven. She walked to the window next. She had a good view from her third-floor apartment. The brown flora and collapsed grass in Rittenhouse Square hung on with stoic forbearance. People crossing through had scarves in place of faces and bodies obscured by masses of cloth or fur. Every so often they looked up at the sky, and Agnes followed their gaze in search of early flakes. *Snow was general all over Ireland.* A line from Joyce's "The Dead." Her eyes pricked. She rarely cried at life, but certain turns of phrase prompted hot tears to sting her cheeks. She squeezed the bridge of her nose, pinching off the emotion. Blizzard, she thought, a word that cooled her off. A blizzard was predicted that would leave a few inches over Philadelphia. The prospect of a rinsed landscape replete with glistening branches and snowmen in the Square cheered her. Refreshed, she returned to her writing room.

Agnes was well aware she could afford to be moved by snow. Mrs. Blundt, her housekeeper, kept her shelves stocked and the domestic details of her winter life on course. Snow would fall over all the living and the dead, and Agnes would have a couple of days of privacy and silence. Perhaps in that quiet she'd find what she needed to begin. An image; a character's voice; a sentence that contained a seed from which the next sentence could grow. Something that would open this cage. Writing had been the one place where she had felt—free. And also on Fellowship Point. Always free there.

She pulled the blank pad in front of her. Fifty-three minutes to go. Frustrated, bewildered, she suffered in silence and could complain to no one. She drew a horse and quickly scribbled over it.

She had a bifurcated writing career, both parts successful, but she was only publicly known for the *When Nan* books. She'd written more than thirty volumes in the series, starting with *When Nan Was a Lobsterman* in 1965 and most recently *When Nan Ran a Wind Farm*. They were published under her own name, as they had been from the beginning, when she'd predicted, accurately, that the books would serve as an alibi for all the time she spent alone at her desk, unavailable. The *When Nan* books allowed her to pretend she was a very slow worker who needed to be left alone. She actually wrote them quickly, in one sitting, after waiting for an idea to present itself whole.

The illustrations took longer, or she took longer with them, because she didn't really have an innate talent for it and drew many versions before she got one right enough. She'd stuck to her style of pen-and-ink line drawings, but had learned to paint on paper over the years and had eventually gone back and added color to the early books. Children liked the way she showed an emotion with a simple slant of the line representing Nan's mouth. She'd practiced that line and agreed she was able to milk quite a bit of nuance out of it. In her social circles, her work was treated as a decent hobby for a woman of her ilk. Being a famous children's book author in her world wasn't so different from anonymity.

Her other series, the *Franklin Square* novels, were popular and, over time, critically praised. She'd written the first one at age twenty-four, mainly as a way to inoculate herself from succumbing to the fates of her friends—reconfigured as the Franklin Square "girls"—as they married or got jobs. It galled her to see them make themselves smaller in order to fit into the roles available to them. Their talents were subsumed into utility and support. She wanted to show things as they were in great detail, to the end of portraying the absurdity of the setup, even for women who had advantages. In her experience, it was harder for girls who'd grown up as she had to notice exactly when they'd been conscripted into the power structure—it was all so seamless and nice. She had been in danger of it herself, her father being kind and on her side, but she'd noticed from the earliest age the hierarchies that existed in every gathering of people, and she'd had a clear visceral objection. It was her subject, in many variations and permutations.

She didn't moralize, or preach, or conclude. The project of fiction was in essence dramatic and sought to reveal what a particular person was bound to do under explicit circumstances. It was hard to figure that out, but when she was able to do so, when after she'd thrown out dozens of false attempts she suddenly saw exactly how her *girls* would act and react, when she was able to make her plots ring the clear bell of inevitability, she'd fulfilled her end of the contract as a writer, and left it to the reader to discover the meaning. She was absolutely sure of her opinions and her worldview and trusted that they were conveyed, palatably, in engrossing plots so that she didn't have to spell out her positions.

She was a novelist. No one knew.

Her potential first editor in Philadelphia praised her manuscript highly but also dropped a disconcerting remark about Agnes not being able to show her face in Philadelphia after it was published. Agnes hadn't even thought of the possibility that she'd be ostracized. She'd had the deceptive sensation as she composed the book, figuring it all out for the first time, that she'd been alone with it and that somehow solitude conferred privacy. In hindsight that seemed naive, but it was quite true that as carefully as she'd worked to make the whole puzzle of the book reach a solution at the end, and with what diamond cutter's tools she'd refined the facets of the paragraphs and made her characters glint under particular lights, it had also not really occurred to her that people would actually read it. As soon as the remark was made, though, it was obvious to her that there was no chance she could be in society and skewer it, too. Without hesitation she asked for the manuscript back and decided to publish under a pseudonym. She had a great time coming up with one, experimenting with every name she'd ever wished for in lieu of Agnes—which ran to the dozens. Finally, she settled on Pauline Schulz.

The name was odd and memorable, and it had served her well. Agnes had often thought of Saint Paul, renamed from Saul of Tarsus, and was moved by picturing him composing his Epistles, writing and crossing out, building convincing arguments to persuade different types around the Mediterranean of Jesus's messages. No matter that none of it convinced her: she liked his effort and his pseudonym. Likewise, she'd be Pauline Schulz! She sent the manuscript to a different editor in New York under this new name. It sounded tough, like a lady reporter. She'd wanted to tell her sister Elspeth, who was so pure Agnes couldn't conscience withholding anything from her, but for that very reason it wouldn't be fair. Elspeth already carried the burdens of many people. Agnes decided if her identity was to be a secret, not one other soul should know about it.

The *Franklin Square* novels were about five women friends and their activities and travails within the context of politics and civic life. She'd written one book each decade and had managed to maintain her anonymity in spite of increasing efforts to solve the mystery of who Pauline Schulz was. There was speculation that she was a man; a committee; or a series of people. Was the author an outsider looking in? Over the years she'd added Jewish and Italian and African American and a smattering of other Philadelphia characters. Could Pauline be from one of these swaths of the local populace? Agnes had even uncovered a drop of Jewish ancestry for one of her women, which led to a second marriage to a Jewish man and a foray into Reconstructionism, which "Pauline" wrote was as Philadelphia as Quakerism. So was Schulz Jewish? Good question. Was Pauline a man? Agnes laughed when that was proposed. Would any man have written some of the scenes she had? The boredom of days with a toddler, the confounding depression at the responsibility for cleaning a messy room, the injustice of being taken for granted, the perceptions garnered by women's sensitive backs of being judged for their shapes as they walked away from work meetings, then later those same backs realizing no eyes were scanning them anymore. Physical pain and its fraternal twin, stoicism. The unsuspected inner life and interrupted sense of self. Pauline Schulz had never gotten a letter from a woman who suspected her of being a man.

For the most part she liked being anonymous and hidden and unbeholden to anyone. The only thing she regretted was not being able to do a *Paris Review* interview. She fantasized about that; she had a lot she wished she could say. But it was a small price for her freedom. As far as the world knew, Agnes Lee was just a children's book author, devoid of the breadth of observation and social acuity and sharp eye of Pauline Schulz. Her three successive editors hadn't even known who she really was—they worked with Pauline always via a PO box in Philadelphia. She planned to take her identity with her into a grave on Fellowship Point. After Elspeth died, Agnes had been tempted from time to time to tell her great friend Polly, who chafed at Agnes's unavailability. Agnes deeply disliked lying to her. It would be fun, too, to have someone know, and transform the constraint of the secret into a shared glance across the room when one of her books came up. Polly would keep the secret, Agnes had no doubt of that, but it would hurt her not to tell Dick, her husband, and Agnes didn't want to hurt Polly. So she kept on keeping the secret to herself.

Finally her hours ended. She set up a tableau of the day's mail in the living room and then tried to read until a call came from downstairs that a visitor was on her way up.

"I'll get it," Agnes called out, and rushed to open the apartment door before Mrs. Blundt could. Polly Wister—whom Agnes had known and been best friends with for eighty years now, since the cradle—arrived smiling on the threshold.

Agnes regretted having to disturb Polly's post-orchestra equanimity, but she needed her to match her own sense of purpose. "We have a problem," Agnes announced, and was gratified when Polly's pretty face bunched up and her watery blue eyes widened. The cold air that had attached itself to Polly's red wool coat made its ghostly way across the threshold and gave Agnes a shiver.

"Good day, Mrs. Wister," said Mrs. Blundt, the housekeeper, from behind Agnes. Her voice trembled.

"What? What is it?" Polly's gloves lifted to cradle her face, a motion that sent her black handbag down to the crook of her elbow.

Agnes turned around. "Mrs. Blundt, will you take Polly's things?"

Mrs. Blundt nodded fretfully and Polly slipped out of her sleeves.

"Thank you." Polly dipped slightly, a remnant of the curtsy they'd learned at school. She'd never learned how to be natural with people who received pay to help her.

Mrs. Blundt retreated to the kitchen and Polly lowered her voice. "Did something happen to her?"

"To her? No, no, no. She's just upset about— I'll tell you later. Come in, come in."

"You have me worried."

As always Polly's concern was marbled with an exasperating innocence. As eager as Agnes had been to talk to her, the breadth of her emotional availability was annoying—because it also was how Polly responded to Dick, her husband. Polly dropped everything of her own to take on his agenda. Agnes couldn't imagine being that cowed.

"I'll tell thee everything. But let's get drinks." She and Polly walked to the bar cart in the living room. Agnes had always been taller than Polly, nearly six feet, though age had subtracted a few inches. She was dressed in jeans, Keds, and an old cashmere sweater, an informality made chic by the intelligence in her green eyes and thin straight mouth. She wore a pair of diamond stud earrings and two of the gold bracelets her father had given her when she turned sixteen; she'd given away the third bracelet long ago. She'd never married and had always seemed fulfilled anyway. She wasn't pretty like Polly and only rarely glanced in a mirror. She liked her hands, though, and rubbed them with creams all day as she worked at her desk.

The lights were all turned on to counter the gray March afternoon. "We need Scotch," Agnes said.

"Just one finger for me. Miles to go and so on."

"How was the concert?"

"So the problem isn't that bad?"

"It is. But I want to wait until we sit down."

"I see. Just tell me—did anyone die?"

"No, it's not like that."

"I am not ready for another death after Hiram."

"I know. Speaking of which, I got a letter from Robert today. I saved it to read with you."

"Oh good, thanks."

Agnes juggled bottles and ice and finally handed Polly a glass. The white sky was becoming pearly, and the street lamps suddenly punctured the gloaming. The living room was spare but plush, all green and yellow, the furniture simple. A thick lemon carpet ran nearly wall to wall. Polly sighed as she sank into a mint sofa. "It's so comfortable here," Polly said. "Unexpected, for you."

"People change," Agnes said. "It ain't over 'til it's over. You may quote me on that."

She looked around at her own design for serenity and was pleased Polly liked her efforts. She'd moved to the apartment ten years earlier, at age seventy. Prior to then, she'd lived all her Philadelphia life in the family house on Walnut Street, a building ancient by American standards and owned by the Lees since the mid-1800s. It had been her Philadelphia turtle shell, inseparable from her flesh. Then she'd had a few falls that gave her black eyes, *and* a few illnesses, mementos of the gross reality that she could no longer take her health for granted. Ease and convenience, qualities for which she'd never had any use, began to make sense. An elevator and a doorman and food that could be delivered up—why not? She sold a great deal of the dark wood from the Walnut Street house and bought new Thomas Moser pieces. Minimalism was her mandate for this last chapter. Whoever was stuck with emptying the apartment after she died would not have much to do. To her way of thinking, that was decent.

Anyway, it wasn't entirely the case that she'd rid herself of her belongings. She'd had her favorite things shipped to Fellowship Point. Maine was her real home now and had been for forty years. The apartment was for the winter months she spent in Philadelphia, to escape the difficulty of being snowed in at Leeward Cottage. Or so she said to people, weather being an excuse that didn't arouse curiosity. The real reason she came to Philadelphia every winter was for research. For a few hectic weeks she hauled herself to her clubs and to luncheons and dinner parties, charity events, galleries, and shops, taking notes on what people did and what they hid, in preparation for writing her next novel. She had years of notes for the present book, but dammit. Was it possible that she no longer had the stamina for a novel?

Her whole chest felt strangled and trampled on, but she affected calm for the sake of her agenda. She needed Polly to see things her way.

"So what's going on? Don't keep me waiting any longer," Polly said.

Agnes reached for the *Cape Deel Gazette*. "This came today. Remember our old friend Hamm Loose?"

"I'd rather not." Polly took a healthy swig.

"It's about his son Hamm Loose Jr. and their development company. Read the article here." She had the paper open to the offending page and handed it over.

"My glasses are in my bag in the hallway," Polly said.

"Use mine." Agnes took a pair from a basket on the side table to her left.

Polly put them on. She gave a quick glance around. She wants a mirror, Agnes thought. For God's sake. The habit of pretty.

"Are they strong enough? Can you see?"

"Yup."

Polly rarely acknowledged Agnes's little digs. Marriage to Dick Wister and three sons had inured her to teasing.

"Hamm Loose Jr. is large, isn't he?"

"That's not the problem. Just read it."

"Aloud?"

"No. It already ruined my lunch."

The story was about the groundbreaking ceremony for a new luxury condominium and marina complex near Deel Town, which was close to her and Polly's houses on Fellowship Point. The resort was being built by the firm of Loose Properties, owned by Hamm Loose and his sons Hamm Jr. and Terrance, known as Teeter. As Polly read the article, Agnes gazed at her, at first in an attitude of waiting, but then with a sudden objectivity. She rarely stepped back from Polly long enough to see her. Twenty years earlier Polly's hair had turned all white, the gleaming kind of white that looked age-less and soft. She still wore it either in a headband or barrettes, as she always had. Her skin was relatively smooth, due to her lifelong habit of keeping the sun off her face. She'd had a few basal cell skin cancers removed on her arms, leaving pale spots behind, but she could pass for being in her sixties. Agnes had read once that men liked women who smiled; smiling was Polly's essence. A good temperament, laughing eyes—easy to be around, as went the com-pliment of their youth. They spent summers in next-door houses on Fellowship Point and lived within blocks of each other in Philadel-phia until Polly moved out to Haverford after her daughter Lydia was born. She'd wanted a backyard for her boys so she could enjoy the baby in peace.

Polly still made her opinions and motives and intentions plainly apparent. She was never confusing or devious or wily. A real Quaker lady, plain and good. When they were girls, Polly was often invited along on other families' vacations and cruises, and on day trips to see plays in New York or monuments in Washington, D.C. Every teacher at school was glad to have her in the room, even the blue-stockings usually resistant to the more social types. Yet for all Polly's popularity, she was also underestimated, her unflappability interpreted as middling brain power. This wasn't accurate. Polly was smart, but she didn't develop her thoughts. Agnes had for a time given her lessons on how to be more penetrating. Polly had listened graciously and carried on being herself.

Odd to have a best friend who was received so effortlessly by the world, when Agnes inadvertently offended more than a few people. So it had always been, and she was used to it—which didn't make it unremarkable.

Polly laid the paper back onto the coffee table and crossed her arms protectively over her middle. "Darn it! I always loved that spot."

"I know. That's bad enough. But how about when Hamm Jr. said he plans to build more *resorts* on Cape Deel, and that his ideal property is Fellowship Point?" Agnes hammered the point home.

"Sickening! And what about when he said *everyone has their price!*"

Polly was upset, thrilling Agnes. It was so satisfying to have horror met with horror. "He's appalling!"

"Like father, like son. I hate them. I don't hate anybody but them, but I do hate them. How dare he even think about Fellowship Point? It means he has looked around."

"We know his father looked around."

Once when Agnes and Polly were fourteen, they'd seen Hamm Loose—Senior, now an old man—and a gang of his pals invade the Sank and shoot an eagle flying back to her nest with food for her cheeping offspring. He'd also kicked gravel at their bare legs on the playground in Deel Town. Polly had tried to understand these actions through the lens of class grievances and the local versus away people conflict, and though Agnes normally adored a good sociological analysis, in this case it was an obfuscation, and she'd gotten Polly back on track by writing a vow for both of them to recite that included preventing Hamm from doing any further harm to Fellowship Point. They pricked their index fingers and pressed them tight to each other's to seal the deal.

Hamm Loose Jr. was a piece of work, too. When Polly's boys were young and taking tennis lessons at the Deel Club, Hamm Jr. had found ways to create disturbances when they were serving, and he peed in the showers with gusto. It was outrageous of him to mention Fellowship Point in a newspaper article. Development would destroy the beauty of the place, of course—but more than that, the hallowed thirty-five-acre tip of the peninsula called the Sank (short for "sanctuary") would become desecrated, and the bird species that had flourished there under the fellowship's aegis for nearly a hundred and fifty years would scatter and potentially go extinct. Eagles' nests, including a towering structure built by golden eagles, had been occupied uninterrupted for decades. The thought of yachts and condos displacing those priceless dwellings made Agnes's heart literally hurt. She had to block the possibility if it was the last thing she did.

A few days earlier, she'd called her lawyer to make certain she had an accurate understanding of how to break the Fellowship Point Association agreement. As she'd thought, Fellowship Point was owned in shares by five families. In each generation one family member held the share. At any time, the agreement could be dissolved if three association members voted to do so. Subsequently the land could be sold or split up more conventionally. The possibility had never before arisen, but circumstances had never been this dire.

Only three families had held a share for a while now. The other two original families had died out and forfeited their shares, which had gone to the remaining shareholders. Two houses had been unoccupied for years and should probably be torn down. Cousin Archie still held WesterLee—his grown children stayed there sometimes, or he loaned it to friends—but he'd built his own house on the other side of the peninsula, a monstrous exercise in why-pay-less. Agnes was sure she could persuade him to break the agreement without much trouble, especially in light of wolves like the Looses

sniffing around. The dismantling had to happen while the two old
ladies were both breathing and compos mentis. Meaning, ASAP.
After Agnes and Polly died, only two people stood to inherit the
shares, Polly's eldest son, James, and Cousin Archie Lee. They loved
Fellowship Point, but how much? Did they have a price at which
they'd be persuaded to sell? It was a better plan to never tempt
them.

"So, Polly. We can't wait any longer to dissolve the association. I
want to start writing to land trusts immediately. You're with me on
this, aren't you?"

"Absolutely. I mean I have to talk to Dick, but yes. I think so, yes."

Polly's deference to Dick irritated Agnes, as always, but she let it
go and pressed on. "There are different sorts of arrangements that
can be made, easements and tax things and so on. I want to make
certain that the Sank is protected forever, even when I'm not here."

"I fully agree."

"Good. Let's get this settled this summer. I'll set up appointments. The land trust people will want to see the place, and we can
figure out what's best."

"We're going in June, as usual. When are you going up anyway?
You're here late this year." Polly looked at her quizzically, as if puzzling something out.

"I'll go soon." Agnes changed the subject as swiftly as possible.
"Now I'm hungry. Mrs. Blundt!" she called out.

Mrs. Blundt emerged from the kitchen, her hands prayerfully
clasped at her waist. She was in her early fifties, ruddy and round,
with an open face framed by a nimbus of gray curls.

"Whatever you created smells irresistible," she said. "Will you
please bring it in?" She turned to Polly. "All afternoon the most
divine scent has been wafting around the apartment."

Polly nodded. "I noticed it the second you opened the door.
What is it?"

"Zucchini cake with vanilla icing," said Mrs. Blundt.

"Oooh," Polly said. "My mouth is watering."

Mrs. Blundt frowned, turned, and left.

Agnes picked up an envelope from the side table. "Now for Robert's letter."

"Me? Or you?"

"You still have my glasses on."

She handed the envelope to Polly, who sighed as she drew the pages out. "It's so sad about Hiram," she said. "Poor Robert. Is he all right?"

"Maybe the letter will tell us."

Polly frowned. "Can you not tease for five seconds?"

"Sorry. Go ahead," Agnes said, thinking of her teasing ancestors, especially her father. A handsome man could get away with it.

"Let me get these pages opened . . ." Polly took a sip and began.

Dear Agnes,

It was good to speak with you the other day. Hearing your voice—well, I felt better. I remember once when a pious visitor expressed shock over you and Polly laughing in the graveyard. "If you can't laugh at death what can you laugh at?" you barked. I have reminded myself of that these days.

It's difficult to know how best to mourn—what's efficient, effective, and honorable. I hit on an answer today. I thought you'd want to hear about it.

I parked my car right off Shore Road at the top of Point Path. It snowed overnight, so the ground was dusted and a light wind blew, rattling the iced branches. I pictured Hiram, and how his gait expressed his essential traits: dignity, caution, sense of purpose. I don't know where he is now, and I, like you, have never been tempted to subscribe to any notion of an afterlife. I am content to remember him as he was. He was so often on Fellowship Point, even after we moved away. Where better to think of him?

I came to the bottom of the hill and stood at the north end surveying the whole point. I looked straight down the full length of the path to the Sank. From that distance, it appeared as an olive rounded dome that made me wish I could paint. It's an Arthur Dove, for sure. Then I took a deep breath, and the full feel of the place came to me—the pine scents, the birdcalls, the booming of the rolling ocean. I headed straight down and checked on the eagles' nests. All looked well, no signs of trespassing or disturbance. I won't check again until after the eaglets hatch, if any do this year. I walked by the site of the summer camp and all around the shoreline, then back up Point Path. By the graveyard I thought of old friends and older inhabitants of what my father— and yours—called God's country. Thank you for offering a place for him there, but my mother wants him in her churchyard. His spirit will always be on Fellowship Point in any case.

I'm looking forward to taking this walk together very soon.

Yours as ever, Robert

"What decent men," Agnes said, "Robert and Hiram both." She looked up and saw that Polly's eyes had filled.

Polly wiped at her face. "Will you excuse me a moment?" She stood.

"Use the one in my bedroom. It has a view."

Polly handed back the letter to Agnes and made her way through the apartment. Agnes skimmed it again. She'd spoken to Robert a week earlier, after Sylvie, her housekeeper at Leeward Cottage, had called her with the news that Hiram Circumstance had dropped dead at seventy-eight. Agnes had known Hiram all her life. He'd lived on Fellowship Point for many years before buying his own house farther up the Cape, which she'd helped him do. He'd been the carpenter and the caretaker and the landscaper, ever reliable, highly competent, and very serious. Agnes trusted Hiram. And she'd liked him so much. He'd treated her with the same respect he'd showed her father when at age forty she took over his share of the association. Her animals had always been happy to see him, either jumping up on or rubbing against his legs, depending on the species. Pets could like the wrong people, she'd seen it, but they loved him for cause. She was pleased that Sylvie had used the phrase *dropped dead* to describe what happened to Hiram. It enabled Agnes to see him loping down a road, looking up at the high branches or the sky, suddenly jerking downward, crumpling, his straight slate-colored hair shading his eyes, his flannel-lined coat wrinkling, his worn corduroys buckling along with his knees. *Hiram dropped dead.* Too bad, but at least he hadn't expired, or passed, or left this world, or gone to his maker, or even had a heart attack. He deserved a straightforward death.

Agnes also trusted Robert, who took after his father, right down to the straight blue merle hair and the cowboy gait. Of the five Circumstance children Agnes had seen in Robert a superior intelligence and had paid for him to go to George School and Penn. He wanted to be a lawyer, but a pot conviction derailed that—Agnes made certain it didn't interrupt for too long, in spite of the Rockefeller drug laws—and he transferred to Amherst to study landscape architecture. Eventually—after a brief marriage to someone who realized she needed more money in a man—he moved back to Cape Deel and went to work with Hiram, and he expanded the business to include design. He had created the outdoors for many of the swells and the new influx of the money-moving rich and celebrities, and became something of a celebrity himself. Robert was nothing if not loyal, though, and he still took care of the Point. He was in and out of both Agnes's and Polly's houses all summer, and he and Dick Wister often had drinks. Fellowship Point relied on him completely. Agnes offered to fly up for the funeral—Polly wanted to go, too—but Robert discouraged it. No sense in coming all that way for ten minutes, when they could think of Hiram from right where they were. "He thinks we're old," Agnes told Polly.

"He's never wrong," Polly replied, and sighed.

Recently Hiram had been doing some tracking and sleuthing to try to figure out who was harassing the eagles on Cape Deel. Several eagles had disappeared over the past few years, to the point where it was suspicious. Hiram wanted to get to the bottom of it. Agnes told Robert she was certain he would have, and Robert vowed to take over the hunt. He would—

"Here we go," said Mrs. Blundt. She set the plates on the coffee table. Polly returned a moment later. "I love that painting of the Sank in your bathroom. And look at this! My dinner is ruined." She sat down and took a bite. "Oh boy. This is dangerous it's so good."

"Thank you." Mrs. Blundt tried to smile but couldn't manage.

Agnes let the cake melt in her mouth. Every pleasure was heightened lately.

"Are your boys set to shovel your front steps, Mrs. Blundt?" Polly asked.

"If they're not, they don't have a mother anymore." Mrs. Blundt had a habit of shifting to her brogue when speaking of her family.

"Good policy," Agnes said. "In any case, no need to come over tomorrow. I'll be fine."

Mrs. Blundt frowned. "You're not fine." She stuck her chin out, as if a jutting jawline entitled her to a breach of boundaries.

"You're not?" Polly asked. "What's going on?"

Agnes held up her hand. "Mrs. Blundt, you may go home now. I have enough food to last a month. If I need you tomorrow, I'll call you."

"Tell her," Mrs. Blundt said.

"I will."

"I'm not going anywhere until you do."

Mrs. Blundt, who'd overheard phone calls to doctors and taken messages, had pressed Agnes for information. There'd been no further avoiding the conversation.

"What is it?" Polly asked, looking back and forth between them.

Agnes leaned forward. "I am having surgery soon. A lump turned out to be cancer."

Polly looked at Agnes directly. "Where?"

Agnes pointed to her chest. "They both have to go."

"You've always wanted that," Polly said, and then, quickly—"Oh no!"

"Ha! That's the upside, and I'm glad you know it. So you won't feel sorry for me."

"I feel very sorry for you. I feel sick—" Polly began to cry. "You'll stay with me after. I'll make your rice and greens for you. Oh, Agnes!" She moved next to Agnes on the sofa and took her hand.

"I'll stay here and so will Mrs. Blundt."

"I certainly will." Mrs. Blundt was crying, too. Polly reached out her free hand and Mrs. Blundt took it.

"I won't need that. But please come visit." The handholding prompted a nervousness she'd pushed off before now, and she wondered how soon she could disengage.

Polly searched her face. "Are you going to be okay?"

"The doctors won't give me a straight answer. I have assured them I can handle the truth, but I get the feeling they can't." Agnes shrugged. "I'll do my best. I have work to do. Including settling what will become of the Point."

"This isn't the time to think about that. You have to concentrate on your health."

"It's precisely the time to think about that. I might die on the table."

"Oh stop it, Agnes, it's not funny."

"I'm not being funny. In fact, I've never been more serious. Going under the knife is good for focus. Promise me you'll preserve the Sank if I'm not here to do it."

"That's blackmail."

Agnes shrugged.

"Of course I promise." Polly shook her head, sniffling.

"Good. Good. The surgery is first thing Monday. I read that was the best slot, when the docs are at their freshest."

At the thought, Agnes placed her hands on her breasts. Soon they'd be gone and she'd be a lean blade again, albeit old and rusty. She'd be flat! At last! Again. She'd toss her bras, torture chambers that they were. She only had to get through the next bit.

Agnes looked out the window toward 18th Street, at the old Barclay Hotel, now condominiums. Hamm Loose Jr. would approve, she thought ruefully. She remembered when the building went up. Her father, Lachlan Lee, had loved construction sites, and could be persuaded to go for a walk anytime if the route led to a deep divot in the ground and girders crosshatching empty space. The Barclay was built in the late 1920s. During the months of construction, Lachlan had reached for Agnes's hand on the doorstep of the house on Walnut Street, and together they'd walked a few blocks to watch the new behemoth rising. People complained about the shadows it would cast, but Lachlan was all for progress. "Presidents will stay there!"

He'd been right about that, and many things. She missed him every day. She'd only loved a few people. Most of those had been dead for a long time now. *Soon I too might be a shade with the shade of Patrick Morkan and his horse.* Joyce again.

This weather. This impending afternoon.

"Remember that crackpot friend of your father's who had a theory that the magnetism in the mineral rocks of Cape Deel scrambled the cells?" Agnes asked.

Polly glared at her and wiped her eyes.

"Polly!" Agnes patted the tweed-covered knee of her old friend. "There are upsides. Cancer is a conversation stopper. And there are very few conversations I don't want to stop."

"Agnes, please."

"Well, what should I say? I can't feel anything in my breast, which is annoying. I attempt to talk to the doctors plainly, but they're obsessed with fifty-cent words, like *diagnosis* and *mastectomy*—four syllables is a bad sign."

"We'll take care of you, won't we, Mrs. Wister?" Mrs. Blundt blew her nose into a handkerchief.

"Yes. We certainly will."

Didn't they remember that they'd already promised that? Agnes longed to move on, but Polly gripped Agnes's hand so tightly she felt in danger of losing her fingers. That was the other thing, which neither of them knew about—Agnes was determined to finish her final novel before she croaked. Maybe the surgery would slice away her writer's block.

"Thank you, thank you, I know you will." Agnes stood, hoping they'd take the hint. Suddenly she was desperate to get back to her desk. "I'll be fine, really. But I'm a little tired now. The doorman will get you a cab. Mrs. Blundt, will you call downstairs for a cab for Polly?"

After several minutes of entreaties and embraces and assurances Agnes was finally alone again.

As soon as she stepped into her study, she felt relief. Where her bedroom was made sumptuous by snowy duvets over fat quilts and a chaise longue upholstered in white silk, her aesthetic here was what she thought of as spare inspiration. She'd modeled it on the cells in the Conventi di San Marco in Florence and had a replica of a Fra Angelico fresco painted on each wall by an art student from the Pennsylvania Academy of Fine Arts. Her hand was no longer steady enough to do the job herself—not that she'd ever had the skill to copy a master. She was an outsider artist at most, untrained and quirky. An illustrator. She appreciated good paintings, though—who didn't? Fra Angelico had made her burst into overwhelmed tears when she was on her post-collegiate European tour.

She had a comfortable reading chair, a desk, a few lamps. A computer and a printer. Supplies. If she wanted to look something up, she went to her bedroom, where she kept two cases of books, mainly reference. In her study there was nothing to do but write and think. She'd always wanted just such a simple room, but it took starting from nothing, and acquiring a space devoid of any architectural interest, to do it right. She loved the space and exonerated it from any blame for the fact that her book eluded her. Though if, as she conceived it, the empty room was a true extension of her mind, what it presently reflected was the image of a ghost. *Cancer was general all over Agnes's breasts.* She wished she could say that to someone who'd laugh in response. But she knew no such person.

And no one wholly knew her. Her books were independent of her charisma—har har—and literary friendships, as she had none. *Franklin Square Seven*, the book she presently wasn't writing, would most likely be the final volume in the series. The Franklin Square women couldn't get any older than they'd be in this book and still be able to turn a plot. She planned to tie up all remaining questions and leave her characters be. No more traumas and dramas. Peace at last.

She'd been looking forward to this for a very long time, but was presently afraid it wasn't going to happen. Maybe the series had ended with Book Six, when the Franklins were in their seventies and reluctantly harboring grandchildren and arguing with adult children and taking big trips. The book had been well received, and Pauline had gotten good reviews and lots of mail, but Agnes had finished it with the sense that she was at last on the cusp of a breakthrough, and of ensuring her work be read beyond her death. So far the Franklins had lived their lives, and she'd charted their hopes and travails and the changes in society astutely. In the last volume, she would make her points. Say what she had to say. Offer up her final words of wisdom. That sounded good in theory—who didn't want the last word?—but the pressure to be profound without being didactic or polemical was daunting, at her age, with no further opportunity to correct herself. She had to get it right. Surely that was part of what was stopping her from getting it at all. Perfectionism. Followed by death.

Which brought her back to Hiram, and Fellowship Point, and Robert's letter describing his walk around the land honoring his father. She closed her eyes and retraced his steps, starting at the Rookerie where he looked down Point Path toward the Sanctuary and then walking forward, past all the houses sleeping now through the winter—Outer Light, Rock Reed, her own Leeward Cottage. She paused there to look over at the graveyard, the stones flat and imbedded in the earth, barely visible from her vantage point, and then at the Meeting Ground where the ancestors had gathered to affirm their values, and occasionally spoke aloud when moved to do so in their hearts. She walked past Meadowlea and pictured Polly on her terrace, and on past WesterLee, the house her great-grandfather had assigned to his brother, dutifully giving away the best location on the peninsula.

Then into the Sank, the place her father had always called "God's country" and where Agnes had gone thousands of times to reset her balance and to affirm what was truly important in life. Thirty-three acres of land devoted to the safety of the birds that nested there and the birds that stopped by on their migrations, and to the cultivation of native woodland flora and trees. It wasn't wild. Hiram and Robert and their crew swept up the needles and pruned back invasive undergrowth and tended the soft paths threaded through the trunks, leading to vistas of deep woods and, in spots, distant islands, and to quiet glens and discreet spots for contemplation or rest. Moose had been spotted there, regrettably not by Agnes, but she kept track of the eagles and had friends among the squirrel families generation after generation. Sometimes she could draw on the beauty so wholeheartedly that she felt as though she had metabolized it, and that it had become an organ inside of her. The next time she was actually among the pines, though, she was apt to be embarrassed that she'd thought she was capable of comprehending what was, by nature, beyond her. Either way, she was determined to keep it safe for the birds, the animals, the flowers, the trees. More than ever, the world needed places free of human notions. She knew what people were like, herself included, and she wanted to make sure the Sank was protected by humans from humans. That would be her great legacy for which she wanted no credit. Anonymity had become ingrained.

She glared at the large manila envelope that had arrived with the mail and pulled out the contents. As she guessed, it was someone's PhD thesis on the subject of *When Nan*. Agnes sighed. This one was called "Performing Non-Traditional Gender in the *When Nan* Oeuvre." By Mariana Wiccan Styles. Of the University of South Lawrence. Wherever that was.

Wiccan? That couldn't be real, could it? Or—hippie parents.

When Penn had first asked for her papers, Agnes had laughed. Poor wretch who had to laboriously catalogue her sketches, and notes scribbled on the backs of envelopes. Little had Agnes known that children's books had become a respectable area of academic inquiry. Every year dozens of requests came in from scholars who wanted to have a look at her papers. Apparently, her character, her protagonist, her heroine, a child called Nan, had become a proto-feminist icon of interest on campus. How could that be? Agnes could see someone eking out a column to that effect that the next morning would be wrapping fish. But a thesis? For which one had to prepare by learning foreign languages and writing rigorous papers on far more heady subjects? Yet the *When Nan* theses started arriving, and Agnes paged through a few of them, learning all about the symbol systems she'd created, the power structures she'd dismantled, the empowering messages conveyed by Nan's oblivion to issues of sexual oppression and sexist hierarchies in the workplace.

No one opposed Nan's personhood.

Her travails were circumstantial, not endemic.

One earnest PhD candidate had noted: "It's as if Agnes Lee had no awareness whatsoever that women might be considered lesser. She writes as if equality were a fact." Well, yup. Was that really so unusual? The authors she loved all believed women were equal. She had a shelf of books she reread over and over, and that concept was intrinsic to them all. The difference with her was the blind eye she turned to inequity. Her true feeling was not that women were equal, as that in itself was a comparison, but that they were whole. Wasn't that indisputable?

All living creatures were whole. End of story. This was one of her earliest understandings of reality, and it had shaped her life.

It wasn't a sacral belief, but a simple recognition. In consequence, she hadn't eaten a piece of meat since she was three and a half, she'd never married, and she'd done her best not to impinge. Nan, a perpetual nine-year-old, sprang from that sensibility. She was seen as being an anomaly to her time and place. An ideal. A tomboy who wasn't role-playing, and far more complicated interpretations that Agnes didn't have the critical vocabulary to fully get. Agnes had done nothing more than portray what a girl was, beyond interference. It depressed her that her simple creation was seen as being such an oddity.

Now Nan was an industry. There was a Nan doll and a couple of Nan movies. What confounded adults was easily grasped by young girls. Agnes reminded herself of that when the theses oppressed her. In any case, she'd made her peace with being the subject of academic speculation, though she liked to joke that she was going to write a book called *When Nan Was Kidnapped by the Academy*. "Be flattered," David Combs, her editor, coaxed her. "It's a good thing. It's attention." As if there were no such thing as bad attention.

Of course, Penn didn't know she had files of correspondence and reviews having to do with all the writing she'd done under pseudonyms. And they wouldn't find out, if she could help it. What a nightmare it would be if people sent theses about her *Franklin Square* series as well.

Poor Polly. This surgery was going to be hard on her.

Agnes had not yet opened the last piece of the day's mail. The return address was her *When Nan* publisher, so it was no doubt a chore. Yet she didn't like work to carry over, so she bit her lip and slit the envelope.

Dear Miss Lee,

My name is Maud Silver. I am the new editorial assistant to David Combs. I will be working on, among other things, the *When Nan* books, so I am writing to introduce myself to you.

I am so excited about this!

It isn't an accident that I have this particular position. Your books have been at the center of my life for as long as I can remember. My mother collected the series beginning when she was a child. She has a first edition of *When Nan Climbed Cadillac Mountain*. It would be worth a fortune but it's missing the title page. My fault for eating it! That's how much I loved it.

My mother was obsessed with the books and says she even wrote her own version of one when she was a girl. She passed her obsession on to me. I was attracted to books, and eventually publishing, because of Nan. I aimed to be David's assistant so I could work with you and on your behalf. I agree with everything important that has been said about the series, and think a lot more will be written, for many generations. You capture what it's like to be a girl. You give girls strength to be themselves.

I feel incredibly lucky to have landed exactly where I want to be. It feels like destiny.

I would love to know more about you and about Nan's origin story. Do you plan to write a memoir?

Yours truly,
Maud Silver

"No," Agnes said aloud. "I do not, and I will not."

She opened the cap of her Rapidograph in preparation for writing about the day. All winter, she'd gotten nothing done. She needed Maine. The salt air. Polly daily. Robert. And the graveyard, where the real Nan had a memorial headstone. That was another secret, and no eager editorial assistant would get it out of her.

CHAPTER 2

Polly, Haverford, May 2000

POLLY'S ATTENTION WAS SPLIT. HALF OF HER WAS KEEPING HER cards close to her chest at the Merion Cricket Club afternoon bridge game, while the other half—really, nine-tenths of her— wanted to go home. Dick was content to be alone all day in his study, and most likely he wouldn't want to be interrupted even if she were there. She'd feel better, though, back at his beck. It was her vocation. She gazed across the room at the scorekeepers, hoping for quick results, but they were comparing papers and frowning.

"Oh, I nearly forgot!" she blurted. "I have to get to the store!"

Three pairs of eyes narrowed and three mouths tightened. Last week it had been the dry cleaner. Before that, an oil change. Patently false, and her friends weren't stupid.

"But I can wait," she amended, in spite of Dick looming in her mind. In many instances over the course of her life, she'd chosen not to bother those around her, hadn't raised her hand with an answer so other girls might have a turn, hadn't gotten up in the movies to go to the bathroom if she'd have to push past people and temporarily block their view. Even when she was pregnant with a bladder so full she couldn't see straight, she'd waited. She never minded making way for someone else, but didn't want to bother others herself. She was charged with making the world kinder, and reciprocity was beside the point.

She was the only one at the table with a husband left alive. The others were all merry widows who went on cruises and bought themselves jewelry for no occasion at all. They pitied her for being tethered.

"Honestly, Polly, did Dick ever leave the classroom to rush home to you?"

"It's not Dick!" Polly protested. "I really have to go to the store. James might stop by." She crossed her fingers under the table. James hadn't made any such plan, but he might. It could happen. He was her oldest, her most dutiful, and their recent lunch had been fraught.

Her table exchanged glances. She was protesting too much, which was unlike her except when it came to Dick. Everything came down to Dick.

"Just wait to see if we won," said Liza Hopkins.

"We didn't win. We never do. Go ahead, Pol," said Greer Jenkins. "I'll call you with the outcome."

"If you're sure," Polly said, pushing up from her seat.

"Goodbye," said True Smith.

The afternoon was chilly, but the clouds were high, and the air scented with flowers. Polly was so relieved to be on her way that she jerked the car door open forcefully and her keys flew from her hand onto the ground. There they were, all the way down there. She looked out over the flat grounds that would soon be grass courts for the season. Magnolias made their effort around the perimeter. She pressed her knees together and lowered down. Halfway, she reached for the help of the door handle. She clenched her teeth against the possibility of her stockings ripping, the new ones were so flimsy. There . . . there. Success! Good grief, that was challenging. She straightened up and found another woman standing by the door of the next car. They caught each other's eye.

"Beautiful afternoon," they said in unison.

The woman was younger, but so was nearly everyone.

"You're Mrs. Wister, aren't you?"

Polly nodded, trying to place her. She was a type from around, with the cantaloupe calves of a former hockey player, wispy brown hair, and an open face.

"I know your son, James, and Ann. I met you briefly at Ann's birthday party?"

"Oh, of course. Remind me of your name?"

"I'm Julia Stevens. My husband is Terry? He works with James?"

Why did the young make all statements sound like questions? "Yes, I remember now." She didn't, but she'd long ago accepted that an occasional white lie made life nicer.

"I hope we'll be seeing you in Maine this summer," Julia said.

"You go to Maine?"

"James invited us. Your place sounds amazing. We are going to look at the houses."

"Houses?"

"Aren't there houses coming up for sale?"

"On Fellowship Point?" Her voice rose. A gust of wind rushed between them.

"I'm sorry, maybe I misunderstood." Julia took a couple of steps backward, peeling strands of hair from her lips.

"What did James say?"

"I can't remember, actually. My husband's family has a house in Stone Harbor, we usually go there. I'm sure we'll end up doing that."

"I'll check with James." Polly was vexed.

"As I say, we're not sure yet. Thank you, Mrs. Wister? Bye!"

A question mark again. Was nothing certain these days?

After Julia pulled away, Polly sat in her car and took a few deep breaths. She pictured James as he'd looked the day before, when she'd had lunch with him in the city. He hadn't mentioned anything then about inviting friends to the Point this summer, but now his demeanor made more sense, and was more disturbing. He'd been a tense baby, as firsts often were, and he was still tense. Too serious. As she thought this, she could hear Agnes saying it was impossible to be too serious, because at a certain point, seriousness converted to a parody of itself, and had to be designated *self-importance*. Yes, James was self-important, and temperamental. He might also be up to something, and she had no one to talk to about it.

He'd wanted to meet at the Union League, but Polly had never felt comfortable there—Agnes kept her abreast of its exclusionary membership policies, and though they'd improved, she still held a grudge about a Jewish friend whom Lachlan had proposed who'd gotten blackballed. James said he didn't have time to argue and made a reservation at a restaurant near the doctor Polly was going to see that afternoon. James was seated when she arrived, looking spiffy in his blue suit and Liberty print tie, and she was proud to be seen with him. They didn't speak intimately—frankly, she wasn't sure they knew how—but it was pleasant to be in the pretty spot, eat the delicious food, and hear about her grandchildren's latest interests. Caroline and Jasper were young adults now, with lives of their own. She checked herself from remarking how quickly time passed, but she certainly felt it.

"How long do you think you'll stay on the Point this summer?" she asked over coffee, no dessert.

"Three weeks, maybe four. It depends how quickly certain agreements move forward, whether or not I'm needed."

He worked at an investment firm, and had been busy since the recent downturn. She'd asked him if he'd lost money, and he'd said, "That's not how it works."

Truth be told, he wasn't all that pleasant to be with.

"I'm so looking forward to it," she said. "You'll stay at Archie's?"

Meaning Archie Lee, Agnes's cousin and shareholder of WesterLee Cottage.

"I assume so. I owe him a call anyway."

"It's nice for you to have privacy." Out with it, she commanded herself. She was slightly afraid of James. "You know," she said, "Agnes and I are hoping to leave at least some of the Point to a land trust. I'm sure I've mentioned this to you before."

The waiter appeared. "May I bring you anything else?"

James scowled and waved him away and Polly quickly smiled politely to make up for it.

"No, you have not mentioned that to me." He shot his cuff and looked at his watch. "You could have brought it up earlier."

"I'm sorry. I wanted you to know we're discussing it, we have been for a long time. As you stand to be the next shareholder from the Hancock family, I thought you should know. I welcome your opinion."

He dipped his head and frowned. She diverted her gaze and passively watched the reflections of the brisk waiters and waitresses in the front windows.

"My opinion. Hmm. Let's see. You're telling me the Point might be given to a land trust before it is my turn to make decisions. What's my opinion about that?"

He dropped his napkin, unfolded, onto his plate. He put the heels of his palms on the rim of the table and pushed backward, then sprang up, a movement that dispersed a cloud of his after-shave.

"I have to get back to the office," he said.

He turned and walked away, stopping at the front and pulling out a credit card. She didn't dare go after him.

She dreaded telling Agnes that James objected to the idea of dissolving the Fellowship, especially as she was recovering from such a big surgery. Polly's inclination was to allow him to rattle his sword and wait him out until he got interested in something else, which was how she'd always handled him. But this was different. This was a matter of money, about which James was undistractable. Polly was suddenly in the middle—on Agnes's side, but James was her child.

She didn't want to think about it.

The roads between the club and hers were, in May, pink and yellow, and scented with lilac growing deeper in people's yards. Children played on lawns and dogs jumped for balls. Dick had never allowed the boys to have a dog, in spite of begging, reasoned arguments, and tears. Was James exerting power now because he'd felt deprived of it then?

Hold on . . . Was that a man in her driveway? She blinked. He moved forward. She squinted through the windshield. Good Lord, it was Dick. Waving his arms! What was he doing? Had something happened? Three sons and five grandchildren gave her a lot to worry about. Her stomach clenched, and she prepared for a rush to somewhere. Dick loped toward her, still waving away. But . . . he was smiling. Smiling!

"I see you!" she called and waved, but he kept on coming as if she might breeze through their U-shaped driveway and right back onto the road again. She half thought *silly old man* and half thought how pleased she was that he'd been waiting for her. That never happened. He was in the dictionary, as the saying went, as the definition of an absentminded professor. So what had lured him out of his study, to look for her?

He kept walking straight at the car, so she stopped short of where she usually parked, and he circled his hand for her to open her window. It was already open, though, and she hadn't had a car with a window crank in decades. He didn't drive, on the theory that old people shouldn't be on the road, the one exception being the old person he needed to chauffeur him around.

Dick loomed at her and pulled at her handle. "Come on, come on!"

"Just a sec." She undid her belt and gathered her things, excited now herself. His strong emotions stirred her. They lived on a quiet dead end in Haverford, where small sounds registered. She heard her sole scrape on the asphalt, and her stockings switch against each other as she clambered out.

He closed her door and pulled at her sleeve. "Come on, I've been waiting for hours! I have something to tell you!"

She laughed. This was marvelous!

He took hold of her hand, and rather than going to the front door, he pulled her toward the side of the house. His strength gladdened her, but she had trouble keeping up in the clothes she'd put on to play bridge. She asked him to wait and slipped out of her shoes. After a second or two the cold of the Pennsylvania earth gave her a massive shiver. This small cataclysm separated her from him, just for an instant, long enough for her to take a step back, to hesitate, to seek to delay pleasure. This was her lifelong habit. She was apt to put new presents away for years before taking them from the box.

"I'll just go in and change," she said, "and put the chicken in." She wanted a warmer sweater and loafers. Slacks, if she dared take the time.

"Polly, will you please, for once, let all that be? I want to talk to you *now*."

"I'm sorry, of course. Here I am." It was wonderful to be needed at her stage of life, especially by him. She was as in love with him as ever. That was what the bridge ladies didn't know. Nor would they believe her if she made the claim. They spoke respectfully of their husbands, but she'd never had the sense that they'd experienced the passion she felt. They even enjoyed being widows, whereas the prospect of that blighted state gave Polly a headache. So if she had the chance to be with him, she took it.

She and Dick—the Wisters—were not young, not young at all at

37

eighty and eighty-two, but had stayed trim and neat and seemed to their three sons to still be their parents rather than a prompt for tours of retirement communities and discussions about how to split up the sticks of good furniture. They'd been married for nearly sixty vital years. Dick still stayed on top of world news, and Polly kept track of goings-on both in Haverford and on Cape Deel. They were often told how delightfully sharp they were, a compliment Dick snarled about in private. *I'm old—not an idiot.* He'd always been a progressive except when it came to fools.

A year earlier Dick had given notice that he intended to retire in the spring—now. "Out with the old, in with the new!" he'd crowed to Polly on the morning he went in to make his announcement. No one tried to talk him out of it, a stance he officially applauded for its realism, but Polly knew that had hurt. To add insult, his chair, Adam Waters, hadn't wasted a moment before saying Dick could retire mid-year. Actually, why not ease up for the fall semester—not teach at all?

"Preposterous! Don't I have a right to my blaze of glory, my swan song?" Dick bellowed when he came home that evening.

"You certainly do," Polly said loyally, but she could predict how this would end, so she added, "if you really want to. But you could use the time in other ways."

"I'm still viable! I have crucial ideas to impart! They'll line up when they hear I'm leaving!"

"Of course they will. But what do *you* want?"

In fact, his students had been grating on him in recent years, a decline he attributed to changing times rather than his own enfeeblement, though his lecture notes were crumbling in their file folders. His sudden sentimentality was a by-product of the chair's shoving him out the door. Dick puffed out his chest. Polly ached for him.

"I'll show them!" he said, when there was nothing else left to do.

He'd been a professor of philosophy and ethics at Haverford, then Penn, and in spite of decades of clamor under his roofs with the children, he'd lived a life of the mind. Though he was often at home, Polly had to plot to get his attention, but she chose to be cheerful rather than bitter about it. She'd wanted more, so much more, all that was possible between two people, but her galaxy of *what could be* ended up as a constellation of bright moments when they'd been intimate. It was just enough to keep her in a constant state of yearning, which Agnes told her was the principle behind dog training. "You're conditioned to please your master," Agnes said crisply. Polly wished she could.

She'd given a party before Christmas commemorating his academic career, spent ages composing a toast, including sending it to Agnes for editing and suggestions. "Dick Wister is the last of his kind, so let's raise a glass to him," it ended. Hyperbole seemed forgivable under the circumstances, and the guests took her cue and whooped and applauded. As they lay side by side in the dark that night Dick touchingly said, "It's true, I am the last of my kind." She reached for his hand, and from there that old familiar coming together. It was as good as ever, if less gymnastic. Her friends, the merry widows, didn't have that.

They didn't have him. For better or worse.

In Haverford, Dick *repaired*—he liked a verbal flourish—to his study for the day, emerging only for meals. At Meadowlea he sat in the old horsehair chair at the desk in his study and worked in the morning when his mind was unsullied. After lunch he wrote letters and newspaper editorials, some of which were printed. Book reviews, likewise. Meanwhile he was putting together a volume of his best correspondence. He'd exchanged letters with some of the most famous thinkers of the twentieth century. Their biographers had come to him already, asking for a look at their exchanges. Surely a compendium of his own letters would be an important addition to the field of twentieth-century philosophy?

All this work seemed to Polly arduous for a man of his age, and

the stream of rejections, which for decades he'd been able to inoculate himself against by means of his occasional publications and
anecdotes about famous books that were overlooked in their own
time, now chafed at his white-knuckled need for a final say and
made him simply miserable. To buck him up, she'd suggested that
until his next book came out he write a weblog to express his opinions. She'd read about them in the paper.

"Are you serious?" He frowned. "A weblog, on the computer?
I'd be laughed out of the profession. And how would my ideas be
protected from being picked up by other people?"

He'd adopted *blog* as a catchphrase rather than an activity. "Time
to work on my *blog*," he'd say for all kinds of transitions—when he
repaired to the bathroom, for example. She was loyally amused.
If what had come of her idea was one more private joke between
them, that was a decent result as far as she was concerned. They
had routines and exchanges stretching back to their earliest days
when they were establishing their exclusivity. Her favorite was when
she asked him, "Would you ever leave me?" The answer was *Nevernevernever*, spoken in a rush as if it were one word, the repetition of
which cast, as repetition can, a spell over Polly that assured her she
had the harmonic marriage she'd envisioned since she was small.
The endearment was atypical of him, but she'd institutionalized it,
attaching it to the end of many exchanges. Usually he responded
by turning away, but sometimes he echoed her *Nevernevernever*. Afterward she felt a twinge of remorse for forcing him to affirm his
attachment, but it was a reprise of some of the loftiest moments of
her life. When they were courting, she'd believed they could have
it all, but she'd long ago accepted that her youthful fantasy that
each partner in a couple encourage the other to do better was not
going to work with Dick. He had no inclination to ask for help or
advice. He wasn't averse to correcting Polly, though. Between him
and Agnes, her path to perfection was well lit.

They turned the corner of their Pennsylvania fieldstone house and walked across the lawn. The spring-blooming trees had recently budded and unfurled, shifting their two acres from gray and brown to pink, green, yellow, and purple. During lilac's brief season she was obsessed with the fragrant blooms, and went out into the cold dawn to soak her face with scented dew.

He pulled her to the middle of the lawn and began to sit down, pitching her off balance, and she flailed her hand to grab an ethereal railing. That was useless, so she thrust out a foot, steadied herself, and grabbed Dick back up instead. Her heart quickened.

"Why'd you do that? I wanted to lie on the grass, goddammit!"

"Oh, Dick, what a nice idea. Let's." She calculated how difficult it would be to get him down and up again. Very.

"Too late. You ruined it." He pulled his arm away from her and brushed at one sleeve, then the other, as if he had fallen into the dirt.

"I'm sorry. I do want to lie on the grass, it's a brilliant idea." The cold earth under her cheek, the blades pressed into her skin, the scent of sun in the crook of her arm—how many hours of her life had she spent lying on the grass? With Agnes, mainly. So many deep conversations had passed between as they lay on their stomachs crushing grass that pressed crosshatched tattoos into their arms and legs.Dick never wanted to do anything like that with her.

"Never mind." He crossed his arms and brooded.

"I really do want to, I just wasn't prepared."

"It's important to be spontaneous!"

She held her tongue. He'd say anything in irritation, not meaning it. She could talk herself into ignoring the words, but a harsh tone abraded her for days afterward. She had to wait him out now. His annoyance with her would soon give way to his greater desire to explain his idea, it always did. In the meantime she looked at her borders, the flowers coming up right on schedule, the earth still dark from a yearly spading in of compost. She'd drop a note to Robert in the morning, asking him how her beds looked at Meadowlea. Did he have any ideas for something new?

It was time to pick the last daffodils, before they began to dry up. She counted them from afar, nine, twelve, seventeen? Some hid shyly behind others. Some leaned. She pushed her glasses up her nose, but rather than clarifying her view of the flower bed, her vision grew misty, as if a fog had rolled in. Then a shift, this world to another. She knew what was about to happen. The state was familiar but beyond her control. In spite of great efforts over the years she couldn't willfully produce it. She had a few moments' warning, that was all, like the pulsing auras she used to feel before migraines pressed her skull in a vise. She slowed, and set aside an acquisitive urge for the experience to come, waiting patiently instead, breathing restraint into the lope of her pulse. Then Lydia appeared.

Polly checked the impulse to raise her hand. No point waving to a ghost, and Dick would see. Lydia, Lydia. Favorite child. A preference she wasn't meant to have, and didn't among the boys—well, Theo—but Lydia was different in kind. Favorite daughter—she could think that without guilt. She looked at her across the lawn, hungry for details. She wore her blue-and-white Liberty print dress, just what Polly would have chosen for a spring afternoon. She gathered a bouquet of ghostly daffodils, shades of the living blooms in the ground, and smiled when the syrup from their stems ran down her arms. Then she swung her eyes around to find Polly, who nodded and smiled back.

Polly glanced at Dick. Had he noticed she'd slipped off for a moment? She half-wished that he'd see the ghost, too, so they could share Lydia again. But Dick was looking up at the distant sky, ruminating, his chin jutted out. She glanced back, but Lydia had vanished.

"I have an idea, Polly, a marvelous idea."

She breathed the lilac scent. Until next time.

"Are you paying attention?" he bellowed.

"Of course. I'm very curious." She ached, as she always did, after the ghost disappeared. Nonsensical as it was, she couldn't fully invest in the unquestionable truth that it wasn't real. Her yearning reified it.

Dick began to rove again. She kept pace by walking and trotting. It appeared he was going to tour the perimeter of the property.

"I've spent the last year looking at all my work and organizing it for publication. You know that." She nodded. "As it turns out I've done a lot of work in my lifetime, most of it better than I remembered. Isn't it too bad that people with the very kind of minds that advance civilization are often so occupied with their work that they don't see what they've done? They forget they are exceptional. I forget! But I am always aware of my effort."

"If only everyone knew how hard you work!"

"They will, soon. After making this assessment, I can safely say I believe, judging by the quality of my work—my thinking!—that I deserve more recognition than I got—"

He glanced at her for a smidge of it, a solicitation for which she was ready with a generous donation. She arranged her face into a reflection of pure admiration. Bolstered, he moved on.

"—but I got a decent amount. I was known in the best circles. People respected me, and still do, I think."

He often spoke to her as if she hadn't been there for every minute of it, didn't know the entire cast, hadn't read every word.

"Yes, they did and they do," she agreed.

His expression brightened but his eyebrows were quizzical. He approved the message but withheld credit from the messenger. "They did and they do. But . . ."—his index finger bobbed instructively—"my real work, my illumination of pacifism—I wrote the definitive work on the subject! Where is my credit for that?"

43

"Oh, but that was just bad timing," she said as she had a thousand times. It was their story, a tenet of their marriage, that World War II had ruined Dick's career.

"Yes, it was. But now I see that I got scared off too easily, Polly! I should have stuck to my guns." He raised his eyebrows at his joke, then went on. "I realize now there is no last word on pacifism. I backed off without a fight. I should have been tougher. I just didn't expect"—he stopped, and she nearly bammed into him—"Hitler," he finished, speaking the name as if it belonged to a relative with whom he'd had an irreparable falling-out.

"You couldn't have, dear," she said.

"Though I could blame Churchill—"

Here he was in danger of going off on a tangent about the true causes of World War II, a lecture that could keep them out until dark fell.

"Churchill has a lot to answer for," Polly said, nipping the diatribe. "I'm just so curious about your *new* idea."

"Yes. Good." He got into a position to face her directly. He put his hands on her shoulders.

"Polly, I have decided to revise *A Pacifist's Primer*. I'll bring it up to date, and I'll take on the Hitler question. I have to. No one else is in as good a position to do it as I am. My mind is as sharp as ever, and I'll have time now. I'll revise the book, add research about what others have said on the subject since my original edition, and I'll add a foreword, describing what happened to the book the first time around. Then—drumroll, please!—I'll make an argument for pacifism even in the face of Hitler."

She listened with an alert expression, nodding encouragingly, but behind the mask she drooped with disappointment. There went her time with Dick. Damn Hitler and Churchill! If only Dick had gotten the glory he sought sixty years ago, he might care to be idle now. She was cold, and hungry. She hadn't eaten much lunch, just half a BLT. It was too late to cook the chicken. "It's a great idea."

"I know." He beamed.

"And you'll be able to work in the library at Penn, and use the pool."

"I won't need to. This will require more analysis than research."

"I thought you just said you had to research the work since then?" She'd open a can of soup and make a cheese omelet. Let's think, she had Swiss, and cheddar—

"Dammit, Polly!"

"Sshh," she hushed him automatically.

"I don't care who hears me, goddammit! That's the whole point I'm making here! I don't care anymore. I have wisdom to deploy. It's important to stand by pacifism. The coming century will surely see a war or two. Finally I'm going to say what I want to say and I'm not going to go hide under a rock if I'm called an anti-Semite for it. I'm not an anti-Semite! I'm a pacifist!"

She tried to catch his arms, to somehow get her own arms around him, to calm him, but he was flailing too hard and she flailed, too.

"It's a great idea!" she said loudly. "It really is. I love it, Dick. Do it!"

He breathed hard and then less hard. "I plan to. Now look, Polly," he said accusatorily, "we've gone down our separate roads in the past, but I'm retired now. I'm home. I thought you'd be here, too. Today is a case in point. I had this idea, and where were you?"

"I've always been here!" The whole phenomenon of welling was set into motion—eyes, throat, and heart. "I didn't know you wanted me to stay home. Why didn't you ask?"

He thrust out his chin and gazed at the house. "I won't waste my breath stating the obvious."

"I would have loved to!" The disproportion and unfairness of the accusation, after all the decades when she'd have loved him to keep her company, was too huge to fathom.

Her distress mollified him, and his gaze softened. "All right. We'll let this time go. But from now on I am going to be working full-time on my book. Which raises the matter of my other projects. I need someone to finish pulling together the collection of my published work, and my letters. Publishers need to be queried, and so on. I could hire an assistant to do that, but it occurred to me today—I have you. You could do this."

"I could. I really could. I want to. There's nothing I'd rather do."

"Good! I need you, Polly. You know that, don't you? I don't say it every minute of every day, but it's true."

It was true. She worked hard to make his life satisfying. Most of her friends had done the same for their husbands, in one way or another. It was what one did. A few had rebelled once feminism took a firm hold in the sixties, and ended up divorced, but she'd never considered it.

"We can get a lot of work done in Maine," she said.

"I'll have to bring more books than usual, and some files."

"We'll make it fit." She began to pack the car in her mind.

"This *is* a good idea, isn't it?"

His face changed, exposing a deeper layer, as if he'd removed a mask to reveal a touching, uncertain hope.

"I believe in you, Dick." She leaned against his chest and he held her and kissed the top of her head. "You'll never leave me, will you?"

"Nevernevernever." He gave her a squeeze.

"I'm excited," she said. "This will be fun."

"To peace on earth!" he exclaimed. "Now, what's for dinner?"

They went inside, and she changed into her slacks. When she came downstairs, she picked up the mail on the hall table and leafed through it. On her way back to the kitchen she spotted another letter on the floor, without its envelope. Dick must have dropped it.

Dear Dr. Wister,

We regret to inform you that the University will not be able to offer you Emeritus status. Your privileges will expire on July 1, 2000. . . .

Polly's heart skipped a beat. How could they be so cruel? This was too hurtful to an old man. Tears came as she pictured him all alone, opening this letter, expecting good news, and finding instead another rejection. How brave he was to come up with an alternative plan, while she was at bridge! What an incredible example of resilience—no doubt beyond the capability of many who'd written him off. There were limits, however. He needed a success, badly. She laid her palm on her chest, holding her heart against its breaking. Dick wasn't just asking for help. She needed to save his life. Not to mention how she needed to preserve the Sank. And mollify her oldest child, who didn't want to let the land slip through his hands.

No more bridge for me.

CHAPTER 3

Maud, Manhattan, June 2000

MAUD SILVER STRETCHED, LACING HER FINGERS AND TURN-ing them inside out, reaching up and bending in every direction. She snapped open the tortoiseshell clip at the nape of her neck and combed her fingers through her hair, releasing it from its professional yoke and over her summer-bare shoulders. She hung her beige jacket over the back of her chair, placed her low black heels in a desk drawer, and slipped into her espadrilles. Finally, she loaded a manuscript into her canvas bag.

"Taking off so soon?" asked Mary, another editorial assistant.

"Umm."

"I'm always amazed you manage to leave at five on the dot. You must be a really fast worker. I'll be here until nine, at least."

It had taken Maud a while to understand that Mary considered her a rival. She was forever taunting Maud and making a point of being a better assistant. She sent David emails time-stamped after eleven o'clock at night. Maud couldn't compete, nor did she want to. She focused on coming up with fresh ideas. David seemed contented with her work, so she decided the best attitude toward Mary was to take her at face value.

"I am a fast worker, thank you!" Maud said. She considered saying she had to get home, but that was really not anyone's business. No one at work knew anything about her private life.

Mary looked back at her computer and tapped at the keys. "I'll help David if he needs anything after you go."

She can't help herself, Maud thought. "Great! Good night!" She sped off before another volley had time to land. No one had told her that the hardest part of a job was the other people.

Maud was as ambitious as Mary. She wanted to create careers for authors in whom she believed. Yet her advisor at college had warned Maud against indiscriminate hard work. Many women forwent the possibility of advancement by being diligent rather than bold. Plus sexism, of course. Maud didn't doubt that, yet she had a very particular way of being a feminist, a central tenet of which was not to mimic traditionally masculine behaviors. There was another way to be in the world, for both women and men. A freer way.

She walked past David's office, hoping to see him, further hoping he had an answer for her about the idea she'd presented that morning. But his door was shut.

Outside, it was June. The air pulled upward, in buoyant invisible puffs, and the entire city seemed to be afloat. New Yorkers had made a tacit agreement to be as civil as the mild weather. In the squares of dirt around the sidewalk trees, flowers bloomed. Dog owners who may have stopped there for relief in February now steered their companions to bleaker spots for a pee. Mothers held hands with their skipping children, and young girls walked three abreast, linked at the elbow. Boys and men made way for women, for once. *Dachshund, sweater, clog, stroller, espadrilles*, Maud named. She rose up on her toes slightly and pushed off with gusto. She'd had a good idea, one that could get her ahead. David would like it, she was pretty sure. She'd have a voice, in publishing, in the city, in the world. *Tree, police car, taxi, truck, traffic light.* Editorial assistant promoted to assistant editor. Then editor, then her own imprint. It was all out there, shimmering.

She wasn't sure if she'd ever make what her father would call "real" money, but she wanted a career. She'd spent a lot of time on the presentation she'd made to David that morning. Her idea was to persuade Agnes Lee to write a book called *Agnes When*, a memoir about her childhood and how she came to write the *When Nan* books. Alongside it the company could reissue all the *When Nan* books in six volumes, both in hardcover and paperback. A new generation of children would become Nan fans. Boys too, now. Marketing could emphasize that. Maud had made it clear that she wanted to handle this memoir project herself—that she'd be the editor, not an assistant.

When she'd dropped it off with him, she'd turned at the door of his office and said, "It's a good idea." Then left. That had been a risk. Who turned her back on David? She'd felt powerful. Now when she pictured it, she winced.

She turned on 18th and walked across to Fifth Avenue. Had she been too assertive? She hadn't seen him the rest of the day. Was that meaningful, or was he just busy?

There were a few crazy people on the walk home. Nothing like when her mother was young in the eighties and the mental hospitals had tipped forward and all the patients had fallen onto the streets. Heidi told Maud that people were frightened of them, but that she never was. "Our minds are made by a weaver. Your mind is a strong tapestry that can't be ripped. My mind is a fishing net with lots of holes where strange notions can enter and get caught." Heidi spent hours chatting, laughing, and commiserating with the unseen people of Manhattan. Maud was proud of her—and jealous of the time she gave away. Like all children, she wanted her mother's full attention.

The fastest route to the Village was across and down, but in the warm months, if she had time, Maud charted longer routes down all the different avenues. Today, Fifth, right to Washington

Square Park. Her spirits invariably lifted as she crossed the street where Henry James had sent carriages rolling, couples flirting, long skirts lifting above puddles, calling cards waiting on silver trays. She passed triumphally under the arch and her spirit expanded. Skateboarders, chess players, street performers, dog walkers, drug dealers. Children, students, old friends, dogs. Every creature touched by the pale green of June. The month of promise, when people married and believed they'd always be happy.

She turned west and stopped at the light at Sixth Avenue. The streets teemed with men. Mesh shirts, motorcycle boots, tattoos. She nodded to a couple she knew. She'd grown up among gay men and had heard their stories of how they realized they were different and how they told their families. "They're ahead of most straight men," Heidi said. "They had to figure out who they are and not take it for granted. You'll figure out who you are, too."

Maud had given the question a lot of thought, but she wasn't sure yet of an answer. She wasn't a free spirit like Heidi. She wasn't social like the men who roamed her neighborhood. She had pursued her love of books into a career, but she still felt there was something essential about herself yet to uncover. But she was already twenty-six. She hoped she'd discover whatever it was soon.

She stepped into the day care center. A dozen sets of searching eyes looked up—*Are you my mother?* She had to disappoint all but one, the nearly three-year-old balancing a block on top of a construction of other blocks. Clemmie—for Clemence, a French name that Maud had loved since she first heard it—looked so small when she was at a distance. A tiny girl in tiny sneakers and shorts and a T-shirt, with large gray eyes like Heidi's and embarrassingly matted dark blonde hair. One of the women on duty alerted her to her mother's arrival, and Clemmie knocked over the block tower in her hurry to cross the room. Maud pushed her shoulder bag behind her back and lifted Clemmie onto her hip.

"Ready?"

Clemmie nodded from her waist, her whole body bobbing forward.

"Let's go make dinner." She inhaled the scent of Clemmie's hair, sweaty and rank. No one told you that you'd be all right with your child's worst scents.

Clemmie reached out a chubby hand to every dog they passed. Some people stopped to let her say hello, and Maud lowered her and lifted her again. "That was very gentle," Maud said. "Good girl."

They turned into Charles Street. When Maud was little, she'd enjoyed the sensation of envious eyes on her back as she walked up the steps and through the dark green door of their house. Then, and now, the first impression inside was the scent of lilies and cool, quiet space. When she wasn't sick, Heidi bought new flowers every week—otherwise Maud did. The house was worth a lot of money at this point. Her father didn't have much to offer in the way of loyalty or thoughtfulness, but he had a knack for being in the right place at the right time. He'd bought this place in the late seventies, when he was a student at NYU. Even then he'd been making money on the stock market, and investing in property seemed like a good idea. Heidi had never criticized Maud's father after their divorce, which had frustrated teenage Maud, who had a lot on her mind already without having to decide what to think of Moses Silver. Now she was glad that decision had been left up to her.

She set her bag on the floor and placed her keys in the ceramic dish on the hall table. A mirror hung directly in front of her, but she didn't glance at it. She wasn't beautiful like her mother, but she had heavy brown shiny hair, and she looked like a girl of the city. She was New York thin. She could either stand out or disappear into crowds, depending on her mood, and she could walk as fast as many people ran.

"Hello? Ma?"

She lowered Clemmie and got her a juice box from the refrigerator. The living room and kitchen and back garden were empty. She called up the stairs. "Anyone home?" she called. "Ma?" Her voice echoed between the walls, and faded to expose the creaks of an old house. She held Clemmie's hand and climbed upward. An old beige runner covered the second-floor hallway. She peered into the rooms but sensed their emptiness even before she looked.

She headed up to the third floor. Halfway up she felt anxious. Before reaching the top step she knew—her mother had turned blue again.

Maud paused to steady herself. She carried within an emotion for which there was no exact word, though it was in the range of well-being—pink in hue, warm in temperature, June-like in atmosphere, feminine in nature. It was her touchstone, her *self*. Her being and beliefs had formed around it, both her conviction that hope was rational and her certainty that the world was moving toward an actualization of noble ideals. She'd once described it to a doctor of Heidi's, who told her it was a memory of innocence—or a dream—most likely from the time before she understood that something was wrong with her mother. Maud couldn't remember that time. What had it been like? All she had left was a sentence Heidi still repeated sometimes. *I loved you before I knew you.* She said it came from the Bible, but Maud wouldn't know.

Once Heidi had appeared on Maud's blacktop playground in the middle of the school day and swung next to the children, laughing loudly yet in a perceptibly joyless way, until a teacher coaxed her to stop. She might stay in bed for days, unwashed, smelling of the jumbled inside of her body. Or she might take Maud on a subway to a hotel uptown and rent a room so they could swim in the pool and order room service and jump on the beds. "No one knows where we are!" she'd say delightedly. "Should we live here, like Eloise?" Or they might go to Central Park at dusk and lie on their backs in the Great Meadow to watch night fall, then not leave until the sun came up. "No one can see us, Maudie, we are spirits of the night." *No, we're not,* Maud thought, missing her bed. She was both exasperated by Heidi and wished she could be less conventional. Maud was rigid and aware. Heidi was fearless and clueless. "I named you Maud because it is a word for meadow. Meadows are the most beautiful places." When Heidi was manic, life was fun, if unnerving. When she was depressed, Maud couldn't find her among the shadows.

Heidi called depression *turning blue.* "What is it like?" Maud once asked. "Good question," Heidi said, as if she'd never before been pressed to describe it, had not told countless doctors where she was on a scale of one to ten with eating, sleeping, bad thoughts, spending, hiding, et cetera. Heidi was the source of Maud's respect for precision.

"Close your eyes and press your palms against your eyeballs," Heidi instructed. "Now cross your legs and lock your ankles over each other. No, don't stop, keep pressing your eyes. Now make a deep noise in your chest, a very afraid noise." Maud did all three. "Keep going." Maud felt trapped. Her ribs vibrated horribly. "Are you feeling anything?" Maud nodded. "What? Don't say it out loud. Tell yourself." Maud felt frightened, and as if she were stuck. Pinned down. Alone. She whimpered.

"Now, now, come back. Take your fingers off your eyes. Shake out your arms and legs."

Maud was crying.

"I'm so sorry, lamb. It was the only way I could think of to explain."

"I'm not crying for me," Maud said.

Their last family time together was at Caneel Bay. Her father, Moses, had told her the story several times, but she believed she remembered some of it firsthand. Maud was almost five. Heidi had gone snorkeling the first day and had been hectic at the tea that afternoon, describing all the fish she'd seen to the other guests. Maud had seen them look pleased at first to be approached by such a beautiful young woman, but soon they were trying to sidle away from her. When Moses led her away Maud saw them notice her limp. Maud wanted to tell them the limp went away in the water— that was what Heidi said—but she was too shy.

On the second day Heidi got up before anyone and swam out into the boat channel. She described swimming alongside a barracuda and seeing his ghastly smile and fanatic eyes. "He recognized me," she said. "He knew me from before." "Before when?" Maud asked. They had never been to Caneel Bay before. "From the past, when we were relatives." Moses frowned. He hired one of the workers at the hotel to keep an eye on Heidi so he and Maud could go to the beach. He needn't have. Heidi was fine for the rest of the vacation, her personality meshing with her pretty face. Maud loved to think of that trip. The temperature and the island colors matched her inner feeling. When they got home, though, Heidi went straight into the hospital. Maud was told she was at a place in the country where she could sleep.

Maud stopped at the threshold of the top-floor room Heidi sometimes went to for naps. "Come on, Clem." She picked her up again and opened the door slowly. Heidi was on her bed, face up. Maud couldn't tell whether or not she was asleep. Heidi's feet were bare, her toenails unpolished. She wore an old broom skirt and a black sweater and the gold bangle she never took off—it had attracted the barracuda. Her hair fanned to the sides across the pillowcase.

"Ma? Are you awake?" Maud leaned over her and arranged her hair. "It's almost dinnertime. Do you want to come downstairs? It's really beautiful outside."

Maud set Clemmie down and sat on the edge of the bed. She

rubbed her mother's arm. Heidi brought a wrist up to her eyes and draped them. She smelled clean, washed and perfumed.

"I just got home from work. Had a lovely walk back, naming the world." She took Heidi's hand. "As you taught me." She looked into the soft brown shadows, and at the wavy pale lines around the blots of shades. "Please, Ma?" She tugged lightly.

Heidi hinged upward via her strong stomach muscles and looked around.

"Hi, Heidi," Clemmie said.

"Hello, you. Come up here." Clemmie reached up, and Maud hooked her fingers in the back of her shorts and lifted. Clemmie hurled herself onto Heidi's lap.

"I had a long nap. I felt a little blue this morning, but I fought it. I took a long bath and did beauty things," Heidi said.

"I'm so glad. You seem fine now."

Heidi raised her eyebrows. "*Fine* might be going too far. But I feel all right. I caught myself in time. This morning I went to a store and stood there staring around, and I thought—*uh-oh.*"

This was a symptom for Heidi. It was also the kind of thing she couldn't tell people without their saying, *Oh I do that too!* No. They didn't. Not in the same way. Her major spiraling symptom was a repetitive thought. She went around the world picturing bad things happening to children at that very moment, and then bad things happening to animals. When she had those thoughts, if she didn't get help soon enough, she ended up in the hospital.

"Good, Ma." Maud was careful not to go overboard. An excess of enthusiasm frightened Heidi. Her detector for false cheer was finely tuned. "Come on, I'm getting hungry."

She held out her hand and the three of them went down— mother, daughter, granddaughter. Maud led Heidi and Clemmie straight down to the garden and headed back up to the kitchen. She cut up vegetables and put rice in the cooker. A stir-fry. A staple.

Maud would watch to see if Heidi ate the green peppers. When she was really getting blue, she didn't like to chew.

As Maud cooked, she checked out the window every couple of minutes. It appeared Clemence was in charge of whatever game she and Heidi were playing. She pointed here and there, and Heidi skipped across the bricks. Maud smiled—her bossy daughter. Clemence had been a person right from the start, with her own preferences and ways of doing things. She'd had colic, and Maud had spent hours walking her, and more hours with her draped like a tense lion in an acacia tree over her forearm, or in the groove between her pressed-together thighs, the baby turned on her stomach, tiny feet pointing toward Maud's abdomen, the rumbling stomach hanging free, the bony back rising on each breath. Or in the same position but rolled on her back, so the baby faced her, and Maud could slip her thumbs inside the little fists and make the hands jig back and forth while she made funny faces.

She discovered that if she removed a layer of clothing when Clemmie was wailing she usually stopped. She also found that Clemmie liked to be set down on a blanket on the floor in a pool of sun and left alone. This perplexed Maud. She'd read about Jane Goodall raising her son, Grub, as she'd seen the chimps raise their young, by always having him in someone's arms and never letting him down or leaving him alone. She'd have tried that if it weren't for her job—she couldn't very well ask the day care to replicate the doings of a chimp mother. But Clemmie wouldn't have wanted that anyway. She had a strong sense of her bodily integrity.

Now Clemmie was nearly three, a solid walker and talker. She'd started talking early and spoke in sentences, and that made her both easier and harder than when she was a baby. Maud hated to leave her to go to work, but she very much wanted to work, beyond the need for money. Her father, Moses Silver, had offered to pay for an abortion, on the theory that having a baby so young and without a husband would ruin Maud's career, but Maud couldn't conscience that, not for herself. She'd asked Heidi what she thought, and Heidi had been her usual fey self, saying she'd loved being a young mother, and that she'd put her creativity into that and the house and missed nothing. Moses's mother also encouraged the abortion on the grounds of her long-term work for abortion rights groups—she'd be proud to have a granddaughter who'd had one. Heidi didn't have any family for Maud to consult, which she was used to—but in this instance the lack, the absence, reinforced her decision. All those people she'd never know would come alive in the baby. Maud made up her mind to go ahead with the pregnancy, and to never regret it. She was sure Heidi had never regretted her.

Now Heidi crouched in front of the brick wall and helped Clemmie crawl up onto her back. Clemmie gave Heidi a good kick in the flanks, which made Heidi laugh. Maud was swept with sorrow, watching this happy scene. Whatever had happened to her mother, to render her mind so porous?

They ate outside on the wooden table, lighting candles when the sky dimmed. When the meal was finished, Heidi excused herself to go read.

"Tired, Ma?" Maud saw that a great strain had appeared around her eyes and mouth.

"Uh-huh."

"What are you reading this week? Anything good?" She glanced over at Clemmie, who was playing quietly now under the table, nearly ready for bed.

Heidi smiled. "Are you doing market research?"

"Nope. Just curious."

"I'm reading *The Emigrants*. Also, *Cold Mountain*. Also, poems."

"Do you think you'd buy a memoir by Agnes Lee?"

"So this is market research." Heidi leaned back and laced her hands behind her head.

Maud laughed. "I guess so."

"Did she write one?"

"Not yet. But I am going to try to convince her to. I asked David if I could pursue it."

Heidi thought about it. "I used to imagine Agnes Lee all the time. When I read her books, I pictured her handwriting as straight connected printing, old-fashioned. I pictured her looking out a window as she wrote—between sentences, that is." She shook her head. "I wanted to do everything that Nan did."

"Me too."

"You are. You will. I never did anything."

There was no point refuting this. A discussion would deflate her. Best to let the words dissipate.

"All right, up I go. Good night, Clemmie." She waved. "Night, Hi," Clemmie said without turning around.

After Clemmie's bath Maud read her two Nan books of her choice—Clemmie had all of them in her room—until the small eyes closed. Maud had taught her how to go to sleep, and how to put herself back to sleep at night if she awoke. It was a great accomplishment, but no one wanted to hear about the triumphant work of mothers. It was a taken-for-granted form of labor, worth little to no money. She had to pat her own back for that.

Before she went up to check on Heidi, she opened her laptop. The sounds of the city seeped in over her windowsill—men's voices, dogs barking, a woman's smoky laugh, leather scuffing on the sidewalk. She never wanted to leave this house.

Emails from Mary that made it clear she was still in the office. Maud rolled her eyes.

An email from David.

Maud. Your idea is good, as you know. But we are a children's book imprint, so we can't do the book. I'm sorry to disappoint you. There are other ways to go about this, however, and New York is full of people who have traveled an individual path toward the future they desire. If I were your age with your determination to be an editor, I'd propose the idea to Agnes Lee, work with her on the manuscript, and then I'd ask my boss to introduce me to people who'd be interested. That is an entirely plausible scenario and can be pursued in the evenings. Meanwhile, a boxed set of *When Nan* is a smart idea. Think of who we can get to write an introduction.

D.

He liked it. But he couldn't give her the go-ahead. Instead he was pushing her out of the nest, or teaching her how to fly out on her own. She knew she better start right in before she scared herself out of trying.

She made a list of pros and cons from Agnes's point of view, and the only pros were A, it was an interesting project—maybe, and B, Agnes could make a personal statement that would seal her legacy as an author for the ages—if she cared about that. Maud had the feeling that Agnes wouldn't be moved by either one, especially without a contract. What might move her was Maud's original idea—a memoir would sell the series. Pure business, nothing abstract or lofty. Nan was decidedly down-to-earth; Maud guessed Agnes admired that mode of behavior.

Maud considered the best approach. She could pretend David had agreed to the idea, but that would backfire. The only sure way forward was to be honest about the circumstances and the gamble this would be. She had nothing to lose by trying. She placed her fingers on her keyboard and began to draft.

PART TWO

A Concern

CHAPTER 4

The Lees, Philadelphia and Fellowship Point, the 1870s

T HE LEES WERE QUAKERS, FRUGAL AND PLAIN, OR SO THEY considered themselves. They didn't decorate like rich people. Their rugs were so thin you could see the wood underneath, and their upholstery had faded from decades of sun and was torn by generations of children. These defects were invisible to the family until that rare moment when someone had a piece recovered—for example, a bedroom slipper chair had been revamped in the 1930s in an art deco diamond pattern, a change under discussion for the next thirty years—but the ethos was nostalgic and historical. On the first day of every summer when the present iteration of the family arrived, the children ran through the house pointing and exclaiming, deeply thrilled by the familiar. They took old sweaters out of cedar chests and set up their rooms and looked through their journals from previous summers. Especially loved was the wicker in the glass room and on the porches, around which piles of paint flakes gathered and were swept away until finally someone thought to repaint.

Wallpaper peeled. Dishes chipped. Silver tarnished. But the underbrush was carefully cleaned beneath the trees in the Sank, and the beds and meadows fed and artfully trimmed to appear Edenically wild.

Since the mid-1870s, the Lees had occupied two of the five large cottages on Fellowship Point, the sizable thumb of the glove called Cape Deel that reached from the coast into the Gulf of Maine. Cape Deel was named, or so went the story, after a deal made between early Scots settlers and the Abenaki, who traded it for the usual assortment of European goods. Why spell it out, however, so the name was changed to Deel, the pair of vowels obfuscating the transaction. The explanation of how the peninsula of Cape Deel had been formed became more cataclysmic over time as the science of tectonic plates and underwater volcanoes and explosions and retreating ice sheets that cast glacial erratics down the coast was proven and accepted. The rock was mainly granite, including a pink variety that became a signature building material of the area. The sight of a pink drive lined with green firs leading to a house with a terrace delineated by a pink wall dripping with ivy and roses in front of a July sparkling sea was the standard set by a rich Philadelphian and copied in whole or in part all over. Mineral rocks were easily found, and generations of children chipped away at them. Mason jars full of brightly colored specimens were a staple of bedroom bookcases and bathroom sills.

For centuries the Cape was the territory of indigenous peoples, who lived on the land without disturbing it very much at all, due to their belief that they belonged to nature rather than the other way around. The Red Paint people arrived by sea and lived along the coast for thousands of years before Europeans figured out how to get there. Then came the Abenaki, a northern band that eventually became five main tribes in Maine. They fished from their birch bark canoes and cooked over fires on the beaches, where artifacts had been found at the sites of their early encampments. One of these was at the tip of Fellowship Point.

People of English and Scottish descent wandered down from the Maritimes and up from the Massachusetts Bay Colony and built

Deel Town, a crossroads with wooden houses in either direction. Soon brick buildings indicated more business coming to town, and a few more lanes sprouted off the main road. Along with the local businesses on the street, small farms, cottage industries, and fishing docks dotted around the peninsula supplied all needs. The new settlers disturbed the land more than the indigenous peoples had, but not much, compared to other places along the coast where logs were cleared, sardine canneries built, and cities erected. In the 1850s a few large summer cottages were built on the eastern side of the peninsula, where ocean breezes kept the blackflies and the mosquitos away and the sunrises were magnificent. The point of Cape Deel was still untouched. William Lee changed that.

William Lee was a Philadelphia Quaker, a member of a rich merchant family that owned a shipping concern, a warehouse on the Delaware, and a large house on Walnut Street near Franklin Square. William worked for the family firm, but his older brother, Edgar, worked harder, and expanded the company by buying four textile factories in Kensington that William was charged with overseeing. Each factory employed about six men, chosen from among the off-the-boat population of English, Scots, and Irish that lived in nearby North Philadelphia neighborhoods, and William did his Quaker best to see that their lives were decent and their children went to school. He was mildly interested in the business and liked walking the streets among all the small factories, finding out who sold to whom and why—childlike questions that garnered him intelligence his brother sought to turn to profit by applying the principles of modernization and efficiency. Edgar Lee envisioned a complex the size of a city block where, rather than each small factory attending to an aspect of a final product, milling, weaving, dyeing, and cutting could all be done under one roof, with no other owner gaining from the process.

William saw the advantage to be had in the idea but argued

against it. How could workers ever save enough from their wages to buy the factory from the owner and become owners themselves if faced with purchasing a massive operation? The brothers stared at each other across a gulf of difference. Edgar was a solid, civic-minded American capitalist whose business acumen was sufficiently bifurcated from his moral perceptions that he managed to believe that the lives of those who toiled for his riches were within a natural order, and all was fair; and William saw himself as an educated, free American man whose lack of constraint and easy path in life afforded egalitarian visions. They couldn't see themselves and their positions clearly enough to dig to the bottom of their difference, which was rooted in personality, a subject that men of their ilk weren't trained to discuss. Instead they argued about the Preamble, specifically the pursuit of happiness. What did pursuit mean, and how responsible was a person to facilitate that pursuit for others? They both agreed that the point of the document—and of democracy!—was that everyone is responsible for his fellow man and woman, but what did that entail? And so on. Edgar despaired of having a real partner in his brother, and William despaired of making so much more money than men he bossed. He believed there was a better way and hoped he could discover it.

He married Verity Hill of Germantown, had children, went to Meeting, and pursued many hobbies and interests. Among those was a category he called Nature, a passion he'd inherited from his father, Andrew Lee, at whose side he'd often rambled through unsullied fields and forests on the weekends. Andrew attended a lecture at the Spring Garden Institute in 1854 given by a man named Henry David Thoreau, who'd spoken about the importance of wild areas and described his solitary walks in remote places. His descriptions stirred Andrew, who immediately bought a copy of *Walden; Or, Life in the Woods*, a book that acted on him like a reveille bugle call.

He became a conservationist and spoke to anyone who would listen of the necessity of a system of national parks where land would be kept pristine and people could go to fill their souls. William took these ideas to heart, and as a young man developed a habit of going off by himself for weeks at a time and coming back having learned new names for flora and fauna that he taught to his children. These ethereal acquisitions led him to an interest in conserving a spot himself, for as much as he was excited by the new, he also wanted to see the same again, and the federal government didn't appear in any hurry to take up his father's idea. William had a dream one night where a bird asked him to protect her eggs. He woke up with the idea of buying a piece of land where birds could be safe. Verity cautioned him to be judicious about describing his apocryphal vision, for fear he might be seen as too emotional. Quakers were meant to be moved by spirit, but only just so far.

In 1872, William took a trip by himself up the coast of Maine—Thoreau claimed it was the only unspoiled land left in New England—to visit relatives at their summer place in Sorrento. By chance he stopped at Cape Deel to rest his horse and buy food. It was a beautiful day, perfect conditions for curiosity to propel him southward. He removed the saddle from his horse to give her a break, then lay down on the grass and gazed up, daydreaming and imagining and reciting poems from memory. As he lazed, watching the birds and marveling at their abilities, he got a sudden jolt. He sighted a male Labrador duck, a rare creature by then and soon to be extinct. It was recognizable by its white wings and black body, a unique pattern that he'd read about in his bird books. He hadn't put it down on his list of birds to look for; it wasn't meant to be here. It wintered off Cape Cod and summered in Canada. But here it was, in Maine, and he might be the only person who knew it. Never before had he felt so essential. Something was happening—to him.

William got back on his horse and did his best to follow the duck, going the direction it went. He rode down the length of the Cape, sticking to the west side, and took a turn down a finger of land, a detour that became his destiny. The place had the feel of a dream, each of its features both natural and symbolic: a salt marsh along the lower side, teeming with wildlife and plants; a wild meadow running down the middle, dotted with trees and wildflowers; a long, flat west side sloping down to a rocky shore; and at the end, a point guarded by cliffs and fir trees where he got another look at the Labrador duck, as well as many other species. This was the land he'd been imagining, he had no doubt. He bought the whole 145-acre point for $7,500, another good *deel*.

The following summer William went back with a group of friends, including his brother Edgar, to camp out, bird-watch, and experience the freedom of life in the wild. The other men loved it as much as he did, and agreed he'd found a spectacular and unique spot, blessedly far away from the social pressures and Episcopalian mumbo jumbo of Newport and Bar Harbor. They ate from the sea and foraged for edible weeds and mushrooms and, after bracing dips in the cold water, lolled naked on the warm rocks and talked desultorily about rabbits and law cases and the future of the United States and birds and their businesses, and how wonderful it would be if this were life forever. William Lee said they all should come every year. They could form a club with that goal in mind. Edgar, who always thought bigger and wanted more, said they should each build a house here, a proposal that aroused cheers. If William felt a twinge at his brother's commandeering of his land, that hesitation didn't make it into the official origin story.

Instead, he was seized, as many Americans had been before him and would be again, by an idea to create a utopian community that conformed to Quaker principles and his own aesthetics. He spent a few months inventing the model, consulting with bankers, architects, and philosophers along the way. It was his opinion that a group of like-minded Friends would be better off having shares in an association than owning individual plots of land. The association would set standards for aesthetics and behavior and events that would benefit all. William would run it. The others could leave things to him and trust that their interests would be well served. He didn't know any other man more willing to work on behalf of others than he was, with less self-interest, a skill he was happy to teach to anyone who would listen. Verity consoled him when crowds didn't line up.

He designed the Point for five houses, one for each of the men on that first camping trip and the man's family—the Dyers' Outer Light, the Reeds' Rock Reed, the William Lees' Leeward Cottage, the Hancocks' Meadowlea, and the Edgar Lees' WesterLee. They would be built on the western side of the spit, with a view to an inlet on one side and across the salt marsh to open sea on the other. The meadows would remain intact, with only a dirt road leading past the buildings and down toward the actual point. He drew the plans so that all habitation would stop about three-quarters of the way down, and the bottom tip remain wild for the birds and other creatures. Many artifacts had been left there by the Abenaki, who had for many decades moved down to the shore for the summer. William and Edgar dug up the leavings and kept them at Leeward and WesterLee. William and his descendants were solicited both by museums and collectors for the items, but he was firm that the artifacts belonged on Fellowship Point, and visitors were disallowed from taking photographs of the collection.

As William sketched where the five houses would go, he thought back wistfully to his initial notion that they should be interchangeable, exactly the same, inside and out. No family would own a particular house but could easily move into any one of them each summer. Little did he know he had invented the idea of time-shares. He liked the idea of people having different views and vantage points and not becoming attached to a plot. It would be liberating to have no house be grander than any other. Even Quakers—maybe especially they—could use protection from avarice, and William believed his plan would provide it quietly; but when he mentioned this to Edgar, he got resistance. Think of the women, Edgar argued. They will want to decorate.

William saw his point and designed five different houses, his own in the middle. He reminded himself that change took time, they were still young enough for moral growth, surely egalitarian sentiments would be stirred by weeks spent in that edifying landscape. He looked at many types of houses and plans before settling on a modified Shingle style for his own house, with six bedrooms, a sunroom that became known as *the glass room*, a screen room for insect-free meals outside, and fireplaces up and down to ward off the foggy chill. He learned enough about architecture to switch professions. He preferred not to trade on his skills, but to pour them into making the human presence on the Point as aesthetically pleasing as the site itself. He consulted with the wives on outward appearance and managed by directing their attention to details to maintain his goal of having no one house larger than any other, as well as creating a sense of unity.

The houses were capacious, yet not absurd. Not mansions! He'd wanted a simple campground, after all. But once he designed for civilization, he realized he couldn't sustain simplicity. He and his friends were used to having servants in their houses, and while they could perfectly easily spend months sleeping on the dirt and picking mussels from the rocks for supper, they couldn't move their households from Philadelphia to Maine for the summer without help. Who would cook? Who would clean? He supposed they could hire local people, but how would they get down to Fellowship Point? It made more sense for everyone to bring their servants from Philadelphia, but where would they live? He pondered this and woke up in the middle of the night with an idea crackling in his head. He'd build a cluster of houses near the top of the Point, in the swath of field on the other side of Point Path from Outer Light. In this environment he would realize his notion of egalitarian interchangeability. The servants would have views of the sea, too, and plenty of room. Beauty and comfort would be available to all.

He conceived of these houses as being more commodious than the narrow, one-room-per-floor Father, Son, and Holy Ghost houses that had been built for an expanding nineteenth-century Philadelphia to billet the non-ownership classes, servants included. His own family had servants living in two such houses, and though he believed the separate quarters more respectable than keeping people in attic rooms, they bespoke inferiority and cramp. He wanted to go a step further and build houses anyone who wasn't rich would be happy to have. It would be good for everyone's morale, good for the children growing up in the association to see a milder delineation between the owner and the servant class than they were used to, and good for the servants, who might, by living well, seek a different life. Nothing would thrill William more than to help people move up in the world. He hoped for long, peaceful, healthy summers on the coast of Maine, communing with nature and family and friends. Fellowship Point had been nameless when the association bought it, with not even an Indian word attached to it. The word *fellowship* was both Quaker and general. It sounded like a generic New England place name. Always better not to draw undue attention.

There was the question of whether or not to build a Meeting House. Edgar was pro, but William had another idea. He wanted to return to older times and ways, when people made do with what they had, and met in rooms or basements of meeting members. On the Point, they had open fields available—why not meet there? Each family would bring their own chairs or benches, and they'd set up in a circle, all facing one another. If it rained, they could all gather in the parlor at someone's cottage.

William drew up a list of bylaws that he renamed *guiding principles* and sent them around to the other shareholders for their amendments and suggestions. It was decided there would be no regular parties, that lack to be mitigated by throwing a large Point Party in August for everyone in the Fellowship, young and old, shareholder and servant, and his or her guests and friends. The Lee Point Party instantly became a tradition, the stuff of winter dreams.

William's finest hour was devising a system for how the property would be passed down to future generations. He wrote an impassioned treatise about the evils of land ownership, how divisive it could be, how neighbors fought about inconsequential offenses, how greed for greater holdings could induce men to break the law. He wanted everyone to own shares only, and to pay dues. Yet once again he came up against some firmly established beliefs and conventions, and once again he conceded when met with an argument. He ducked conflict of any sort, a trait Edgar worried about from a business standpoint, though it was convenient when he wanted his way. It was finally agreed that William would sell the land to an association owned by the five men, to be shared and cared for by all; but that they'd have rights to own their houses and a share of the whole, with the stipulation that a house could only be passed to a blood relative, one at a time, so that no more than five people would ever have shares. If no inheritor existed, or wanted the place, the house and its value would return to the association and the number of shares would shrink. If there were only four or two shareholders, and an issue devolved into a tie vote, it would be broken by flipping a coin thrown by an impartial party. It occurred to William to include a clause describing how the charter might be nullified, the Fellowship broken up, the land sold: three owners of sound mind would have to agree to it. If it came to that, so be it. He wouldn't be around. The system was straightforward, equitable, and promising of a long intact future ahead.

The first summer, 1879, was hot and dry, and the association was able to be outdoors most of the time and established many little traditions and games. Everyone, women included, agreed they'd found Eden, and they eagerly invited friends and cousins over from the fleshpots to experience communal harmony and simplicity. They learned to fish and sail, and they took picnics out to the islands and strung up hammocks between soughing trees. They all liked walking through the meadows to the meetinghouse on Sundays. The wet morning grasses soaked their skirts and trouser legs, and children rubbed their cold toes together like paws as they fidgeted on the benches. People were moved to speak far more than they ever were in Philadelphia. William Lee positively expounded.

There was a debate for about a decade about whether or not to allow other birders to come down to the Point. William Lee was eager to show what he'd created to experts, but no one else wanted strangers in their front yards. Finally it was decided the experts could come in spring and fall to observe the migrations, and William went up with a group he bivouacked in the servants' houses, an area that came to be known as the Rookerie. He loved these weeks, and became an early and generous member of the Audubon Society. He bought two sets of Audubon prints. One he looked through so often that they lost most of their value. The other he had framed and hung on the wall of his study in Philadelphia.

William had no belief in heaven but he respected bones and paced out a graveyard in the meadow between his Leeward Cottage and the Hancocks' Meadowlea. He wanted to abide by the old Quaker practice of putting the body into the ground in a simple shroud with no stone to demarcate one from another, but he bowed to the association's desire for stones; they'd walked past the graveyards of Philadelphia too often not to want a stone for themselves.

Over time a number of the Point's residents and pets were buried in the graveyard, and in his old age William liked to walk among them. He aged gracefully, which was no surprise. He'd always had everything he wanted, including a handsome and high-minded son, Clures, to take over his share of the business, his houses, and his duties. He was briefly ill before he died, and gave explicit instructions on his deathbed, an idea man to the end. Unfortunately, his teeth had been taken out for the night, and the nurse, a local girl, who sat by him for the hour the family went to the dining room for supper couldn't understand his Philadelphia accent, so his last words were left to the imagination. Afterward, whenever a member of the Lee family made a plan, he or she invoked William's final intention, often as a joke. William Lee was all things to all family members, and miraculously wanted what they wanted. If only all ancestors and spirits were as accommodating.

If only all members of his family were as high-minded.

Like me, thought Agnes Lee.

CHAPTER 5

Agnes, Leeward Cottage, June 2000

"DAMMIT!" AGNES WAS UP ON TIPTOE, IN THE PANTRY AT Leeward Cottage, frustrated at being unable to reach the local pottery on the pantry shelf. Since having her four-syllable mastectomies, she couldn't lift her right arm higher than her waist. "Sylvie, I can't reach!"

"Hold your horses, I'm coming," Sylvie responded, without a trace of matching urgency.

"It's not my horses I'm worried about, it's the ducklings." Agnes couldn't see the beach from the pantry, and it worried her not to know what was presently happening in the war between the ducks and the gulls. She was eager to get back upstairs to monitor the situation. Every morning all week a mother eider duck had swum into the harbor with a flock of ducklings so tiny Agnes had to focus her binos for a clear sighting. At first there had been nine, then seven, six, and yesterday five. A heartbreaking decimation of the ranks. This drama occurred every year. The ducks were, well, sitting ducks when it came to the birds of prey—perfect snacks. The gulls, otherwise adored by Agnes for their schemes and lengthy conversations, were horrible on the subject of the ducklings. Murderous and cruel. She could not stand by and let nature have its way, not on her watch. Every year she did her best to intervene.

"I need Robert to persuade those gulls to go pick on someone their own size. I'm too old for this job."

Sylvie was in the kitchen only a few feet away. She was as old as Agnes and no more swift. She'd been the housekeeper at Leeward Cottage for nearly forty years, ever since the Circumstances moved off the Point and up the Cape. Mrs. Circumstance had continued to come in to cook for a while, but eventually Sylvie took over that chore as well. She and Agnes were alike in more ways than either of them cared to admit. Both were tall and thin, both stubborn and abrupt. Sylvie wore her scraggly gray hair chopped—possibly sawed—at her chin, and this year, she'd given up on bras. Was that solidarity or an act of rebellion? Agnes couldn't very well tell her to put one on, though her dangling bosom was unsightly. They did well together, though—neither of them needed compliments or hand-holding. The business of running Leeward Cottage was accomplished with little drama.

Sylvie clomped into the pantry. She'd taken to wearing heavy clogs, amplifying her presence. Agnes's cat, Maisie, didn't like it. She was a Maine coon with a particularly fat and feathery gray-brown tail that she used to express a broad range of disapprovals and displeasures. She sauntered back toward the hallway, tail thrashing.

"That one, please." Agnes gestured at a blue Rackcliffe plate. Sylvie reached up easily and pulled it down.

"Show-off," Agnes said.

Sylvie shrugged.

They went into the kitchen. Agnes took an orange from the fruit bowl and slipped it into her pocket.

"Fruit, eggs, toast, marmalade, coming right up."

"Thank you. You'll eat with me?" Agnes eyed the plums in the fruit bowl. They were hard as stone, merely decorative this early in the summer. But the color, purple and red, with a yellow pulse beneath the skin, made her mouth water. She felt a pang of sympathy for William Carlos Williams and his swiped plum.

Sylvie poked her head in the refrigerator. "I have to go to town for some things. Add to the list if you want anything special."

Agnes pictured a bag of M&Ms. That meant she was on edge. She didn't write it down. "I hope Robert can help with the gulls."

"Nature red in tooth and claw. That's what your mother always said."

"She wasn't a pacifist." Agnes had thought the expression was *nature redintooth and claw*. It made no sense, but she loved the sound of the word *redintooth*. She'd had the pleasure of giving it to a Franklin character's suitor as a last name. Chauncey Redintooth. She amused herself naming her people. Dickens must have laughed all the time—once he got out of the workhouse.

"Good thing everyone isn't. The bad need to be dealt with on their own terms."

"I'm not sure we can say the gulls are bad, but I want them banished. All right, I'm going up. If Robert comes and you happen to be here, will you tell him?"

Sylvie made a noise in the range of an assent, but short of true acquiescence. That was their state of relations. Two old coots cooting around an old house. Agnes had told Sylvie many times that she should retire. The house in the Rookerie was hers for the foreseeable, and beyond that Agnes would cover her expenses into the grave. But Sylvie, like Agnes, had no interest in a life of idle comfort. She liked running the house, and running Agnes, and she was still good at it. Good enough.

"Shall I carry the plate up for you?" Sylvie asked.

"Nope." That Agnes could manage. Nothing above the waist. She'd been told by her surgeon in Philadelphia that if he ended up removing a lot of lymph nodes Agnes might lose some range of motion along with her breasts, but she hadn't imagined what that would be like. She brushed her hair by bending forward and batting at whatever strands she could reach.

Accompanied by Maisie, who was careful not to get in her way, she returned to her rooms and ate while peering out the window. All quiet so far. Maisie watched with her, and Agnes offered her the plate to lick. Maisie slowly dropped her gaze to the smeary surface and its few flecks of egg, then slowly raised her head again and turned to look at Agnes. Maisie's look was one of affectionate indulgence, as if Agnes's efforts to please and charm were appreciated but jejune. Maisie lived with Sylvie all winter, and it showed. They both believed they were necessary, and they were right.

Agnes set the plate on the table in the hallway and moved to her guard post on the chaise. The water was motionless and etched with reflections of boat masts. She breathed the scents of brine, seaweed, and fish. Intoxicants.

When she'd gotten up to Maine six weeks earlier, Agnes had gone to see William Oswald, her oncologist in Portland, who'd told her she had between a 70 and 75 percent chance of a five-year and onward survival if she did nothing further. Radiation and chemo would improve her chances but negatively affect her quality of life in the present. Dr. Oswald's point of view was that death was natural, and that chemo was a lot for an old body to handle. His advice to her was to live a healthy life, as she was used to doing. She was grateful to him for not being spooky about death and was happy to play the odds to avoid the poisons.

She'd been getting stronger and feeling more robust, but her novel was still a joke, albeit a private one. Her writer's block—awful phrase—was confounding and painful, and she couldn't tell a soul about it. Her letters and her gardening column for a syndicate of New England papers—written under a pseudonym, Gertie

Weedie—flowed, as always, so it wasn't that she couldn't write at all. It was her Franklin women who eluded her in their old age. There was nothing to do but keep at it. Do what she'd always done. She wasn't going to start in on a memoir, that was for sure. That had been an easy decision, dispatched in a postcard. Maud Silver hadn't reared her head again.

Her condition was one of comfortable desolation. She was never lonely when she was in a book, no matter how solitary her existence, but this stasis made her aware that others were enjoying themselves, and she envied that—even as she disdained their enjoyments. She was somewhat mollified by working on *When Nan Wrote a Book About a Friendly Bear*, a sly nod to the academics who'd elevated her status.

It helped that Polly was back. Agnes liked having her next door and counted on their routine of meeting every late afternoon. They knew each other so well that their speech was as vertical in nature as a good poem, and a glance could stand for a dialogue.

The night before, as they spun around the graveyard, Agnes had complained of her physical limitations.

"I have dinosaur arms now." She hung them in front of her at rib height, like a tyrannosaurus.

"Remember my mother used to walk around that way? Carrying her dangling hands in front of her."

"Like Frankenstein," Agnes said. "If he bent his elbows."

They wandered over to Posy Hancock's grave. It was comforting to have known each other's family so well, and the ambiance of each other's house. The Hancocks' atmosphere was gentle, thanks to Posy, a mild, pleasing person who'd lived in a mild pleasant version of the world because everyone went out of their way not to upset her, for fear of seeing a reflection of their own imperfections mar her tranquil face. Even her snobbish and limited husband, Ian Hancock, had been sweet with Posy. Polly missed her, and from the foot of her plot spoke to her as if she were still alive.

"Why did you carry your hands that way, Mummy?"

"Did she answer?" Agnes teased.

"Yes. She said it was to provide a role model for thee, Agnes Lee."

"Har har."

Polly also stopped before Lydia's grave, as always, but she never said anything there, not in front of Agnes. Similarly, Agnes stopped by Virgil Reed's grave, and Nan's, though in hers there was no body present. Polly in turn left Agnes alone with these private, deep griefs. They were open with each other about visiting and talking to Elspeth and Edmund, Agnes's younger twin siblings, and Teddy, Polly's younger brother, and Lachlan Lee, head of the Point for so long, and they shook their heads over Grace Lee's insistence on being buried in Philadelphia. Who would want that?

As if to cement the point, a golden eagle soared overhead, toward the Sank.

"So what day should I set up a luncheon?" Agnes had asked. She'd already told Polly that she'd made contact with several land trusts. They were falling over themselves at the prospect of Fellowship Point.

Polly visored her eyes and looked up at the sky. "Soon. I have to talk to Dick."

"That's what you said months ago. You still haven't done it?"

Maisie brushed against her legs, as she did when she sensed Agnes was upset.

"I brought it up." Polly looked at Meadowlea.

"What did he say?"

"Not much."

Agnes felt her blood come up hot and angry in her jaw. "Come on, Polly. We have to get on this."

"He's not doing very well, Nessie. Retiring wasn't easy for him. Then he had the TIA . . ." Her chin quavered.

"Well, I'm sorry for all that, truly, but none of it matters to the eagles. Do I have to play the cancer card to get you to agree to a meeting? Because I will." Sometimes, Agnes wanted to throttle Polly for the exact opposite reason as the gulls. They were too much; she, too little.

Polly looked stricken and her eyes filled. "You think I haven't played it already? I think about it every minute of every day! I'm frantic about it! I can't lose you both!"

"I'm sorry," Agnes said quickly.

"You should be. Sheesh." Polly reached up and threaded her arms into the sleeves of her sweater.

"I am."

The subject had changed after that. Agnes would have to try again later. Why was everything up to her?

She cringed. That was one of her mother's queries of the universe, never uttered with the irony her family heard in it. Cosseted Grace Lee. Lately she'd been swimming up through the dark aquifer of Agnes's subconscious, asking for attention, as if she'd figured out that Agnes's block was a chink in her defense against memories of her mother. It was hard to believe there was anything left to say about her beyond what Agnes had already worked into her novels in a disguised form, where judgmental, forbidding, narcissistic mothers reappeared over and over. But there was always more, wasn't there? Recomposing the familiar was apt to expose a fresh interpretation. Memory was hazy and capricious, but bearing down on a memory with words, examining it with all the senses and representing time with light and technique, this shook up the past, unfixed it, kneaded it, and bent it into a new shape.

Sitting alone at her desk, or on her chaise writing in her journal, she went deep into life. She felt vividly involved with the entire world when she was writing. Alone, literally, yet she was choosing words with the intention that they serve as stepping stones between herself and the mind and heart of another person. It was a miracle that this was possible. Small black marks on a page, a code called the alphabet, and she could read a story written hundreds of years earlier, or write a book read thousands of miles away. Why get excited about gods and ghosts when writing and reading were so supernatural?

When she was with another person, the choice of words wasn't so crucial. She could point to a flower and smile, and trust that her appreciation had been communicated. But she couldn't write the word *flower* and expect a reader to know what she meant. What flower? Red, white, yellow, blue? What size, what scent, what season? To draw a scene wholly from her mind and draw it well enough that a stranger might see it, too—this was her way of living, and it didn't seem any less active than commanding troops or performing a surgery. Or having children.

Her mother hadn't agreed. When at age twenty-three, after a disastrous romance, Agnes came home to live, Grace Lee further refined what was already an effective glance of disapproval, flashed whenever Agnes said she was going upstairs to read. Grace prodded Agnes to be more social, but once was enough. There had been high hopes for the match and the future, and Agnes was tacitly but clearly blamed for the implosion. Grace's squared shoulders and her clipped departure from a room spoke for her.

Agnes made a great point of proclaiming she'd dodged a bullet. To whoever would listen, mostly Elspeth and their indulgent father, she railed against marriage as an institution unfavorable to women, not to mention unnatural and antiquated. Even if women were protected by marriage—a main argument in its favor—they were paradoxically infantilized by their own security. The equality of women was a Quaker tenet, but Grace let that slide. Instead she dwelled on visions of brilliant matches, inheritances, great houses, and social standing, all the furniture of the nineteenth-century novel. Lachlan had always jollied Grace, embraced her around the shoulders like a pal, made faces at her until her frozen expression broke and a genuine if self-conscious smile made a brief appearance. He never seemed to take her stiffness to heart. Had he known something about her that her children didn't? Was she vulnerable or sensual or playful when they were alone? It seemed unlikely but not impossible. Agnes, now, hoped it had been so, for both their sakes.

Assuming a modern sensibility was Agnes's form of rebellion. She was curious about psychology—Freud was a good writer, Jung too—and unflinching before the hard realities. She could never live the lives her friends did, propping up silly men and caring about propriety and breaches of etiquette. Elspeth, too, had managed to escape Grace Lee's Victorian hopes for her daughters by acting so much like a nun it wasn't possible to conceive of her being with a man. So the Lee girls were to be spinsters. Free of men in close quarters.

The idea that Dick had a say in what happened to the Point—that Polly gave him a say—made Agnes nauseous. It was annoying that every conversation with Polly on the subject, and on plenty of others as well, ended with the statement that she'd have to talk it over with Dick. Dick, Dick, Dick. He was really such a small man, so inconsequential, and without the sense to know it. How many people had he discouraged from pursuing philosophy? How often had he poisoned it with pretentiousness? It was a stealth pretension, too, one that masqueraded as an aversion to snobbery, swapping it for a knowingness offered with such a light touch that its elitism was barely detectable. And yet—detectable. She would have seen through him, even as an eighteen-year-old, and she wasn't special. A lot of students surely had. Why couldn't Polly, after all these years?

It rankled. Aside from Dick's general unworthiness of as good a creature as Polly, Agnes had always had to stand aside for him, always had to go along with the convention that he was more important to Polly than she was simply because he was married to her. What sense did that make? Every afternoon at a certain point—it could be right in the middle of a sentence—a look came across Polly's face, followed by a tip of her head, like a dog hearing a whistle out of reach to humans. Whatever expression she had on her face at that moment shifted to one of some complexity, different features showing different emotions. Her forehead was concerned, her chin weak, her jaw eager, her mouth compliant, her eyes—they annoyed Agnes the most. Her eyes had a look of fanaticism. They shone as if they were being treated to a vision. A vision of . . . Dick Wister?

Agnes banged her fist on the arm of her chaise. Where were the ducks? They were behaving like tourists, sleeping late. The water had turned from pink to blue gray, and the sky had whitened. Dick no doubt was preening. Rereading his own words or carving a semi-clever sentence into a letter. Lord, she was glad not to be saddled with supporting that! She heaved herself up and began to pace, keeping an eye out. Aware of her footsteps. Aware of being alone.

No matter what she'd claimed to her mother and the world, Agnes had never felt entirely relieved that her engagement had come to grief. She had been interested in John Manning. A bicycle bore down behind her in Fairmount Park. She turned, and there he was. She was twenty-two, recently graduated from Penn, and working in an arm of Lee & Sons as a glorified secretary. He was older, an officer at Girard Bank, and he looked the part—solid, dark-haired, a war veteran. She picked her bike off the grass and they walked side by side. He claimed he had his position because he'd studied economics at Penn, but there was something about him that brought out her mocking response. Do you think if you were Italian or a Negro that an economics degree would have been as persuasive? This flustered him. They parted ways, but the next day, he called the house.

She liked it when he shot his cuff to look at his watch and she saw the light brown hair stop at his wristbone, and when he cut his chicken and chewed it firmly, raising his finger to tell her she had to wait for his response to whatever she was saying until he swallowed. It was exciting to think a grown man might eventually belong to her, and that these gestures would become beloved by her alone. She already had love in her life, with her siblings and her father and Polly. But that kind of love didn't reveal her to herself in the same way. After they began to kiss, she wanted to see John naked, and told him so. She had no experience and knew next to nothing about what men and women did, sex, but she wanted to touch him and to explore every inch of him with her mouth. She'd never before felt this way, but then, she'd only walked out with boys before.

"Heavens, Agnes," he said. They were sitting on a bench in Rittenhouse Square. She was invigorated by the change of season, summer to fall, and wanted to be outside as much as possible.

"Is that wrong of me? I don't think so," she answered her own question. "It's an impulse coming up naturally from here." She touched her abdomen. "Shouldn't I tell you when I feel something?" She moved her hand to tickle him, but he caught it midair.

"Impulses to kill come up naturally too." He frowned at her.

"Exactly. Many times people are asking for it. You're asking to be licked."

"Whoa! Where did you learn to talk like that? You're an unusual girl, do you know?"

"I'm not, really. It's only that most girls don't act like themselves around boys."

"I promise my sisters don't have thoughts like yours."

"Ask them!"

He turned pink. She wrested her hand free and moved closer to him, laid her head on his shoulder. He glanced around him.

"Sit up. We're in public."

She let go and moved playfully all the way to the other end of the bench. Her spirits were too high to understand that they'd reached an impasse. "You're an old fuddy-duddy already, John Manning. Lucky you met me before it's too late."

What went wrong? There was no definitive answer. One day she called him at the bank and asked him to meet her for a walk at lunchtime. It was the first time she'd made an overture. He called her so often she never felt the need, but she didn't think twice about being the one to initiate a meeting. He was her friend now. He agreed and was perfectly pleasant when they spotted each other by the Liberty Bell in Independence Hall. He held her hand as usual, threw his head back in surprised laughter at her remarks as usual, but she sensed an undertone that confused her, and the next time she saw him she asked him about it. It seemed, she said gently, as though you didn't want to be there. You could have said no, she offered, but his eyes widened with suspicion, and for a split second, they looked at each other as total strangers. He recovered swiftly and the mask of affability settled back over his face.

She didn't know how to discuss it further, and had the distinct feeling that, if she pointed it out, he wouldn't know what she was talking about. There was a part of him immune to her, and he could withdraw to that place at any moment. This was a cold, stark realization, akin to the sense of insignificance she felt under the night sky. She wondered if it was possible this impasse could be reached with anyone, if a nerve was touched, or if this was a problem unique to John Manning. She'd been happier alone, even if her contentedness was based on a delusion about the closeness of her ties. Or was this vast gulf between people a feature of romantic love?

They went on as if nothing had happened, but in fact the relationship had ended then and there. He began to show a temper, and became angry with her if she went away, which at first she took as a compliment; but he became angry at her, too, if he were the one to go away, and their reunions were far from happy. She often displeased him. He shouted at her in a tight, controlled voice, his neck reddening. She had to remain calm until he relented and forgave her. She supposed out loud that this furor would end when they'd known each other longer, a remark that once again prompted a suspicious glare. He declared he wanted to be free to go places and see people and for her to display a cheerful willingness to wait for him to return when he was ready, a proposal so absurd she chalked it up to naivete. Whoever would think a woman would want such an arrangement? Had his mother taught him to expect that?

On the other hand—he had a keen sense of duty and was on hand for all the events he should show up for—but that seemed more to do with his opinion of himself than with wanting to share Christmas or a birthday with her. He placed great value on being beyond criticism, and believed if he hit his marks, he was square with the world. But she began to feel that because he loved her he hated her. His attachment to her represented a weakness to him rather than a broadened source of support. It made no sense, and she kept hoping she was imagining it. He kept getting angry. Yet they became engaged, and she imagined that would calm his fears.

She told her sister about her misgivings, the only person she could confide in without feeling she was being disloyal to John. Elspeth had had no experience of men and never would, but she was wise and smart and believed in love. She listened carefully to Agnes while tactfully pretending to be busy dressing her hair. She asked for time to think it over, which Agnes granted. Two days later Elspeth came back saying she thought Agnes should break the engagement.

"He's a lost soul," Elspeth said, her large eyes revealing the trustworthiness in her own soul. "He will always find a way to believe he's right—even if he offers an apology. He's broken, Ness. Everyone is—we all fell and broke when we were born. Some are lucky enough to understand this and devote themselves to making repairs. Others don't see it and blame what is around them for pain that is universal in nature. John is one of those. I'm so sorry."

Elspeth was exactly right. How did she know so much? Yet Agnes couldn't give up. She rededicated herself to John and did all she could to anticipate his moods and reactions and to keep him even. He grew more and more restless, however, and rejected her touch. One night when they were alone in the parlor at her house she decided to take a chance. She didn't have a plan when he came over, but after about an hour she unbuttoned her shirt and removed it, lifted her chemise and removed it. He stared at her and she smiled. "John." She reached out her hand. "Let's." She was certain. So sure that she didn't notice for a moment—probably only a second—that once again, he hated her.

He twisted his hand out of hers and flung it away. He jumped up and turned his back.

"Get dressed, Agnes. You're behaving like a prostitute."

She barked a laugh, surprising both of them. He frowned. She laughed again. It was funny. It was really terribly funny. Even in the moment, she was sorry there weren't others there to see it. She was showing him more of who she was and he was seeing her less clearly than ever. Yet he was utterly revealing himself.

"No," she said.

"Do it right now or I'll—"

"You'll what?"

He raised his arm and curled his hand into a fist. He could really hurt her, she was fully aware of that, but she couldn't help laughing. This gesture—all his gestures—seemed grandiose and false. How had she gone this far with such a husk of a man?

"All right." She put her shirt back on.

"That's better," he said. "What got into you?"

"Please leave, John."

"What?"

"This is over."

He opened his hand. "Give me my ring back."

She pulled the ring over her knuckle and handed it to him.

"Bitch," he muttered on his way out.

"Gentleman!" she hurled after him.

She went up to bed feeling strangely elated. She had stood up for herself. Many people in her life would say she always did, but that wasn't entirely true. She voiced her opinions and she said no to invitations, but that wasn't the same as sticking up for herself. John had tried to shame her, and she'd refused to feel shame. That refusal was for her own good. She left the relationship whole.

She'd known only a little at the time about psychological pathologies, but knew she was not the cause of his explosion. Marriage should be a long conversation leading to freedom. She might have had true communion later, with Virgil Reed—but no point thinking about that. None at all. Especially as the speculation had no basis in experience. It was the last trace of her interest in romance, beyond her work. Best to leave it there.

She saw John many times over the years, but he never gave the smallest acknowledgment of having once been attached to her. If he had to speak to her, he offered the fewest number of words possible and walked away.

She shook herself back to the present. The ducks were already at the shoreline! She'd missed their approach. There were still five tiny windup toys paddling along, looking as though they had no idea what they were doing or any sense of danger. But danger was right there, on the beach. Two gulls stood quietly on rocks several feet apart, waiting for the targets to come to them.

"Get away!" she shouted, to no effect. Agnes wished she could run, but that had ended a long time earlier. Instead she lurched down the stairs careening between the walls. "Come on, Maisie! Sylvie! I'm going into the fray!"

Sylvie appeared in the front hall and handed Agnes her walking stick. "Don't knock your brains out."

"Thanks."

"I'll come."

Agnes glanced at her clogs. "No—keep watching for Robert. Send him to me as soon as he arrives."

Agnes went down the front steps and across her driveway and the meadow and finally reached the shore. It wasn't easy to get down the bank. The path was narrow, cutting between sturdy rugosa rosebushes that sent bulging roots snaking through the dirt and causing her to stumble as her heart skipped with fear. She reached out and grabbed a branch and yelped when the thorns pricked her hands. Dammit!

"Get the hell away from here!" She crashed onto the rocky beach. The gulls took a few steps, and then turned toward her. "I mean you!" she yelled. "Get away!" They tipped their heads and blinked. She approached them with as much vigor as she could assume, but she was not what she used to be. She turned her stick upward like a sword and brandished it from her waist.

"Go! Scat! Scram, ya bloody blackguards!"

They rose into the air.

"And you!" She turned to the mother eider. "Could you do a better job watching your kids? You're giving me a heart attack!"

The eider craned her neck and spun around. She paddled off nonchalantly, considering the danger. The ducklings followed, equally unconcerned.

"Morons," she said. Yet she was glad they were safe. She'd prevailed for one morning. She turned back toward the house and walked up the path, the wall of rugosa rose scratching at her jeans. Robert's truck was tooling down the road. In spite of her agitation, it made her smile to see him step from the truck. She often teased him that he could have been the Marlboro Man, with his gaze trained on doings high on the mesa. He took after his rangy father, where his siblings were stocky like Mrs. Circumstance.

"It's about time you rolled up. You missed the drama."

Elegantly, he shut the door behind him. "Oh? What was that?"

"The gulls!" She poked her stick at him. "What can we do about them?"

"Whoa! Put that thing down." Robert leaned against his truck and looked at her fondly. He was deeply tanned. Outdoor work. "What do you think we can do? Or let me rephrase—what do you want to do?"

"I don't want to see them snacking on the ducklings while I am trying to work in the mornings. Anything that will put a stop to that."

He nodded slowly, as if thinking the problem through from every vantage point. As he did when he planned a new garden bed. His hair slipped down over his forehead, just as Hiram's always had. Robert now sported a few grays. "I can understand that. I could shoot them."

"Har har. What else have you got? I want them gone, but not dead."

"They are regulars here. This is their favorite restaurant. I don't know that I can interfere with nature." He squinted rather than wearing sunglasses. Cowboy.

"Excuse me, but aren't you a landscape architect? Isn't interfering with nature your métier?"

He laughed. "Agnes, I can rely on you to keep things honest."

"So you've got nothing for me?"

"Beyond applauding your efforts? Nothing that I would feel good about."

"Oh, all right."

"Nature can be harsh." He gave her such a sympathetic look that she felt better. It always gave her a jolt when men could be of comfort—though Robert often gave her that jolt. "Speaking of which, what's news on the eagles?"

"I'm concerned about the nest near the Deel Club. I haven't seen as much activity as there should be around it. We'll see."

"Fingers crossed they're all right. And how's my cousin Archie? You were working there yesterday, I take it."

"I was, for longer than I expected. The boxwood I put in last spring isn't happy. Which was predictable. But a certain someone is insisting on having topiary in her garden." He raised his eyebrows playfully. "Seela Lee is a tough customer."

"Dammit, Robert, there's plenty of work for you here, and all over the Cape, and all over Maine, and the world! Seela is going to eat up all your time, on purpose. Polly and I will be picking weeds by August." Agnes's blood came up again at the thought of Robert being monopolized by Seela. An image of her bony wrist encircled by chiming Lee charm bracelets came to mind. She gritted her teeth.

"No. I'll be here. Don't worry about that."

"Robert! What aren't you telling me?"

Robert crossed his arms and twisted around to look up at the sky. His movements were easy, graceful. He always seemed to be doing things slowly and deliberately, but he accomplished more than anybody. "We could use some rain."

"Robert!" Now she was enjoying herself. A little flirting lifted her spirits. She saw Polly get giggly around her sons. Well, Robert was like a son to her, if fondness were the measure.

"All right. You'll find out anyway. Mrs. Lee has asked me to make her a white garden, modeled on Sissinghurst."

Agnes banged her stick on the ground. "You have got to be kidding! If she's ever read a single book by anyone in the Bloomsbury group, I'll dig the garden myself. Honestly, there's no excuse for her. Once again I wonder why they don't buy a house in the Hamptons and be done with it. Especially after the great wampum belt robbery of 1999." She couldn't think of the mayhem Seela had caused the summer before without feeling a wave of disgust.

"They're having a security system put in," he taunted.

"Oh, for God's sake. Can't he just accept that it was one of his light-fingered friends who took it? Or that he threw it out himself after a few drinks?"

The summer before, when Archie Lee took a visitor into his library to show her his treasures, his version of the *Let me show you my etchings* routine, he noticed that an extremely valuable wampum belt was missing from the display case. He wasn't exactly sure when it had disappeared, but he remembered having shown it to another houseguest not long before. The belt was one of his favorite belongings, a classic and symbolic pattern—though it didn't come out what the symbols stood for. When he noticed the object was missing, Archie called the police—Bobby and Joe, boys well known to them. They were flummoxed from the beginning, their line being DUIs and thefts from the campgrounds, barking dogs and loud parties, and lately, meth labs in trailers. Art theft was an unprecedented incident on Cape Deel, and the belt was easy to abscond with. It could be anywhere, and anyone passing through the house could have easily pocketed it.

Archie could talk of nothing but the theft. Seela was as aggrieved as Archie. Her degree of upset and devotion to his cause illuminated the reasons for his attraction to her. Agnes knew the type—a woman who took over without the man quite knowing what happened—and ran his life, well. She loved to write about such women, who by all rights should be running the world. Seela was older than Archie by fifteen years, but that was of no consequence compared to the easy existence she made possible for him. Yoko, Agnes joked, without the creativity. A shrewd helpmeet in a disaster, such as the theft of the wampum belt, as she laid her arthritic fingers on the pulse of every party and sensed when the time had come to limit the subject to a few answers about developments in the case. She didn't want Archie to become known as a bore.

But Archie rejected her concern. As certain as Dick was of his erudition, Archie was of his allure. "How could this happen?" he asked, with the incredulity of a person who'd never come in touch with rejection. He didn't feel the need to add the words that obviously came at the end of his question: *to me?* It went around that he was thinking of hiring a private detective from New York. "That places him," Dick said. Agnes was always bemused when Dick lapsed into snobbery—his bleeding heart pumping out its true colors.

"Tell me you're not going to do it," Agnes said now. "Robert, please quit them. It's a waste of your time."

"It'll be all right. I told her it might be hard to get the right plants." He didn't seem at all put out.

"But she didn't *hear* you. Don't forget that. She can only hear what she wants to hear. And dammit, Robert, you can have all my money! You know that."

He grinned. "And I won't take any of it except what I earn. You know that."

Agnes looked down toward the Sank. "Then at least let's take a walk. I'm going to have land trust people come soon, and I want to imagine seeing the Sank for the first time, as they will. You can make sure I don't fall and crack my head open."

She meant to be funny, but he neither rolled his eyes nor smiled. Instead he hesitated. She saw his entire to-do list flash through his eyes, weighed against his desire to be in a favorite place. She pressed her request.

"I forbid you to torment those poor boxwoods today. Archie and Seela can stew together in their truffle-infused juices. You'd be doing them a favor, making them wait. They like having something to complain about."

Now she earned a grin. "So this is really for them, not you?" he teased.

"Of course! Selfless is my middle name."

"All right, then. Are you coming, Maisie?" he asked.

Maisie looked up and gave Agnes a slow, acknowledging blink. She sauntered back to the house.

Agnes pointed down Point Path with her stick. "Your job is to chase off the snakes," she said to Robert. "And please don't tell me not to be afraid because the snakes around here are harmless. It's not harm that bothers me, but the sight of them."

"I know that, Agnes. But you have given me an idea. Why not create a row of topiary snakes for Seela?"

"Promise?"

They headed down Point Path. He walked at her pace, which was respectable, considering. She liked that they were about the same height, or had been.

"I'll say it again, Agnes. You're doing the right thing with the land." He reached out and linked arms with her. She gave him a squeeze in return.

"I'm not doing it yet. Polly has to talk to Dick about it. Same as it ever was." She rolled her eyes. "Maybe you could tell her I'm dying, but I've been sparing her the bad news?"

He pulled back and looked into her eyes. "That's not true, is it?"

"It's always true, Robert."

He was visibly relieved. "I'm not going to lie to Polly."

"You know," Agnes said, "the very reason I like you is the very reason you can get on my last nerve."

Robert squeezed her arm again. "Thank you."

CHAPTER 6

Polly, Fellowship Point and Deel Town, July 2000

Polly, too, needed Robert. Dick had finally agreed to her plan to widen the path from the house to the rocky shore and plant it with bluets and Kentucky bluegrass seeds to transform it into a blue river. She wanted Meadowlea to look its best when the family came in August. She'd tried to catch up with Robert over the past few days, but he'd been scarce. Agnes said it was *effing* Seela. Polly, who made a point of finding the good in everyone, didn't like Seela either. She practiced a set of showy good manners that were actually bad manners, such as explaining why she couldn't accept an invitation or complimenting someone's dress. She'd even brought some sort of loaf to a luncheon at Gay Burk's. "It's a pound cake with lime zest," she'd said to the assembled group. Gay received it as if she'd been handed a dead squirrel, and rushed it to the kitchen, where it disappeared and was never heard from again. Polly wished Agnes had been there to see Gay's face, but Agnes never went out in the day due to her writing. She'd shattered the afternoon peace with laughter, though, when she heard the story. "I'd call her a Philistine, except the Philistines have been misunderstood, and she hasn't."

Robert would be excited about creating the path, she was certain of that. He'd told Polly that Meadowlea was his favorite of all the cottages he cared for. When the original structure had been expanded, the additions were simple, with an eye toward bringing light inside and affording views of the landscape. Polly's mother, Posy Hancock, found Victorian taste oppressive, and resisted it even as Grace Lee next door was putting up velvet curtains and having mahogany shipped from Philadelphia. Lachlan Lee had looked around wistfully when he came over to Meadowlea.

This morning Polly was determined Robert be hers. After breakfast she walked up to the top of Point Path to get a jump on Agnes. Agnes liked to believe she was closest to Robert, and maybe she was, but Robert and Polly's boys had played daily during the summers and later shared a love of hiking, often driving over to Acadia for the day. Dick had had Robert as a student and always said he was one of the best—broad-minded, brilliant, curious, and calm. Sometimes Robert had a Scotch with Dick in the late afternoon while Polly was over nipping the white with Agnes, after which sessions Dick was stimulated and robust with ideas. Polly saw both sides of the argument about what Robert should have done with his life. He could have been successful on Philadelphia terms—lawyer, banker—but he was successful here, too. She and Agnes agreed he had made the most of his education by being a decent and reliable man. Not to mention that he made a great living and created beautiful gardens. He'd never remarried after his brief early attempt, and, predictably, Polly examined the young women at the club and around town with him in mind, while Agnes made pointed remarks in his presence about the pleasures of solitude.

"Neither of us are having any effect," Polly observed one day as he drove off.

"Dammit, Polly, you are so right!" Agnes said, with warm exasperation.

The Circumstances had moved off the Point in 1962. There'd

been deaths that winter, the town librarian and that odd young relative of the Reeds—Virgil Reed—who had been a source of fascination for her and Agnes right after Agnes's father died. Virgil and his little girl, Nan, had lived in what they'd always called the Chalet, a cabin by Rock Reed. Agnes had gotten close to Virgil—maybe more. Polly had never known exactly what happened between them. After his death, Nan had been whisked away by relatives and had sadly died herself when she was still a child. Polly had always wondered if there were any connection between that tragedy and the Circumstances' departure. Perhaps the place felt haunted afterward. She'd never asked Agnes about it. Somehow, the whole topic shimmered with an aura of taboo.

Never mind. The past couldn't be retrieved, much less fathomed. No more than one could fully know one's closest friends, or partners . . .

Even after Hiram had moved farther up Cape Deel, he'd remained attentive. Robert, too, when he took over. But if he lived on Fellowship Point all the time, it would be easier to catch him.

She waited until ten for him to show up, but he didn't, so she walked home, checked on Dick, and left for town. She had a daily habit of doing her marketing, getting the mail, and maybe having a chat or two if she ran into anyone. She thought of it as her time, which sounded very women's magazine, but nevertheless. If she said she wanted to be alone, the boys got anxious and found reasons to ride along. But the word *shopping* made everyone scatter, Dick included. He had a horror of being the man in the store sitting on a settee while the wife tried on dresses. He wouldn't hold her handbag for her even for a minute.

Deel Town was quiet. That was often the case if there was a morning breeze on the water. People went sailing or were drawn out to walk. Polly did her errands and chatted with the counterboy at Harney's. He'd gone to the high school and was back from UMaine

Farmington for the summer. Polly told him he must be very smart and was immediately glad Dick hadn't heard her say that. He was apt to find her interaction with the public inane. She put her food in the car, thinking she'd done things in the wrong order. Oh well. She looked in the windows of the shops, at the clothes, the jewelry made of local stones set in gold and silver, the gift items, and patted a placid dog tied up in front of the hardware store. A bowl of water had been set out for just such dogs, a thoughtful touch. "You're a good boy," she told the dog, who seemed to return the compliment. Then she gathered her mail at the post office, and Agnes's too.

A letter from James—her heart sank a bit, as he generally wrote her to tell her what to do about something or other; a forwarded bill from the Cricket Club, which she'd quietly pay lest Dick question why they needed a membership anymore; and then two exciting envelopes, one from Agnes's publisher, and a letter from Dick's chair! Perhaps they'd changed their decision about his emeritus status—realized their mistake.

Polly picked up her pace on her way back to the car, eager to deliver these missives. Then wouldn't you know it, she got stuck trying to cross the street. Traffic was backed up behind a wide truck laboriously hauling long logs. Polly wondered who was building what—something on the east side, no doubt. She grieved at the sight of cut trees and shorn meadows.

The police car—there was only one on Cape Deel—was in the line behind the truck. She rapped on the glass, her hand raised to wave hello to Bobby and Joe, both boys she'd known as children. Joe glanced at her swiftly without smiling. Bobby kept his eyes on the road. She was embarrassed and took a step away. But as the rear of the car came abreast, she took a swift, reluctant look into the backseat. To her shock, she saw Robert Circumstance, bending forward, his hands cuffed behind his back.

"Robert!" she called out. He turned and their eyes met and exchanged disbelief. She stepped off the curb and rapped on the window by Joe. It whirred down. "What is going on, Joe?"

"Can't discuss it, Mrs. Wister." His words were carried on a plume of fruity scent from an air freshener hanging from the rearview mirror.

"But why is Robert Circumstance in your car?"

He looked ahead, stony as the shoreline.

"Joe, you know Robert. Whatever this is, it's a mistake."

The window closed. Polly touched Robert's window, and he offered her a bleak smile and a rueful shrug.

"Don't worry," she yelled. "We'll get you home today."

He nodded and dipped his head forward again.

She made it to her car, heart pounding, sick in her soul. It was hot, hot as hell. Her back cooked against the seat. Right now Robert was being pulled out of the car and walked into the town hall—in handcuffs! Everyone would stare. They all knew him. He'd been there a thousand times on a thousand errands—as had Polly, who'd seen men brought in before, mainly for a spell of drying out. The municipal building held one lone cell in the corner like a zoo cage. Was Robert being put into it now? She rocked back and forth, pressing her fists against her abdomen like she used to do when she had cramps. Rock, rock, rock and a hard place. Why had she had to see, and to be the one to bring the news to the Point?

She headed home the faster way through the backwoods, down what they'd always called Dump Road; the town dump was off a side road, and marked by gulls and other birds of prey circling overhead. The cramped, potholed track ran between an unofficial, uneven allée of pine and maple trees that cupped a gloom, even on glittering days. There wasn't a view to be had from beginning to end. Dick sometimes told her to go this way, and when she resisted he lectured her that the rural scene was as true to the Cape's character as where they lived on the water. He interpreted the denizens for her via literary references. The Beans, he'd say, pointing at a clot of trailers and unkempt kids running around, or The Misfit, when they passed a menacing, big-bearded man in a rusty pickup truck.

Hers wasn't an aesthetic shudder, though, and it bothered her that Dick would say it was, even as a joke. Yet she couldn't explain her disturbance well enough to set him straight. It was too interior, too private, too in the same range as how she'd felt when Lydia died. The road filled her with a profound desolation. She struggled to swallow from a dry mouth. Part of it was poverty. She was sure these people had a culture they were proud of—humans made the best of things—but that was the point. They had been born into a situation where they had far to go, but that unfairness didn't cause the deep distress she felt being in this place. It was something more elemental—like the inverse of the miraculous sense of smallness she felt when she looked up at the sky. There was nothing miraculous in the enclosed, fated atmosphere of Dump Road, and she was eager to get through it and out the other side—where she felt she mattered.

A passel of grimy children chased a ball out of a yard dotted with dead cars and two immobile trailers, slowing her down. They stopped their game as she passed, and their inscrutable gazes landed on her. She waved. They stared harder. She blushed and pulled her hand down abruptly. What was she doing? She wasn't creepy. But she was a stranger, and O-L-D. In other words—creepy.

She pressed forward along the road in hiccupping leaps, unable to keep her foot steady. The scent of burning leaves penetrated her windows and her shirt dampened from nerves. What in God's name was Robert doing in the back of that police car? Mistake, mistake, it had to be a mistake.

She looked sideways again. The nearby yard was choked with dandelions and trash, a half dozen strewn tires, the rusty body of an old green sedan, a ghoulish gathering of filthy plastic climbing toys and bikes, tinsel gum wrappers. There was something else as well, that she could not understand immediately. She slowed to puzzle it out. The shapes were familiar, but their relation to each other wasn't. She stopped. Squinted. And suddenly she shivered a cringe that reached all the way down to the nut of her.

A dog—a thin, gray creature with a wide heavy head—stood perched on top of a large wooden box. The box was next to a tree. A maple. A rope led from a branch to the dog's neck. Polly stared at the rope. Something was wrong. A grim, sad dirtiness hung in the air. Her gaze measured its length. The knot over the tree branch, the knot at the dog's neck— Oh, she gasped, oh Lord.

The rope was taut. If he tried to jump down to the ground he'd strangle. And what was he supposed to drink up there? Polly put the car in park and rocked against her stomach. What could she do? She was close to her home—a walk, if she were younger. How could this be going on so nearby?

Part of her counseled she should just go on home and forget she'd ever seen this. But that wouldn't stand up on Judgment Day, if there was one.

She unbuckled her belt and worked her way around until she could reach into her brown paper shopping bag. She groped for the packet of hamburger, sat back down, and opened the brown paper, exposing the pink squiggles of top-of-the-round ground. Chances of her throwing it accurately enough that it would land on top of the box were zilch. Should she get out of the car? The idea was insane and reckless. But it was that or leave having done nothing, which was intolerable.

Her eyes stung from smoke. Did Bobby and Joe even come out here? Why were they arresting Robert instead of putting out these fires and rescuing this dog? She opened the car door, inched gingerly out of her seat, and straightened up. Lord, she was stiff! Step, step, around tires, across trash, between the scrappy dandelions.

Blood rushed through her head but she put one foot in front of the next and pressed forward. Pellets of mud and grit hopped into her old Pappagallos and gravitated below her sole, tormenting her, but she kept her gaze on the dog. Its horrific condition overwhelmed her. Sores ringed its neck and bugs crawled on its back. Jesus wept. She wanted to run. But she pushed on, good boy, good boy, and held the hamburger under his nose. The creature responded so slowly she wondered if he were alive. Pitifully, he took a tiny lick. She proffered the meat firmly, and the dog mustered a surge of life force and ate the entire half pound in one continuous bite.

"Good boy." She slid her hand underneath the rope around the dog's neck and felt her way along it to the knot without any plan in mind about what she'd do next. One thing was clear; she had to rescue it. But Dick loomed at the other end of her plan, forbidding a dog in the house. The immobility of the animal added to the difficulty.

A shout cut through the roaring of her own blood in her ears. "Get the hell off my land!"

Polly trembled. The trailer was shouting, spewing a string of curses. The screen door slapped and twanged, followed by louder shouting.

"This is private property! There's a sign!"

Polly didn't even look to see who was saying this. She made a fraught, bony run for the car. When the engine caught, she glanced over and saw a huge man flying a fist.

"Don't come near here again!" he shouted. *Ne-ya he-ya.*

She mashed the accelerator and shot off, ducking low over the wheel in case of bullets. "What the hell?" she said aloud. She couldn't shake the sensation of the dog's lips, that hunger, oh that hunger, elemental and frank. She recognized it, but there was no time to think about it now. She raced to put distance between herself and the ugly scene, the menace. Finally she emerged from the road and turned onto Shore Road, where a field of grasses hummed and swayed, unperturbed by leaping butterflies. She pulled over and parked, laid her hand over her heart and took deep breaths. It was hard to believe what had happened—that she had seen Robert in handcuffs, rushed home the back way, and fed the starved dog. She couldn't tell Dick she'd fed his dinner to a dog. Though he probably wouldn't care about anything else once she'd told him about Robert. Polly hoped that situation was all straightened out by now.

An eagle hung above, hunting, no doubt, for helpless rodents. Did Robert's arrest have something to do with his efforts to protect the eagles? Had he done something bad in the name of good? The bird swooped low. She gunned the engine in hopes of scaring it away. *Fly, eagle, fly*, she thought, and found in the phrase a reason to cheer up. It was the Philadelphia Eagles football team pep song. Dick and the boys—and Robert, who'd kept the Eagles as his team from his years in Philadelphia—would be belting it out together very soon.

Without deliberately making a choice of who to tell first, she let geography decide it and pulled into Agnes's. She walked around the side, and spotted Sylvie in the kitchen. Sylvie poked her head out. "She's not receiving. It's work time. You know that, Polly."

Sylvie unnerved her.

"It's an emergency." Polly meant to be firm, but her errand engulfed her with its enormity, and her voice quavered.

"What kind of an emergency?" Sylvie challenged.

"The real kind. It involves Robert."

"Car accident?"

"No. He hasn't been hurt. Will you please go tell Agnes I need to speak to her?" She clenched her fists at her sides.

Sylvie regarded her coolly. "You're going to take the blame for the interruption."

"Yes."

"Go around to the porch. If she's willing to see you, I'll send her out that way."

"Thank you so much, Sylvie," she said with a touch of irritation, though it came out sounding sincere. She wasn't sarcastic often enough to be good at it.

As she was already halfway to the porch, she kept going rather than turn back around to cross the driveway again. A flag path ran the perimeter of the house, on the outside of a ring of old dusty blue hydrangea. She ran her hand along the blowsy blossoms and felt a wave of nostalgia at the whisper of the petals on her palms. Just like that, there was Lydia! A few feet ahead, also caressing the blooms. She tipped her head and smiled at Polly. Her long light-brown hair slid over her arm. *Having a nice day?* Polly asked, in her mind. Lydia nodded. Polly knew to stay still, she knew how this worked, but she couldn't help herself. She took a step forward: Lydia vanished.

It would always be so sad.

A few minutes later she arrived at the porch steps. Agnes rushed toward her.

"What about Robert?" She grabbed for Polly's arm, a level of alarm that roused Polly's tears. She gripped Agnes in return.

"Oh, Nessie, I do not know! I was in town, and I saw him in the back of the police car!"

"Robert? Are you sure?"

Polly nodded. "I spoke to Bob and Joe, but they wouldn't speak to me. I told Robert it would be okay."

"But what would be okay? What happened?" Agnes let go and began to pace. "Let's think, Polly. He wasn't here this morning, and he wasn't at yours, either. He was probably at Archie's. Damn her! I smell Seela Lee's slime all over this!" She laid her face in her hands for a moment and lifted it up again. Polly saw a combination of resolve and bewilderment—a look she'd seen many times before. "Who shall we call first?"

"Maybe town manager?"

"Good idea. Come on, let's go in."

"I have to go make lunch for Dick." Polly braced herself for a scowl. But Agnes only looked sympathetic.

"Go. Then come back."

"At the usual time?"

"Anytime. I hope I'll know more by then." Agnes reached for an embrace. Polly registered her newly flat front. They clung for a longer moment than usual.

"Oh! I have a letter for you. It's in the car." Polly jerked her head in that direction.

"Set it on the steps, will thee? On your way out?"

Polly went home and barged in on Dick, too. How had she attached herself to two writers? She stood in the doorway of Dick's study and told him she had news. He held up his hand—just a minute! She shifted from foot to foot, and then had the idea to slap the envelope that had come for him against her wrist—a recognizable sound. Crack, crack, crack. It worked. He twisted his swivel chair around.

"Mail?"

She handed him the envelope. As he read it, he pulled his hand down over his face. "Adam is not going to write a foreword to my book," he said.

"Oh, Dick. I'm so sorry. After all you did. And the book is a classic. He should be thrilled to be associated . . ." She took in what she was saying as she said it. Adam should be thrilled. Why wasn't he? Had something happened she didn't know about? Maybe she should write to him privately to ask what was going on.

Dick tossed the letter in the trash. "This is a relief! Now I can ask better people!" he bellowed.

"Like who?" She felt a wave of regret as soon as she said this. "Never mind. You have time to find the perfect person."

He turned back to his work. "There are a lot of people."

"Yes. Many will want to be associated."

He bent over his keyboard. She lingered.

"Dick?"

His shoulders stiffened. "Can't you see I'm in the middle?"

"I have something else."

"Save it for tonight."

"It can't wait." Before he could object again, she said, "Robert's been arrested."

He spun around again. "What makes you think that?"

"I saw it. I saw him in the police car."

"It's a mistake, of course. You mistook someone else for Robert. You don't see very well anymore."

"No, it was Robert. I was as close to him as I am to you now. I spoke to him." Polly wanted to get past this skeptical portion of the program quickly. The fastest way was coolness on her end. Though his disbelief stung. And she saw well enough to run his world.

"You spoke to him?"

"Yes."

"Did he see you?"

"Yes."

"Well, I don't believe it!"

"Neither do I!"

They stared at each other. They both believed it. She took a seat on the sofa.

"Maybe he's a witness to something."

"He was handcuffed."

Now Dick looked to the side, bewildered, as if he had lost the thread. His TIA had occurred on Memorial Day weekend. They'd been told that he'd probably have more and not to worry about it, they were no more than "a brain fart"—the doctor had actually said that. They'd slow him down and perhaps be depressing. "Farts are the opposite of depressing!" Dick had joked afterward. He wanted to put it behind him.

"Speak more clearly!" he shouted now.

She raised her voice a notch. "We were talking about Robert. Agnes is calling the town to see what's going on."

"Oh yes, yes." He pressed his temples. "Yes, you said that."

"Coffee?" she offered.

"Mmm."

Was he having another TIA?

"I'm sure Agnes will straighten everything out."

"Yes, yes." He rubbed at his forehead, and her heart pinched.

If she thought staying by him would help, she would, but he did better collecting himself when he was alone. On the way to the kitchen she slowed by a table and smelled a bouquet picked from the garden. She scooped the beans from an old red pottery bowl and poured them into the funnel of an appliance the DILs—daughters-in-law—had given her the summer before. They thought her ill-equipped and gave her items out of the Williams-Sonoma catalog, supposedly to liberate her but really so they could cook at Meadowlea as they did at home. Polly didn't want things like giant mixers on her kitchen counters, so the appliances stayed—the DILs said "lived"—in the closet or the basement until they were due to arrive. Then Polly brought the flotsam of gadgets out and arranged them to look appreciated. The coffeemaker, however, was miraculous. Such good coffee. But Robert! She wondered if she shouldn't have done something more right way. Gone straight to the town hall and reasoned with the powers there. And freed the dog—somehow. Was she a coward? She'd never felt like one—she'd advocated for her boys as heartily as was polite. But she retained a horror of getting in trouble.

"Here you go." She placed the cup on Dick's desk.

"Thank you." He looked up. "I'm hungry," he said.

"Oh! I should have made lunch. I'll do it right now."

She hovered.

"What?"

On the one hand she'd have liked to leave it at that. On the other . . . She swayed from foot to foot. "I saw another awful sight on my way home. "

He moved his eyebrows to show curiosity, so she told him the story of the dog, omitting, of course, the bit where she trespassed and gave away their good hamburger, emphasizing instead the misery of the animal. He shook his head at her description, just as she hoped he would.

"It's being treated unjustly." She chose the adverb carefully, for the best chance of a concerned response.

He frowned.

"I know you wouldn't want it here, but . . ."

He clucked his tongue rhythmically, ticking off seconds of thought. These days a small problem got the same treatment as a major inquiry. She sensed his mind turning over, like the tumblers in a combination lock clicking and falling, until the safe in his head swung open.

"Isn't there an animal shelter just above the Cape?"

"You're right! You'll call today?"

He brightened. *You're right* were his favorite words. "I'll call right now."

"I'll go make lunch."

"What are we having?"

"Grilled cheese?"

"Would you just put mine on the desk, and I'll eat *a seule?* Though tell me when you hear from Agnes."

"Of course." She walked briskly back to the kitchen, buoyed both by the thought of the dog being rescued and by having brought Dick a focus. She had trouble holding the heavy cast-iron pan—her old wrists had weakened—but she got it on the stove and dropped a wad of butter on the bottom. It melted in tentacles, and with a spatula she raked the butter to an even coating. She set the sandwiches in the pan. Cookies, too, would be a good touch for a mid-afternoon snack. She pulled out her old green bowl and a wooden spoon. She didn't need the DILs' fancy mixer to concoct what Dick liked.

The phone rang.

"Goddamn Seela!" Agnes bellowed. "She accused him of stealing!"

"No!"

"It's insane. I want to wring her neck. Come back over as soon as you can."

"Just after I feed him."

"You eat too. I can't have you fainting during our walk."

So they'd be taking a walk. That was welcome. She took the food in. "It's Seela. She's accused him of theft."

"No. I don't believe it."

"Of course you don't believe it. He didn't do it. It's Robert!"

"I know that!" Restlessly he shifted around in his seat. "I meant I don't believe Seela! What happened?"

"I don't know, and I don't think Nessie knows. I'm going over there now—after we eat. What did the shelter say?"

She saw a look flash across his face that she couldn't quite interpret. He seemed to have new looks since the TIA. "I know it pales in comparison," she said, "but not for the dog."

"It's fine," he said.

"You told them where?"

"Yes. What you said." He rubbed his forehead. "Yes, I spoke to them."

He looked tired. "Dick, eat your lunch. Then have a nap. I'll find out what Nessie knows."

"I should call someone. I'm known around here."

His whole face dripped and dropped. He was suddenly so old.

"I'll find out who you should call. You'll definitely be needed."

She ate her sandwich quickly. He licked his fingers between bites—also new.

"I'm going to make cookies later," she said.

"The peanut butter?"

"Yes." She'd been thinking of oatmeal. "Do you want to nap on your sofa here or go upstairs?"

"Dammit, I'll decide what I want to do!" He banged his fist on the desk, and his plate jumped.

"I'll be back soon," she said, and took both plates back to the kitchen. She crossed the desire line between Meadowlea and Leeward Cottage and knocked on the front door this time.

Maisie appeared next to her ankles and Polly reached down to stroke her. Her long coon cat fur was silky and kempt. *That poor dog.*

"Shore?" Agnes said, startling Polly, who let out a shriek. She was jumpy and undone.

"Sorry! I mean sure."

Their old formulation. *Shore? Sure.* Which should have been reassuring, but nothing was at the moment.

Agnes had come out prepared with her hiking rod/snake stick. She planted it firmly on every other riser as she descended and then every fourth step ahead of her, pulling herself up alongside it as if it were an oar. She claimed it had nothing to do with her old lady concerns about falling, which she'd done twice, both times on her face, resulting in much dramatic bruising. They headed out to the road and crossed over onto the shore path away from the houses, and then they both spoke practically at the same time. Maisie looked up at the voices. Agnes claimed the cat knew over three hundred words, including the names of several kinds of fish.

"So what happened?" Polly asked.

Agnes sighed. "It's absurd. Seela accused Robert of stealing a piece of jewelry. I'm not sure what. They want to charge him with stealing the belt, too."

"No!"

"It's nuts."

"It's sickening," Polly said.

Agnes crunched across the rocks for a while, huffing audibly.

"Is this too much?" Polly asked, meaning after Agnes's surgery.

"Whatever it is I'll bail him out tomorrow. I called Gabriel Marin. He can go to court with Robert, too."

"Court?" Polly had assumed Agnes would fix it today.

"Who knows? If he has to stay in jail for a night, they'll all take care of him over there. They'll certainly be on his side."

"I hope so." Polly took a deep breath of the salt air. "I feel old this afternoon." She gauged where to step, raising her arms for balance. Her sneakers cupped the round rocks. "And here's something else I have to tell you." She described the dog.

"I know about that dog," Agnes said. "He's been there for years."

"You know? And you never helped him?"

"Polly, I wouldn't last very long as a year-round person if I judged how people live."

"But you love dogs!"

"Yes. And I deplore putting them out on ropes, or throwing them in ditches, or drowning kittens, or separating calves from their mothers. I despise all of it. But you can't fix everything."

"You can do your best."

"I do. I don't eat them. And I'm not stopping you from helping."

The ocean rearranged the rocks in quick raining sputters, deep drumrolls, and a sustained syncopated clacking as the sea pulled back. The gulls spoke adamantly, and an engine vroomed.

"Dick called the shelter about it," Polly said.

"Good for Dick."

Polly looked at her for signs of mockery, but Agnes had shifted. She was appreciative. She was so predictably unpredictable!

And that was the last word for some time. They drifted into the mammalian comfort of being together. Stones, plants, birds, and well-known spots heralded the next stage of the year. It was all reassuringly familiar. The gray sea looked as cold as it was, the heavily wooded land across the harbor as inimical to habitation as ever. When the wind shifted, the buoy bell clanged, and then another shift carried the sound out to sea.

"I couldn't get Archie on the phone. I'm going over there first thing in the morning," Agnes said. "I won't abide this."

They rounded the point of the Sank and climbed from the cold sand onto the narrow path along the cliff. Quickly they were a story above the water and looking down on flat granite ledges and out to a sea flecked with small islands, hunched and bristling with green spines. This was free to all. The coastline was open to everyone. Not true of the path, which belonged to the houses behind it, but the shore, the beach, the ledges, all public, all America's, and no person's. The horizon and beyond it, the sense of infinity and the sensible conviction of democracy, intertwined. Agnes was right about deeding the Sank to a land trust. Polly would have to find a way to square it with James.

She'd wondered as she opened James's letter earlier if there was an argument inside. But he only wrote a newsy note and the dates of his visit. Did that mean he thought his objection to breaking the trust was the last word on the subject?

"I'm tempted to go look in the windows," Agnes said of Wester-Lee, Archie's house that sat just above the Sank. When they were little, they recited the names of the houses from the bottom of Fellowship Point to the top in a singsong. WesterLee, Meadowlea, Leeward Cottage, Rock Reed, Outer Light. Polly taught the ditty to her children. It hurt her heart that she couldn't remember Lydia's voice. They hadn't even made a recording.

Polly looked over at the large gray shingle-style cottage with its deeply sloped roof and angled wings and walled porches and half columns set on shingled balustrades. It was thought to be the best house on the Point architecturally: William had done his brother that favor when he drew the designs. Polly knew it well from going over daily when James was in residence every August. "I'd rather not," Polly said. "It's trespassing."

"On Archie? You actually care about him today of all days? Anyway no one's there. Wait—is that what I think it is?" Agnes pointed.

Polly followed her gaze over the cliff, down to the ledge. She knew what she was seeing, no matter how little of it she could actually see. It was a rope swing, a piece of rope with a log tied at the bottom to make a seat. "Who hung that up?"

"Beats me," Agnes said. "Who even knows the spot anymore? What am I saying, though? If there's anything that endures it's the lore about spots like this. Shall we walk down and have a swing?"

"You first."

"Oh, Pol, how has it happened that we can't even get down there now? Do you remember the last day you went onto the ledges?"

"No." Polly heard her friend's mournful tone, yet her focus was elsewhere, in the past, on the rope swing, flying back and forth while the kids shouted *let go, let go* with every trip out over the water.

"But there was a last time. An unforeseen and uncommemorated last time. I don't remember it. That, more than anything, describes aging to me—the letting go of one activity after the next, with no fanfare. Just realizing later that the last time has come and gone," Agnes said.

Polly hadn't been able to do what they shouted at her to do: let go. No one ever described it beyond coming up shrieking at the shock of the freezing water, or saying they felt something against their leg. No one talked about what it was like. But she often imagined it. Darkness, the gelid pool, no sound, no voice, no breath— obliteration. It occurred to her that the prospect gave her the same feeling she had when she drove along Dump Road. On the day she finally volunteered to go on the rope swing, she couldn't bring herself to loosen her grip on the rope. She swung back and forth until the swing slowed enough for the other children to grab it. She ended up as dry as she'd begun, on the ledge.

Everyone was decent about her failure and said she'd do it soon, but she'd never again called a turn. She'd watched the others take the plunge over and over for years and had been there when a visiting cousin had let go on the backswing and crashed into the rocks, breaking several bones. His accident overshadowed her shameful swing in the annals of failure and Polly was guiltily glad of that.

Yes, she was a coward, to answer her earlier question. Coward then, coward now.

"I was a coward," she said aloud, "don't you agree?" She and Agnes had lived through all of life together.

"It ain't over," Agnes said ruefully.

The sky was pink and red along the horizon now, the chop settling. The afternoon wind had given way to the cool, calm evening, and the wildflowers were closing up shop. Polly looked up for the moon and the North Star. She gestured slightly, and Agnes looked, too, quickly spotting the bright distant touchstones in the sky. Then the mosquitos rose from the grass.

They parted at the graveyard. When Polly got home, Dick was sitting in the shadowy living room.

"Where were you?" he said anxiously.

"Very close by." She snapped on a light.

"Well, I called you and I got no answer."

She wrapped her arms around his neck and kissed his head. "It's been a long day. Eggs for supper?"

"What about Robert? It's been a long day for him, too."

She chose not to tell him that Agnes had spoken to a lawyer. "You'll help him tomorrow."

Dick nodded. "I'll get him out. Dammit!"

CHAPTER 7

Agnes, EasterLee, July 2000

THE NEXT MORNING, AGNES WOKE WITH A STARK FACT IN mind: Robert had had a prior run-in with the law. He'd been arrested and convicted for marijuana possession when he was in college. Caught with pot, wrong place wrong time, a youthful dumb moment that had cost Agnes time and money and Robert his ambitions for law school. The insane drug laws could have meant Robert would rot in jail for fifteen years. Agnes managed with the help of certain friends to get him released on probation. He transferred to the Landscape Architecture program at Amherst and promised to pay her back every penny. She'd let him give her money, but not as much as she'd spent. She'd owed others favors in return, and they had come due over time. Such was the way of the world. But she never blamed Robert. People made mistakes.

She hadn't thought about it in ages—never imagined he might be arrested again. Who would think it? Robert was the most honest person around. But that old conviction could hurt him now. He'd surely realized it, too.

She could kill Seela. She was worse than the gulls.

"Oatmeal?" Sylvie called upstairs.

"Yes, please. I'll eat in the kitchen today."

She dressed and went down. Her place had been set. Maisie lay down beside her feet.

"What a morning," she said to Sylvie. "Sit with me."

Sylvie cocked a hand onto her hip. "I'm too busy to sit, but I'll tell you this. There's not a soul in town who thinks he did it."

"What did you hear?" The scent of the freshly cut herbs on the sideboard reinforced her determination to make the world right.

"That Mrs. Seela Lee accused Robert of stealing her diamond necklace."

"That's a detail I didn't have before. The necklace. I hate that necklace. Of course he didn't do it."

"Suspicion creates suspicion. Also, everyone's saying Mr. Archie Lee will stand up for Robert."

"Archie better. I'm going to talk to him this morning."

"Good. Nip this in the bud. Nip her head off." She made a quick, decisive snapping gesture. Agnes didn't want to think what she'd used that for. Sylvie had been a farm girl and had never approved of Agnes's ethical vegetarianism. "Am I driving?"

"Nope. Going alone."

Agnes braced for Sylvie's disapproval. But Sylvie only said—"Just talk some sense into him, that's all."

"Thank you, Sylvie. I plan to. He's a Lee. He knows what's right."

The inland road from the Point to the east side of Cape Deel cut through farmland, small places devoted to local produce, mainly vegetables and eggs. Cows and goats were fenced in with room to be stimulated by life. Agnes put her window down. She'd driven past Robert's house many times but never turned in the driveway. The attractive and creative landscaping served as an effective advertisement for his abilities. She slowed to have a look at his beds, and a car came down the driveway. Agnes pulled over smack in front of the entrance. Robert's right-hand man, Jeff Glynn, got out of his car and came to Agnes's window.

"Good morning, Jeff. Is Robert here?" She knew he wasn't, but she erred on the side of being open to fresh news.

"No, he's not here." Jeff said carefully. He was a few years younger than Robert, and had worked for Hiram since he was a kid.

"I'm driving over to talk to Archie."

Jeff nodded. "I checked on things here. It's all locked up now. I got the perishables out of the fridge."

"That was smart, but he'll be home soon." Agnes's stomach fluttered.

"Yup, well, anyway. Do you need anything over your way?"

"Not today, thank you, Jeff. Do you know what happened?"

"Not from him, so I don't know for sure."

"That's exactly right. Thank you, Jeff."

As she drove away, a line came to her, the way lines often did, even when she was occupied with the immediate. *He knew very quickly his marriage was a mistake, but he stayed out of a sentimental fondness for his error.* She wished she could write it down. She tried it out changing the pronoun to *she* to see if it brought up any of her Franklin Square women. Yes—there was Neve. *It was very like Neve to stick to her story rather than try to make her life better.* She felt a moment's satisfaction that something had come through. She repeated the sentence, hoping she'd remember later.

In spite of her upset, in spite of her errand, she was moved by the beauty all around her. Cape Deel always pulled her mind down into her heart and through her feet into the ground, through the soil and rock. She had no interest in writing a memoir, per Maud Silver's request, but if she did, she'd write about Cape Deel. Even the name stirred her, the sounds. Maine only peripherally figured into the Franklin Square series—she'd never given it its due on the page. She should. She wanted to.

Maud Silver was certainly persistent. Her tone had changed a great deal since that first note. Letters arrived regularly. Confident, persuasive letters. Her pitch was that a memoir would serve as an excellent companion piece to the repackaged editions of the *When Nan* series, which were in the works. The one could sell the other and vice versa. Agnes had rolled her eyes when she read that. "Don't kid a kidder," she replied. That should be the end of it, she thought, with a twinge of regret—she rather liked Maud's letters. But it wasn't over. Maud wrote back that Agnes should do it for her own reasons. What was that line from *Lawrence of Arabia*? "He will come because it is his pleasure." Clever, but Agnes saw through it. Yet she didn't end the correspondence, either. Maud Silver was bright. And—no reason for the girl not to get some mileage from the idea. Let David think she was considering it.

But—Robert! How could her mind wander under these circumstances?

She hadn't driven up the east side of Cape Deel—known as the Diamond Coast for the sparkling sea, though the wags said it was a jab at the rich residents—in about a year, and now noticed the changes. Spiffing up, mainly. Signs of away people encroaching. Additions, fences and gates. Pickup trucks everywhere, men at work. Volvos, Volkswagens, Saabs, and Mercedes whizzed by her. Even a Porsche!

The enormous cottages on the Diamond Coast were downhill of the road and could only be seen from the water. By land, one might spot an occasional roofline behind the tips of the pines. Driveways were ruthlessly unmarked and nearly undetectable. The houses had names, and all one had to do was say one, and name a time, and guests would arrive at lawn parties, fireworks viewings, afternoons of croquet and picnics on the rocks to which the social group was invited, including babies in arms. The babies became children became teenagers who had their own clandestine parties, by which time they all knew who lived down every hidden ingress along Shore Road, perpetuating the whole system of initiation into an invisible realm of money and beauty that was inculcated without those involved realizing it wasn't organic or natural or simple. They took it for granted and felt misapprehended when they were called exclusive. They simply liked one another's company and desired privacy. What could be wrong with that?

Agnes had a strong opinion on the subject that she largely kept to herself. But once at a dinner party, prompted by a particularly disingenuous conversation on the subject and a few glasses of burgundy too delicious to moderate, she said she supposed it was all right for all the ethnic groups of Philadelphia to belong to their own exclusive clubs if it were agreed that no business be done anywhere on the premises. She saw brows furrow when she used the word *ethnic* to include present company, and it took a moment for her meaning to sink in. Then one of the women at the table told Agnes she'd gotten that from Pauline Schulz! It was in the Franklin Square novels! Agnes was, for once, struck dumb. What could she say? It rankled her to be accused of a borrowed opinion, and the fact that she was borrowing from herself didn't allay the pique of being so accused in front of a table full of her erstwhile kind.

There were exceptions to the rule of hidden mansions on the Point. A few properties were conspicuously marked, and Archie Lee's EasterLee was one of them. He could very easily have chosen invisibility, with all the advantages and good manners it offered. For that matter, he could have chosen to stay at WesterLee. Instead, after his marriage, his second, to Seela, her third—Agnes hadn't had time to memorize her last name, so eager was she to swap it for his—he built a behemoth on the Diamond Coast and had the name "EasterLee" carved into two wide stone pillars at the end of the drive. It reached him that he'd caused perturbation in his circles by announcing his presence so loudly, but he was of the modern mind that there was no such thing as bad publicity. He felt this sincerely and robustly, and the two traits combined to create a charm persuasive to all but the most conventional of his neighbors. The others adapted, for nothing quelled a revolution more quickly—wrote Pauline Schulz—than the prevailing powers inviting it in for drinks. The final verdict was that Archie was eccentric, and his penchant for being easy to find was turned to their advantage, with EasterLee serving as a marker to offer directions to deliverymen or visitors. Grudgingly, the neighbors admitted it didn't hurt to have it for orientation after a sodden club dance.

Agnes tootled along Shore Road, shifting her intelligence, which she could turn on and beam like the Fresnel lens in a lighthouse, to how to handle Archie, her young cousin. She must prevail.

When he was a boy, Archie had once told Agnes that he wasn't going to stay at WesterLee when he grew up because he loved it too much. That had endeared him to her forever. His personality was playful and wry and droopy and finally louche. In his fifties now, he still looked boyish, his sandy hair having grayed but not retreated, and his thin figure still assuming postures and poses that suggested agility. He paid his Fellowship Point bills and taxes on time, loaned WesterLee to his children and his friends, and always checked with Polly about when her sons were coming so they could spill over into his bedrooms.

This all reflected well on him, and she pointed it out when others made note of his ostentatious ways and faults. Her opinion of him had formed decades earlier, and she didn't believe people really ever changed. She'd forgiven Archie for his divorce from a person Agnes liked a lot, and his inexplicable marriage to a sour woman fifteen years his elder that Agnes couldn't bear. Who knew what people really needed? He had three children, an apartment in Manhattan, EasterLee, WesterLee, a partnership at an investment bank, a seat on the board of Lee & Sons, and friendships and habits and hobbies that kept him amused. She was arriving with an agenda—drop the suit against Robert, first, and agree to dissolve the association for the purpose of donating the lands to a trust—but coached herself that it would be wise to consider his concerns before she asked for anything. Archie wore a gilded cape of male vanity and would need it admired.

She frowned as she turned through Archie's massive plinths and headed up the slope on his pink granite drive through an allée of flashing silver beech trees. Just beyond them, walls of fir covered the terrain, and the spicy cool heavy air settled on her arms. At the top of the rise the sea rolled out miles and miles to a soft horizon. In between stood the house, part stone, part weathered barn wood, all festooned with flowers and vines and trees and bushes. She pictured the formal gardens in the back, where she presumed the topiary was a vaunted feature and the white garden would be dug in, and she shook her head. *Versailles sur mer.* So many people wished they were king.

As always after a drive, Agnes needed the bathroom first thing. Thank God Nora O'Connor answered the door, so Agnes didn't have to directly ask Archie. It embarrassed her to reveal to men that she inhabited a body—it was none of their business! Agnes had known Nora for decades and made meaningful small talk while heading straight for what Seela called "the powder room." Agnes opened the door and, though she'd been in there before, gasped at its sumptuousness. Pink granite again for the sink table, and an inset sink of jade marble. Brass fixtures—she hoped. What if they were gold? Soaps and lotions that all smelled divine. She could have whiled away half an hour if she weren't embarrassed by the thought of Archie imagining her occupied with the room's central function. She dried her hands and got out.

Archie materialized, a vision of how aging men delude themselves into believing they have achieved peak allure. He was groomed to the crown of his head, clothes pressed to the point of stoniness. His face, sweet in childhood, now sported lines revealing pastimes of predation. So, he was at that stage. Poor Seela, or lucky Seela, depending on how much she hated the way he ate and snored.

He was smiling, as if nothing had happened. Agnes used all her will to disguise her upset and smiled back. He opened his arms to her.

"Cuz! Please, please come in. I have a feeling I know why you're here. An awful mess. And here we are before I've even come over to visit. How are you?"

"I have cancer," Agnes announced. She hadn't been able to contain her rage after all. She didn't expect it to come out that way—it just had. Her hands rose to the sides of her rib cage, a gesture left over from when there had been drains there.

"You got the flowers we sent?" He'd been coming straight toward her but stopped, as if she'd announced a contagion.

"Probably. Did I write a note?"

He laughed. "Probably! How did this happen, though?" He shifted gears, stepped closer to her, looked her in the eye, and asked—intimately, wittily—"Have you been smoking, Cousin Nessie?"

"Wouldn't that be nice!"

"Yes. I'd love to myself. I always say I'll pick it up again at eighty. But you are eighty!"

"And now I'm saying I'll start at ninety."

"Oh, is that how it goes? I don't know if I'll last that long."

"That makes two of us."

His face crumpled. A little boy again.

"Oh come on, Archie, if you can't laugh at death, what can you laugh at?" She gave him a light punch on the arm.

"I'll be lucky to live to the age you are now," he said awkwardly.

"Yes. It is fortunate. Everything becomes very clear."

"But you still feel young, don't you?"

"Are you kidding? I feel old as the hills and twice as dusty, as my mother would say."

"You better come see the view immediately, in that case." He hovered his hand under her elbow and moved her forward.

His living room was too tasteful, too clean, too decorated, too self-aware, too beige. He hadn't lived like that during the reign of his first wife, who'd been as slapdash as all the Lees and had fit in easily at WesterLee. If only Archie could have kept his hands to himself and her, Robert would be at Fellowship Point, doing his chores. But no. Seela had taken over and hired decorators, a rarity in houses where all the furnishings were antediluvian. Archie's old pieces were back at WesterLee, while here reigned the new. Coral pillows, turquoise throws over sofa arms, against a landscape of beige and what Seela had educated Agnes was called "greige." Looking at it, Agnes could have fallen asleep standing up. Seela had told her on another visit that her decorator claimed beige was the *classiest* color, a phrasing that repudiated the statement. "I always think of beige as more a backdrop than a color," Agnes said, and realized she'd hit on the point. The décor of EasterLee was a backdrop for Seela, who tended to wear beige as well, her house and clothes the equivalent of a jeweler's cushion where she displayed her tightened face and bedazzled ears, neck, and hands. "It's so easy to redecorate and introduce variety," she'd said, in awe of her own ingenuity. "All I do is add splashes of color." If only Seela knew how funny that was, Agnes might forgive her for her unassailable good taste. As it was, Agnes wanted to assail her, especially now.

Agnes's sweeping gaze made a spot inventory of all the Lee family heirlooms in the room. There wasn't much. The old Philadelphia Chippendale had appalled Seela. Agnes had divested herself of hers, too, but that was her choice, and it had landed in good homes. She hoped Archie's had gone straight to his likable children, though apparently the youth wanted pale wood now. Agnes certainly understood that.

"We've just had everything redone," he said, pointing his hand around. "I know you're thinking it looks the same, but the materials are far better."

"Diamond dust?"

"Costs as much. The fur of rare goats." He nodded at his furniture, as if the pieces were the peoples of his kingdom.

"The fur of rare goats. That would make a great book title."

"You may have it. Or should I ask for a share in the royalties? Your girl—what's her name?"

"Nan."

"—has done well, hasn't she? She could use a stint as a goat farmer."

"There's an idea." Agnes couldn't venture into public without being told what Nan should do next.

"How many more are you going to write anyway?"

"I have no plans to stop working, if that's what you mean. I'll go until the clock runs out."

"Of course you will." He grinned at her with their old familiarity. "I am happy to see you, Cousin. As I always say, no one is like you. But tell me straight out—is this a social visit, or have we matters to discuss?"

"A bit of both. But I come as an ally."

"I know that." He saw her over the raised marble threshold between indoors and out. "Come. This will make you happy."

She stepped out, and immediately she noticed a wind that hadn't been apparent on the other side of the house. Her heart lifted, in spite of her mission, at the sight of how straight and high the old firs stood among the branching oaks and silver birches. They created a carefully groomed natural frame for a view out to the untamed ocean. Today the water was navy blue and rippling. The terrace hung over a garden that perfumed the air. She gave in to it and deeply inhaled the rich scent.

"Beautiful," she pronounced.

"We think so."

We. She despised couples who referred to themselves as a unit. Polly, who thought as a *we*, nevertheless always said *Dick and I.* So much better. "Is Seela here?" She glanced around.

"She's out."

"That's fine. It's best we speak alone, I think."

"Come look over this way." He pointed. "Our new garden," he said. "It's going to be all white."

"Like Sissinghurst."

"Ha! Cousin, you never fail to know everything."

They settled into chairs far more comfortable than any outdoor furniture she'd ever encountered. A sigh escaped her. "So this is what it's like to be *comfortably* rich."

"Ha, yes! Who knew comfortable furniture even existed?"

Nora O'Connor appeared.

"Coffee or tea? Water?" Archie asked. "Something stronger?"

Agnes thought of the drive back and guessed she'd better resist. She didn't want to ask to use Archie's toilet again. "No, thank you. I won't be long."

"Iced tea for me, thank you, Nora," Archie said. She vanished abruptly.

"Then let's get to it." Archie shifted to business mode. "I'm very confused, I must say, by what happened with Robert." Archie looked down at his hands, his brow furrowed. "I always trusted Hiram. And I have liked Robert, too. He has been an excellent designer and gardener in general. I'd never have expected him to do anything like this. But here we are."

Agnes felt a flash of rage. "Here *we* are. Robert's in jail."

"Yes, true. I feel sick about it, actually. But Seela caught him red-handed, and then—well, it was awful."

Agnes gripped her fingers into tight fists. "Why don't you tell me exactly what happened?"

"Yes, yes, first things first." Nora arrived with the tea, and he took it from her and had a sip. "Thank you, it's delicious. Perfect amount of mint."

Nora gave a nod that said, *Of course it's the perfect amount of mint.* Agnes caught her eye, acknowledging her burdens.

"I was in my study, working. Money never sleeps, and all that. I heard her scream. I ran out to the driveway and there was Robert, holding her necklace. Seela was on the ground, where he'd pushed her. She'd just gotten back from a trip to town." He rubbed his cheeks. "She could barely move. We had to help her up."

"You and Robert? Robert helped her up?"

"Yes."

"And what became of the necklace?"

"He handed it to me."

"After you accused him?"

Archie looked up at the awning that shielded them from the worst of the sun. "Actually, no. Seela hadn't said anything yet. She was injured."

"When did the accusation happen?"

"Just after that. Seela called him a thief."

"So you came out and saw Seela on the ground and you and Robert helped her up and he handed you the necklace, all before she accused him?" She let that sink in. "It seems to me," she said calmly, "if Robert *were* going to steal something, which he never would, I've known him since he was a child and so have you and he's always been the best of humans, he'd hardly be stupid enough to show Seela what he was taking. And pushing her? That's crazy."

He shrugged. "You think you know people."

"I do know Robert. He's pure integrity."

"Seela has bruises."

"Archie. You can't possibly believe all this."

He wiped his hands down his face and shook his head. "She's my wife!"

Agnes worked to steady herself by means of deep breaths. For a moment the only voice belonged to the wind.

"You, Cousin, are a Lee. You must understand that this situation is bad for everyone. And it's not how we are. We give people the benefit of the doubt, and we give good people a second chance. And a third chance, if they need it." She paused. "Let's say Robert did do it. Even then, would you want him to go to prison? His mother depends on him now, with Hiram dead. He has all those siblings who count on him for leadership. He's an important part of the community, always on this or that board or committee. I am not denying Seela her perception. I'm sure she did see him carrying her necklace. And that she tripped and fell. But may God strike me now if Robert deliberately pushed her."

"What about the wampum belt?"

"The belt! What about it?"

"That might be part of this. He was here off and on."

"Archie! Stop this right now! You are making yourself ridiculous!"

He leaped up. "What am I supposed to do? I don't know what you want from me!" His hair came loose and spittle clung to his lip.

"I want you to drop the charges."

"I can't do that! It's up to Seela."

Agnes pushed herself upright to meet him. It was time to command him. "You drive her to the station. Get her to tell the police that she made a mistake. She did make a mistake. You know it and I know it. It makes no sense."

"But Seela—"

"Oh, for God's sake! Does she scare you that much? Stick up for yourself!"

Archie pushed his hair back into place and pulled a handkerchief from his pocket. He wiped the lower half of his face. "Do you really think he didn't do it?"

One, two, three, four, five . . . "I really do. Don't you? Wait a minute—Seela is at tennis?"

"Yes."

"After being attacked yesterday? You made it sound as though she'd be at the hospital, not the club."

"Thank God she didn't get hurt."

Finally Agnes could no longer keep her temper. "Call the station! Fix this, Archie!"

They stared at each other, and he visibly relaxed. She had lost her advantage. Why were women never allowed their legitimate rage? She watched Archie realize that he had the history of civilization on his side, and all the laws made against women, all the burnings and incarcerations and jokes. She had made herself dismissible if not worse. Guilty.

"Calm yourself, Cousin," Archie said coolly. He looked at his watch. "Seela will be back momentarily. I suggest you not be here then. What was the other thing you wanted to talk about?" he asked, all affection gone.

"That can wait. I want to be sure you understand now that you will be ruined in this community if you let this happen, Archie Lee. Your favorite uncle Lachlan would be deeply ashamed of you, as am I right now. This is a man's life and his reputation. If you pursue this, you and Seela will not have a social place on Cape Deel."

"You think you have that much power? People can hire another landscaper, you know. The first rule of work—everyone is replacable."

"We shall see." Agnes was tired now.

Archie called out, "Nora!" They waited stiffly until she appeared. "Please see Miss Lee to her car. Goodbye, Cousin." He clasped his hands behind his back and bent slightly forward from the waist. Pretentious fool. He fled down the steps to the garden.

"This way, Miss Lee."

"Thank you." She walked just behind Nora, steadied by her deliberate gait. Suddenly it occurred to her—"Nora? Did you see what happened?"

Nora shook her head miserably. "I only saw after. When Mrs. Lee told Mr. Lee to call the police."

"All right. Don't worry. This can't stand."

She sped down the driveway to avoid running into Seela Lee coming the other way. On the drive home she tried to remember the line she thought of on the way over, but it was gone, wiped out by conflict. If Seela stole her book, too—

She pulled over to the side of the road and cried for the first time in years.

CHAPTER 8

Polly, Meadowlea, August 2000

Polly's garden came in well, campanula and globe thistle, cosmos and Queen Anne's lace, hollyhocks in the sun and hosta and astilbe in the shade. She weeded with the help of a kneeling pad made of gel that buffered her joints. Every afternoon she walked to Agnes's across the desire line, a routine she felt duty-bound to maintain but that she'd grown to dread. Agnes was furious and aggrieved about Robert, and in a permanent bad mood. The instant Polly arrived, she'd start in on it, especially on Seela, but if Polly chimed in, Agnes would retreat, saying she was too upset to discuss it—as if Polly weren't. Agnes wasn't going out at all, and rolled her eyes if Polly asked about her work. "Visiting the graveyard is the one cheerful part of my day," she said belligerently. The only relief was that Agnes wasn't obsessing about the Point as much. Polly didn't want to talk about that. James had once again made his position clear in his letters to Polly, saying he was trusting her to be loyal. She was always loyal—but how to choose between the entities that deserved her allegiance?

After her glass of white wine and visit in the graveyard with an uncompanionable Agnes, Polly walked across the desire line back to Meadowlea, and as they had their ginger ale on the terrace, Dick sucked pensively on salted pretzels, and she told him what she'd done that day. He was aggrieved as well, and constantly snappish. Everything had happened so fast—Robert's arrest, his taking a plea, his imprisonment. Dick had been incredulous, and Agnes had come over and told them both about Robert's marijuana conviction. That had come as a shock to Polly and Dick, who'd never before heard of it. No wonder Robert hadn't gone to law school. Agnes apologized to Polly for never telling her, but Robert had asked for privacy.

Also—he wouldn't let Agnes help him. Not even a little bit. Not like last time, when he'd been a boy who didn't want to upset his father. Robert put his house on the market so he could cover his legal expenses, maintain his payroll, and give money to his mother while he was gone.

The plea deal was considered a fortunate outcome, though it was hard to feel anything but depressed about it. Robert would be in the state penitentiary at Thomaston for two years. For nothing. Polly was more sad than enraged. She couldn't bear to think of him in that place. Locked up, when he should be building her pink wall with her.

But life went on. She didn't want to become as embittered as Agnes was. Occasionally she and Dick went out, to old friends and safe places. When invited, she overcame her manners to ask a necessary question—were Seela and Archie invited as well? If so, she declined.

Dick often went back to work after dinner, and she walked down to the Sank. The evenings were full of bats and the calls of the night birds. Sometimes her mind vanished, and she became the black trees. She would like to think that was what death would be like, that you become one with the trees, but who knew? No one knew.

Lydia knew.

Polly had taken to thinking of all the dogs out there, alone, hungry, in pain, miserable. How did everyone not notice? But people had noticed, the shelter existed, and other shelters and organizations for animal welfare. *She* hadn't noticed, was what she meant, not before now. What else had she missed?

She'd been raised not to dwell on such injustices, because dwelling made it difficult to be good company in the present. Perhaps it was necessary to dwell, though, even to be obsessive, for any real change to occur. Plenty of Quakers dwelled—the American Friends Service Committee, for example—and hadn't that done the world a lot of good? When she got back to Haverford, she'd volunteer for something to do with animals—if Dick could spare her. Agnes would approve, though Polly hesitated discussing it with her, knowing it would bring on a lecture about vegetarianism. *If you want to help animals, don't eat them. They really appreciate that.* Polly could supply Agnes's lines from afar.

One night Dick came upstairs to bed with energy still in his step. He didn't say hello but launched straight into a rant. He dwelled—it was his whole way of life.

"How have we ignored our prisons? We are no better than the Germans who lived among the camps. There's no such thing as rehabilitation anymore. The conditions are monstrous!" He changed into his pajamas. He was at the age when wrinkles were smoothing out, and hair was disappearing on his limbs. Even his personal hair was nearly gone. "I believed that men were in prison learning a trade or studying law books to secure an appeal, but there's virtually none of that now. Prisons are cages! I have never been so disgusted with this country in my whole life. I must work harder writing letters to the editor about it. People need to know."

He looked at her beseechingly.

"Oh," she was able to offer, "I have been thinking nearly the same thing, except about all the dogs being mistreated. That dog I found—and you saved—was only ten minutes from here. We all have scales over our eyes."

He picked up the envelope of covers she'd turned down and slid in. "I think Robert has the stuff to endure it, though. And it won't go on too long for him, anyway. I feel sorry for those poor bastards who are in for life. I don't care what they've done, no one should live that way. It's bad for the whole of society to have people made invisible. It weighs us down subconsciously. We know we are being cruel, and we have to push that out of our minds."

His words stirred Polly deeply. Robert's arrest and Dick's disappointment at the lack of fanfare on his retirement—aside from the party she'd given him—had stripped him of a protective layer. Speaking of which, she still had to write to his chair to ask why the department had turned against him. She reached over and rubbed his bony shoulder, and he reached up and touched her hand.

After a moment she asked—"Do you think the dog was adopted by kind people?"

"What?"

"The dog. The one I found on Dump Road. Do you think he found a good home?"

"Yes, yes. It was a good-looking animal, didn't you say?" He rolled on his side, lacing his hands under his cheek. "Okay to turn off."

"I'm still dressed." Not to mention sitting up.

"Well, get undressed."

"That's all right." She clicked the switch and lay back. After a moment the walls swam with shadows. What if she slept in her clothes? What harm?

"I want to write Robert as often as possible," Dick said. "I wrote him about visiting. Do you think he can get good books there? I'm going to bring him some books. The new Philip Roth, I think—*The Human Stain.*" His face was a dark drop of night.

"That sounds like a good idea."

"I will. I will! I'll go to the bookstore tomorrow."

Which meant she'd drive him. "Good idea," she repeated, a

phrase that had kept him attached to her for sixty years. He had the ideas, or the acknowledgment of ideas. Credit didn't matter to her. Peace did.

He fell asleep quickly, but she was restless and stimulated so she went on with the conversation.

ME: *If we had it to do over, I'd want us to travel more.*

HIM: *I never became as famous as I'd hoped.*

ME: *I'd have taken Lydia to the hospital right away in spite of what the doctor said.*

HIM: *I wouldn't have been so squeamish about writing my books for popular audiences rather than academic ones. In the end, no one thinks poorly of those who do so, if they are successful.*

ME: *I'd have been braver. I'd have insisted the boys have a dog. Or maybe several.*

HIM: *Believing in pacifism didn't mean I was anti-Semitic.*

ME: *After everyone leaves, I'd love for the two of us to drive over to Campobello.*

HIM: *That'd be nice.*

ME: *I'd like to stay here until Thanksgiving this year. We can walk the trails under the bright leaves.*

HIM: *I don't see why not.*

ME: *The main thing is to spend as much time together as possible.*

HIM: *Alwaysalwaysalways . . .*

She'd invested in the spell of a promise by making especially significant words like *always* and *forever*. There was no such thing. To believe in nothing, to have no need of belief—that was growing up.

What would she give up for that sober maturity, where all was dispelled but the present? What would she give up to truly believe *always* was only an idea, and not even an intelligent one? Nature was right out the door, offering a daily example of flux and impermanence. What was the biological purpose of humans having such a vast capacity for denying reality?

She rolled over, her mind too active for sleep. Agnes got up if she couldn't sleep, thereby forestalling the fretful thoughts that came when lying in bed. Polly agreed with the good sense of that method, but she couldn't bear to leave Dick alone or risk waking him up. She considered what to think about, and naturally, her children clamored for attention. She tried not to think of them as she lay in bed, for she was bound to worry, or wish she had a second chance to redo particular decisions or respond differently to a question or an upset. But they insisted on being seen, even in absentia, and she opened her eyes and looked out the window, at the stars, settling in for a long night.

Polly's children. When each was inside of her she learned what they'd be like. She felt it in the way they moved. The sweep of a hand across the inside of her abdomen, the tossing and turning or kicking in distress or glee. From the very beginning she wanted to experience them, share with them, but otherwise leave them be to grow into individuals. Other women seemed to feel the opposite— as if their children were miniature versions of themselves, sources of pride and shame. They encouraged sameness rather than difference. Polly supposed that kept a society coherent, but her own feelings were too yielding for that. She was a good herder, and she was strict, too, in her way. But she was also squeamish about interfering too much.

James was conceived at Meadowlea. One moonlit night, when Polly was very tired from a day in the sun and an evening dancing at the Deel Club, she and Dick made love, not for remarkably longer than she'd so far experienced, but more languorously. She relaxed, sensing that he wasn't pushing toward his climax. She became more and more liquid as it went on, and there seemed no reason to ever stop—they might eat and sleep and live this way.

Her thoughts drifted past, nothing sticking or catching, a river of notions and sensations, placid and cool. She had no capacity to make an emotion. *She* was a feeling. She herself. She was in life, a thread in the pattern. Yes. It was real, and true. Most of the time she was a jumble of states. Emotions latched on to her. They separated her from nature, from this languid flow. Now she and her feeling were one.

When it happened, she knew it instantly.

It was like—a ping. A timer going off in the kitchen. A sonar sounding. A distant thunderclap. *Oh,* she thought. *Oh!* Two vast sets of information meeting and combining, a new and powerful brew. Dick kept going, but she was in two places at once, and she had the presence of mind to have the prescient thought that she'd be that way from then on. Dual loyalties. In the next moment she sank into a stupor. When Dick moved away, she was already half-asleep. In her last moment of consciousness she told him what had happened. He assured her she couldn't possibly have felt it, the process was microscopic. She couldn't explain, but at the same time how could she be unaware of what had changed? "You'll see," she told him. "We aren't alone anymore."

"But I'll always come first," he said.

She should have heard in that remark a howl of storms on the way, but she only said, "Of course."

Marriage was based on trust, she'd heard that all her life. Trust bypassed questions. Trust operated on the premise that all would become clear in time. She'd never asked about lovemaking or childbirth. She'd gleaned that both would hurt to some degree. Otherwise she trusted and was ill-prepared. Lovemaking stopped hurting very quickly, thank God, but childbirth hurt before she was knocked out and afterward, and she assumed the worst pain had come in the middle. It was cruel that no one had told her what it would be like, especially her doctor, who'd seen her over and over. He betrayed her, she thought darkly, in the delivery room. But afterward, beyond the pain, she was a mother. She had presents to open and notes to write and new routines to figure out and establish, and above and beyond all that was the real consideration—she had the baby to take joy and pleasure in and to marvel at, the incredible baby. She searched for joy.

He looks like your father! He looks like Dick! He looks like a Martian, what funny faces!

She smiled and agreed he looked like whatever was suggested. She couldn't see anything in him but himself. Sometimes she wondered if he really was her baby, and sometimes if she'd even had a baby. Crazy ideas. Yet she couldn't shake them off. Her flat stomach persuaded her that nothing had happened, it had all been a dream. She was miles away from the people who made faces and noises at the baby and reached for him, cuddled him, kissed his cheeks. All she wanted was to be left alone and to sleep.

She pretended, though. Enough so that no one knew but the baby. He knew and reacted by not relaxing when she held him or crying until Mrs. Bailey took him away. Mrs. Bailey knew, too. She gazed at Polly sympathetically while telling the world how well everyone was adjusting. Nor did she remark when they were alone that Polly would feel like a real mother soon enough. Polly noticed these considerate attentions and appreciated them immeasurably. She'd never before understood the value of being left alone or met a person who knew how to do it thoughtfully. She let the care roll over her and slept for weeks.

One day while the baby was lying next to her on the sofa, he lifted his foot and pointed it toward her. She leaned toward him and the foot wobbled, but with great effort he pushed it closer and closer and finally pressed it against her cheek. How had he done that? Did he do it on purpose? It had certainly seemed deliberate. She closed his foot in her hand and jiggled it—and he laughed. She tried it again and he laughed again, and when she let go, his wobbling foot pressed forward again toward her face. She played the game with him until she was convinced he knew what he was doing. How clever of him! What a brilliant baby! She called Bailey in to see.

"He wants attention, like all men," Bailey said. She bent down to coo at James and emitted a puff of powder from inside her dress.

"I don't mind giving it," Polly said.

"That's how they rule the world." Mrs. Bailey sighed and ran an efficient finger into the front of James's diaper. "Time for a change." She bent to pick him up.

"Show me how," Polly said.

After that, all Polly wanted to do was to wake up in the morning and see James again. Once he entered her mind, he never left. She couldn't think without engaging him, couldn't speak without finding a way to mention his name. She could turn any subject in James's direction. Agnes told her that her mother, that battle-axe Grace Lee, remarked that Polly needed to beware of becoming boring, which embarrassed her. She, who was acutely aware of the feelings of others, and who thoroughly fulfilled the dictate of her upbringing not to draw attention to herself, had become a chatterbox. She *knew* nothing was more boring than talking about one's children. How often had she been on the other end of it, and had that fact proved to her? But, besotted, she rattled on hectically, crazed with love.

Eventually Bailey determined that Polly didn't need her anymore—until the next baby. Polly found a sitter who'd come three days a week so she could get out and see friends, pick up her volunteer work again. She'd have been just as happy to have no sitter and take James out with her—people did that, at least for the market—but the sitter insisted Polly needed time to herself, and that that was better for the baby. Soon she was back in her regular round but elevated above her characteristic high spirits by knowing her husband and baby were ahead of and behind her—that she now had everything. She hired a housekeeper and quietly paid for it, meanwhile thanking Dick for being such a good provider. As she gathered advice, most of it unsolicited, she heard many tips. Your child needs discipline, he's basically an animal, always keep your eyes out, he's going to try to get away with all kinds of nonsense. That couldn't be right, could it? Why be suspicious of your own child?

Her mother, that gentle person, never once criticized Polly's mothering, and waited to be asked for advice. So Polly realized where she'd gotten her ideas. Her wild love for her baby encompassed her mother, too, who had gone through the very same incredible things. Why didn't people talk about this?

James was mischievous. He climbed up the Christmas tree, pulling it over and smashing all the glass. He hid under beds and bit his own hand to keep from giving himself away with giggles. Dick insisted on disciplining him—he didn't share the liberal theories about child-rearing that Polly hewed to. This only meant that James kept an eye on Dick and saved his pranks for Polly. That was genius, wasn't it?

The second time she got pregnant it was under the same circumstances, on a night when once again they made love after a long party and were nearly asleep, and she was completely relaxed. Again she felt the small explosion in her abdomen, and this time, Dick believed her—or said he did.

At the birth she insisted on only the smallest drop of knockout drugs. She'd never said so aloud, but she wanted a girl, very badly, and she wanted to be conscious when her daughter entered the world. But she had another disappointment in that regard, whom they named Knox. He was a pretty baby but colicky and miserable a lot of the time. He couldn't settle for a nap and screamed when he was dressed, especially when she pulled socks onto his unblemished and unused feet. By age two he was more at ease, in no small part because James wanted a companion and taught Knox how to play. Polly was grateful for that, and a bit jealous. Her fervent domesticity also yearned for companionship. Daily she attended to her plants, watering, fertilizing, stroking, and talking to them; she poked a needle through a needlepoint canvas, taking on a years-long project of making chair seats for both her dining rooms; she made birthday cards, Christmas cards, Christmas ornaments far beyond ho-hum orange and clove sachets and popcorn strings; and she decorated carefully, with much thought going into proportion and color. The boys swirled around her whatever her pursuit, happy to be in her orbit but without any interest whatsoever in helping her, or learning. She taught them the names of every bird that came to both houses, and all the flowers both wild and cultivated, but they only learned *robin, blue jay, hawk, eagle, daffodil, hydrangea, hawkweed.* If she had a daughter, it would be different. A daughter would stitch her into a long line of women who had quietly made the world beautiful, stretching back to Eve. A daughter would make fresh stitches.

Pregnant again! She cast spells for a girl, but the pregnancy felt no different than the other two before it, and she prepared herself to be a good sport in the delivery room. She was in Philadelphia when the baby made it known it was time. She had the normal pains in the normal way and didn't think anything of it and went to the hospital when her water broke and liquid rushed down her legs. She waited to be told when to push, but many faces peered and poked at her, and when she asked what was going on, no one told her. Instead voices barked overhead and she was wheeled swiftly into a light-flooded room where metal chimed and rattled and her doctor introduced another doctor and a black saddle plunged to her face and she slipped from consciousness.

When she woke, she understood nothing. Frantically she scrabbled back through recent memory to figure out where she was, but she couldn't find her name. She lay in limbo for eons. Dinosaurs were born and their species extinguished. Leaves became coal. Magnificent civilzations sank under the ground. Then a woman in white handed her a small creature—b-a-b-y, she spelled out in her mind—and asked her what she'd name him. *Him.* A man came in and handed her flowers. They gave her a glass cylinder and showed her how to plug it into the baby's mouth. Bottle! The word announced itself and she spoke it aloud. Yes, the baby's bottle, the milk warmed up. How did she feel?

She tried to sit up, and they pushed her back against the pillow. *You had a caesarian section, Polly. You couldn't get the baby out yourself.*

She reached down and discovered a big bandage across her lower abdomen. Everyone told her that all that mattered was that she had a healthy baby boy. But what about her? She'd failed miserably and had been horribly violated. The slicing of her uterus gave her nightmares. Ten days after they released her, five days after the baby was "born," she was back in the hospital with a high fever. Her belly had puffed up into a bready dome. *You have a puerperal infection. Childbed fever. Women died of it in the past, but we can treat it now, so you're lucky. Who knows how you got it, it didn't happen here, the hospital is sterile. Maybe you did something at home? Do you always wash your hands after using the bathroom?*

And she'd believed her doctor was a good man.

Her parents and Dick and other friends came to see her, but she was too depressed to speak. Then Agnes came, and Polly wanted to talk.

"You have to get better, that's all," Agnes said.

"I feel as though I'm being punished for wanting a girl so much."

"You could have died. Your blood was poisoned and it could have gone all through your whole body."

"Why can't I have a girl? Everyone I know has a girl."

"I don't," Agnes said.

"You know what I mean. I have so much knowledge, and who am I going to share it with? How to arrange flowers, how to divide hosta, how to set a table for every occasion. Boys don't want to know any of that."

"Polly, you sound spoiled, and you're not spoiled. So what you don't have a girl? You have a new child, a healthy child, and you are sick. Focus on those two things. You have plenty of time to feel sorry for yourself, though don't do it around me."

"You're right," Polly said. "You're right. Thank you, my friend."

"Call me anytime. Even in the middle of the night, when I'm out flying on my broom," Agnes said.

Polly giggled.

When Dick came in later, he sat down by the bed and took her hand.

"Polly, I've made a decision. There will be no more children," he said. "I'm not risking this again. This boy is the last."

He was just upset, worried about her. "I want to call him Theodore," she said. "After my brother. But we'll call him Theo rather than Teddy."

"Fine by me. From now on we'll be a lot more careful."

"Even after parties?" She grinned at him.

He looked at her quizzically, and then kissed her on the forehead. "You just rest, my dear. We'll talk when you're well."

An unexpected feeling developed as Polly got to know the tiny infant. She adored him in a way she'd never adored anything before. Here was her own child, her true love. She felt no guilt about this deep affinity. She loved James and Knox unconditionally. It was just that Theo and she knew each other, so well that their intimacy embodied a paradox—they constantly surprised each other. She never had the confounded feeling with him that she often got with

Dick and James and Knox of not being able to make sense of their actions. She had to adapt to them, but not Theo. From his first days on earth they moved forward in tandem. Bailey sized up the situation quickly, and attended to Polly more than to the baby, hovering around the two of them, protecting them from the rest of the world. Polly now felt she had more than a purpose, she had a destiny. It went beyond being a mother, into the realm of souls.

What was a soul mate? She had dreams, strange dreams of music she'd never before heard that required instruments that didn't even exist. In one dream a filament connected each person on earth to a speck in the universe. In another dream, she was plunged into the barrenness that preceded existence. It was impossible to put it into words, but she was determined to do so, not just leave it to tumble around inside of her, amounting to nothing. But not the same nothing that she was trying to describe. Her nothingness was something. Even the word *nothing* was something! She decided to figure out how to talk about it.

On a visit Dick paid her in the nursery it occurred to her to ask his advice. She hadn't thought of it earlier—or had, but didn't want to bother him. He might be flattered, though, to be needed by her in this new way.

"Dick, this is going to sound strange, but I've had an idea. I don't know how to express it, though." She leaned forward, careful of sleeping baby Theo, who lay cradled between her legs on the covers.

"An idea?"

"A discovery, really."

"A discovery? Have you found money in a drawer?"

"Har har, you wish! No, nothing so fortunate. My discovery occurred in a dream."

He raised his eyebrows skeptically. "Ah, a dream. You know there's nothing to them, don't you? They're just electrical impulses firing off during sleep."

"Yes, I'm sure. But this was more the kind of dream people have in the Bible, where you're somewhere between awake and asleep and you hear words. You tell yourself that they must be coming out of your own mind, but you hear them as if another person were speaking. It was strange, and I don't even know if I believe in messages or visitations, but it happened. So I want to tell you about it."

"What did this voice say to you?" He was kindly, humoring, but unaffected, poised on a ledge, peering down. Yet she had to make him understand.

"This is what I heard." She sat up and lifted her head, affecting a posture of authority. *"Nothing owes its existence to something, and vice versa."*

"That's it?"

Upon saying the main thing, her shyness became excitement. "That's it, and everything! Nothing owes its existence to something. And something owes its existence to nothing."

"You realize you're toying with one of the central arguments of philosophy—the argument from contingency."

"I am?"

"Yes. Perhaps you heard me mention it."

"No. I'm telling you my vision."

"The vision that came in a dream." He raised his eyebrows.

"Oh, Dick, I know I sound like a nut, but I have been having these dreams and seeing and learning things. It's so marvelous. I feel as though we'll be able to start talking about ideas now, this kind of idea, the kind you work with. What did you call it?"

"The argument from contingency, which has been refuted by many famous people. And I said you were in that ballpark, not hitting a home run. Philosophical arguments are developed through work and thinking, not in dreams."

"But ideas can come that way, can't they?" There must be a way to secure a fair hearing. She sifted back through moments when he'd paid attention, searching them for a common denominator, but her findings showed caprice more than any specific action she could take. She turned to other examples for support. "I'm sure I've read about scientists who saw things in a dream."

He hesitated. He picked up one of the Maine lucky stones she'd laid out on the bedside table, satin black with a white circle around it, and rolled it across his palm.

"There have been such cases. Are you taking up science now?"

She looked down at baby Theo, who, sensing the maternal countenance tipped toward him, opened his eyes and searched her face. Perfect trust, or something even deeper than trust—faith, perhaps. Or a word that didn't exist. Whatever it was she drank it in, took courage from it, and this enlarged him in return. When they two were alone in the room they completed each other and she whirled through space with him.

But they weren't alone in the room. For once Dick's nearness was unwelcome. She had a soul mate, and that gave her the wherewithal to see that Dick wasn't one, after all, and that he was gearing up to belittle her with skepticism and disdain. There it was, configuring his face, bent on rendering her whole experience inconsequential. This had happened many times, she realized now, but she'd scrambled so hard to be close to him that she'd never seen it clearly. He was small, and petty. Just as Agnes said. Her idea was good, she was sure of it. Philosophers had thought something like it, he'd said so himself. But he would not compliment her. She was sitting in bed with her baby, experiencing an unprecedented firestorm of cerebral activity, and his plump pink lips, indecently protruding below his mustache, refused to acknowledge it. What was he, what was this? Words floated past, ephemeral as soap bubbles, each one popping as she tried to grab hold. How had he managed that, and how had she allowed it to happen? She was in danger. He could eliminate a true part of her right now.

"Never mind. It was just a dream. Maybe I'm still a little delirious."

He looked at her, assessing her sincerity, and she had a sudden comprehension of what he was like in the world: competitive, in a stealthy way; belittling of good ideas that weren't his; suspicious. She organized a childlike expression on her face, and he relaxed, seeing it, and accepted her demurral with magnanimity and a loving smile, and rewarded her by kissing her cheek. From far away she viewed the charming portrait of a contented threesome and doubted anyone would wonder what the woman was thinking.

"You need to rest. This one took it out of you." He reached for Theo's foot and rolled it in his palm in the same way as he had the stone.

She thought Dick was probably right, yet the thoughts and dreams persisted, and she was as besotted with them as she was with baby Theo. Each mode required her to inhabit it, and she imagined dressing herself for these different roles; either as a blue-stocking, like the women who'd taught her at Miss Dictor's, in tailored no-nonsense suits, or like a modern version of a mother in a Mary Cassatt painting, an innocent and cosseted Madonna dressed in the frilly and the floral. On her mother days she played with the boys and pottered around the house and outside, setting flowers everywhere. On her bluestocking days she went to her desk and tried to elucidate her visions on paper. She'd assumed it was easy for Dick because he did it all the time, but she understood now all the hours he spent in his study. The ideas were *right there*, clear and simple, yet when she tried to write them, there seemed to be a gate or a barrier between her mind and her hand that made the visions vanish, like the uncatchable rainbows cast by the crystal pendants in the dining room. She ached to think of Dick battling with this all the time, but was afraid that if she discussed it with him again he would say she should stop.

She didn't stop. Instead she pressed until she got her entire idea written down. The piece was formed, the argument made. She stacked her notes in an ordered pile and copied them onto her letter paper, numbering each paragraph as she went along. When she'd seen how it would appear on the page, she began to copy it again, but her work was interrupted by Theo waking up and wanting his food and embraces. As he sucked with his cheeks and tapped at his bottle with his tiny hand, it occurred to her that her work would look more important if it were typed. She rarely had cause to use the typewriter and didn't know how to use more than her index fingers, but she'd manage. When Theo was satiated with milk and affection, she handed him to Bailey for a walk outside and took her pages down to Dick's study. Briefly she caught a mental picture of his eyebrows raised, but she'd finish before he got home and wouldn't touch anything in his office but the typewriter.

She threaded three sheets of typewriter paper with carbon sheets between them into the slot behind the platen. One keystroke at a time, slow progress, mistakes that necessitated starting over, swearing in a whisper, and finally, done.

Soul Mates

1) What are soul mates?

Two people connected invisibly. Two people fully aware of their connection and how it differs from all their other affinities. Two people separated yet belonging.

2) How are soul mates created?

Soul mates were created during the Big Bang. They exist materially. The feeling soul mates have of being halves of a whole has a material basis.

3) What basis is that?

The splitting of atoms into two parts, destined to search for their other half through eternity, until all matter is restored to its original state. Then the universe will shrink again into a dense dot.

She tapped on, writing out her idea. All the time she was working she thought of Dick. What would he make of her dreams now? It seemed unbearable to ask, and unbearable not to know. How could she put this before him without incurring skepticism? Wait—she had an idea. Impulsively she put one of the two carbon copies in an envelope and addressed it to him at the university. Then she ripped open the envelope and replaced it with the original. A carbon went into another envelope, for Agnes. She neatened the environs of Dick's desk until she was untraceable and walked the envelopes to the mailbox. But the postmark would be a giveaway to Dick, and she'd never know what he really thought unless he judged it impartially. She happened to be expecting a visit that afternoon from a friend who was going to New York. *Mail this, please? Oh yes, of course.* Her whole body tingled from the thrill of making a plan.

She put the other carbon copy in the bottom of her blanket chest, where it would never be found.

The days passed in silence, however, and her excitement about the project dwindled. Dick said nothing at all about the letter. She hadn't thought of that possibility, but—of course. He rarely mentioned his work mail, unless one of his articles was accepted for publication. She fished once or twice by asking if he'd gotten any interesting news lately, which elicited an eye roll. As time passed, she let it go, dismissing the episode as a fever dream of childbirth and nothing more. She wasn't a philosopher, or a seer. She ripped

153

up her handwritten copy and stuffed the shreds under the garbage in the kitchen can. It was an episode, and over.

When a letter from Agnes arrived, she was in the middle of such a busy day that she left it among the envelopes on the hall table and forgot it until after Dick came home and handed it directly to her. Agnes made an immediate excuse for brevity; but she didn't want to wait any longer to say a few words about Polly's essay. Polly brought the paper closer to her face, curious. She could barely remember writing the essay—a curtain had come down. But having Agnes's mind on it brought it back, even if it didn't seem to be exactly about her.

Your ideas are brilliant, cogent. The notion that every soul has another half floating somewhere in the universe is a galvanizing insight, and convincing. The simple profundity of the concept takes me back to one of my oldest sources of contemplation—the sad specter of all the gifted people who perish or live lives without fulfillment of their talent. People in prisons. People with debilitating illnesses. The enslaved throughout history and especially in our own country. People with no access to the official channels of information. People with singular languages unknown to others, or people locked in their own heads by an injury or an illness. You, too, are in a category of thwartedness, Polly. You aren't a scientist or an academic, so how can you develop or disseminate your idea? But don't feel discouraged about that. You told me, and sharing a gift with one other person has the power to make a change in the world. Now you know, and I know, and that will ripple outward.

But listen, my friend, whatever you do—do not share this with Dick. I know you will be tempted to do so, but he won't be a good audience. I realize you might be angry with me for offering this advice, because it tacitly speaks against him. I am not speaking against him, though. I am speaking out of my respect for what is probable. Your ideas are worthy of consideration, Polly, and I wouldn't want them to be dismissed.

Thank you for sending me to this.

That was the end of her period of heightened vision. Agnes was right; Dick would never admire an idea of hers, and if she pursued that path, it would come between them. That she did not want. He made sure Polly got a diaphragm and checked that she used it, an embarrassing exchange, and Polly's enthusiasm for living was greatly diminished for a few years, though she didn't show it. She behaved as happily as ever and remained a good friend, wife, and mother. But she'd lost a dream, and felt it gone—felt the phantom limb of a daughter.

Then she became pregnant again, in spite of her sincere efforts not to, but she lost the pregnancy at three months. Her grief made it clear to her that she needed another child, and she was more ardent toward Dick than ever while preparing herself to act surprised when she felt the ping. With the easier birth of baby Lydia, the most purposeful and happy years of Polly's life began. Where she had had a deep soul affinity with Theo, Lydia was on a continuum with Polly, in affinity and also in body and spirit. The same, but different. From the first moment she held the baby, Polly had the sensation of talking with her. Lydia lived on her hip, and all the things Polly had imagined doing with a daughter came to pass.

They spent hours in the gardens at Meadowlea and in Haverford, and they made the beds together and cooked and thought up new ideas for holiday decorations and generally enjoyed the gratifying work of keeping house. Polly had little interest in social life, except for events with her other mother friends, such as going to the zoo, or to Wanamaker's at Christmas to watch the light show and the dancing fountains, or to a performance of *Peter and the Wolf* at the Academy of Music. Most of her friends wanted to talk with her on those outings,

155

though, where Polly only wanted to watch Lydia. Never was there a face she loved more, nor were anyone's responses to the world as riveting. She made certain her fervor didn't detract from Dick—the main part of the day was over by the time he came home, and he was happy to give the children a good-night kiss downstairs and wait for her in his study while she put them to bed. The boys had each other and got quite enough of her. Polly felt at the center of her small world, and it made her proud to keep everyone happy.

When Lydia got a fever at age nine, Polly was only mildly concerned at first. It was winter, when illnesses were regularly passed around the schoolroom. A week later Lydia was dead, of a cause never explicitly determined, as Polly wouldn't allow an autopsy. The grief was unbearable. If Polly hadn't had the boys, she'd have followed Lydia into the ground. Never again would she disapprove of suicide. Agnes and Polly's mother both sensed that dark pull and watched Polly carefully until she began to "take an interest" again. But she was never really interested in much until Lydia appeared as a ghost.

Polly returned to the present. The sky was turning from black to pearl, and she was still awake. She may as well get up and make herself useful. The boys and their families were coming soon, and their rooms needed final touches. The Theos would stay with her, and Knox and Jillian, too. James and his fam would be at WesterLee, as always. The five grandchildren, all in their teens or twenties, would be lively and great company, the DILs would offer dozens of suggestions for what she could be doing better, and her boys—well, her boys. Theo was unfailingly kind to her, but Knox could be moody, and James—bossy was probably the right word. *Just smile*, she could hear her mother say. She always had. But leave it to Agnes to have the last word—in her mind, Polly heard Agnes instruct, *Don't let them walk all over you.* As if *she* didn't!

CHAPTER 9

Agnes, Gulf of Maine, August 2000

AGNES HEADED OVER TO MEADOWLEA, AS INSTRUCTED, WITH her jacket and hat secreted in a bag, also as instructed. A welcoming committee greeted her in the driveway.

"Hi, Aunt Nessie!" A chorus. "Are you ready?"

Three golden sylphs, Maeve, Maddie, and Margot, the M girls, Theo Wister's daughters, along with their dark-haired cousin Caroline, who belonged to James. They smelled of suntan lotion and orange juice, and they all spoke at once, over and around each other, laughing and gesturing, swinging their pretty hair—except for Maeve, who'd chopped hers short. Polly gave the M girls the run of Meadowlea, ignoring Dick's pleas for a quiet house. "He doesn't mean it," Polly said, and Agnes believed that. Even a stickler for control like Dick couldn't resist this glorious youth.

"We've hidden all our gear in the car. Nanny doesn't know a thing. Here, hand over your bag, quick!"

Agnes did as told. They stashed it away just as Polly appeared. "What are you doing here?" Polly's eyes widened and she splayed her hand over the top of her chest. A bit much, Agnes thought, which made her wonder if Polly was onto the plan.

"I don't know," Agnes said, dyspeptic on purpose. She had a

reputation to live up to, and her orneriness amused the girls. "I was taking a walk to think and these reprobates waved me over. We're being kidnapped, apparently."

"Now, Nanny," Margot said. "You are to do as we say all day."

Caroline, who had a job at JPMorgan, said, "And don't even think of pulling out your wallet. This is all on us."

"I certainly take no issue with that," Agnes said. "It's a rare treat for me to be paid for."

The girls glanced at each other. There'd been no understanding that they'd treat Agnes, too. She gave them a wink, and they visibly exhaled.

"Am I properly dressed?" Polly's hands got cold very easily.

"No, no, no gloves," Maddie said. "You're fine as you are."

Margot gave Agnes a return wink. Rarely did Agnes think she might be missing something without children, but these girls, now that they were older, made a good argument in favor of reproducing.

They piled into Theo's monster of a van, with Agnes and Polly given the whole middle seat. Maddie got into the driver's seat, with Margot beside her, and Maeve and Caroline in the way back. They whipped past Leeward Cottage.

Polly turned to Agnes. "I'm so glad you're coming."

"They made me an offer I couldn't refuse."

"Can you believe it, Nanny?" Maeve said. "Nabbing Agnes—it's like we have Halley's Comet with us on a day trip."

"Or a seventeen-year locust," Polly said.

"That's more like it," Agnes said. "I identify with the bugs of the world. They are the survivors."

The girls went into gales at this and discussed what bugs they each were. They all agreed that Maddie should be a daddy longlegs; she had been stopped on the street in New York and asked if she were a model. They went on through ladybug, firefly, and cicada, but Agnes only half paid attention, having been carried back to a time when she entertained Nan Reed with comparing everyone on the Point to a bird. So long ago, nearly forty years now, yet she recalled all of it.

"I guess we're going to miniature golf," Polly said.

"We really should blindfold you."

"Don't guess—you'll ruin it."

"You're going to be so happy. This might be the best day of your life."

"All right. Everything's out of my hands," Polly said.

"That's the spirit!"

"Are you writing a new Nan book, Aunt Agnes?" Maeve asked. She was the middle girl, labeled as the good student, though they all did well.

"I'm trying out a few ideas. Please don't make suggestions. I hate suggestions."

"One of my friends wrote a paper about her." Maddie.

"I want to be as adventurous as she is." Margot.

"Maybe you should branch out and have her try being a financial analyst or something like that." Caroline.

Chatter and jokes, finishing each other's sentences, leaping subjects with a graceful coordination.

"Okay, here's a question," Caroline said. "A lot of times when I go to a dinner party I feel like the men talk over me."

"That's not a question. . . ."

"I hear an implicit question about what to do," Agnes said.

"Men?" Polly exclaimed. "Why are you around men?"

"Young men," Caroline said. "My age."

"That's all right then," Polly said.

"They talk over you because they want to hear themselves talk." Maddie glanced at her cousin in the rearview mirror.

"Here's what you need to know," Agnes said. "Men have a bad habit of forming opinions based on no facts and thinking about what they want to say next rather than listening. And they interrupt! As soon as they have the gist, they want to have their say before someone else does. Sound familiar?"

"Exactly!" Caroline sighed, and the whole car sighed with her.

"Just become a lesbian like me," Maeve said. "It's better this way."

Agnes glanced over at Polly to see if this fazed her. At the least she expected Polly to stick up for Dick, who was the king of blowhards. But Polly just smiled, along for the ride.

"Short of becoming a lesbian, what should I do?" Caroline asked.

"You can make them listen to you, which will require some trick of force or seduction or need—nothing within the realm of normal conversation. Or you can just think about more important things while they are talking and save your breath for women, who know how to converse." Agnes felt for them, she really did, and was so glad she'd left all that behind while she was still young.

"Take that with a grain, girls," Polly said. "Remember the source. Many of my favorite people are men, and I love listening to them."

"To be fair," Agnes said, "everyone is interested in what he or she has to say. But women are taught better how to listen."

The conversation went on, but Agnes succumbed to the wildflowers along the roads, the white dottings of Queen Anne's lace, the houses, the trees, pedestrian thoughts, pleasant. The tentacles that held her to her pen and her desk loosened. The girls were right. It was good for her to have a day away.

Polly read her mind, as always.

"We do need this." She squeezed Agnes's hand.

"We do," Margot said, as if the remark had been general. "Poor Robert."

"Margot!" Maddie scolded.

"Sorry."

So that was what this was. An effort to cheer the old ladies up. How thoughtful these girls were, and how right.

Maddie parked in a spot on Front Street in Bar Harbor, Caroline disappeared into the building on the pier, and the rest of them got in a line leading to a gangplank. "What is this?" Polly asked. She was still pretending, for the girls' sake, though signs announcing "Whale Watch" were everywhere.

The morning harbor was calm and windless, yet Polly put her hand to her hair as if it were being blown around wildly. The girls grinned. "A whale watch, Nan! Your very favorite!"

"Oh, how wonderful!" Polly hugged them all.

On the boat—a large catamaran—Agnes suggested they sit in the cabin until they were out to sea, but the girls cajoled her up the steps to the open top deck. Just as they were settling, a member of the crew came along—a handsome young man, if a bit too bearded— and suggested they go back down and spend the long trip out to the whaling grounds below deck.

"You can get really burned facing the sun. On the way in, the sun will be at our backs. That's a better time to sit up here."

The girls had their faces tipped up to him like a bouquet of pansies. They did as he said, and all trooped back down. They commandeered a spot, and Maddie pulled out a couple of decks of cards.

"Who said to stay below?" Agnes teased.

"Sorry, Aunt Agnes," the girls chorused.

"What shall we play, Nanny? You choose."

"Go Fish, of course," Polly said. Again they all went into gales as if no one had ever said anything as funny.

They played for a while until the girls got bored. Agnes wanted a word alone with Polly. "Come on. Let's go check out the snack bar."

Polly hopped up. The girls asked them to check for various items. Cracker Jack!

"I guess we really do have to check out the snack bar," Polly sighed, when they were at a distance. "My face hurts from grinning. How about you? I can't believe you're actually doing this, though. What got you out of your lair?"

"Maeve told me not to be a dull boy. She had a point. I am all work, and all rage since Robert." They got in line. "How was Dick's birthday party?"

"It was fine. Dick made a great observation—everyone likes his or her own feet."

"That's a known fact!" Agnes made a face. Polly was always positioning Dick as being a singular sensibility.

Polly sighed. "It would be easier if you could approve of him just a little." She fixed her blue eyes on Agnes and gave her a patient look. "I've heard that about feet before, too, but the girls loved it. They slipped off their shoes and studied their feet. Dick showed them his and they gave gratifying screams." Polly smiled. "It was an old-fashioned night."

They hovered in front of the snack bar, examining the offerings. A group of tourists muscled up and moved Agnes and Polly aside.

"It was a nice break for Dick. He's writing to Robert every day."

The boat glided smoothly beneath them, moving them up and down enough that they had to keep their stance wide and shift their balance in response. They both loved the feeling. No seasickness.

"I keep imagining Seela crowing in glee, thinking she was right," Agnes said. "I really hate her."

"Don't hate," Polly said automatically, having said it to children a thousand times. "Wait—I take that back."

"Don't you hate her, too?"

Before Polly answered, the young woman behind the counter leaned forward. "Can I help you?"

"I don't know, can you?" Agnes said.

The girl dropped her jaw, startled. Was she going to cry?

"You should say *may* I. You are asking for permission. It is assumed you can help. How else would you have gotten this job?"

"I applied to work on the boat in general. This is what I was given."

Agnes sized her up. A pushover, if she ever saw one. "What did you really want to do?"

"To teach about the whales."

"Do you know a lot about the whales?"

The girl nodded.

"All right. I'm going to order a few items, and every time I ask for one, you tell me a fact about a whale."

"I feel funny."

"Which is exactly why you don't have the job. Prove that you can do it. I'd like four boxes of Cracker Jack."

"Whales eat eels."

"Good one. Keep it up. Four potato chips."

"Minke whales average eighteen feet in length."

"Six bottles of water, please," Polly said.

"Right whales consume enormous gulps of seawater and filter out the krill through baleen plates in their mouths. Krill are an excellent protein source."

"And six Cokes," Agnes said.

"They're called right whales because they were considered the right whales to catch. The females give birth to one calf every three to five years."

"And a pack of M&Ms."

By the time Agnes and Polly had finished their transaction, Emily—they'd traded names along the way—had offered them and the people in line behind them a crash course, and everyone was talking and laughing.

"Who's your manager?" Agnes asked. "I'm going to put in a good word. Everyone, let's put in a good word for Emily!"

When they walked away, Polly said, "You're the life and soul. I forgot you can be charming."

"Don't say that. Don't even think it. Charm is a bad sign."

"All right. But you did a nice thing."

Maddie came running up. "We're supposed to go out on the bowsprit now. The whales are close."

"Coming!" Polly said. Polly turned to Agnes. "Dick keeps agitating to see Robert. This morning he was particularly insistent—"

"Naturally. Because you are doing something beyond his control today."

Polly gave a small wave, clearing the remark. "Do you think I should take him?"

"No. Robert doesn't want anyone to see him there. He made me promise."

"Dick doesn't believe that."

"I'll tell him."

"No. I'll figure something out. He's not himself these days, he still hasn't—"

The girls swarmed around and pushed them outside.

The sun stunned them at the door, and they scrambled to put their sunglasses on, then filed behind one another along the deck and out onto the right side of the hull. The captain spoke over the microphone, guiding them to spot the distant whales all around them, teaching them how to look for spouts, and the whole boat pointed here and there, exclaiming triumphantly at each geyser of a blow. The pontoons sliced quietly through the water and the bow rose and fell. The girls repeatedly asked Agnes if she were okay; she repeatedly reassured them, yes, yes, more than okay! The wind took all but single words and tossed them overboard.

"Look starboard!" the captain called.

All heads turned, and all jackets billowed like sails. A hundred feet away the water parted. The whole boat gasped as the curved lunar back of a whale broke the surface. "Oh, they're just getting started!" the captain said. "You are in luck!"

The crew knew all the whales and introduced them by name as they appeared. A few came close and communicated with the boat, soaking up the admiration of the oohing and clapping audience. Over and over, a patch of water swirled and imploded, then sucked back from its center to make way for a huge bright body to leap into the air, streaming from head to tail gallons of the sparkling sea. The whale lofted and, airborne, paused, miraculously defying gravity so easily that the watchers invented a fresh hope that the great creature with its huge staring eye might live among them, like a cow or an elephant, so they could encounter each other at leisure rather than in brief and unpredictable flashes. Or maybe it was she, Agnes, alone who could easily be persuaded of a different possible outcome to the same old story.

Just when they thought the show was over, a whale appeared between the two arms of the hull. She rolled on her side and looked up at everyone on one pontoon, then rolled the other way to look at the rest of the crowd. She stayed with the boat for fifteen long minutes, and Agnes stayed with her wordlessly. The girls let out *Aws* every time the whale moved, and the air whirred with the winged sound of cameras snapping photos. Finally she dove, but reemerged a hundred feet away, easing the sorrow of parting. They were all about to head back inside when a mother and calf swam close and breached! The boat applauded, and the whales repeated their trick again and again. Every so often one of the girls asked Agnes if she was all right. On cue, Agnes snarled, and they laughed.

"Time to turn back," the captain announced. The assembly moaned, but Polly looked relieved. Agnes could almost see the invisible rope that bound her to Dick cutting into Polly's waist.

"Let's go upstairs now," the girls clamored. "All right, Nan?"

"You get seats, I'll be right there."

Polly led the way. Halfway up the galley stairs she twisted around. "Wasn't that incredible?"

"Very," Agnes said. "I'm still dazed."

"I know, I—" Polly twisted further and her foot caught on the lip of a tread. She hung suspended for a moment, and Agnes, for whom time had slowed, had a split-second fantasy that the error would end well—that against all odds, Polly, like the whales, could soar. But that wasn't reality. Polly crashed down hard, and when her ulna snapped, Agnes jumped. Polly rolled from side to side, grimacing instead of screaming. Agnes didn't scream either, but emitted the hoarse sound usually called forth by snakes. "Hold still, Pol. You'll be fine." Agnes directed the people around her to get help, with hand gestures so Polly would not hear the urgency she felt. Some alerted the girls, and they all came down and carefully moved Polly away from the stairs that everyone needed to use to exit the top deck. The boat headed for harbor and sped faster than Agnes had ever felt it go. "Goodbye, whales," Polly said wistfully. "It's not your fault," she said to the girls.

"Time to shut up, Pol," Agnes said, and pinched her feet to distract her.

At the hospital in Bar Harbor, a physician's assistant tended to Polly's knees and elbows with antiseptic and bandages. A shot dulled the sting. Her broken arm was casted, her sprained ankle wrapped up, and she was issued a pair of crutches, returnable when she no longer needed them. She'd asked the girls not to call back to Meadowlea to report the mishap—they'd be home soon enough, and she didn't want to worry Dick.

An orderly pushed her to the car in a wheelchair. Maddie brought the van around to the exit and helped Polly in, everyone cooing "Poor Nanny," and "Are you okay?" over and over. Agnes felt off balance after a day at sea and braced herself by planting her legs apart on the floor of the car. Every turn or small bump in the road was jarring.

"Can we do it again?" Polly asked.

There was a pause in the car.

"Girls—I'm kidding," she said.

A further pause. A moment of suspended animation, like storm clouds full overhead. Then the burst! "Ha ha, very funny. That was crazy, Nanny, you were so brave!" And they went over and over the accident, and the whales, lofting the story and watching it soar above them into the realm of family lore. When they got back, Agnes insisted on coming with them into Meadowlea. They were all still laughing and chatting, but they stopped abruptly when Dick appeared, groping his way along the wall.

"I'm late for class," he said.

Polly hurried to step in front of him, but not before all of them saw that Dick had had an accident. The front of his pants was dark and wet.

"Dick, go upstairs," Agnes said.

"You go upstairs!" he barked.

The girls looked downward, embarrassed.

"It's all right, dear," Polly said. "Let's go up."

She reached for him with her casted arm and it slipped out of its sling. She yelped.

Dick took her in, finally, and returned to his senses. "What happened?"

Normally the girls would clamor to fill him in, but they were too embarrassed.

"Let's go upstairs and I'll tell you."

"Why are you rushing me off!" he shouted.

"Come on," Polly coaxed. "We both need to change."

Truer words, thought Agnes. "Go on, Dick," she said.

He looked down at himself and was bewildered by what he saw. He looked at Polly helplessly and she pointed to the steps.

The rest of them watched the couple, attached at the hip again, make slow progress up the steps. Then Agnes turned to the girls. "Make certain she eats and takes a painkiller tonight. She'll heal more quickly if she isn't in a lot of pain."

A car pulled into the driveway. "They're back!" Maddie called, then ran out to be the first to deliver the news.

Agnes said her goodbyes and left via the terrace, down the back steps. She was still a little dizzy from the boat and placed her sneakers carefully, playing around with finding balance by switching her L.L.Bean bag back and forth. A wave of distress passed through her thinking of Polly in pain, and then having to come home to Dick standing in the doorway with wet pants. Agnes startled suddenly, and lost her breath. *Snake*, her alarm system warned, and she forced herself to look. But it was only a stick. A stick and Robert in handcuffs being led from the courtroom, and Hamm Loose Jr. leering out of the front page of the *Cape Deel Gazette*. There were snakes in the grass, if not now, soon, and always. Never had she felt as helpless.

CHAPTER 10

Polly, Meadowlea, Late August 2000

POLLY WAITED UNTIL DICK WAS COMPLETELY SETTLED IN HIS study—there had been a few false starts interrupted by need of a coffee or water or the bathroom—and then limped upstairs, dragging her broken right arm along the railing. She'd had the plaster cast on for three weeks and had figured out how to work around it for most things. She wasn't strictly allowed to drive, but she'd gone into town a couple of times without difficulty. A lot of people drove with one hand—she always had, to be honest. She couldn't write, which was frustrating. Letters to be answered were piling up. And she could only make rudimentary meals that didn't involve heavy skillets or pots. Her housekeeper, Shirley Mcquellan, a mother of five from Deel Town, brought over casseroles, and though Dick complained that they were tasteless, he ate them. Sylvie brought dinners as well that were far better. Polly made sandwiches and Dick opened cans. Honestly, they didn't need much.

What she did need was a nap in the morning. She was already tired from getting up with Dick at four, when he woke into an agitated fretfulness. This had been happening every morning. He was never fully awake, but he couldn't get back to sleep, either. He didn't want to get up, but he didn't want to read. What he wanted was to have her sit by him as he talked. It wasn't clear that he even knew who she was in those gray hours before dawn. Sometimes he seemed to be talking to his mother, which she feared meant he was near death. What death, though? The death of the mind or the body? His body was fine as far as she could tell, and the doctor confirmed it. He had the issues of someone his age—macular degeneration, stress incontinence, arthritis, and so on—but he was free of cancer or heart disease. Healthy, except for his transient ischemic attacks—TIAs. They could occur swiftly, without Polly even noticing. He might look as though he were dropping off when his brain was actually seizing. She wondered if this was what brought on these early morning episodes. She hadn't exactly explained them to the doctor because she didn't exactly want it to stop. He was talking to her.

The first time it happened he talked about Jingle, his childhood dog, a story that was new to her. One day his father had walked into town with Jingle and returned without him. "Where's Jingle?" Dick asked. His father tipped his head and looked quizzically into space. "I don't know. Let me think." His father frowned. "I must have left him tied out in front of the post office." Dick pictured Jingle there, alone, waiting, trusting, faithful, innocent. Perhaps Jingle had watched his father walk right past but had been so trusting that he hadn't even jumped or pawed, just sat as he'd been told to. Instead he waited. Maybe. What if someone stole him? Dick felt ill, thinking of it. He asked his father to go right back to get Jingle. His father said he'd go after lunch. Dick spent a torturous hour imagining Jingle's confusion and feeling of betrayal. He pictured people shoving him into a car and driving off. They wouldn't know what Jingle ate. Would they even get a bed for him? Would they kick him? Finally his father walked back into town. Dick waited on the front porch and tore down the sidewalk when he saw his father and Jingle coming toward home. "See? No harm done," his father said. Oh, but there was harm! By Dick's reckoning his father's oversight revealed all of human carelessness, and lack of seriousness. He knew who his father was after that. Serious people didn't make such mistakes.

"I'm serious," he said to Polly, or to the gray room. "I'd never do that."

Dick's dentures floated in a glass on the bedside table. He gummed his words.

"I know," she assured him.

Sometimes he sang, always the same song, "Old Man River."

Old man river
Dat old man river
He must know somethin'
But don't say nothin'
Dat old man river
He just keep rollin' along

Dick could sing. He had a beautiful baritone. He told her one shadowy morning—this was a story she already knew—that he'd considered learning how to sing opera, but his father forbade it. Dick thought he could have been successful to some degree, but he would never have been Paul Robeson. He admired Paul Robeson above all men. He, too, was a pacifist. He, too, fought for his principles. He, too, had lost his career for his beliefs. He was ruined by McCarthy. Had his passport taken away.

Dick saw Paul Robeson once. It was after he was investigated by the House Un-American Activities Committee. Dick defended Robeson to anyone who would listen. Robeson was a fellow victim of intolerance toward pacifism. What was that song he wrote? Something about springtime, and war. Ironic lyrics, Dick remembered. *I wonder if there will be a war next spring?* Something like that. He'd bought the record, must still have it somewhere.

"It's in Haverford," Polly offered.

"Oh good."

Dick was invited to the only concert Robeson booked after his denunciation. In Peekskill. It was in August, though, so Dick was at Meadowlea, and it didn't make sense to drive down. As it turned out, there was a huge riot, and it was doubtful he could have even greeted Robeson. He regretted not going for a long time.

"I'm glad you didn't go," Polly said.

"But I've never done a thing to act on my beliefs."

"Not true. You wrote *the* book on pacifism. Anyone can learn what it is because of you."

"It's hopelessly out of print."

"Not for long. Your new foreword."

She stroked his forehead, arranging his silver hair becomingly. His cheek rested on both his hands, like a child.

His father wanted Dick to be a businessman, but Dick had no mind for numbers or for sales. He'd always been attracted to Quaker philosophy and at college found he was good—the best in his class at Harvard—at formal logic. Polly asked if he'd made the right decision becoming a philosopher. This was the magic of these morning talks—she could ask questions that would make him impatient in the light of day.

He said he studied and practiced philosophy because the world was a confusing place and he wanted to further what understanding humans had come to and why, and how things might be better. The deeper in he waded, however, the more he suspected that he might be seeking an answer to a question he had about an indentation in his own being, as palpable to him as if a meteor had hit. He had a hole inside him like a deep black pool surrounded by rock. For a while he assumed everyone did—wasn't that original sin, or the other way around?—but during late-night dorm confabs he discovered other men felt whole. They had no suspicion, as he had, that they might implode into their own depths one day. He was always teetering and exhausted from keeping himself upright.

Polly couldn't have been more shocked. She dared not respond at all—dared not remind him she was his audience. He wouldn't want her to know any of this. She sat absolutely locked into a stillness akin to invisibility until he dozed. When he woke up, she'd pulled the curtains open, and he talked mildly about the weather. But she pondered what he said when she went upstairs after breakfast to take her nap. It seemed to her he'd spent his whole life hiding this central motivation. Whether that was good or bad, right or wrong was beside the point now. What was left was to add pieces to the puzzle of him. Maybe this was what Agnes meant when she said Dick had a classic narcissistic wound. Poor Dick. The word *wound* was so sad. How did such a thing happen? Dick's parents had been like everyone's as far as she knew.

A few mornings later he spoke about an afternoon in the fall when he was about ten. His mother collected him at school, and they walked home through the city in their companionable way. He looked at dogs and people and things on the sidewalk, waiting for her to ask, *What was the most interesting thing that happened today?* She always asked, and knowing the question was coming encouraged him to sort through dozens of little happenings for what might be most entertaining to her. His brother Peter, too old by then to be met at school, interpreted his day through a prism of wit, and noticed moments of hypocrisy and treachery, sneakiness and subterfuge, that he told about hilariously, causing their mother to laugh. Her laughter changed the world; to be able to make her laugh was the most desirable talent a person could have. Dick couldn't do it. He wasn't funny or witty. Yet his mother met Dick's choices of what was important with astonished admiration that made him feel brilliant. "You must be the only little boy in Philadelphia who cares about . . ." whatever it was he had said interested him. Cicadas. Past imperfect tense. The formation of river deltas. It was all extraordinary!

On the particular day in his memory his mother had seemed on the verge of asking him the question, when instead she stopped abruptly and turned to face the house at their side. She was in general a sanguine person, calm and unflappable, so it riveted him to see a shock ripple through her body. *Mummy?* But he had receded and was part of the background. She stepped closer to the house, looking up into the window and raising her hand, her five fingers splayed, pressing them forward as if they might meet a reciprocating hand. He shifted his gaze and to his shock saw a hand pressed back against the window from the inside. Between the hands, one inside, one out, rolled waves of feeling, sluicing and churning. He couldn't see it, but he saw it. The rolling feeling transcended what was naturally possible. His mother began weeping. He looked up at the face in the window and the face was weeping, too. The face of another lady. His mother's hands folded, fingers curling in toward the palm. She bowed her head and stepped backward again and walked into a man who made a fuss of apologies, and then they chatted while Dick waited in worry to have her back to himself.

"Mummy, are you all right?"

She turned her face toward him, her eyes full of tears, and she shook her head. "No, no, no, no. I am not all right."

Then she shrugged. She smiled. She reached out her hand to him and he squeezed hers, molded his body to her side. He was surely the only one who ever knew, and he didn't really know anything, except that she lived in anguish. He didn't know exactly what the pain was, but understood both that she couldn't tell and that she hadn't minded sharing her secret with him. Sometimes he took that to mean that there was something trustworthy about him. Or that she saw in him a maturity that had been waiting inside to come out and be useful. Yet neither of these interpretations, flattering as they were, produced much feeling in him. It was the sharp lurch of his own spirit in the moment when his mother turned toward him, her cheeks wet, and offered him a shy smile that acknowledged what had happened, but in no way attempted to defend, interpret, shield, or explain the event, that afforded him an expansion of heart and soul.

Polly ventured a question. "Did you ever find out who the woman was?"

"No. I never saw her again."

"What do you think it was about?"

"No idea. It's one of those mysteries of life that is never explained."

"I suppose the explanation is that the feeling between them struck you as being remarkable."

"True. I was a boy. I'd never seen anything like it before."

Polly hesitated, but was too curious to hold back. In this instance she felt protected by the dark. "Do you think they were lovers?"

"I've considered it. Would they know how to do that, though? In those days?"

"People figure things out. We did."

"We knew we should and could, though."

"Things went on at Miss Dictor's."

"Huh. True. My school, too."

He yawned. Time to drop it. Polly's greatest skill in living in a house full of men was knowing when to stop. There were no medals for it, no recognition, but it kept the peace. "I hope she found peace, don't you?"

"Is Agnes like that?"

"Like what?" Polly answered automatically, though his meaning was clear.

"Women," he said.

"Why do you ask?" Polly wanted to say it was none of his business, but she was never harsh with Dick.

"I always thought she might be."

"Just because she never married—"

"That's not it. It's something else about her. She seems more like a man."

"I know what you mean," Polly said. "I also know she would say that what you are calling man-like is—" She stopped. She was going to say *your own limited perception of what women are like.* But battle was over.

Anyway, he nodded off.

He often talked about his betrayal by the department and how unfairly he'd been treated after all he'd done. All those years. He'd kept his head down and prepared his lectures and taught his courses and spent a preposterous number of hours carefully reading and grading papers and exams, seeking in even the laziest and most slapdash of them a trace of conscience or intellect that could be developed. He circled words and salutary rhetorical choices and wrote careful arguments as to why they were good. Arduous work! Time- and mind-consuming work! And most students didn't even read his comments, or not thoughtfully. They turned to the back of the paper to look for the letter grade and that was that. Dick knew this—he wasn't stupid—but pressed on anyway. He learned by error and disappointment to treat all students equally and put in his best effort each time out. He thereby became decent, almost by default. His approach was just and it honed his character. He would be unsung and unknown, but he had to believe that spending your life becoming decent made a difference to the world.

"Of course you made a difference," Polly said. "A huge difference. Your students will never forget you."

She brought this up again later in the day, but he had no idea what she was talking about. From then on she made little tests, but it always turned out there was a wall between his early morning life and his waking day. For the first time since she'd known him they were developing an intimacy beyond the physical. He was agitated and sometimes incontinent, but he was opening like a bud, and she was there to see it in slow motion. A fresh chance, a new freedom—how true it was that one should never give up.

One morning he told her something so astonishing and so private she could barely believe he'd remembered it much less said it aloud. He remembered knocking on James's door and when he didn't get an answer opening it and finding the boy, his eldest, age twelve, lying on his side on the bed, naked, one leg up in the air, looking up at his toes as if they were stars. He was humming. He was in private. Dick recalled that thinking the word *private* had led his gaze to his son's privates. He looked away immediately, of course, but he'd taken in the few curled hairs, the maturing flesh. He backed out of the room quietly, undetected, and felt, as he walked gingerly down the hall, a new emotion, an elation, grasping in a visceral way something he'd never felt before—he was a father. He'd made that beautiful curve of flesh and bone, that James, that happy hum in his boy's throat, that gaze cast upward at his own toes. He was a father!

He didn't quite know what to do with this new understanding and had gone to look for Polly—*I wanted to tell her*—but when he spotted her out in the garden troweling soil into a hole, Lydia beside her dribbling clumps of dirt from dimpled fists—he was embarrassed to say what he felt. Who was *he* to tell *her*? What could she do but look at him as someone a little stupid and a little immature? She wouldn't say *I told you so*, but she had a right to. So he'd backed away and gone into his study to get ahold of himself. He basked, a fat seal on a slab, reveling in the flesh that had made other flesh. He hadn't counted it as being much—anyone could do it. A tugging urge, a female partner, and it was accomplished. Natural. Basic. But simplicity turned out, over and over, to be the most obscuring disguise. What greater intellectual challenge was there than to recognize the simple?

This moved Polly beyond measure. He was who she'd wished he was.

Dick spoke about the children, and his own father, and old friends, all in fleeting comments, but never Polly. Why not Polly? Shamelessly, she prompted him. "What did you think of me when you met me?" But he didn't register that, or ignored it. Then there came a morning when he told a story that had Polly digging her nails into her palms. He told of meeting a girl named Polly Hancock, who wasn't coy about her strong feelings for him. He didn't believe he warranted such devotion, but he thought it unfair if he felt only affection for her rather than passion. She loved more than convention taught her to. All the aspects of her that might have grown strong and effective if she hadn't been so early on trained to be normal—they all rocked quietly, like boats tied to buoys in a calm harbor. He had to admit, he liked that. It made sense for a woman to throw herself into love, into her husband and children. Yet he couldn't love reciprocally out of a sense of fairness.

Or so he came to understand. At first it baffled him to see how she looked at him, as if her face were the representative of a thousand suns, all beaming at him. He wanted to save his thinking for work, and to have a woman for solace and pleasure. She assured him that she was as invested in his work as he was, and she didn't desire or expect the kind of romance some women did. She believed in the life of the mind, and that to serve as his partner while he advanced the course of human knowledge would be an honor. And he felt that with such a calm, faithful champion beside him he would achieve a significant contribution. It all seemed workable. Yet he still felt squeamish about being loved so much. He wasn't truly moved by her, and so he held off on asking her formally.

Then one weekend married friends of Polly's invited them

to visit. They took the train down to Cape May, New Jersey, and jumped right into a round of beach mornings and afternoons, boat rides, cocktail parties, dinners with the sun giddily gilding the sky, sleeping to the sound of the waves. They could have shared a bedroom, as no parents were present, but Polly had a sentiment for waiting, which was fine with him. They met at the table each morning. A cook came in for breakfast and dinner, but they were on their own for lunch, free to go into the kitchen and pull out the bowls of chicken salad and tuna salad and egg salad. They were excited by the freedom these lunches represented, the sensation of being in charge in the kind of house their parents owned. They spun around, still salty from the morning swim in spite of a rinse in the outside shower, drunk on the sun and sea, and dipped big spoons into the bowls of mayonnaise salads. Lifting them, lofting them, proffering them for sights and tastes, they enameled the sandwiches and carried them out on the porch, feasting, laughing, showing off tan lines, growing sleepy, seeing sun spots from gazing at the sea. Eventually they decided it would be nice to read for an hour, or walk, or do needlepoint, or nap.

Polly reached for Dick's plate and carried it back to the kitchen, the others carried their plates out, then everyone returned to the porch, all but Polly. The conversation went on, desultorily, everyone swearing they were about to make a move, but no one did. "Where's Polly?" Dick asked. "I think she's in the kitchen," someone said, so he headed back there, through the quiet empty rooms, brown and cool, noticing the light scents of salt and mildew. He remembered his way through the dining room around the corner and through the swinging doors into the pantry and then a left into the kitchen—and there she was. Standing at the sink. Humming. The water running. Beads of water bouncing off the bottom of the ceramic sink and back up against the side before running down again, circling the drain. She hadn't heard him come in, so he saw her

179

as she was, without her love coming at him. Her hair in bunches, her nose pink. Shoulders peeling, feet turned out like a ballerina's, holding a plate in one hand and a sponge in the other, soaping it dreamily, making it look as though being alone in the kitchen washing dishes was the most exquisite thing a person could do. She had a private life, a source of pleasure other than him. He would be able to love her now, and not feel guilty that she loved more. A gentleman loved his wife. He asked her to marry him shortly afterward.

All through this story Polly had wanted to shake him and say, *You're talking about me! I am that same Polly, right beside you!* Yet she resisted, she couldn't help but ask one small question. "And did you always love her, after that?"

He had drifted off. How silly of her anyway. Fishing again. He had. She knew he had. That was the whole point of these predawn musings—to leave his life in the care of someone he trusted. And loved.

Today he'd been restless and fitful, and Polly had really needed a nap. She slept until a noise interrupted her. A car door?

"Dick! Dick!" Polly called from the bedroom window. What was he doing sitting in the car? He didn't drive! He never left his study before she went downstairs again and told him to come eat.

He poked his head out and peered up at her. "I'm back already?"

"Back from where?"

"The prison! I went to visit Robert."

"You did?" For one second she thought he might have. "Come inside! Tell me all about it!" Old fool. "It's time for lunch!"

She watched to make sure he got out. He moved stiffly, especially after he'd been sitting down. Then she went down to the kitchen, and Dick came in to watch her preparations.

"I miss the girls, don't you?" she offered.

"There is a season, Polly." He rustled in a drawer for twine. His discard bundles of mail and papers were thoroughly secured, as if they were to be kept rather than thrown away. He went out the door to put them in the trash, and she prepared two trays, working with her good hand. She chose the lightest plates she owned but she had difficulty lifting them. Her bad arm still hurt.

"Why two?" Dick asked suspiciously.

"Two people?"

"Where's Robert?"

Polly's heart thumped. "He's in the prison at Thomaston."

Dick computed this, the machinations showing. "I know! Why are you stating the obvious!" He banged his cane. Then he rubbed his forehead. "I have a bad headache," he said, and slumped against the counter.

"Let me get you some Tylenol."

She opened a lower cabinet where she kept a shoebox of pills. Knock wood they hadn't needed many so far. She shook him out two Tylenol and coached him on how to place them on the back of his tongue and swallow. He gulped them down.

"Good!" She applauded him.

"Dammit! It's stuck in my chest."

"Swallow again." She held the glass out to him.

"No! Ouch!" He rubbed at his ribs, making her nervous. But he never could take pills. "Let's eat. I'll wash it down with food."

"I'll make just one tray." She turned her back to him so she could breathe.

He carried the tray outside and set it down on the iron table. She followed closely. He teetered for a moment stepping over the door saddle, but he made it and set the tray down. His capabilities and limitations were so confusing.

"We're getting casual in our old age, Dick."

"We can file that under it ain't over 'til it's over, as Agnes would say."

He grinned at her. It was hard to keep up.

"I wish the children had stayed for the Point Party. They never do anymore. I'm going to ask them to stay next year. They really should. It might not happen much longer."

"Why not?" He lifted his sandwich with his wrist curled and shoved it in his mouth. His manners were gone.

"Agnes wants to dissolve the Fellowship, remember?"

He drew back and gasped. "Why?"

It was as if she'd never told him. "To make certain the Sank is preserved."

"It is preserved. It has always been preserved. She should leave well enough alone."

Polly looked over at the great hulk of Leeward Cottage and wondered if Agnes were eating with Sylvie. It was so hard to tell if Agnes really preferred eating alone, or if it was her way of not being a burden.

"It can't be done without Archie, so it can't be done right now. I hope he doesn't show up at the party. The thought of seeing him . . ."

"We'll leave." Dick shrugged, as if it were simple. She supposed it was.

They ate quietly for a while, but Polly could only tolerate silence for a short time.

"I had a call from Theo today. He said Philadelphia has emptied for August, and that he can park anywhere in Center City. I don't like the term Center City, do you?" She ate a forkful of chicken salad.

Dick banged his fist. "Archie is the one who should be in prison!"

"Oh, dear, I know, but don't upset yourself now."

"Archie is the thief! Seela is the thief! How dare they come to the party!"

Dick's eyes widened alarmingly and he gripped the arms of his chair. A sudden pungent stench bloomed from behind his back. Polly flinched at the same time as instinctively she began to stand up, to both go to him and back away, but Dick jerked sideways, tipping the table, and Polly's plate slid slowly over the edge and sailed to the ground. Her hand flashed to a sting in her calf and she pulled out a shard of her shattered plate—it must have smashed when she leaped from her chair—and blood ran into her shoe. Dick jerked violently. She went around behind him planning to hold him still, but he crumpled over heavily. She spread her legs wider and squatted and tried to heave him upright, her hands in his armpits, but when she moved his torso, his legs turned sideways.

"Help!" she called out. "Help, someone!"

He fell all the way down to the ground and convulsed, kicking the table leg rhythmically, clang, clang, clang, clang. She heaved back upward, call 911, call 911. But—leave him? Have to, have to. "Come fast! He's turning gray," which she hadn't grasped until she said so to the operator. "Fellowship Point, the fourth big house down, white clapboard, he's out back on the terrace. No, yes, no. Only me. All right, I understand." Run back out. Push on his chest. Nothing. Keep pushing, more nothing. She raised her hands over her head and brought them down hard on his sternum and he folded up for a second and then went limp. His skin, dark gray and purple, darker and darker. *Dick! Don't! Please please please please please.*

Soon the moment arrived when she knew there would be no result. Then she kneeled down beside him and wrapped her arms around him as well as she could. He was a dark gray-blue, including his lips, but she kissed them anyway, over and over. The ambulance men came tearing around the house but slowed when they saw him. Though everyone present knew it was useless, they worked to revive him, and she watched patiently as they pushed on his empty chest, not trying to stop them. *After great pain a formal feeling comes.* She was aware, even in the thick of it, of having a formal feeling. It gave her the equanimity to understand that everyone had a role and it was best to go through the motions, even if they were futile. Finally the men stood up with their heads bent, and she wondered which one would turn to her and tell her that Richard Wister, her husband of sixty years, was dead.

Nevernevernever. An impotent spell, after all.

The oldest man stepped forward.

"Thank you for telling me," she said. "I am glad we are in Maine because in Philadelphia he would be taken to the hospital and everyone would pretend there was hope." Had she said this aloud? She wasn't sure.

They asked if she wanted to keep him for a while and call the funeral home to pick him up later, but what would that do for her, to sit with his dead body? He would still be dead. She had liked him alive. So she had them take him.

"Anyone you can call?" they asked. "You shouldn't be alone."

Polly looked across the field. Agnes was on her way, trotting along the desire line. "My friend," she said, pointing.

From the time they'd sat down with their lunch to his body being loaded into the truck was under an hour.

She and Agnes looked at each other with a mutual resignation. It was a moment they'd been waiting for. Someone eventually had to die.

"Come on," Agnes said. "Let's go inside. Where's your address book?"

"Wait a sec." Polly watched the car until she couldn't see it anymore. "Kitchen drawer," she said.

Agnes linked arms with Polly and together they went inside and Agnes sat Polly in the living room, the phone between them. Agnes got one boy after the other on the line and told them what had happened, then handed the phone to Polly. The conversations were brief, and Agnes made notes about when each one planned to arrive or when he'd call back after he made plans. She went out to the terrace and cleaned up the lunch and the broken plate. Polly stayed inside. Her mind couldn't think. The beautiful afternoon light came in the window and waved across the carpet.

For decades she'd feared this day, so she had prepared by picturing being alone in the living room, alone in the bed. Now she saw that her imaginary preparations were useless.

"I'm staying over," Agnes said.

Polly nodded. She had been wiped clean of all opinions, manners, will. She napped for a while, and then she and Agnes walked out to the graveyard and had their Meeting for Worship, as always.

"Where will he go?" Polly asked, looking around.

"Right here. Next to Lydia. You're on her other side."

"Yes, yes. That's good."

Sylvie walked by on Point Path carrying a basket—dinner—and Agnes waved at her. She and Polly went back in and ate supper, or Agnes did, and sat up, answering phone calls, until nine o'clock. Then Agnes guided Polly upstairs. "Get undressed, wash your face, brush your teeth."

Polly did as told. Agnes took her to her bedroom, but she balked at the door. "No! No! Close it up!"

Agnes took her to Theo's old room. She opened the covers and guided Polly in.

"Is Dick dead?" she asked.

"Yes," Agnes said.

"Maybe he's just napping."

"No."

"He tried to go see Robert today. He sat in the car but he never left the driveway." Polly could still see him in the front seat—only his arm and then his face turned up to her.

"He was loyal to Robert."

"I feel so sorry for Robert," Polly said.

"Can you sleep, do you think?" Agnes lay her hand on Polly's forehead.

"I don't know."

"I'd get in bed with you but Sylvie says I snore. Call me if you need me. I'll sleep next door."

He is napping and still alive.

Both of us are alive and always will be.

I, too, am dead.

PART THREE

2001

Moved to Speak

CHAPTER 11

Polly, Meadowlea, May 2001

A T THE POST OFFICE POLLY ASKED FOR HER WINTER MAIL AND
went through it in the lobby, throwing the coupons and re-
cycling into the bins along the wall. Circulars, catalogues, nothing
important; or so it seemed, so she expected, until she came across
a packet of letters that bore a return address of Thomaston, Maine,
and a PO box. From Robert Circumstance, addressed to Dick. Jarring to see them. Nothing had come for Dick to Haverford in a
few months. He'd want these immediately, she'd better go—skip
her other errands. Then she remembered and went through a now
well-honed routine of reminding herself that he was dead but she
was alive and had to go on. This happened less often than it had,
but still—at least four times a day.

Should she send the packet back to Robert? He had written her
a beautiful condolence note. She may not even have written back,
not properly. The DILs had helped her send out cards. That was
the best she could do. It was one of her intentions for the summer
to write back to people more fully.

She'd sorted through the business involving the houses and the
taxes and asked questions of her boys until she learned what she
needed to know now to manage things herself. James wanted her to

sign a power of attorney, but she'd always managed the checkbook and the household finances. "I understand, Ma," James said, "but it's time for you to just rest." Who did he think she was? Didn't he remember her running around after all of them, all those years? Organizing their schedules, making certain they got their homework done, throwing baseballs and footballs, endless driving, driving, driving. Plus, managing the money. "I don't want to rest," she said. "Just go over these papers with me so you know what is happening, too." James put this off, and it was Theo who ended up sitting over the accounts with her. She'd have gone to him in the beginning, but James would have been wounded if she'd skipped over him. Was it true that therapy could sort out these ancient jealousies? If so, she wished he'd go.

Back from town she walked down through the lupines and unmown brown winter grass to the water. The islands farther out were socked in by the sea gray. A pillar of pale smoke rose from Agnes's chimney, and the straight pine on the water's edge struck its lonely pose. She lay down on the rocks. No one would see but maybe Agnes, who would surely understand—and leave her alone. Polly made croaking noises. *Dick, Dick! Tide, take me. Take me to him.*

Songs came, hymns. He'd always made fun of her voice, so she sang, now, for his mockery. *"Bring me my bow of burning gold. Oh come, oh come, Emmanuel. Way down yonder, in the meadow, poor little baby's crying Mama . . ."*

She rolled to her side. She was alive to see the white sky, how she loved a white sky! Gulls hung frozen overhead, who knew how? The same old lobster buoys and the boom of the ocean and the whistles in the treetops had confounded her all her life—they were too beautiful. Way too beautiful for now, when she was smeared with sorrow.

She pushed herself up. Pain; blood. She'd cut her hand on a barnacle. Her hand found her mouth, the blood tasted clean and rich. As she licked her wound, she marveled that Robert Circumstance hadn't known Dick was dead right away. But he hadn't known and so had kept writing. He'd been writing to a living man while she was already in her weeds, and he'd gone on writing way after Dick was in the ground. She envied him for that. She hadn't had a minute of delusion. She and Nessie and Elspeth had made a joke once upon a time, when they learned about Freud. *Denial is a river.* Her grandchildren told her everyone knew that joke, but she informed them it had been made up right here, on the Point. She wished she were in that river now, but she was only at her seaside, lying on the rocks, an unwild old woman.

She rolled onto her knees and awkwardly pushed herself up. God, it had gotten hard. She had to spread her legs and squat, push her hands against the ground, then squeeze her thighs taut. She slogged through the high grass, resoaking her pants.

The pale blue sky was pinking by the time she went back inside. A newspaper sat on the kitchen counter and Polly picked it up. A raccoon had bitten a child, everyone should be on the lookout. Hamm Loose Jr. had bought another property on the coast. Polly ignored the casserole Shirley had left and instead cracked two eggs against the edge of a skillet and drew them back and forth across the hot steel with a spatula. Eggs and an English muffin with orange marmalade. Same old. She ate standing up then soaped her plate. Three books on her shelf were possibles to keep her company later: *The Country of the Pointed Firs* by Sarah Orne Jewett, *Death Comes for the Archbishop* by Willa Cather, and *Little House on the Prairie* by Laura Ingalls Wilder. She pulled them all down, and their lonesome content weighed on her hands. She put them back and chose *Jane Eyre*. Perhaps it wasn't going to be better to be here. Perhaps nothing would ever be good again.

She opened the book to find her marginalia. Her Miss Dictor's connected script.

* * *

When she learned that writing marginalia was a legitimate response to a book, she read with a pencil in hand, noting the parts where the women wrote pining letters and eagerly ripped open the replies, and the parts where their hopes were dashed and they wept into the crooks of their arms. She loved the loneliness that walked alongside love, eager to waylay and suffocate it at any moment. An examination of the women around her showed no signs of a secret life. Was it so rare? To be sure of having one, she had enacted the signs herself: long walks in the rain, a diary hidden beneath her underwear in her chest of drawers, and when she could get hold of a candle, wax dripped on the back of her own letters to friends. None of these were remarked on, but she cultivated them just the same, for a little while. But by the time she was fourteen, Polly had educated herself enough in the possibilities of love to know that what she wanted wasn't the grief that leveled her favorite heroines but the deeply loving marriages that belonged to many of the minor characters in her books. She wanted to fall in love once and to stay in love forever. A marriage built on love that comprehends seemed to her the pinnacle of human potential, and something even a person like her—quiet, pretty not beautiful—could have. She wasn't a subject for romantic tragedy. That was fine with her. What made for enthralling reading didn't seem so appealing in life.

Ian and Posy Hancock, her parents, conveyed without ever saying a word against him that Dick Wister wasn't what they'd imagined for Polly. They didn't have to. Her entire upbringing told her so, especially the guiding principle of her childhood household that it was imperative for women to be gay and social and bring light into the world—a philosophy that weighed against the brooding addition of a future professor of philosophy to the family. Just as they didn't voice their objections, no doubt assuming that their mild rightness would hold sway, Polly didn't explain herself. No one wanted a scene. All she could have said, anyway, was that she adored Dick.

Her family mitigated the detour in their plans with the fact that he was from a decent Quaker family—as Polly had known they would.

He courted her casually, an attitude she found suave. He was as ardent as anyone, she explained to her friends, it was just that he was squeamish about showing it. He got taken up by ideas, taken up and away, as if he'd climbed into the basket of a hot-air balloon and lifted into the sky, except the balloon was his mind and the flame was an idea and the sky was the universe. Once she teased him by asking which came first, the absentmindedness or the professor? Poor thing, he hadn't much of a sense of humor. He walked off to ponder this.

"Dickie!" She ran after him. "I'm joking!"

"Oh!" He looked at her curiously, as he might look at a dog that suddenly spoke. She wasn't sure he'd like this side of her, but from then on he mostly appreciated her wit; it wasn't a trait he considered truly essential, so he wasn't competitive about lacking it. Over time, he learned some humor from her, and developed the ability to recognize even the driest jokes, which made her feel she'd brought him along. She also brought money into the marriage, though he didn't care about that. He was in the clouds, conjuring up fresh dilemmas and sorting them through. Did animals feel? Did evil exist? What was free will? Or freedom? Or will? Questions she could answer in a snap took him years. He explained that his questions weren't like a regular person's, and nor were his answers. He made inquiries, and came up with proofs—which, after months of toil, often ended up in the same place as what she had believed all along. Ah, but he could argue and back up his point, whereas she could only say what she felt. Making sense without proof was ultimately useless, according to Dick. Proof reigned supreme. Feelings, common sense, and intuition—until he made an inquiry into their nature, they were in the limbo of phenomena that might not actually exist. "Old bear," she teased. *My own old bear.*

She was besotted with Dick, though, a feeling located in her stomach, a thrill akin to what occurred on a roller coaster, or when she had to travel alone to an unfamiliar place, or talk to a person who had authority. She didn't have that stomach all the time, of course. She couldn't have gotten anything done if she did. It happened often enough, though—when he came home from work, especially if he were a little late, or if she were the one who'd gone out and on her way home pictured him in his study, sitting in his green leather chair, reading and lost to the world. She was excited to see him again, and nervous, over and over. He stepped into that place in her mind she'd perceived as a fallow field, waiting to be planted. For years she'd had faith he would come, and then he came. He was the fulfillment of a central wish. It wasn't exactly the same for him. He blinked at her when she entered a room, as if she were someone half-forgotten whose name had slipped his mind. He seemed surprised and confused by her, and she knew it was because he didn't feel the need to figure her out, as she did him. She made a point of finding her own happiness. His moods, once she learned them, could be shifted by her subtle adjustments. She could make him happy. There was nothing in the world she wanted to do more than to give him the feeling that he had a happy life.

They married on Flag Day in 1940, and she immediately threw herself into the project of being even more in love. Her in-laws gave them a honeymoon at the Hamilton Princess in Bermuda, a perfect spot. They took walks along the harbor in the mornings and drove out to moonlit pink beaches every night. Sex had barely been awkward at all. They both wanted it, enjoyed it, and were encouraged that it got better day by day. One night Dick exuberantly jumped up and down on their bed, making his penis whirl around like a pinwheel. He leaped to the floor and jumped up and down in front of the window while she laughed helplessly. She found she liked being naked. She never had been, really, not even as a child. As soon as they went up to their room, they always took off their clothes.

He was a little bit stingy, certainly compared to her father, who always pressed a few bills into her hand when she left the house, but that was easily made up for when Dick's back was turned. He didn't notice much, either, not a flower, or a meal, but he discussed ideas avidly. He threw his racket down if he missed an easy shot, and became distressed if any food on his plate touched. Once she grasped that she could modify these flaws over time, or look the other way, she found most of them endearing, the poor sportsmanship excepted. She'd never seen a Miss Dictor's girl behave that way, no matter how heated the contest. But men had something in their makeup that made them less even and less ashamed of it. How else to explain war?

They arrived back in Philadelphia and moved into the wedding gift from her parents, a house on Delancy Street. Polly had money, but Dick made a point to her and Posy and Ian that he intended to run the household on his salary, and they politely kept up that pretense ever afterward while making sure Polly had what she needed. Soon the true adjustment began—the lull of daily life after the hectic wedding whirl. What she'd thought of as an original pick of a husband became a realization that her choice was about as original as asking for a whiskey rather than a sherry. All she'd done was to marry at age twenty-one, like everyone else, and if her husband liked to read more than play tennis—the joke was on her. The finality was shocking. She'd live with Dick Wister for the rest of her life. It was what she'd desperately wanted, but now that she had it—no, it wasn't as simple as being stymied by gratification. She was unsure what it was, but she caught herself feeling odd, as though she was a glass full of clattering ice cubes, chilled and melting at the same time.

One day Polly headed to Gladwyne for a tea with other Miss Dictor's alums who'd married—Agnes wasn't included—to be held at the new house of newlywed Carol Burns, a girl in the class above her. She and her mother drove out early for lunch at the Cricket

Club. The grass tennis courts were brown, the porch closed off. She wanted the lemonade of her girlhood, but it was off the menu, too, so she ordered a ginger ale. But as always, a chicken salad sandwich.

Posy behaved differently toward Polly now that she was a married woman. No matter what they discussed, Posy brought Dick into it, mainly by asking about his opinions. How does Dick feel about Churchill? The Selective Service Act? The fate of the globe was more up to Dick and Daddy than it was to their better halves, for men's opinions might reach influential ears. After the world was out of the way, mother and daughter shared the real news, talking about other people in their discreet manner, forgoing gossipy excitement in favor of tender, forgiving probes.

"And what about Teddy?" Posy asked, as if she didn't see him most weeks.

"He's being young," Polly said. "I'm so glad he loves Penn."

"He seems enthralled with Mask and Wig." Posy ate a spoonful of soup in the normal way. Her table manners were plain, and didn't include what she considered affectations, like pushing her spoon to the opposite rim of the plate. Polly was torn—fanciness made her feel knowing—but she kept to the old way for her mother's sake. "I'm not sure comedy is called for at the moment."

Polly nodded. The War in Europe.

"And I've never found it funny when men dress up in women's clothes. Aren't they making fun of us?"

"I don't think so!" Polly said. But then she pictured it. They were.

"I don't know why Teddy would want to do that." Posy was truly stricken. There was a pause in the chatter around them.

"Yes, it's a dumb form of humor, and Teddy will realize it soon enough."

"I hope so. I don't want him getting caught up."

"Teddy will always land on his feet." Polly cajoled her mother until they were once again laughing. It was entirely new to her to be the one to bring her mother around. Posy's feelings had always presented themselves as a calm, united front. It seemed that marriage had conferred on Polly a confidential role—unexpected, but a fresh source of pride. In Carol's driveway, she leaned across the seat and gave Posy a warm hug goodbye. "I'll call you," she said—as if speaking to a friend.

Carol Burns gave the group a tour of her house. Not that there was anything exceptional to see. She had many of the same Colonial pieces they'd all grown up with. The novelty was that it was her own house, and she was in charge. They all sat down, and Carol poured the tea into her wedding china, a very modern pattern. She poured as they'd all been trained to, half a cup of the dark brew and then water to fill up. She asked each girl about milk and lemon, and dropped two cubes in each cup without asking. Soon sugar would be rationed, but they were oblivious in the present. Soon husbands and brothers and friends would be dead, but they still felt free to be boastful about how well they were making their way in the world. They kept up with the news, but not one could imagine what was to come. Dick was bewildered by Hitler's outrageous opinions and aggression. Polly considered repeating some of his pronouncements, but held back. This was not the time or the place. This was about another kind of change.

Polly felt camaraderie with the young marrieds. They all knew now the great secret of sex and what it was like to see a man around the clock. They wouldn't discuss that, of course, but they communicated it in the new way they sat and moved, as if their bodies had been unlocked. It was a code tapping out messages within their conversation about who had seen whom, been to whose wedding, and had dinner with each other. Like Polly, the girls had been encouraged to be gay creatures, and to laugh at life and themselves. They laughed in many registers as the afternoon passed.

Then, suddenly, Helen Vaughn began weeping. She bent forward and wailed.

Carol, being the hostess, went to her first and quickly, and the others followed. They all huddled around, worrying their necklaces.

"What is it? Are you sick?"

Helen shook her head. She bawled, and everyone pulled back an inch. They'd never seen a friend act this way.

"Do you want to lie down?" Carol asked.

Helen pitched herself out of the chair, and Carol waved to three of the guests to vacate the sofa. Helen flung herself along its whole length. The women couldn't help but notice that the blue velvet showed off her red hair perfectly. Helen's beauty was outside the normal range, a bit New York for their crowd. She wept loudly for a while longer while they all huddled and waited. What could be so dire? Nothing bad, they hoped, nothing really bad.

Virginia Monroe leaned down next to her, and touched her back. "Helen, we are all your friends."

Everyone confirmed this in small murmurs. Helen kept on weeping. Carol asked someone to go to the kitchen for a wet towel. Polly began to go, but Mary McClain was quicker.

Helen couldn't cry forever. She simply couldn't. The thought traveled around the group telepathically. They wanted to help, but her behavior was out of their realm. This wasn't fair to Carol. They shot her bracing glances.

"Helen, would you like to lie down in a bedroom?" Carol asked.

Abruptly Helen sat up. "I want a divorce!" she wailed. "I made a mistake!"

Virginia settled on the sofa next to Helen. Polly maneuvered for a chair across from them. She could barely breathe.

"Why don't you start from the beginning?" Virginia said.

Helen wiped her eyes and blew her nose. Her delicate skin had thinned to a translucent rosy membrane. She looked up and gave a weak, unconvincing smile, ran her fingers through her hair.

But tears began again, though less violently. "I don't know, I don't know," she said. "I didn't expect it to be like this."

"Like what?"

Polly clutched her chair as if she were about to be in a car wreck.

"So . . . so much like a prison. And so permanent."

Virginia opened her mouth, but closed it again. Carol picked up the hot water pot and set it back down.

Helen brushed beneath her eyes and crossed her hands in her lap. It had been all right for a while after the honeymoon. Then without even noticing she began to change. She had moments when she felt as though she wasn't in her own life. She had the sensation of watching herself say things and go places, as if she were eaves-dropping on a woman who wasn't even interesting. It was discon-certing, to say the least. Helen raised her eyebrows, trying to joke, but the small returned smiles of the group were belied by worried eyes. A current ran in every direction around the room, connect-ing all of them. The sensation, Polly later told Agnes, was one of those movements of soul that showed you what had been missing. Everyone had surely had that same odd feeling of being two feet away, watching her own performance, but no one had dared notice it. Once named, though—they listened, uncomfortable and rapt.

Helen had a few weeks of walking around the city—she and Chauncey lived just off Rittenhouse Square—counting the slabs of gray pavement and running the tip of an ungloved finger along the sharp rims of ivy leaves frozen without recourse against Colonial brick walls. When they went to parties, she felt as though she were tracking in a clod of earth blown up to a full-sized brown smudge that distracted the hostess with thoughts of remedy rather than repartee, and imposing work rather than play on the other guests. When they were alone, Chauncey disintegrated from being a whole man into mechanical parts. When he ate, his teeth clicked against his fork, and when he took off his pants at night, he scratched the strange hairy seedpods that were his thighs. He spent hours shining his shoes and paring his fingernails, staring at them with great concentration—or did he only spend a minute, but it seemed like hours to her? In a movie theater she was aware during the whole hour and a half of his viperous arm, sometimes around her shoulders, sometimes rubbing his own leg until she wanted to be sick.

What was happening? Why didn't she recognize him anymore? Wasn't it way too soon to be disenchanted? She was a newlywed! So why did she want to eat chocolate before breakfast, and spend her afternoons either at the zoo or at the library researching Benedict Arnold's tunnel to the river under Strawberry Hill, or standing outside Catholic churches defying whatever eldritch powers that lived inside to suck her through the doors? Why did she feel as though she were hearing everything from deep underwater, and seeing everyone as if they were wearing a mask? Nothing felt right, or real. Nothing made sense. The girl she'd been, that hearty, positive creature, so game and full of fun—she'd been scraped away, like kernels off a cob. Most confounding of all, she'd stopped laughing. She recognized situations and sentences that would have made her laugh before, but the impulse had vanished. She remembered her old self with a sense of homesickness. She didn't want to have children with him. Or do anything to attach herself further. He wanted to buy a house, but she found flaws in every house they saw.

She was doing all she could to sabotage the marriage, and Chauncey noticed nothing. But wasn't love bothered by everything? People thought it was the opposite, a comprehensive besottedness that smoothed all wrinkles; but Helen said she thought real love was always upset. She didn't mean irritated by the roommate problems of married life; that was to be expected. She meant the deep disturbance caused by vulnerability and attachment. It was quite awful to care about somebody, it left you naked and needing things you never knew existed. She'd felt that, at first, but she was alone in it. She didn't bother Chauncey, and that was horrible! They were *friends*. But she had *friends*. She swept her hand in a semicircle, indicating everyone in the room.

"So I am ruined," she concluded. She reached for a blue velvet pillow and held it to her front. "Who is Chauncey speaking to when he talks? Not me."

"Now, now," Virginia said, "of course he's talking to you. You have a case of the newlywed blues, that's all. It's perfectly normal."

"That's right," Carol chimed. "It's the adjustment. Sleeping in your own cozy bed all your life and then suddenly—a man!" She hadn't meant to be funny, and was startled at the rain of laughter she inspired. Everyone needed to laugh.

"It is normal," they all concurred. Normal as the sun rising and falling. Normal as liking baby animals. Normal as Friday afternoons at the orchestra! She was adjusting to marriage, that was all.

"So you have all felt this way?" Helen asked, wishing for it to be true. She looked around hopefully. "Is it nothing?"

"It's nothing!" they chorused.

Helen smiled hectically and clapped her hands. "I'm so glad I asked. I was really afraid I was losing my mind."

"Not at all," Virginia said.

"I feel better. Thank you all so much."

The women broke into spontaneous applause, and Helen beamed. Everyone seemed set to rights and happy again—so why did Polly sense she'd just witnessed a burnt offering? The conversation went forward, but she was stuck remembering all the times she'd tried to get Dick's attention and had ended up kissing him on the cheek and calling him a bear. And what of gathering up his underwear from the bottom of the sheets? What of noticing without daring to name it that they were not entirely clean?

"You're Chauncey's partner now. Partnerships are rocky."

"He'll be able to get much further and do much more because of your efforts behind the scenes. You'll be the making of him."

"Our job is to wreathe them in the fresh greenery of domestic happiness and the spicy scent of good counsel!" Virginia said. This got a laugh, but an appreciative one.

"Think of the widowers who remarry as soon as it's decent to do so. They can't live without a woman, whereas vice versa is not the case."

They named examples. Helen looked at each speaker intently, hungrily. When the reassurances died down, though, she had a question.

"I know I can do a lot for him. But what will he do—for me?"

"He'll take care of you, and he'll appreciate you. His happiness will make you happy. And he will give you children."

Helen considered this, and Polly did too. It was the case that she was happy when she made other people happy. She liked the idea of being taken care of, and wanted children. She felt, though, there was a missing piece to all that had been said.

In the hallway Helen thanked them all sincerely and promised to think carefully about their encouraging advice. The plan was for Carol to drive Helen and Polly to the train station. They sat beside each other on the train and Polly hoped Helen would say more, but the conversation was general and typical. At 30th Street Station, they decided to walk across the bridge and down to Rittenhouse Square. They were quiet, each in her own thoughts, until Polly had to speak.

"Helen—you were brave to speak out like that."

"Oh, I was a bore, for certain."

"No. You were saying what others feel but don't dare notice."

"But it was nothing. Everyone said so. Newlywed blues. What a perfect phrase. Something borrowed, something blue."

"No. Helen—if they told their own stories, our whole society could fall apart. They have to think it's nothing. But—"

"All I know is I'm going to a psychiatrist," Helen said.

They turned west to go along 24th Street, and the episode was over, just like that. As they headed down Walnut, Polly caught glimpses between houses of back gardens dotted with snowdrops and crocuses. Spring was coming! Helen would feel better then, Polly was certain. Her own certainty grew new roots on this walk. This was familiar to her, this groundedness. She wasn't Helen, and didn't want to be. She'd never go so far as to consider she'd made a mistake marrying someone whose interior furnishings and emotional tastes were so hopelessly different than her own—for Dick was innocent, too. She knew what she'd wanted in a husband, and he was all those things: tall, handsome, smart, sober, from Philadelphia, grown-up, respectable, and he liked Maine. That there was more to it than that, and that her empathic disturbance in Carol's living room might be a cairn along the way toward growth, wasn't an idea that had any precedent in the life she'd led, so she chose not to go on pursuing it. When they passed a Catholic church, Helen said she felt nothing more than the usual admiration for the glass—no pull toward spirituality outside her usual purview. Polly wanted very badly to get away from Helen Vaughn.

"I have a feeling I will have a happy life, thanks to you," Helen said.

"No, no," Polly blushed, "not me. And here's where I split off!"

But she stood for an embrace, shriveling inside.

She'd rarely been so shaken, and the disturbance shook a new feeling loose—*I want children. Now.*

That night she told Dick about the afternoon, in the spirit of sharing everything as husband and wife. She even described her feeling of alienation from and doubt about him, which now seemed utterly bizarre. He was so unperturbed by her confession that the incident seemed nothing more interruptive than an unfortunate piece of gristle she'd leave at the edge of her plate. "Better now?" he asked, wiggling his eyebrows. "Better!" She kissed him, and made her own vow—that she'd never again indulge in doubting her love, even if she did. What was the point?

At five she walked over the desire line to Agnes's, avoiding the graveyard. Enough was enough for one day. Sylvie led her to the living room, where a fire had been lit and they caught up on the events of the winter. In her dry way Sylvie detailed power outages and sunken boats, wringing the drama of small-town catastrophe from these non-events. Polly was glad to hear all the news, as she had nothing to say for herself, nothing had happened between last summer and now. Just grief, which was dramatic, but incommunicable.

Agnes, in her sneaks, walked step by step down the stairs. Polly had thought she looked thinner, and now confirmed it.

"You look like an old lady," she said to Polly.

"That's the pot calling the kettle black," Sylvie said and left the room, shaking her head.

"Thank you. I'll pay you the same compliment," Polly said to Agnes.

"Must we hug?"

"That's the custom."

"God forbid we of all people forgo the custom."

They embraced. Agnes led them to chairs by the fire. The room hadn't changed in decades, not since the fertile period when Agnes first owned the house and had gone on a mad dash of renovation, jettisoning or painting over all the dour mahogany and adding bright paintings and murals on some of the walls. This frenzy of decoration had stopped when Agnes became serious about writing the *When Nan* books. The wood had been painted again and again, the murals occasionally touched up but also allowed to fade. They were fantasies of the landscape, inspired by Gauguin, but with the flora and fauna of Maine.

"Let's be silent."

They looked within for a few minutes as they usually did in the graveyard every day. Then Agnes reached out her hand to shake Polly's, ending the meeting from heart to hand.

"I am insanely glad that you've arrived," Agnes said. "I've had no one I like to talk to—except Sylvie, of course. No one is you, though."

Polly was moved by this rare declaration, and she nodded her agreement. She, too, had had no one to talk to, though that was less of a *Neither did I* than it may have been in other years. This winter she'd had nothing to say. They'd only met twice when Agnes was in Philadelphia over Christmas. Polly wasn't up to it, and Agnes didn't press. She'd been through enough loss to know when someone honestly needed to be alone.

They'd been in touch since, but it wasn't possible to replicate sitting together, seeing the face of the other, the small shifts of muscle, the flicker of surprise. Agnes had never once bored Polly, though she was sure that couldn't be said the other way around.

"What's so funny?" Agnes asked.

"Nothing. I'm just relieved to be here."

"The Main Line isn't conducive to widowhood?"

Polly's eyes widened. "No one has said that word to me."

"Is it bad?" Agnes searched her face.

"No, I like it. I mean, I don't like being one, but saying it is better—thee knows what I mean."

"Thee can count on me to call a widow a widow."

"Yes." Polly noticed again how old she was, but they'd get used to each other soon, and Agnes would look the same to her as ever, and it would be perplexing that they couldn't tear across the meadow anymore. "How's work?"

"I've spent the winter writing something new. A memoir of sorts."

"Really? What brought that on?"

"That pain in the neck I told you about, name of Maud Silver. She bothered me about it until I wrote it to keep her quiet."

"I can't even understand what it must be like to work on a long-term project. I can only think in the day."

"That's completely untrue. You had children, which is a feat of long-term thinking if there ever were one. And what of your needlepoint? All those dining room chairs. They're a masterpiece."

There was nothing to replace an old friend who knew everything, who'd spent enough time in the childhood home to know the atmosphere and how emotions and silences transpired—to know how the other had really grown up. Polly felt the power of this truth as she sat in this room that she knew before she had language, with this person with whom she was a friend before friendship even began.

"Are you well, Nessie? All clear?" She'd asked this in letters but had never gotten an answer.

"No one has said anything different."

"But have you gone to be tested recently?" Polly pressed.

"Yes, I do as I am told."

"So I don't have to worry?"

"No. Absolutely not."

"Good. I have to die first. Promise me."

"It will be all right," Agnes said. "Not the same, or as good, but all right in the absence of what was better."

Polly teared. Her doctor had told her she could expect to be *emotionally labile.* And she was. But she didn't like to impose tears on Agnes. Agnes knew this, and got up and poked aggressively at the logs, sending sparks flying up the chimney and popping onto the rug. Polly wiped her cheeks and settled deeper into her chair. The Lees had always had Christmas in July, right up until Elspeth died and there was only one child left, Agnes, by then a woman in her thirties. No grandchildren, no point. A moribund tradition.

Yet it was easy to see the great tree where a sofa sat now, decorated with summer finery, flowers and shells and feathers. They'd wanted to make it a Maypole, but Grace Lee said there was no room to dance around it and anyway *You can't have everything*, a formula Polly accepted without question until Agnes pointed out the deep dangers inherent in it. What happened when people applied this to the poor? Where was the line drawn? Polly was always shocked to learn how complacent she was, when she was certain of her good intentions.

"A funny thing happened at the post office," Polly said, and heard in her own voice a testing of the waters. "A slew of letters from Robert to Dick . . ."

She pushed on, describing the packet and her dilemma, and Agnes sat down and nodded as she spoke.

"I wonder how long it was before he knew Dick died? He sent a condolence letter but it's in Haverford. I think I wrote him back." Polly clasped her hands and squeezed her fingers together tightly.

"I'm sure I wrote him right away, but who knows how long it was before he received the news?" Agnes said.

"True. Maybe he was in solitary for a while."

Agnes was amused. "I like your lingo. Where'd you learn to talk like that?"

"TV." Polly giggled. "I didn't even realize."

"Robert's no doubt learning a new vocabulary."

"I can't even think about it. And I can't open them," Polly said. "You agree, surely."

"Nope! I would read them," Agnes said.

Polly sat up abruptly. "I don't believe it."

"I would. My curiosity would overcome my scruples. Oh, not normally. I'd *never* read *your* mail. But Dick is dead."

Polly flushed. *Dick is dead.* The phrase elated her, strangely. "Thank you! You don't know how often people say he passed, or he went to the angels, or something that completely confuses me. He is dead. That is correct. But—it is Robert's mail, too, and he is alive."

Agnes shook her head. "Pretend we're not speaking of *Robert* Robert. He isn't the point here. These are your letters now. Or maybe not, but in any case I would be overwhelmed by curiosity and somehow justify my giving in to it by means of some sophistry. I'm not saying I am right. But you asked, and that's what I'd do."

"I asked what *I* should do. There's a difference."

"True."

Agnes took her seat and brought her glass into both her hands. She had a very bad haircut, the same one everyone around had, a style that Dick had called shingles-falling-from-a-roof. But she'd given up on that side of life, the pretty side, long ago. Polly thought the lack of concern for her appearance helped Agnes be certain in other ways. Prettiness is a distraction for everyone. Polly had been having funny thoughts like this lately.

"You should throw the packet out," Agnes said.

"No!"

"See? You're going to read it. You may as well stop pretending."

"Pretending is how I've managed all this time. I pretend everything is fine."

"I know. But life is short. It ain't over 'til it's over, but when it is . . ."

Two hours later, back at Meadowlea, Polly took the envelopes into the living room and sorted them by date. There were eight of them. She opened the earliest letter first, with her finger, ripping the envelope jagged—so unlike the clinical seams Dick cut with his letter opener. She got a paper cut—two cuts in one day, better put some peroxide on them—as a rebuke for her haste, but it was the first time she'd ever opened a personal letter addressed to him. The paper was lined, from a notebook, the writing very neat. She glanced up at the lamp, wondering why it wasn't brighter. The pages had to be held high to see them.

Dear Dick,

She hesitated another moment, mousing with the last of her will-power the high-minded option of mailing them back to Robert Circumstance in a manila envelope. But greed had gotten hold of her right from the moment she saw the letters; yes, it had been there, even if she hadn't admitted it then; and she felt greedy for whatever she could get of Dick. His name, someone addressing him who believed he was alive, someone else's mind on him . . . She read.

I reread your letters daily and am lifted by them. I never gave
much thought to the idea of justice before. I believed in it,
and fairness, and equality, but without stopping to consider
the assumptions made about those words. I supported those
good ideas, and many others that thoughtful people believe in
and practice. They all seem based on common sense. That's a
wonderful phrase, isn't it? Common, suggesting an agreed upon,
simple standard, and sense, the collective mind connected to the
universal body that gathers data from the real world and not only
from itself. Common sense, grounded in the real. It seems to me
that people across the globe and the centuries have arrived at the
same set of good ideas that honor life and promote well-being for
all. Truth, with or without supernatural guidance or intervention.

Justice isn't an idea in a place like this. It is concrete, literally,
meted out in ponderous footsteps as men think about whatever
they can manage to put their minds on. A lot of the time it is
justice. I don't believe a single man here agrees with his capture
or his sentence, his treatment or the food; everyone disagrees
with some aspect of our present life. The worst off among us,

the men in solitary confinement, are living under entirely unjust conditions. To be alone involuntarily is surely torture. In the outside world there are so many distractions. Here there are few, and those few are pathetic or vile in nature. But to have none is misery on a scale that is evil.

No one thinks this is justifiable. Nor does anyone say why he is here, though the news gets around. It doesn't matter. Everyone has his reasons for whatever he did or did not do. Few want to go back and think about it. Better to live in the present, complain about the present, make trouble or not in the present.

In a just world, there would be no need for conscience, and no cause for regret. I think about that a lot—how people would behave if they fully understood how their behavior affects others.

It must be hard to keep up a correspondence with me and to think about the specter of prison every time you sit down to write. I should say, please don't write again, but I can't do that. I look forward to your letters. There may be a stack of them somewhere in this place, languishing undelivered. The guards and wardens here test people beyond any reasonable limits, then punish them severely for their human responses.

Please give my regards to Polly and your family.

She opened another.

Thank you for the Hemingway. The piece that strikes me hardest, right between the shoulders, is "Big Two-Hearted River." I've never read it before. Hemingway came to me at school. I had the same response as I guess most do—I was wildly excited by his style. We read some of the famous stories in class, in eleventh grade, and learned about the iceberg method. It had never before occurred to me that there could be much more to a story than what I was reading. Good books always seem complete and inevitable. How could satisfaction of curiosity be only the tip of an iceberg, with most of the vast truth, and the entire basis for the truth, out of sight? Yet I instantly grasped the idea. It's an innocent perspective; the smallest child knows there is more to his surroundings than what he is seeing. Much is above his head, for one thing. Things are behind closed doors. The sun disappears. Hemingway's iceberg fathoms these things that are mysterious for being invisible. They make his stories tragic. . . .

Polly read through the letters slowly, losing her place over and over in favor of strangling sorrow, but returning until she grasped what Robert was saying. She placed each letter back in its envelope and into the pile on her lap. When she took a break and closed her eyes, she found in that darkness a memory of Dick sitting on a bench in town, reading one of Robert's letters. She'd never once wondered what Robert was writing. Her thoughts had only been about Dick. And, even now, reading Robert's words, she wondered if Dick had written back in kind, with an equal offering of self? She looked into the shadows in the direction of his study, feeling the presence of a cabinet of letters there as carefully kept as the ones in Haverford. None were personal, not even to his children.

Today one of the guards came in with a bright red wet maple leaf pasted to the back of his shoe.

Isn't that like a Zen koan?

She'd always noticed the same thing, wet leaves on her bare legs, the rush of adrenaline as if a thing alive had leaped on her. It was in the category of small mishaps, and not a memory she'd have ever drawn up for pleasure, but she saw that for a person in prison the sight of a bright red maple leaf pasted to the back of an ankle could be a conduit to a storehouse of sensations missed now, cut off.

What must Robert have thought of Dick before he knew of his death—for not responding to such searching thoughts?

In the morning she wrote a letter of her own.

Dear Robert,

I arrived back on Fellowship Point just yesterday and picked up several letters from you to Dick that had been held over the winter. The postmarks were after he had died, and it bothered me to think that you were writing to him but not receiving any response. Your last letter is postmarked October 14. I know Agnes let you know about Dick, and I did receive your letter of condolence. If I didn't write back—I was useless, truth be told. I am planning to make up for my months of blurriness.

It is only this gap in time that concerns me now, and I am writing to reassure you that Dick had every intention of maintaining a robust correspondence with you until you came home.

Please tell me if there are things I can send—any book you'd like, or whatever comforts you are permitted. Nothing feels right with both you and Dick not here. But soon you will return, and we can build the pink wall, only if you want to, of course.

A week later she received a reply from Robert Circumstance. He wrote back sympathetically, reassuring her that he hadn't had a moment of doubt about Dick. For all he knew the return letters had been lost or withheld—it happened. And Agnes had written, and he had grieved. The letter went on, pondering the baffling nature of a patterned life, be it marriage or a job or prison—and the exposure of the soul to equally baffling, wilder elements when the pattern was interrupted. Contrary to the accepted idea that all experience was valuable, he hadn't been able to find any good or lesson or utility in many of the sorrows in life, especially not from Dick's death. Nothing good or wise or bracing had come of it. She agreed. She hadn't found she had the strength to go on, she merely went on. Life was mere, now.

She took her time making a tuna sandwich. Mayo, pickle relish, red onion, toasted bread. She set a place for herself at the dining room table and ate slowly. After lunch she sat down to write Robert back and tell him how her own feelings mirrored what he'd expressed, but when she picked up her pen she felt shy and wrote instead about the garden, going on about her plants, and how she made decisions about which flowers to pick for the vases, be it eeny meeny miny mo or copying the palette of a famous painting. And then, finally, in a burst, she wrote how oppressive it was that she was supposed to more easily accept Dick's death because he was old. They'd been together for sixty years! The time she had on her hands now gave her the sensation of waiting. She made the best of waiting, that was all. She guessed it was disbelief—secretly believing he'd come back. At first she'd thought she could tell no one this, it sounded so crazy. Then she realized she could tell nearly anyone who'd had something bad happen to them, some setback, accident, disease, death. Everyone who'd lost something of crucial importance wished he or she could go back to the moment when it was still theirs. The wish was so powerful it seemed it might reverse the direction of time. It bore apparitions and ghosts.

It bore Lydia. She did not write about that.

She read her reply over, wincing at its intimacy. She considered not mailing it, but what did it matter? These weren't truly secrets, only the private feelings of an old invisible person. She drove the envelope to the post office the next morning and placed it in the Out of Town slot.

Robert wrote back at length about the quality of food in the prison—haggard meat and mute vegetables. He wrote of the difference between solitude and loneliness, and how he had to work harder and harder to feel the former. He wrote of the pets men kept, the mice and bugs, and a snake, hidden in a bed. No one knew how the snake had gotten in, but the impossibility of it appearing in a prison had made it into a deity of sorts. He said how much Dick's support had meant to him, and that this would always be true. He was very sorry Dick had died.

Polly read the letter twice, and again later in the day. After dinner she sat down with a fresh sheet of letter paper, marked MEADOWLEA on top and began what became a habit. They both had the time for a correspondence—a silver lining, she wrote. She didn't think of herself as a replacement for Dick, didn't imagine she could offer Robert much stimulation. She was new and lesser, but probably better than silence. She woke up in the mornings writing to him. It was almost like writing a diary, a very honest diary, except he was the presence looking over her shoulder rather than the anonymous confessor she'd always pictured. That cold presence had been inhibiting. Robert was unfailingly kind, and she surprised herself over and over, discovering her thoughts on many subjects. If she'd lived alone all her life, she would have been a vegetarian, like Agnes, but males had to have meat. She liked staying up until the sky pinked before dawn, or getting up then. She had never felt as happy as when she was a girl on the Point with Teddy and Agnes and Elspeth and Edmund, except during her years with Lydia. They were happy.

Robert wished he'd had children; traveled more; met the right person, or at least someone companionable. He wished he hadn't been curious about weed in college, and had been more cautious about friendships. Polly was well aware that these yearnings and regrets were prosaic on both their parts. Dick would scoff at their sentimentality. She liked knowing this, and mentioned to Robert that she felt as though Dick's opinions of their opinions were a part of the correspondence, and he suggested she include what she knew Dick would say about what they said. This added another layer, and sometimes she laughed aloud when she was composing; she described Dick's liberal stridency, which freed her from her vigilant defense of his faults. He was gruff, unsentimental, judgmental of the unrighteous, and even a bit selfish. No—he was selfish. She'd polished a sheen even on his shortcomings, but now she laughed warmly at them, as she probably should have when he was alive. Perhaps laughter would have shored him up better than reverence did. Agnes would have laughed at Dick had Polly allowed it. She was an old friend, though, and knew what was sacred. It was a red flag, Polly and Robert decided, not to have old friends.

CHAPTER 12

Agnes, Leeward Cottage, June 2001

Dear Agnes,

I'll come in August, if that's all right. That's when David wants me to take my vacation. Your memoir isn't official business, so I have to come on my own time. I think it's important to do so now. I enjoy our correspondence, but we're not getting to the bottom of anything. I don't think we will this way. I am hoping that in person your manners will work to my benefit and you will answer my questions about the manuscript.

Truman Capote said that all literature is gossip. That's an efficient way of saying that literature provokes and astonishes. Your current version of *Agnes When* is gossip withheld. There's tension beneath what you've put on the page—I almost just wrote "deigned to," because that's how it feels. There's good holding back, and then there's deliberate withholding. No one likes that, not in relationships, and not in memoirs—unless it's dramatic, such as when food is withheld in *Oliver Twist*. But Oliver Twist figures out ways to get food, yet the reader can't get any more from you than what you give. All right—I worked that metaphor a bit hard. I'm confident you know exactly what I'm pointing to. Your choice to tell only a partial truth is clear. It frustrated me and it will frustrate many readers. How can we fix this? Let's discuss.

Please tell me what airport I should fly into, and the name of the nearest town where I could get a room at a bed-and-breakfast. I'm looking forward to meeting you, and to hashing this book out once and for all.

Yours,
Maud

Hashing this book out? Once and for all? What delusion was this?

Agnes lay the letter down on her desk. She went to her official study down the hall where she kept her papers and carried back the folder of her correspondence with Maud Silver. Unbeknownst to all but a few, she had learned how to use a computer and a printer and printed out copies of her important correspondence. Polly had described to her Dick's careful system for filing his correspondence, and she'd been sincerely appreciative of it—not that she thought it would ever come to anything in his case. No one beyond himself and Polly and possibly a grandchild with an archival bent would ever want to read Dick's letters, she'd put money on that. Probably true of herself, too; she had no fantasies about posterity, the archive at the U of P notwithstanding. Her records were for herself, and practical, but every so often she wanted to be able to reread a passage she'd expressed well. She often thought it would be best if everything was thrown out upon her death, but you couldn't count on that. A Max Brod might emerge—possibly called Maud Silver.

She opened the folder on her desk and reread Maud Silver's letter chain.

Dear Miss Lee,

I have read your manuscript, *Agnes When*, twice, and have sat with it for a week before gathering my thoughts. Now I will do so.

First of all, your writing is gorgeous. The sentences are sophisticated and fascinating. Many made my heart lurch, and I paused to stand under the waterfall of your words. Please excuse my metaphors.

The depiction of Fellowship Point and Leeward Cottage, and the life you lived there with your neighbors and siblings, is nostalgic and a dream of summer. Who wouldn't want to spend a few months every year in an unspoiled place, living a life of simplicity without hardship, having constant companionship, being subject to laissez-faire rules and attitudes, with an available, kind father arriving from his office for a few weeks? I hope you are immune to being the subject of envy, because you will be. I envy you already. How could your life have been any more perfect?

When you look through the manuscript, you will see all I loved, underlined, and showered with the initials FSP, which stands for Fresh Summer Peaches, meaning the very best. You'll also see suggestions, which are few. As you are aware, the manuscript is tight and irreducible. It's as if you have been writing prose forever. It's astonishing. I can't figure out how the children's books correlate to this piece of work.

Har har, Agnes thought.

Now we come to the part where you sit down and brace yourself. Are you ready? In addition to all I said above, there is the added fact that I wasn't satisfied by the book. I'm going to be blunt, because I sense you would prefer that, and it's far easier for me than hiding my critique in the middle of a bouquet. So please sit down or get a glass of whiskey or whatever you need to do to fortify you for this next paragraph.

Miss Lee. Last summer I wrote to you asking you for a memoir about how you came to write the *When Nan* books. What you sent me ten months later is a highly readable and very beautiful portrait of a summer place that you know well. I love it and admire it deeply.

What it is not is a book about how you came to write the *When Nan* series. There is nothing in these pages that answers that question, except by an oblique inference, which I can't count on most readers who are curious about you to make. You do depict small girls who have great freedom and large ambitions, and you were an unusually self-aware feminist in spite of being close to your father. But how and why and when you became more than a child diarist is nowhere shown. That leap is what is interesting. It's what the majority of letters you receive ask you about. Who is Nan? Was she a real little girl, or did you make her up? Why did you decide she should have so many adventures? And many more.

This isn't an official editorial letter, because I think the manuscript is in early stages. You can do a lot more with this, and I hope you will.

What do you think? Or—tell me something. When did you write your first story?

Warmly,
Maud

Dear Ms. Silver,

As you did, I have taken some time to mull your letter over. It was hard to read, of course. No one wants to have her work so easily dismissed, or to be sent back to the drawing board by a few strokes of the keyboard. I have veered between incredulity and rage. I am calm now. Which you might like no better.

I spent the entire winter writing that book. I agree, it is beautiful. I put in exactly what I want put in. The manuscript explains why I wrote the *When Nan* books, and if the explanation is too subtle for most readers, as you seem to believe, then I'd say the fault lies in an educational system outside of my responsibility. Anyone with a jot of sense of direction will be able to go from Point A to Point B, between my past and my books. Answering your blunt-force questions will drag the pages down. Drown them.

Dear Miss Lee,

It's always disheartening to have to do something over, especially before you figure how to go about it.

You will figure this out, I have no doubt about it.

Shall we discuss possibilities?

Dear Ms. Silver,

If I remember correctly, and I do, David isn't on the hook to publish this book—no one is. Nor are you doing me any favors. You are hoping it will advance your own career. So you are being awfully choosy for a beggar.

I sent you a perfectly good book.

If you don't want it, I'm sure there are others who will.

Dear Miss Lee,

It may be true that there are other publishers who'd print this book as is. Your name and brand would sell a certain number of copies before the word got out about the gorgeous yet slim pickings inside. I wonder, however, if you want to use up this chance without making the most of it? The book I suggested you write is meant to be a companion to, or an elucidation of, the *When Nan* series. I am not sure it would work the same way if you took it somewhere else, or how it would be marketed. I was hoping to time it to a major redesign of the whole series, and hoping that David will make the connection when the time comes to another imprint here that we could work with. Or maybe he'll do it!

Apparently Laura Bush is going to focus on literacy as her First Lady project.

Dear Ms. Silver,

I realize you are young, so rather than rise to your bait I'm going to view your recent letter as a mentoring opportunity. Your tone is threatening. You mean it to be. Your fantasy is that I will read your letter, suddenly come to my senses, and do things your way . . . because you threatened to link my compliance with the reissuance of Nan. This, my dear, is not a good tactic. I am eighty-one years old. I am interested in the continuation of the series, but will I be here to see it or promote it? That isn't as clear to me as it would have been thirty years ago.

I am still invested, however, and if you came up with a way to convince me that doing the work you are suggesting on the manuscript would be a good way to spend the remaining days

of my life—that might be effective. Be a little smart, why don't
you?

Call me Agnes.

Dear Agnes,

Point taken. Let's both draw down our arms. I'll start over.

I don't think I told you I did my senior capstone project on
feminist portrayals in the *When Nan* series. I realize I do have a
very particular agenda in asking you to write this book. I myself
am curious as to how you think about your work from that
angle.

However, even if you don't want to address feminism, I still
want you to write more about how you came to create these books.
And how you create them, for that matter. That question is at the
center of the memoir. The 200-page description of your childhood
summers in Maine encapsulates your inspiration to you. Not to a
reader. And, it isn't a question of your portrayal being too subtle.
It's a matter of fulfilling the premise of the book.

Why do you write? When did you start? What does it mean to
you to be a writer? How did you think up the character of Nan?
Did she come to you all at once, or did you work at imagining
her? Why did you decide to write about her for children? Did you
always draw? How do you choose the professions and activities she
engages in for each book? Which one is your favorite so far? How
do you understand children so well, when you don't have any?
When did you realize you are a feminist? (I'm hoping that one just
slips in . . . !)

You get the gist. Interview yourself on these matters and see
what you come up with.

Dear Maud,

Are these the kinds of things you want to know?

1. I never realized I was a feminist. I realized I was a person, a human being, with desires and needs and talents and abilities—the same as everyone else.
2. I understand children because I remember what it was like to be one.
3. My favorite is *When Nan Never Ate Animals Again.* It is moldering in my drawer—unpublished.
4. I choose Nan's occupations by whim. Whatever I happen to be reading about or thinking about is apt to become a book. I aim to choose active pursuits that involve movement.
5. As you know from the manuscript you find wanting, we had our habits on Fellowship Point. We kept extensive notebooks at our house, and my father encouraged each of us to contribute to them. I often drew what I saw outside. Trees, birds, flowers, people. I had no knack for it but I enjoyed it.
6. Nan is based on a child I once knew. That is all I want to say on the subject, now and forever.
7. What does it mean to me to be a writer? That I have found a method of thinking that reliably moves me forward. That I have developed a system of logic that resembles reason while containing my emotions which are by nature unreasonable. That I know I can express myself clearly if and when I need to. Above all, that I have a private space where I can wander and play and dream, where I can be scathing and cruel and reprehensible, where I can love and expose myself completely, without any interference from anyone other than my private projections. Writing is how I live even when I am not writing.

8. I write because I am a human being, and to make art is to be fully a human as distinct from the other animals. Art is human. So am I.

9. You see? I have answered all your questions in a few pages. This has all the excitement of an interview. How do any of these answers explain me better than my descriptions of the Point, or of trees and eagles? What is there to be gained by adding this material to the manuscript I gave you? I don't see the point.

The next letter in the series was the one that had just arrived. Agnes considered. She wouldn't rewrite the book, but perhaps that was a message more successfully delivered in person.

Anyway, Polly's family was coming and Agnes would have no playmate for a few weeks.

She went to the back room again, typed out a letter, and printed two copies. She reread it again before putting it in the envelope.

Dear Maud,

As we live in a semi-free country, I can't stop you from coming to Maine. There's no bed-and-breakfast nearby so you may as well stay here. I have a lot of room, as you may have gathered. I'll give you more info about travel shortly.

A.

Agnes found Polly in her dining room playing with place settings. She'd asked Sylvie to come along, but she'd declined. Sylvie was aware that Polly felt inhibited in her presence.

"Is that what you're wearing?" they said at the same time.

Agnes was dressed as usual—jeans, an old family sweater, sneaks. Polly had on a skirt.

"What if we walk around the Sank?" Agnes said.

"I can walk around the Sank in this. It's about a hundred yards of material." Polly pulled the sides apart—and curtsied. They'd curtsied to the headmistress every morning for years at Miss Dictor's.

"You can still bend a knee," Agnes said.

Polly rubbed at her leg. "Not really."

"I'm going for rustic yet elegant." Agnes put her hair behind her shoulders.

"You achieved the rustic part."

"They aren't going to care how we look if we hand over the land."

"You make a good point," Polly said. "Now come help me. I thought I'd serve from the sideboard."

Earlier Polly and Shirley had made a crabmeat salad, a tomato aspic mold, corn muffins, and iced tea and set it out on the sideboard.

"Where is Shirley? I see her drive by but I never run into her."

"I sent her home for the afternoon. She's coming back later to wash the dishes. I don't need that, of course, but I want to pay her." Polly adjusted the placement of the serving dishes. Agnes would have separated them by another half an inch—but it wasn't her house.

"Butter. I'll get it." Agnes felt strong and eager. That wasn't the case every day anymore, and when it was she sought ways to apply her vigor.

The two guests arrived, and after brief introductions they sat down. The meal began with the usual sort of small talk, a sighting of Martha Stewart in Northeast Harbor and reports of nearby moose. Agnes had spoken to the person called Jane on the phone and was gratified to see that she looked exactly as imagined: slightly stooped, wiry gray hair, dressed like a hiker, knowing. Her partner, Nathan, was tall enough that the height of the rooms at Meadowlea seemed necessary, and he was a handsome man. Fiftyish, boyish slenderness, relentlessly polite—the better to coax people to part with their property. An Archie Lee type.

They had come armed with a plan, and many examples of successful people who'd recently donated lands. Had Polly or Agnes heard about the gift of Aldemere Farm in Camden to the Maine Coast Heritage Trust? "The Oreo cookie cows," Polly said. Yes, they'd heard. Polly asked how it worked with the houses on a property and was assured that it could work any way the owners wanted. The houses could remain privately owned, and only the land put into trust; or they could be put into a conservation easement whereby the family could use them in perpetuity but they would belong to the trust; or they could be donated but remain in the hands of the present owners until their deaths. There were also many options for how the transfer could work. The land could be directly donated all at once, or it could be donated a bit at a time, or it could be sold to the trust and bought with funds raised by the trust for that purpose, or the transfer could be structured so that the family would get an annual annuity to live on. And so on. Basically, it could work any way they wanted.

"This place is so well cared for," Jane said. "Who is your caretaker?"

"Robert Circumstance," said Agnes and Polly in the same moment.

Nathan paused, fork and knife held in midair. "How do I know that name?"

"He's a landscape architect. He's done a lot of gardens along the coast," Polly said.

"The gardens here as well," Agnes added.

"No, that's not it." Nathan looked at his plate for the answer.

Agnes and Polly had the discipline to not even exchange a glance. Agnes watched Nathan pursue the question and felt a flash of hate toward him. Immediately she corrected herself. Ire might push him toward what he sought—a memory of Robert on the front page of the *Portland Herald*, being led out of the courthouse in handcuffs. Agnes wished she'd never seen that image.

"Well, it's just lovely in any case." Jane smiled at them. She's like Polly, Agnes thought, always seeking equilibrium.

"And we want it to remain so," Agnes said. "It should be obvious that that must be done, but there are those who only care about development." Spoken as if it were a curse word, as she believed it to be. "We are most interested in how the birds would be cared for."

"In other places the U.S. Fish and Wildlife Service oversees the care and well-being of birds and animals on trust sites," Jane said. "Do you know what birds nest here, specifically?"

"That would be good to know, wouldn't it?" Nathan asked as he stood to forage for seconds.

"We've kept records for over a hundred years." She didn't offer to show them.

"That's good, that will be very helpful," said Jane.

Nathan had the habit of running his thumbs over the pads of his fingers. He even did it between bites. He also hid his cherry tomatoes under a piece of lettuce. Sexual tells? Evidence of secret greed? Agnes made a mental note of these gestures.

"Are the U.S. Fish and whatever people good at taking care of birds? We have a system. Will they follow our system?" Agnes picked up a tomato in her fingers and popped it in her mouth. "Oh, that's so good. I wonder if we have more tomatoes in the kitchen. I'd love to have another right now."

Nathan glanced at his plate. Mens rea.

"I think they'll do as you ask," Jane said. She had the sheepish look of someone who knew things weren't going very well.

Leave it to Polly to feel sorry for them. "What projects are you working on now?" she asked encouragingly.

Nathan piped up. "We are planning to purchase a several-hundred-acre tract near the Penobscot River, don't you know. We're sorting out the rights. There is another group interested, too, a Wabanaki group, but it doesn't seem as though they'll be able to raise the money."

"I didn't know the Native Americans buy land," Polly said. "I thought they lived on reservations."

"It's complicated," Jane said, setting down her fork. "I have never been able to follow all the treaties that were made and broken in New England. It comes down to the Wabanaki in general seeing themselves as sovereign peoples and wanting to self-govern. The concept of land relationship is different, too. They have the idea of peoples and tribes having rights to hunt and fish in specific places, but traditionally they don't believe anyone can own a plot."

"I must say I am sympathetic to their view," Agnes said. "As you must be."

"Yes," Jane said. "That's one of the reasons why I am in this line of work."

If it were only her, Agnes thought, maybe. But not Nathan.

"There were legal cases in the 1970s claiming that the old land treaties had been violated," Jane went on. "The distress was about too much land granted by treaty to the indigenous people having been transferred to non-Natives, and the Native people wanted both the land returned and restitution. I don't know all the ins and outs of it, but basically the Native Americans received money with an option to purchase lands for market value, but they also had to give up some lands. And not all the tribes were included in the suit."

"The tract we are interested in was once sacred land," Nathan said. "But we figure if the Wabanaki group can't acquire it, better us than a developer."

Agnes sliced her corn muffin in half—pointedly. "Certain people have their eye on this place, too, for development."

"Actually, Native people had a summer camp in the Sank. Lots of artifacts have been found there," Polly said.

"It wasn't a burial site, was it?" Jane said.

"No. My father had someone come look at everything. It was a campsite, if you want to put it that way."

"That's all right then," Jane said. "Burial sites are in a different category. The legalities are complex and, to be frank, subject to change."

"We have our own burial site just across the road," Agnes said. "My father is there, and Polly's, and many others of ours. We have to figure out what to do about that, too."

"We can manage that." Nathan rubbed his finger pads.

Unctuous, Agnes thought. One of her father's few but effective put-downs.

"Do you have a timeline in mind?" he asked.

He looked like Robert, not Archie. That was it. He looked like him but wasn't him. And so she was resentful. That wasn't mature, but it was understandable.

In her preparation for the meeting, Agnes had considered describing the setup of the trust, and their present estrangement from a principal shareholder, but she saw no reason to share that information with the members of the Dirigo Land Preservation Trust, because she wasn't going to sign any part of Fellowship Point over to them.

"Not exactly," she said. She delivered a big, ugly yawn. "I must apologize, but suddenly I am exhausted and need to go home for a nap. I just had cancer surgery."

The table commiserated and fluttered. Agnes stood, Polly stood, leaving Nathan and Jane no choice. Meal over. No tour of the Sank. No promises. No let's-talk-again-soons.

"It was nice to meet you." Jane held out a comprehending hand. Nathan frowned.

That was the end of that.

After they drove off, Agnes asked Polly about dessert.

"Thou art tough, Agnes Lee," Polly said. "Come on." They went out to the kitchen and ate lemon cake standing by the counter.

"Mmm. Did you make this?" Agnes licked her fork.

"I did."

"I should accept more of your dinner invitations. Anyway, it wasn't a waste to have them here. I learned that we have to find the right people to take over the Sank. People who really understand how special it is. Did you notice they never praised the land?"

"Oh, yes they did, Agnes! They had plenty of nice things to say."

"But not the right things. I'm just so eager to get this settled. How many dopes are we going to have to talk to?"

"It was never going to be easy," Polly said. "And there's still the problem of Ar—"

Agnes held up her hand. "Do not speak that name."

"Fine by me," Polly said, and cut herself another thin slice of cake. "Meanwhile I've been getting ready for the hordes to descend. Want to see? When was the last time you were upstairs in this house?"

They both remembered—the day Dick died.

"I meant before that," Polly said. She led the way up the stairs. "It's so odd—we are in and out of the downstairs of each other's houses all the time."

Agnes shrugged. "Old-fashioned."

The doors were all open but one. The master bedroom. They passed by without remark.

Polly led the way down the hall, giving a tour. The rooms were very plain, each containing a bed or two, a chest of drawers, a chair, and either a table or a small bookcase or both—more to do than in a nun's room, yet congruent with Quaker values. The point of Meadowlea was that it didn't change.

"I like these pictures," Agnes said. "How do you know about all these artists?"

"Nessie, unlike thee, I actually leave the house! There's a painter every two feet in Maine."

"Well, that's good. Artists are benign, more or less. Maybe not this one." Agnes pointed to a painting of a Maine island, done in fastidious pointillism. "I don't think dots were art's finest moment."

Polly looked at it. "I see your point. Har har. Why don't I replace it with one of yours?"

"I'm not legitimate."

"So what? I love your paintings. Your murals."

"I can't very well give you a wall. But . . . how about a Nan illustration? A pair of them. They would look nice in one of these bright rooms. Great-grandchildren will be along soon enough."

"Thank you, Nessie. I'd love that."

"I wish I could really paint," Agnes said.

"I wish I could sing."

"These kinds of confessions call for each of us to assure the other that it's not too late. But we can't do that. It is too late."

"We will never be gymnasts," Polly said. She opened a window in one of the guest rooms.

"Nope. Nor go to Egypt."

Polly was walking ahead so didn't notice when Agnes stopped and turned the knob to the master bedroom. But she sensed Agnes wasn't following and turned to see where she was.

"Pol," Agnes said. "It's time."

"No—"

"Yes. It has been a year. Come stand by me."

"I guess you're right." Polly hung her head but joined Agnes.

The opening of the door. A great blast of heat! Surprised giggling—out of the era of their lives when they were girls together and new intense physical sensations altered their moods radically, usually in the direction of joy. Blasts of joy. Blasts of cold or heat or fear, blasts of pleasure in eating a peach or caramel, blasts of pain from wearing new shoes to an endless party or tripping and land-ing on your face. Blasts of life. They giggled more, and Agnes took Polly's arm while they were still giggling and led her into the room where Dick had last slept.

A swift assessment. The room had been cleaned. Cleared of daily life. Both bedside tables were cleared off. Agnes crossed to the win-dow, her modus operandi in any room. This was the best view, tradi-tionally reserved for the person who held a share in the Fellowship.

"Dick loved this view."

"It's awfully close in here." Agnes unlatched the sash and lifted the window. The screen could wait.

A fly roused itself and buzzed drunkenly around the room and they both swiped at it, its loopiness dangling the prospect of an easy, one-handed catch. They watched and listened to the dipping and buzzing as if it were all that existed. Incredible how one tiny creature could command all the attention in a room. Like a baby. Before they had a swarm around them, Agnes gently brushed the sill clear of other trapped insects.

The fly lighted on the wardrobe door and walked ponderously, diagonally across its surface. Polly lunged forward, hitting Agnes accidentally.

"Ouch!"

Agnes urged the fly toward the window, this time successfully. "There!" she triumphed, and banged the screen shut.

"My heroine." Polly nodded appreciatively as the fly disappeared. She gazed around at everything. "I don't know why I was so worried about coming back in here. It's actually comforting. This is where Dick talked to me. Did I tell you he talked to me?"

"I don't think you did, in the way that you mean now."

"He did, last summer, in the early hours of the morning. He told me things he never told me before."

"That's funny, Daddy did that, too, before he died."

233

"It's nice, isn't it?" Agnes ran her hand over the old smooth wood of the wardrobe. "Thine?"

"No. His."

Agnes pulled open the doors and was enveloped in the scent of cedar and the odor of old man. Dick's clothes hung just as they had, according to his own method. Polly gasped.

"You didn't expect this?" Agnes asked.

Polly reached out and touched a shirt. She shook her head. Agnes remained in the room quietly as Polly looked around. In the distance a motorboat buzzed. Polly explored like a child, with her left hand, her sense of smell, her remembering gaze. Feeling it all. She came back to Agnes.

"Thank you, Ness. I can fix this up nicely. It's my room again. I'm going to move back in tonight."

"Good." Agnes was very moved, which brought out the brusque in her. "I'm going home and I'm taking some cake with me. I have to set up another luncheon with another pair of vultures. Are you going to town?"

"In the morning."

"I brought a letter for you to mail. I'll leave it on the hall table."

"Mmm."

Agnes walked home. Maisie met her partway, swishing against her leg. Sylvie met her at the door.

"The meeting was a bust, but Polly is doing better. I need a drink!"

CHAPTER 13

Polly, Meadowlea, August 2001

T HE CHILDREN AND GRANDCHILDREN ARRIVED, SETTLED IN, and were active all day, sailing, playing tennis, heading over to Acadia to climb. The DILs took over the kitchen and admired the gadgets they'd bought for Polly over the years. They wished *they* had such a good mixer/grater/blender—she was sooo lucky! She wanted to say, *Take it*, but instead she thanked them and exclaimed that she couldn't live without all the machines. It was all a part of the pageant of summer at Fellowship Point, an old show.

The days together took the same form as days spent by many families in many houses nearby. Picnics. Hikes. Shooting stars. The words out of Polly's mouth were doubtless similar to those of other grandmothers. She felt a robust bonhomie around her grandchildren and inhaled their energy. She kept up!

They thought she was doing well with her widowhood, but she missed Dick fiercely.

One day they had a ceremony down by the water, in remembrance of his death. The notion to do so had come from the grandchildren, based on their exposure to the wider world. Their Jewish friends unveiled the gravestone after a year, and they liked the custom. Funny how young people both wanted to be original and loved tradition, especially when it wasn't their own, and satisfied both tendencies by borrowing the traditions of others. Polly had grown up celebrating birthdays modestly, and had never gone in for the nonsense of differentiating zeros and fives as being the big ones. How was one year different from any day in between then and now?

The ceremony was sweet, though, dominated by the impulses of the granddaughters to pick meadow flowers and float them out to sea. Each of the boys spoke. The grandchildren had asked her to say a few sentences, and she did so, for their sake.

"Dick believed in seeking peace and he came closest to finding it here in this beautiful place. He always found peace in his family."

It didn't make much sense, was really just a jumble of words along the expected lines, but many cried. The widow's words had gravitas.

The weather was of the best kind late summer had to offer, warm and yellow. The high and clear sky pulled the world below it upward toward heaven. Up soared the flowers, the sea, the moods of the people. A day incongruous with death. Perhaps the train of thought that elevated death into an affirmation of life owed its origin to exactly this kind of weather. She'd have shared that thought with Dick, and he'd have explained why that was wrong or, if he agreed, he'd have narrowed his eyes, clamped his lips, and muttered *Hmm*. Either response was fine. Either would be welcome now.

Death revealed new aspects of people. She'd have thought James's wife Ann would be the most sensitive, but Knox's Jillian was the one who called regularly and made her laugh. Afterward she couldn't even remember what was said, but she felt better, and found herself doing something—working out in the garden or taking a walk. Or even driving over to the library to browse the shelves of new books. Yet now that they were here, Theo's Marina was the more attentive, while Jillian took long solitary walks. Polly had often heard Agnes say that everyone had specialties when it came to others. Some people loved celebration, some loved funerals, some people liked taking care of the ill. Polly had found that to be true. She herself was all three—she showed up all around. A brick, a good egg. She'd skip funerals if that were a choice, but of course it wasn't. You had to go—it wasn't about you.

One evening, at the end of the meal the young scattered. She should have suspected something then, at least Maeve usually lingered, but Polly was drowsy from wine and two weeks of company and having little time alone. The red sky in the west once again inspired a contemplative mood. She glanced over at Leeward and saw Agnes's bedroom light on. Already winding down. Agnes got up earlier and earlier in order to see the full sunrise, starting with the pearly light.

"Mother," James said. "We have something we want to talk to you about."

"You're not about to be serious, are you? Because look at the night." She smiled fondly at him. He was really too easy to tease. It was ridiculous that he called her *Mother.*

"Mom, it's about the houses," Knox said.

"What houses?" she asked placidly.

"Your houses. You have two large houses now all to yourself. That's a lot to take care of."

Marina leaned forward, her hand stretching toward Polly across the table. "For you to manage, that is."

"On your own," Ann said.

"You're alone so much now. What if you fall, and no one finds you for hours, or even days?" James shook his head, lugubrious as if it had already happened.

Polly looked at him. "Fall? I never fall." The hair on the back of her neck prickled.

"Excuse me? The whale watch?" James frowned.

It was an ambush.

"We were thinking you might want to look at Beaumont or Waverly," Ann said. "I could take you for a tour. You could be with your friends, and you're fit enough that you'd still be able to enjoy all the facilities."

Polly began to shake her head at the mention of the fancy old-age homes near her in Haverford. "No. I'm not moving to one of those places. I like our house. My garden." Shadows obscured their features; they were an outcropping of stones arranged around the table. "If it comes to it, I'll have nurses in my house. Or here. I'm planning to stay here longer now that I am not on your father's academic schedule."

James jerked backward, as if he'd been stung. Had he thought she'd just go along with this?

"It doesn't make any sense," she went on. "If I'm here eight months of the year, I'd be paying Waverly a lot of money for nothing," she said.

"Who knows how long you'll be able to be here eight months of the year?" Knox asked. "Things could change on a dime."

"What does that expression even mean?" Marina asked, glancing at Polly with sympathy.

"Just something to think about, Ma," Theo said.

"Theo? You think so, too?" Her plaintive tone made him wince.

"I don't know," he said. "I suppose it never hurts to consider new things."

James rolled his eyes. Knox tapped impatiently on the table. "Mom, Dad would have wanted us to look out for you."

"I think he'd want you to be on my side." Polly looked around the circle, at faces either eager or uncomfortable. "I'm only eighty-one. And who do you think looked after whom in our marriage?"

"You'd still have this in the summer, when we could be here with you," James said, waving his hand to mean Meadowlea. "This garden is extraordinary. You don't need two."

Polly had wondered if she were going to say something while they were here. She'd found ways to avoid it, wanting to keep the peace. As it turned out, it had been a matter of finding the right moment, and this was it. "I want you all to know that Agnes and I have decided to dissolve the Fellowship Point trust so we can give at least the Sank to a land trust. Agnes—we—are concerned about the birds—"

"But you said you weren't going to," James said. His tone, almost a whine, made everyone turn to look at him.

"No," Polly said. "I asked what you thought about it, and you gave me your opinion. I am of a different opinion."

"There would be major tax advantages to doing what you propose," Knox said.

"Easily said by someone not in line to inherit." James crossed his arms sulkily. "Dad did not want that, I know for a fact."

"That's all right. Dad and I didn't agree on everything. But the share in the trust is mine. It is the Hancocks'."

"Yes, and how emasculating that was for him," James muttered. Ann lay a hand on his arm but he twisted away.

"What about the house?" he asked.

"There are options. I'd like to leave the house to all of you, and you can share it or buy each other out or sell it. That's more fair anyway, don't you agree? We are concerned above all with preserving the Sank."

"What will happen to the rest of the houses?"

"Again, options."

"Archie will never agree to this," James said, squeezing himself harder. "When did it happen?"

"We've been talking about it for years," Polly said.

"When were you going to tell us?" Knox asked.

"Soon. Now. Listen, it will all be all right. We will have a proper discussion about it later. I'm tired now, though." She felt dazed with tiredness, suddenly.

"So what peak shall we climb tomorrow, group?" Theo asked, baldly changing the subject.

She didn't tune in to that conversation. Instead, she reeled, quietly. Her boys, with their chosen mates, had been planning this for who knew how long. They'd decided, all of them, to suggest this. They'd considered it, communicated with each other about it, planned how they'd present the idea to her, and when. None of them saw her as the head of the family in Dick's place, but as a dependent, and at any moment an incompetent one. Perhaps already. Had she slipped? Physically, yes, but she was strong and well for her age. Her mind felt fine to her. It was true that grief had made incursions, and she'd had periods of blankness or fog. That could be described as stress, though. Was there more that no one had told her about? She'd check with Agnes.

Younger people always thought they'd never change, and that the diminishing eyesight and hearing loss and groping for names that was typical of everyone who lived long enough wouldn't happen to them. Yet Polly saw these changes all around her, in all her friends who were perfectly fine, just older. She'd have to be more on her toes around the boys. Not relax, after all. She studied them as they talked, and saw their unease, their attempt at being hearty after their failure. They'd been certain of their success in the matter, she realized. They'd taken into account her possible objections, had waited until their visit was nearly over, when fresh good memories had been born, certain that her devotion to them would prevail. Her famous easy personality.

She stood. "Excuse me, please."

"Shall I help you upstairs, Ma?" Theo asked.

He was only being thoughtful, as he always was, but now an honest answer seemed a trap.

"No." She channeled Agnes for a commanding tone. "I'd like the table cleared now."

Everyone jumped up. Chairs scraped back, napkins flapped softly as they were folded and set next to the places. Jillian took charge of the cleanup operation. She hadn't said a word in the discussion. Was she against it?

"Do you want to watch TV, Polly?" Marina asked.

"No, thank you." She'd had enough of voices for one day. "I'm going to take a walk. Don't suggest that it's too dark. I do it all the time, and you're not here to worry then." She went to the front door and let herself outside.

Oh, that was instantly, immediately better. The night air was heavy with moisture and salt. A starry night. She placed her hand firmly on the dew-wet railing. The door opened behind her.

"Ma? Shall we take a stroll?"

Theo looked like her side of the family—like her fair mother, shorter than his siblings. James was the handsomest, but she liked to look at Theo most. When he was young, on a Eurail pass trip, he'd bought a little house near Urbino that he visited once a year, often alone. He'd learned Transcendental Meditation at college and had kept up with the practice ever since, and he felt he could ready his mind for a whole year of stress by means of a silent week in the Italian hills. He'd always told her she should go use the house, or better yet, go with his family. The girls all loved Italy, and Margot planned to get her PhD in Art History, though that was far off. She'd love to show her grandparents around. Dick had never wanted to go, however. No one knew this but Polly—he was afraid of flying, and couldn't conscience the expense of a transatlantic cruise.

"Come now," Theo said. "This fall."

She looked at him. "If you think I have the wherewithal to make a trip to Italy, why do you believe I need to sell my house?"

"Don't be angry with me." He linked arms with her to guide her down the stairs.

"I'm not sure I'm angry. I'm really asking."

241

"It's worth raising, isn't it? You're so social. If you moved to one of those places, you'd have friends all around."

"I see them now. They're three minutes away. I go over to those places. They're not for me."

They stepped onto the gravel and headed out the drive. "Ma, I don't want to go against my brothers."

Polly stopped and turned to search his face. "Is that it?"

He took her hand. "Uh-huh. But I do want you to do what's right for you."

"So you are caught in the middle. I'm sorry for that. Frankly, I wasn't expecting to be put out to pasture, though."

Theo nodded. "No. Too soon for the pasture. What do you think you do want to do?"

He was sincerely curious. He was the child who'd always sat on the kitchen counter to talk to her when he came home from school.

"Oh, sweetie, I'm eighty-one. My options are limited."

"What about Dad's papers? Wasn't he looking for a publisher?"

The question astonished her. How had she forgotten?

"I haven't thought about that at all. He was working on a revision of *The Pacifist's Primer.* I couldn't find his revisions in Haverford, so they must be here."

Of course they were here! He'd been working on the revision the summer before. How had it evaporated from her thoughts? She certainly couldn't reveal that.

"That's a good idea. It might be a good time for it. And did he ever find a library to take his papers?"

"I think he made an arrangement with Penn—he gave some already—but the rest are still here, or in Haverford." Embarrassment traveled her body. She looked up at Theo. "Thank you for reminding me. I have been so out of it and also so busy. It's hard to explain. I do have my work cut out for me, don't I?"

"I think so, Ma." He put an arm around her shoulders and they began to walk again. The ocean lapped at the shoreline, and the buoy bell clanged.

"Well this is certainly a new lease on life! He asked me to help him. We'd just gotten started, really."

"Get going on that. Forget we ever brought this up."

So he was rooting for her. He would help her behind the scenes. "Ah. Excellent point. You might have been a diplomat."

"I live with four women. My whole life is diplomacy."

They'd reached Point Path. Lights shone in the houses across the harbor. She squinted and made them elongate and shimmer.

"I really want you to come to Italy! Please please please? I dare you not to love it."

"I'll see. I'm sure I'd love it." Why hadn't she gone alone? She'd never considered it. Now it seemed nonsensical that she'd held back. It wan't fair to Theo.

"Listen, Ma—the house is yours. Don't do anything you don't want to. James is just being like Dad."

She flinched. "What do you mean?" She had that sense of suspension between life and death at the mention of Dick's name—even as *Dad*.

His eyes widened but not to the point of alarm. It was a minor gaffe. "James doesn't give you enough credit sometimes."

"Oh."

"I'm sorry. That came out wrong."

He was nervous because she was not smiling or reassuring him it was all right. It wasn't that she was holding back from him. She was thinking of Dick. It was true. He didn't give her enough credit sometimes. She had worked her way around that. She was sorry Theo knew it, though.

"I understand, dear Theo. You have never offended me in your whole life."

"Nor you me."

Her eyes swam. "Do you think we should get back? They might be worried."

"Oh, soon. Not yet. Are you good to walk down to the Sank? Let's go listen to the owls."

Polly shrugged. "Why not? What's the worst that could happen?" She poked him in the rib.

"Ouch! You're strong!"

"You're making my point." She lifted her gaze toward the Sank and there was Lydia, about twenty feet ahead down the road. Polly immediately hoped she'd remember to be cautious on the slippery rocks at night. She had on a green Fair Isle sweater and jeans. She waved. Internally, Polly waved back.

"Theo—what do you remember about your sister?"

"Oh, Ma, so much. I think about her all the time."

"You do?"

"Maddie thinks she's all around here."

"She does?"

"Well, you know, Maddie's got powers. She'd like to live among the psychics at Camp Etna."

Lydia picked up a stone and skipped it over the water. Then she faded away.

"On second thought," Polly said. "I really am tired. Do you mind if we go back?"

He took her arm and steered her around in the opposite direction. There was Meadowlea, lit up and floating on the grass like an ocean liner.

"Do *you* want to keep the house?" Polly asked. "If we break the Fellowship agreement and keep the house, you'll have an equal share."

"I'll come to Maine no matter what," he said diplomatically. "It's in my bones."

"Yes. It is."

When they returned to the house, she asked Theo to send Maddie up to her room for a chat. Polly had to know more.

"What is it, Nanny?" Maddie hesitated in the bedroom doorway.

"Come in, come in. Have a seat."

Polly had taken a spot at one end of the chintz chaise, and she gestured Maddie to join her. Maddie flopped down and stretched her long legs out. She pulled her hair forward over one shoulder and fiddled with it. These girls with their easy ways. Polly half wanted to correct her and half envied it.

"How are you doing, dear?" Polly began. It was hard to bring up a ghost.

"I don't want to leave," Maddie said. "I like it here."

"That is good to hear. I do too."

"Are you and Aunt Agnes really going to give it away?"

"We want to be certain the Sank is protected. Beyond that, no decisions have been made."

"Oh." Maddie split an end expertly and dropped the peeled wisp in the scrapbasket. "You should tell Uncle James. He thinks we're losing Meadowlea."

"Always ask me about such things. I'll tell you the truth."

"Okay, Nanny, sounds good."

"Maddie, I have a question for you."

"Uh-huh."

"Your father tells me you sense spirits on the Point."

Maddie dropped her hair and sat up. "What about it?" Wary. Well, Polly didn't blame her. Women had been burned for such perceptions.

"I'd like to hear about it, if you don't mind. Because I sense spirits, too."

"You do?" Maddie was fully engaged now. "Like what?"

"The spirit of a young girl. I see her sometimes. I even talk to her."

"Oh wow, Nanny. That's so cool."

Polly reached out and took her hand. "How about you, dear one?"

Maddie nodded and took a deep breath. "I think mine are people who lived here before."

"Who?"

"I'm not sure. People. Sometimes I think maybe . . . the Red Paint people. The oldest ones who spent summers in the Sank."

Polly nodded and smiled in spite of a searing disappointment. "What are they doing?" she managed.

Maddie shrugged. "Nothing. Kind of. Just living, I guess? I don't know. It's just a feeling I get." Her green eyes shone.

"Living. Yes. I think that is what my spirit is doing, too. Thank you, Maddie. And by the way, you're welcome to stay as long as you want."

When she'd gone back downstairs, Polly spent a long time looking out her window at the night. *Come to me.* She concentrated, calling for Lydia. But the night was still.

On the second-to-last day, she sat her sons down to have another talk about her future.

"I have given thought to your idea about the nursing homes—"

"They're a lot more than that! The apartments are as nice as—" Ann said.

"—and my decision is that I don't want to move now. I want to be in my own places. I am fine. If I have a stroke, you can make decisions then. I want to be buried in the graveyard here, next to Lydia and your father. I hope that goes without saying."

"Whatever you want, Ma," said Theo. He chewed at a cuticle.

"I have written instructions down for my funeral, too. You'll find them in my desk."

"Mother, we didn't mean to upset you, we're trying to do what's right," James said.

"Oh, I know, I know. But I will tell you now for future reference—no one wants to be eighty-one, and at the stage of being a potential liability. No one wants age to be the most important thing about her. You won't like being this old when you are, and have your children explaining to you what is right."

She stood.

"Mother!"

"I'll be down later." She waved at them from behind her back.

Maybe James thought better of saying more, or maybe the others signaled him, because he stopped there. A blessed silence followed, a space for her to hear the still small voice.

She turned and faced them, framed by the doorway. "This is my house, you know. It always was. Your father understood that. I asked his opinion about things, and I shared it with him completely, just as I have shared it with you, but he never forgot for a moment that it was mine. Why have you all forgotten?"

She went up to her bedroom and closed the door.

CHAPTER 14

Maud, Manhattan and Fellowship Point, August 2001

*T*HIS IS ILL-ADVISED, MAUD SILVER, ILL-ADVISED INDEED. SO, SO, ILL-*advised.*

Maud shook her head at her reflection. Her freshly washed hair hung in waves around her bare shoulders. Her skin was flushed from the shower. She started in on the critique—skin too pale for this stage of the summer, eyes too small, blah, blah, blah. All the usual hideous girl stuff. How could she still be doing this to herself? Why had she ever, when it was such a colossal waste of time and didn't help? And why would she even for a moment look at herself through the eyes of Miles Warren, her nemesis? Correction—her past. That was all he was—her past. She'd one hundred percent finished with him nearly three years earlier, when he refused to take responsibility for Clemmie. So what was she doing?

I want him to see what he's missing. No. He either knew that or he didn't.

I'm dressing up for my own self-respect. Okay, except—not entirely true. Self-respect had nothing to do with makeup or a blowout or clothes.

I need a bit of glamor in my life. True, but having a drink with Miles hardly qualified.

I'm curious. Getting closer.

I'm exhausted and can't help it. Yup.

I don't owe him anything, especially not an effort made for his sake. That's more like it.

Cancel! Don't go! That was the best plan. Could she do it?

She put away her hair dryer unused and dressed in her regular summer outfit of a loose dress and flip-flops. Her hair could frizz up as it wished. She removed herself from her mirror and her supplies and headed downstairs.

It was so odd to be alone in the house. She couldn't remember the last time. She didn't know quite what to do with herself. That morning she'd dropped Clemmie off at her grandparents'—her father's parents—in Livingston, where she'd stay while Maud was in Maine. Heidi was in a bed at Payne Whitney again, which was—awful to admit—a relief. Maud could go away without worrying about where she was or if she were safe. She kept expecting to see Heidi lying on the floor or in the fetal position on a sofa. But she was gone. Maud raised her arms overhead and did her usual side bends. Then she stretched her hands out and swung them down to touch her toes. Her stomach was jumpy.

So this is what happens when you are alone for five seconds? You consort with the enemy? How very ill-advised.

At least she got to repeat the phrase *ill-advised*, which she liked very much. She poured a pre-drink drink—okay, so she was going—and went down to the garden to mentally prepare. Not that it was possible to prepare for Miles Warren. He was a living, breathing ambush. The best policy when it came to him was to keep your enemies farther away. Well, she had, until she ran into him the day before at Souen. What was he doing at Souen? He was as far from macrobiotic as anyone could be. A BLT guy, extra mayonnaise and bacon please, just to drive his Jewish parents nuts. Like Moses did with his parents. Moses. Miles. How could Maud have dropped a bigger clue to herself?

There he'd been, talking with another man, noodles hanging languidly from a pair of chopsticks as he diatribed. They'd waved. She paid for her takeout and fled. But when she got home and logged into her AOL account, her stomach flipped. m.warren was top of the list.

> hey you. it's me. amazing to see you. I can't stop thinking about you. I really messed things up. I'm an asshole! but I was at my best around you. so may I be around you again? for a drink? don't answer. don't make up your mind. I'll be at the Rose Bar at the Gramercy tomorrow night at 7. I miss you like crazy. you look really pretty.

Pretty. The oldest trick in the book. In any case he was married and always had been. She flushed with shame when she thought how little she'd considered that when she was in love, but he'd told her his wife didn't understand him and that he'd get a divorce as soon as the kids were old enough. Second-oldest trick in the book. No way she was going to the Rose Bar. He said it himself—he was an asshole.

But the following twenty-four hours had done a number on her resolve. So much weighed on her at the moment. Her father was threatening to move back into Charles Street because his precious daughter Astelle was starting at NYU. Heidi had offered that Astelle move in with her—she and Maud were half sisters, after all—but Moses said they—he and Kimmy, his newer wife—wanted to keep an eye on Astelle, who was wild. What constituted wildness in the other Greenwich, where they lived? Toilet papering the neighborhood on Mischief Night? Playing drinking games? Maud asked him to reconsider, and he said she and Clemmie could stay with them. What about Heidi? That was where the discussion had ended. But she knew that once he'd floated the idea, it was a plan, and that he and Kimmy and the kids would be moving to Charles Street. Moses practiced *maximum follow-through*. It was, he believed, the source of his success.

Maybe it was. She had spotty follow-through and mixed results. She was doing well with Agnes Lee—whom she'd be meeting the following day, at long last—and felt sure she could get a book out of her, but she could feel herself caving to Miles. Maud sipped her Scotch and thought about Clemmie's face and sweaty head and about Heidi's unwashed hair. Something tickled her arm. Automatically she swatted at it. Dammit, it was a ladybug! She picked it up and set it on a blade of grass. *Please be good luck.*

She went back upstairs and pulled her red dress out of her closet. She fiddled with her hair. She painted defiant black lines under her lower lids. Why would she ever consider seeing him again? When they first broke up, her grief had been all-consuming. She'd been miserable and made bargains at every step. *If I do not cry, he will come back. If I see three white cars in a row, he will be on my doorstep. If I picture us together, we will be.* But in spite of all her concentration, Miles stayed away. So Maud changed. Incrementally. She was one person, and then she was another, not entirely different but enough so that she wasn't a person who loved Miles Warren anymore. A doppelganger. A tougher twin. Naming the world, naming the buildings, her old strong self. *Cornice, balustade, plinth.*

It wasn't that she did things so differently that people noticed. She kept the same schedule with the exception of the holes left open by Miles's absence, but they'd become few and far between anyway and it wasn't hard to fill them. Ironically, she was more like Miles post-Miles. More cool-headed and decisive. As a result of her buffered internal rearrangements, the world around her changed. After years—a whole life—of being careful and watchful, of figuring out how to fly under the radar, get the teachers to like her, land the job, keep her mother on track, sustain a relationship with her judgmental, bossy, shallow father, she'd ended up nearly alone, except for Clemmie. Miles had left her for a woman four years younger. She'd gotten too old for him, too demanding, not adoring enough. Her stomach had sprouted a few stretch marks during pregnancy. She was . . . wifelike. And he already had one wife.

No matter what he said about never having loved his wife, he stayed. Maud finally understood—he was never leaving her. Why should he? She took care of him, the house, the children, their social life, their money, their vacations, their reality. Miles had his professorship and his occasional publications. Who would forgo that deal unless there were something truly awful going on at home—and there wasn't. He was bored by her, she told the stories of her day in a childlike manner, *and then and then and then*. They didn't have a sensual connection anymore. Typical married-man-having-an-affair complaints. Now she knew—if a man said he'd never loved his wife, he was reinterpreting his story, and he'd do so again whenever he wanted something new.

Going would be strong, not weak. And she'd have a night out on the town, in a dress. Some fun before rumbling with Agnes Lee. From what she'd gathered, there'd be no call for dresses on Fellowship Point.

Maud was in sore need of some amusement. That was the deciding factor. She was tired. Heidi had been slipping all summer. She came downstairs less and less and was dreamy and forgetful when she did. Once Clemmie had walked up to her and stroked her arm and said, "You *are* real," as if she weren't sure without the physical evidence of touch. A baby's keenness.

When Maud was small, she'd loved Heidi so much that she named her favorite doll Heidi. Maud followed her mother around and watched with amazed rapture how Heidi folded the paper towels for napkins and pressed the seam flat. She watched her iron her white eyelet skirt, spending hours working between the cutouts until the material was crisp and flawless. Heidi smelled like fresh mineral-rich water and sunny skin. She wore bells around her ankles and put bells around Maud's and taught her to pretend they were a herd of goats prancing gracefully down Waverly. She was tough, and cool, and fun when she was well.

Yet Heidi also got in bed sometimes and didn't get up. Maud sat on her bed and read to her, inventing before she knew what the words were, and then later, once she learned phonetics, reading books way above her level of comprehension. She read *Housekeeping*, which Heidi loved because the odd people were the good people; *The Handmaid's Tale*, which she understood was terrifying even if the details were fuzzy; *Giovanni's Room*, which made her sigh, because people were so stubborn; *The Professor's House*, which she loved for the spooky dress form and Tom's trip to the old Southwest; and *Anywhere But Here*, which was Maud's favorite, because it starred a girl. All of this helped until it didn't. When Heidi was getting depressed, she succumbed to a series of thoughts and images, the same every time, that had to do with children and animals out alone at night in the snow. Panicked and freezing, they'd run back and forth, calling for help without anyone hearing them. Heidi pictured this in different places all around the world, even in hot countries. In the logic of depression there was snow in the desert, too.

She'd told Maud about this when Maud was five. They walked over to the river and sat on a pier looking across at New Jersey and down into the water.

"I have to tell you something," Heidi said. "A few things, actually."

Heidi had always talked to Maud as if they were equals.

"First thing is, Moses is going to go live in another place."

"Where?" Maud asked. She wasn't upset yet.

"Close enough that we'll still see him. You will."

A couple they knew, two burly guys, stopped to chat. Then the talk resumed. Maud had had time to think about it. "Why is he moving to another place?"

"Because he wants to live with another person."

"Not us?"

"Not me. He isn't moving away from you. He is tired of how sad I am. This other lady isn't sad."

"You're not sad." Maud knew that wasn't true, but she had to defend Heidi.

Heidi kissed her where her hairline met her forehead, as she always did. "You will have to be a detective now," Heidi said. "If I start talking about dogs who are cold or children who are hungry or frogs on a hot road, you need to call Moses. Then I'll go away for a rest and come back."

"I'll go with you."

"We'll see. You could also stay with Moses."

Maud shook her head. But she had ended up doing so. Many times. Kimmy was an idiot, but all right. Maud's half siblings were innocent children, and they had the sense to think Maud was cool.

She still called her father when Heidi had an episode, but now she got in touch after Heidi was in the hospital, all arrangements set. She'd made the call the week before to Payne Whitney, where Heidi was well known. Heidi had tried to kill herself several times. She couldn't help it. Those incidents were frightening and horrific, and Maud and Heidi both wanted to get her to the hospital before Maud had to cope with a real emergency. Maud felt awful leaving her there, but Heidi knew there was no choice and always thanked Maud for helping. In turn, Maud thanked Moses for handling the insurance and picking up the tab. She loved Moses while being aware of his self-ishness. He had primed her for a man like Miles. Moses, Miles. Denial is a river, and she had floated down it for a long time. No more.

She called Clemmie at her grandparents' to say good night, and then she was free.

She'd been to the Rose Bar with her father a few times, one of those old-fashioned places at the heart of New York that Moses thought existed for men like him. Dark wood, plush banquettes, people murmuring worldly secrets. Miles was more a White Horse Tavern guy. What was he trying to prove?

She arrived first and had the liberty to acclimate alone. But not for long. Shortly a pair of hands covered her eyes from behind. "Boo!" Ha ha. Did he think that was cute? Was he trying to be cute?

She spun around and held out her hand for a shake. "Hello, Miles."

"So formal? You know me."

"Do I?" Half-flirting, half-warning.

He had on a pink shirt. He knew she loved pink shirts, on men, women, dogs—any living thing. But especially on him. As their relationship deteriorated, he would not wear the pink shirt for her. When she asked, he'd say it was at the dry cleaner's, or that he threw it out. Now it was back. Hmm.

He asked for a booth and got one. Maud ordered a Manhattan and he gave her a look that said—*That's interesting*. She returned with a look that said—*I'm full of surprises, your loss*. He ordered a Manhattan, too, and he raised his glass to—old friends.

She clinked and looked him in the eye so as not to garner bad luck, but she said, "You were never my friend."

"No. I guess I wasn't. I was too attracted to you to feel friendly." He shrugged and wiggled his eyebrows, pleased with his inverted compliment.

"There's no conflict that I know of between attraction and friendship. I was friendly to you. For example, I never told your wife about us, not even when I was pregnant."

She'd never talked like this to him. She'd always gone along with his requirements for controlling the narrative. His eyes widened.

"Oh good, good. No, she wouldn't like that I got you pregnant." He blushed. Giggled!

"No, I suppose not. I have two things to say to that. A, good for her, I should hope not. And B, you did not 'get' me pregnant. The rubber broke, or so you said, which was unfortunate, and even more so was the fact that your sperm fertilized one of my eggs. That was not a 'get' for you. It was an accident."

"You're in a mood," he said. He was surprised and hurt. Did he think time healed all wounds? Or that she'd been waiting patiently and quietly like a girl in a song for just this moment?

"Why would that be, Miles? It couldn't be because when I told you I was pregnant you immediately said you wanted nothing to do with it, nor could it be because you dumped me for a newer model. How could I be mad at you?"

"Is that why you came tonight, looking as you do? I mean, a red dress? You made an effort."

Maud nodded. He wasn't stupid. She had to remember that part. "Honestly? I don't know why I came, but I'm sure the decision didn't come from one of my better sides."

"I know why. You miss me and you want to know if I miss you. I do. In fact, I made a mistake."

"No shit, Sherlock."

He wagged his finger at her. "Ha! Maud Silver said shit. I thought you had a policy against swearing, especially the word *shit*."

Maud did have that policy, and she found it distasteful to hear the word spoken, but she looked at him steadily. "I've changed."

"Have you? How?"

"Well, most importantly, I'm a mother now. I have a three-year-old daughter named Clemence. Actually, I'm a single mother, which is mothering at a whole different level. Would you like to hear about my child? We have been sitting here for twenty minutes and you haven't mentioned her. Not once." She pressed her cold drink to her wrist. Cutlery clinked and ice rattled in glasses. A woman laughed. A waiter bent at the waist.

"I'm not sure I want to know," he said, "unless we are going to be in each other's lives again. Is there any chance of that? I'd like it, but you seem incredibly hostile. You were nicer in Souen yesterday. I don't understand what's going on now. You're sending mixed messages looking so pretty but being so mean." He drummed his fingers on the table, but when he saw her notice, he pulled them into his lap.

Maud slipped her feet out of her flats and rubbed them together, her old habit that Heidi said was like a cricket. She had an embarrassingly Pavlovian response to being told she was pretty and squelched it. She knew better.

"Miles, I have no business being here, so I'm going to leave."

He wrapped his hand around her wrist. He tipped his head and he looked at her in the way he had of making the rest of the world vanish, the look that won him teaching awards and jobs and women. "Let's get a room upstairs."

"What?"

"Isn't that why you came?"

Dammit, it was. How could she not have been aware of it, and allowed herself to think she was curious or any of the several other excuses she'd made? It was obvious—why else? It was what they'd had. She hadn't forgotten what it was like to be with him, how the slightest touch had made her shudder. In the beginning she'd been so constantly ablaze she could barely think or breathe. They'd never done anything acrobatic or pornographic—they hadn't needed any embellishments. It had always and only been about an elemental desire, and the consummation was usually quick. Then they lay in bed and talked until the desire overcame them again. He said it was like being young. She was young.

Not anymore. She was old, careworn, responsible. She pictured how she'd feel tomorrow if she went upstairs now. She had to get on a plane to Maine. Agnes Lee would be waiting for her. All that, with a soreness between her legs and all because . . . because she missed her mother.

"Miles, this was a mistake. I'm going to go now, and we won't speak again. If we run into each other, let's not say hello. And don't worry about Clemence. To be honest, I'm not even sure you are the biological father." This was a lie, a complete lie, but she would have to expiate this violation of her moral code in some other part of her life.

He gaped at her and she saw his rage begin to swirl. A visceral panic gripped her in response. She jumped up.

"I've already paid for this drink many times over," she said. "You can pick up the tab."

She rushed away so she wouldn't hear his words. The sun had not yet set, but the evening cool was lowering onto the flowers in Gramercy Park, and the windowpanes that had glared at passersby only a few hours earlier were now a burnished dignified topaz. Glorious evening! It gave her strength. For all Maud had hated Miles and worked on herself to believe she'd deserved more, she wasn't sure she'd really known that until now. Deserved wasn't quite the right word, however. She was equal to more than what Miles offered. Capable of a real love. She'd wait for that, if it ever came. In the meantime, she'd go see a woman about a book.

On the way to Fellowship Point from the airport, the M girls—"See like all our names begin with M and we're sisters, our grandparents call us the M girls, it's okay if you do, too"—gave Maud a scenic tour, taught her the best way to eat a lobster—"You won't get a drop of meat at Agnes's"—and prepared her for what to expect. Agnes sounded fearsome indeed, but at the end of every story came a declaration that she was actually really nice. Which was it? The sufferno-fools warrior who terrorized every flabby-minded, trumped-up, entitled dumbass east of the Pecos? Or an intelligent, humorous great-aunt type who quietly helped dozens? "It depends if she likes you," the girls said.

That wasn't reassuring.

They turned into the grass driveway of Leeward Cottage. An old woman stood in the doorway, looking cross.

"Is that Agnes?" Maud asked. The woman looked different than the picture of Agnes Lee that smiled from the back of every *When Nan* book, but authors often looked different than their pictures. The girls waved and the old woman frowned. Maud thanked them and they made her promise to come over soon and she thanked them again and they gunned it out of there. The old woman shook her fist at them, her expression full of disgust. Maud put a smile on her face. What had she been thinking? There was no chance she'd change this person's mind about writing a memoir. She could be home with Clemmie. She could have skipped the whole humiliating scene with Miles, too.

She always made mistakes when Heidi went to the hospital.

"Agnes Lee, I presume?" Maud held out her hand.

"You presume wrong. Agnes is inside."

Maud dropped her hand—the woman had made no move to take it. "Oh! I apologize. I am Maud Silver and I am expected." She hoped.

"I know who you are. Come in."

Maud focused on each step of the way and memorized the layout of the lower floor as best she could at the end of a long, tiring trip. If she lay down now, she was likely to sleep through until morning. But it was only three o'clock, and that would make an odd first impression. Instead, she took deep, reviving breaths.

Sylvie stopped abruptly and Maud nearly mowed her down.

"Agnes?" Sylvie called.

"In here!"

"Should she put her things upstairs first?"

"Don't shout at me from Antarctica!"

Sylvie turned to Maud. "Would you like to put your things up-stairs?"

Maud understood the question as a euphemism for using the bathroom, brushing her hair, generally cleaning up. "Yes, thank you."

"She's going to put her things upstairs first," Sylvie called, hands cupped around her mouth. She shook her head. "Old bird is get-ting deaf. Come, I'll show you."

Maud saw the woman clench her jaw at the prospect of the climb. "Please, I'll find it. And I'm sorry, I missed your name?"

"Sylvie Godreau. Got it?"

Maud nodded. Sylvie gave directions that Maud repeated to her-self until she found it—she doubted she could remember anything. When she walked in, she nearly squealed. It was a room from her fantasies. Old-fashioned, in a good, simple way. Creamy yellow walls and a very thin yellow bedspread probably a hundred years old. A framed set of drawings of flowers on the walls. Old furniture painted white. The bed pulled at her, so she laid out her clothes all over it, no room to lie down. Her desk faced the sea. She organized her papers and pens and touched the roses. To live in a room like this would make a person feel she deserved to be treated fairly, and if she weren't, at least she had a refuge. Heidi had tried to create such a room for Maud, but Heidi's wounded spirit had marked the space and Maud could always sense her mother's state of mind. She'd made a simple pretty room for Clemmie and did her best to keep the world out of it. Clemmie would have a room of her own.

A surge of fresh energy and a feeling of eminent capability led her to push the sash as high as it would go. The specter of Agnes waiting for her downstairs didn't interfere with her sense of free-dom. On the contrary, she looked forward to getting to know her. Her big project, her plan for changing her life, was underway.

She found a bathroom, peed, and splashed water on her face. She brushed her teeth and hair and went back to her room to change into chinos and a striped shirt. By then fifteen minutes had passed. Any longer before going down and she might try Agnes's patience.

Agnes stood by a table in the glass room, looking through a pile of books. Though she was bent over, her elegance made Maud stand up straighter.

"Knock, knock," Maud said. "Hello?"

Agnes stiffly straightened up. "Welcome to Leeward Cottage."

"Thank you for having me."

Maud held out her hand and they shook. Agnes gave Maud a penetrating look—no surprise there.

"I can't even remember the last time I had a houseguest. How did you manage to convince me to let you come?"

As Agnes spoke, Maud collected a swift impression. What was it about her? She wasn't youthful, she was too old for that to be said of her. Her neck was curled forward, and some of her knuckles were swollen and knobby. She wore jeans and gleaming-white Keds. Who polished sneakers? She was a force beyond the details that comprised her. Dignified. A personage.

"You wanted me to come to discuss *Agnes When*. You want it to work as much as I do."

"It does work. I wanted you to come to impress that on you once and for all. Come sit down."

Agnes led them to two wicker chairs at a table facing outside. The seats were low, the toile cushions thin and threadbare. Maud had read about the penurious affectations of certain of the rich, Philadelphians and Quakers being ardent practitioners of the style, and it gave her a small thrill to see such affectations in the wild.

Sylvie appeared and Maud asked for coffee.

"That's youth! Coffee in the afternoon. Good for you," Agnes said. "I'll have an early start on my white, in honor of your arrival."

Maud gazed down toward what she recognized as the Sank. From Agnes's solarium it looked like an area of dark woods. And that must be Meadowlea, where the M girls were staying. Polly's house. These people were so lucky. Maybe when her father kicked her and Heidi and Clemmie out, they could move here. As if.

In the meantime, she'd better give Agnes her money's worth. "The book does work, yes, but not well enough for the purpose. I'm not the only one who will feel you're hiding something. The whole point is to reveal who you are. But we've had this argument before. The question now is, how do we advance the conversation?"

Agnes drummed her fingers on the arms of her chair. "You have a lot of energy for someone who just got off a plane."

"This has been at the top of my mind for months now."

"Look down there," Agnes said. "That's what we call the Sank, short for Sanctuary. Lots of birds' nests, moss, et cetera. Take a walk down there while you're here, if you'd like."

Maud peered down the road toward the woods. "Is it safe?" Immediately she regretted asking. The last thing she wanted was for Agnes to think she was easily scared or weak. "I mean, the footing," she added.

Sylvie returned with a tray and set coffee, wine, and snacks on a table. "Let's ask Sylvie. Sylvie, is the Sank safe?"

"Not for interlopers. She'll shoot an interloper." Sylvie nodded toward Agnes.

"Has she?"

"Hasn't had to. Everyone knows about her. I hope you do, too, Ms. Silver." She emphasized the zee sound. Maud had the feeling she'd been made fun of.

"Please call me Maud."

"Thank you, Sylvie. We'll eat at six-thirty," Agnes said.

Sylvie left.

"She's scary."

Agnes snorted. "She's been with me for a long time." She pointed out the window. "That's the bay. The other side is the ocean, although also a bay but called a harbor. My great-grandfather named it Bay Lee, which I suppose he thought was funny."

Agnes reached for a handful of Goldfish.

"It's beautiful," Maud said. She took a Pepperidge Farm cookie.

"It is. We are working now on preserving it forever. I'm hoping to leave it to a land trust."

"Are you going to move?"

"I have no plans for that. This is for the future. My father would want me to preserve it before I kick the bucket."

"I know something about your father. I looked him up. He sounds like he was an enlightened person. A fair-minded businessman."

"That's right," Agnes said. "He believed in helping the people who worked for the company to rise in the world. That was a strain of thought coming down through the line from my great-grandfather, who founded this Fellowship. The other strain was more conventional capitalists—or so I see it—who kept their hearts and minds on profit. My cousin Archie is from that strain. It's a real difference of approach, and it caused a rift in the company that resulted in my father retiring early. He was sorry about what had happened, but he had plenty to do without going to an office."

"He loved it here." Maud could feel it.

Agnes nodded.

"Your fans would like to hear more about him in the book."

"You're persistent, you know that?"

"Sometimes." She thought of running out on Miles the night before. She supposed that could be interpreted as persistence in maintaining her own integrity and not succumbing to his fleeting desires anymore. She was persistent about trying to help Heidi, and about Clemmie's well-being. "I guess I am."

"What if I want to maintain privacy about certain things? Certainly that's my right. Isn't there a difference between a memoir and a tell-all, or whatever it's called?"

"I think that's what I'm here to figure out with you. What more you could comfortably tell that would give the reader a clearer sense of how you came to write the *When Nan* books. It's a lot to ask readers to surmise how you became a writer just from beautiful descriptions of Fellowship Point. They want specifics and—"

Agnes pushed her knuckles against the chair and, with effort, stood. "Yes, yes. So you've said. Come. Let me show you around before dinner. And let's shelve this conversation until tomorrow. I'm tired by this time of day."

Maud was sorry she'd pushed. "Of course. I would love to see everything. Especially the Sank."

"Stay here, Maisie!"

The cat sat back on her haunches and looked up at Agnes placidly. Agnes gave Maisie an exaggerated blink. Maisie blinked back. They repeated the routine three times.

Agnes got a walking stick and repeated to Sylvie they'd eat at six-thirty but Maisie could have her supper now. The screen door slapped behind them, and there they were, in a kind of heaven. "This is Point Path. It runs the length of Fellowship Point. We'll go this way today, but you can walk by the water, too. The water is frigid and the rocks are slippery, but it's always a balm to be so close to the sea. Oh look—there's Polly. Shall we invite her to join?"

"Sure." Maud was torn—she'd just met Agnes, but she didn't want to be disagreeable. When she saw Polly's kind and open expression, though, it occurred to her she might be an ally.

They waited until Polly caught up and fell into step.

"Your reputation precedes you," Polly said. "I hear you are a taskmaster." Her eyes shone with a warm teasing. Maud found her lovely right away.

"I'm trying to help, I think."

"But you must push this old bird! She's very stubborn. She scares everybody."

"She does?"

"Oh yes. Even me, and I know how tenderhearted she really is."

"I'm not deaf yet," Agnes said. Polly raised her eyebrows at Maud, and Maud in turn felt a rush of elation. They were letting her in.

They passed into the woods and the temperature dropped. Light filtered through the trees, making a case for celestial magnificence.

"But don't let her scare you," Polly went on. "She was very close to her father, you know. I have found that girls who have that kind of backing are often fierce."

"That's interesting. What about the backing of mothers?" Maud asked. Heidi had backed her as well as she was able.

Agnes sighed. "I wouldn't know about that."

Maud's elation ebbed. Her scalp prickled. She'd said something wrong, but she didn't know what.

Agnes put her arm out and a finger to her lips. "Shh—do you hear that? That's an owl," she said quietly.

"I didn't hear it," Maud said. She knew nothing about being in the woods.

They all stopped and listened. Shortly Maud heard a sound like air blown through a pipe.

"Is that it?" she whispered.

Agnes and Polly nodded. They smiled at each other. They'd had a long life of such surprises and sharings.

"Many live here. They're predators, like the eagles, but they leave each other alone in the Sank."

"I'm so glad to see this place," Maud whispered. "It's just as you described it. Will we see the eagles?"

"Maybe," Agnes said.

They walked deeper into the woods. The mossy forest floor, the dun-colored needles, the expressive tree bark, this slowed-down world—Maud wished Heidi and Clemmie were here to see it. She hadn't shown Clemmie enough of the natural world. She made a vow to change that. And Heidi loved Maine. She'd only been here once, for her honeymoon, but Maud had grown up on the *When Nan* books, supplemented by Heidi's stories of pine-needle paths through the woods and rocky beaches. One year when she was old enough to order a present, she got Heidi a subscription to *Down East*, and had been renewing it ever since. Heidi always exclaimed when it arrived, and turned every page slowly. And she read the *When Nan* books to Clemmie from the moment she came home from the hospital.

Agnes planted her walking stick and pulled herself forward while Polly stepped nimbly over the tree roots. Maud thanked her for the M girls coming to pick her up, and Polly explained all her children and grandchildren. Maud's eyes pricked as they always did when she heard stories of big families. She had watched *The Sound of Music* many times, imagining she was Brigitta.

They walked across the Sank to a clearing on the edge of a gently sloping cliff. "Notice anything?" Polly asked.

Maud looked around. It was a ludicrous question—there was so much to notice. The shimmer off the sea made her wonder if she was seeing islands or optical illusions. If she lived here, she'd stare at the ocean all day.

"Be still. Wait."

Maud nodded. After a few moments her feet became warm, and the heat traveled up her body. Should she mention it, or was she imagining this, too? The weariness of travel was catching up with her.

"This was an Abenaki campsite, and possibly even older," Agnes said. "The Native people rode their canoes down the river and came here for the summer."

"Wow."

"Wow is right," Agnes replied. "We have artifacts we collected here, well cared for if I do say so. Polly and I once came upon a group of boys who were digging around and hurling things out of the hole. We chased them away."

"How old were you?"

"Fourteen," Polly said. "Agnes was the brave one. I thought one of the boys was cute."

Maud laughed. "Agnes was never boy crazy?"

"No, that madness never gripped her."

"She got off easy," Maud said. "Where are the Abenaki now?"

Agnes took over. "They don't exist under that name anymore. There are a number of people—groups—in Maine that are all together called the Wabanaki. But the people that came here for the summer before we did—they are gone."

"That's sad," Maud said.

"Yes," Agnes said. "By the look of the things they left behind, though, it was great while it lasted. Okay, let's go. I need my tipple."

They turned around and headed back the way they'd come, which Maud was to learn was the quick way. Everything looked radically different going in the opposite direction. The sun filtered through the trees now, making magic. Clemmie really should be here!

"Shh! Look." Polly pointed to the right and upward. At first Maud focused into the distance, then realized the ten-foot-high mass in her way was the nest itself, nearly close enough to touch. It sat heavily in the crook of a tree, supported on each of four sides by a branch. There was a messiness about it, as if the eagles had better things to think about than where they lived. Two white heads bobbed out and jerked around.

"They were born late," Agnes said. "Eagles hatch in the spring."

"There are more permanent nests in here as well," Polly said, peering up.

"All golden eagles?"

"Bald eagles, too. This is what Agnes's great-grandfather sought to preserve when he set up the Fellowship. A safe habitat for all."

"And it belongs to the two of you now?"

"In a sense, yes. And my cousin Archie," Agnes said. "It's an association."

"We don't think of it as ownership," Polly explained, "more as a kind of stewardship. I must say ownership sits lightly on my shoulders. I can't fully grasp that this land is mine."

"Women weren't allowed to own land until recently," Maud said. "Only a hundred years or so."

Agnes gave her a pleasantly surprised look. "That's exactly right. We have less history of thinking of ourselves as landowners," Agnes said.

"Look!" Maud pointed up at a great flurry overhead. An eagle's wings whapped the air, stirring a breeze. She turned in a circle to see it best. "How glorious!"

"I'm here to protect that gloriousness," Agnes said. "If it's the last thing I do."

"As God is your witness?" Polly teased.

"To hell with Scarlett O'Hara, and to hell with God," Agnes said. "As usual, it's all up to me."

Maud and Polly laughed.

They never discussed what they were going to do, or how they were going to go about doing it. They simply settled into a routine, as if they'd lived together forever and had their ways. Maud had her breakfast in the solarium—"the glass room"—and reread Agnes's manuscript stretched out on a chaise, picking out points to discuss. She explored the cabinets full of artifacts from the Sank, and studied the maps hung on the walls that showed all the scattered islands she'd thought she might be imagining the first time she saw them. She hadn't been—there were lots. She poured through the books left out on the tables, about the flora and fauna, and the family notebooks of lists detailing what had been spotted where and when. All of it fascinated her even beyond what might appear in the memoir if she had her way. She loved it here. Sometimes she had the sense that she could simply not go home and live here forever without looking back. That if she never saw New York again she wouldn't mind. It was this place—a match for something she hadn't known she was missing. She hoped she'd discover what that was.

Then suddenly she'd think of Clemmie, and her whole fantasy would implode.

Agnes stayed upstairs in her study, writing. At the end of the morning she came down, they ate, then took a walk around the Point. Agnes loved wind, and Maud found she did, too. Nor could she get enough of watching the ocean shift in patterns that repeated on a large scale but were unique close up. On their return they had strong cups of coffee and went to work, or played tug-of-war, depending how you looked at it.

Agnes's many years mostly alone hadn't erased her early social upbringing. She was an excellent conversationalist, and Maud was quite likely to find herself back up in her room with every question she'd meant to ask in that session still unspoken. She was so sure, so clear, yet Agnes got the better of her again and again, with obfuscations hard to catch due to her seeming candor. Agnes made a good show of examining the minutiae of her feelings with disarming frankness and remembered breathtaking details of the distant past. The children of Fellowship Point came even larger to life for Maud. Still, she wanted more for the book.

"Have I told you about my career as a child playwright?" Agnes asked one afternoon.

"You know you haven't." Maud knew enough by then to know Agnes's mind never faltered for even a second, she showed no mental signs of old age, and therefore she kept a perfect running record of her conversations.

"I suppose they were my first creative writings. Morality plays of a sort. I had a sense of the character flaws of my siblings and friends, or what could use improvement, and I wrote roles for them so they would act differently than they did in life."

"That was manipulative of you." They had a teasing tone available as part of their exchanges. "How old were you?"

"I started at eight. My play was about the day before the first Thanksgiving. The girls got to be the Indians, and the boys were the colonists. Both sides talked about what to expect."

"Really? You wrote that at eight?"

"You are imagining more nuance than it had. The drama left much to be desired. I didn't write things down at that point but 'directed'— more like bossed around—my cast with great zest. They weren't as impressed with me as I was with myself. The one thing that came out of it and that got me hooked was that I assigned Elspeth to play a mean person and I assigned Teddy Hancock to play a shy person. Their character's goals and actions were alien to their natures, and they were forced to take on another point of view. That was fascinating, and it shaped my ideas about how fictional characters worked."

"You're saying that at age eight you found their acting struggles fascinating?"

Agnes shrugged.

"It's a good story anyway. Will you write about that?"

"Maybe. Maybe not."

And so forth. Up, down, back, around, sparring and circling. After two hours of this Agnes went back up to her room, for unspecified activities. Maud went out then, usually, and walked around exploring by herself.

Sometimes on her way back from her walks she stopped in at Meadowlea for an iced tea and met more of the family. The M girls could chatter and giggle forever, it seemed, without growing tired of each other. Being here, Maud could see Agnes's point about writing a memoir evocative of the place rather than one focused on gossip about the denizens. She was getting the sense of the whole.

One afternoon when Maud got back from her walk Agnes was waiting at the door.

"Your father called. He wants you to be assured that it's not an emergency but to please call him back." Agnes touched Maud's arm lightly and guided her to the phone in the library. She shut the door and left Maud alone.

Maud was nauseous and terrified. Why would he call? She dialed him back with trembling fingers and a throbbing chest.

"Dad! What's going on? It's Clemmie, isn't it?"

"No, Clemmie is fine. I told that to your author, but she didn't seem to understand."

No, she wouldn't. Maud hadn't told her she had a daughter.

"It's Heidi. She had to be put in restraints." Moses sounded tired. "Why?"

"She acted out, whatever that means. But she sank into a deeper depression, and now they want to do ECT."

"I hope you said no." Maud couldn't bear that Heidi was in restraints.

"Yes, I know how you feel, and I said no, for now. But I think we should consider it."

Maud rarely felt sympathy for him, but now that she was older it was sinking in what it must have been like to have Heidi as a mate. At what point had she stopped being able to be a partner to him?

"I'll come back." Maud looked around, as if for a means of transportation.

"Yes, that's a good idea," he said. "I'm really busy right now."

"You added me to her health care proxy, didn't you?"

"I'll double-check." Meaning he hadn't.

"You know she got depressed when you said you're going to take the house away from us." Lucky he was five hundred miles away. She'd like to punch him.

"So you've said. She always knew it wasn't a permanent arrangement. I'll pay for another place."

"Go to hell, in the meantime."

"Got it. Let me know when your flight gets in and I'll book a car."

Maud brushed her cheeks dry and finger-combed her hair, then found Agnes in the glass room.

"It concerns my mother," Maud said. She flopped into a wicker chair by the chaise where Agnes lay regally.

"He said another name I didn't recognize," Agnes said.

"Clemmie. My daughter."

Agnes took it in. "How old?"

"Three."

"Her father?"

"AWOL."

"So you really are holding up the sky. And your mother?"

"They want to give her electroshock. I have to go home to make sure that doesn't happen."

"All right," Agnes said. "We can continue by mail."

Maud appreciated how low-key she was about all this.

"Do you think I can fly out tonight?"

Agnes shook her head. "Tomorrow would be the soonest."

Maud sighed. The few days she'd been on Fellowship Point seemed like her real life. She was eager to see Clemmie, but otherwise had no desire to leave. She was glad to be forced to have a little more time. "I guess I have to wait, then."

"Let's have a drink."

Maud moved to stand, but Agnes raised her hand, *stop.* "You stay here. Wine or whiskey?"

"I don't know much about whiskey."

"I have some tasty Scotch. Not like a bog."

"Thank you," Maud said. *Why doesn't Heidi want to live?*

In that way she knew what her mother had done in the hospital.

"Here's your drink."

Maud took a big gulp and sneezed. Agnes smiled.

"You'll get used to it. It's a medicine you can have in your cabinet for life."

Maud set the glass down. "My mother tried to kill herself."

Agnes frowned.

"My father didn't say so, but he wouldn't tell me that. He has no sense of what's appropriate to share with a child." She gave a rueful laugh. "When he left us, he told me his sexual urges were too strong to be with one woman. I was five."

"Good riddance."

"Yes. It hurt my mother, though. Made her permanently wobbly, though when she's good you don't want to be with anyone else. I hate to go. The book—I can taste it," Maud said. "Are you going to give an inch?"

"I don't foresee that."

"Me neither. So why did I even come?"

"You wanted to see with your own eyes what a cussed old woman looks like. Now you know." Agnes raised her arms as high as they'd go to portray her glory. "I'm a vision of your own future, Maud Silver."

"Kill me now," Maud said. Then she heard herself, and swiftly covered her mouth with her hand.

"It's all right," Agnes said. "Slip of the tongue. Tell me about your mother."

Maud sighed. "That's kind. But I don't want to impose. I'm here to listen to you."

"Nevertheless. I'd like to hear."

"The only people who ever want to hear about my mother are her doctors, but they only want to hear symptoms. Or maybe that's all there is. I don't really know that much. She never talks about her past."

Agnes nodded. "No wonder you're intent on getting mine out of me."

Maud was taken aback by this and couldn't respond. Agnes was insightful, or shrewd, she wasn't sure which.

"Why do you think she's depressed?" Agnes asked, changing the emphasis.

"It's not entirely clear, but I know her parents were killed in a car accident with Heidi in the backseat, asleep. She was four. Afterward she went to live out in the country near Tallahassee with an aunt, her father's sister. Aunt Sally. She was an evangelical, but in more of a cult than a church."

"Awful. Not much worse than a cult in rural Florida. Snake handlers, no doubt."

"She left when she was sixteen and got a scholarship to Columbia and met Dad. She had me when she was still a teenager."

"Tell me, what do you think of her doctors?"

"They seem fine. I don't know what's possible for someone like her."

"I used to be on the board of Friends Hospital in Philadelphia. Would you be willing to take her there to be examined? For a second opinion? It's an excellent place. Read up on it. It was way ahead of any other hospital in America on humane methods of treatment and never succumbed to the horrible ideas that came into vogue."

"That sounds like a good idea. Thank you."

"I'm going to make a fire, and then I want to hear about your child," Agnes said. "Tricky of you not to mention her." She pushed herself up and crossed to the fireplace.

"Okay. I think I better make a plane reservation first." Her head was full of tears she needed to get out, but she didn't want to sob in front of Agnes.

"Go right ahead."

Maud trudged upstairs and went into her hallowed room, where she collaped on the bed. She pressed her face into the pillow and screamed. Screamed and screamed. It probably lasted thirty seconds, but she traveled through time being so enraged. She hated everyone! The world. It was so unfair. Frying Heidi's brains? No. She hoped Moses could be trusted, but she'd never counted on that before.

Nor had she taken Heidi for a second opinion. She still had a foot in the world of dependence, of going along with decisions that were made when she was young. But she was twenty-seven years old. So many people had died at that age—Jimi Hendrix, Jim Morrison, Janis Joplin, and Kurt Cobain, deaths that had bruised the heart. Maud couldn't die, because she had a child. And she had Heidi. So she had better grow up and make a plan.

She washed her face and went back downstairs into the den and called the airline. When she rejoined Agnes the fire had caught and was popping. Plates of food sat on the bench in front of the sofa. Maud sank into the cushions.

"Did you ever want children?"

She looked at Agnes, who could not have looked more maternal than she did at that moment, handing Maud a blanket and pushing the plate closer.

"I have Nan," she said. "She has been a very satisfactory daughter."

Maud picked up the plate. "You put her to work at a young age. I don't know about that."

Agnes threw back her head and laughed. Maud would take this laughter back to New York with her. The trip had been productive after all. It produced a new friendship.

CHAPTER 15

Agnes, Leeward Cottage, September 2001

AGNES GOT UP AROUND THREE A.M., THE HOUR OF THE WOLF, and spent a few hours fooling with a scene about the past, inspired by her conversations with Maud. It felt good to write, even if the pages would go in a drawer. Maud hadn't changed her mind—though it might not be awful to write the book Maud wanted to publish without publishing it. A potentially posthumous book, or one that could be burned with no loss to a soul. Maybe it was something that would engage her if she couldn't find her novel. She deeply missed being immersed in a book. She wrote with focus, oblivious to the passage of time. Toward eight thirty, she was interrupted by Sylvie whacking a rug with a broom below her window. Agnes lifted the screen and popped her head out.

"Do you have to do that here?"

Sylvie looked up. "She lives!"

Ah. Sylvie had been worried. "I'll be right down for breakfast."

Agnes looked out at the sea and the quiet meadow. Everyone who'd been on the Point that summer was gone except for Polly. Now for the golden days. The sky was so blue it looked chewy. She took five deep breaths, dressed, and went down.

She walked into the kitchen, where Sylvie was clomping around. "I'm going to eat in the den today, Sylvie."

"Why?"

"I'm as surpised as you are. Let's call it inspiration."

"I'll bring a tray in."

"If you call me, I'll come get it."

"Humph!"

"All right. Thank you." No doubt they would wrangle forever about Sylvie's notions of service and Agnes's need for far less of it.

Agnes walked across the first floor toward the den. On the way she glanced into the glass room and smiled at the light spilling onto the floor. She was rarely downstairs at this time of day and didn't realize it was so sunny. Perhaps she should have eaten in here, but she'd already said the den. To her surprise, it was also light-filled. She glanced at the bookshelves, all the old tomes on history, gardening, philosophy, Maine, Native Americans, Quaker writings. She didn't feel like reading just yet; impulsively, she turned on the TV, and because she was still thinking about her scene, she didn't turn the volume up. She rarely watched TV, but sometimes liked it as background company. It wasn't much to look at, either—an old black-and-white Motorola, bought to replace the TV—the first in the house—she'd gotten for her father when he was sick. She settled with her legs bent to the side on the sofa, Keds on, all bad behaviors. What perverse god had made being bad so enjoyable? But she didn't believe in any god. The reason she gave herself was that she was allowed to do whatever she wanted because she'd had cancer. *Play the cancer card, Agnes!* It was an ace and trumped everything.

Sylvie nodded approvingly when she came in with the plate.

"Good. Relax!"

"I'm not dying," Agnes said.

"I am," Sylvie replied. "And so is everyone else, all the time. Good for you if you're not, but you'd be the only one." She turned her scolding back, and Agnes shook her fist at it. But she had to admit that she and Sylvie were alike in some basic, annoying ways. Know-it-alls. Last worders.

She poked the tines of her fork into a slice of honeydew and watched the juice emerge and spread, like lava. Lava—Vesuvius. She and Elspeth and Edmund had invented a game called Vesuvius. They played it over a whole winter. Any of them could say the word at any time and they all would have to freeze on the spot. Edmund chose to say it when he was already in a contorted posture that deserved further notice. Elspeth said it when they were walking down the street in Philadelphia, so they'd become living sculpture. Agnes obnoxiously said it when she was reading, so she could go on reading. If she was interrupted, she claimed she wasn't unfrozen yet.

She couldn't remember who'd been the last to say it, but like all the games it ended. Eventually she visited Naples and Vesuvius. All those people, caught doing what they were doing with no warning, or running away if they noticed. Their grimaces and twisted postures caught forever. She didn't go see the corpses when she was in Italy. It felt to her to be a violation of privacy to gawk at the pain of another.

She spread jam on a piece of toast and took a bite. First bite of the day, almost as good as the first swig of coffee. She felt no pain at the moment. Heavy fatigue, though. Today would be a nap day. Cancer, like lava, freezing her on the spot, even in so-called remission.

She glanced over at the TV and saw fire coming out of the top of the World Trade Center. A new movie, she supposed, a disaster flick. She took a few more bites and looked at the TV again, hoping for a bit of stimulation, but the picture was the same. Flames coming out of the top of the World Trade Center. This was certainly a long movie review for short-attention-span TV. But wait a second— what about the words moving across the bottom of the screen? *LIVE.* What did that mean? *LIVE. PLANE CRASHES INTO THE WORLD TRADE*

CENTER NORTH TOWER. Her stomach responded before her mind, executing a flip. She felt oddly self-conscious at having been caught with the TV on because of what was on TV. Nothing was sensical. Smoke billowed from the skyscraper.

Agnes put her plate down and went to the door. "Sylvie? Would you come in here, please?"

"I'm in the middle of cleaning the kitchen!"

"Never mind that. Come in here quick!"

"Hold on."

Clomp, clomp, clomp. Sylvie appeared holding the end of the dish towel she'd slung over her shoulder. "What now?"

"Please, and watch this with me? I can't understand what I'm seeing."

Sylvie frowned. "It looks like a fire." She leaned over and squinted at the crawl. "A plane hit the World Trade Center?"

"Oh no." Agnes had gathered that, but she needed to hear someone else say it. She went and stood next to Sylvie, and together they listened to the reporter. A plane had flown into the World Trade Center, no one knew why, they kept repeating the same information and showing the picture of the smoke.

"What happened to the plane?" Sylvie asked.

Agnes shook her head. "I thought you weren't allowed to fly over Manhattan."

As they watched, another plane appeared on the screen and they clutched at each other. "Swerve!" Sylvie yelled.

"Jesus," Agnes said softly. "I'm going to Polly's."

"I'll come with you," Sylvie said.

"Yes. Do. We'll leave Maisie, though."

It was warm but clouding over. The grass had lost its green, its sap, and was shriveling and a lovely beige. Not many wildflowers left. The scent was as heady as ever, wheaty and warm. Hard not to notice beauty, even in shock.

"You think Maud is all right, don't you?" Agnes just wanted to hear it. "Say yes."

"She's nowhere near," Sylvie said firmly.

"I should have called her. Sylvie—will you go home and try her? Then call me when you have spoken to her."

They were opposite the graveyard. Sylvie put her hands on her hips. "Yes. I'd like to do that."

"You don't mind being alone?"

"What difference does it make?"

And that is why I can live with this person, Agnes thought.

She walked into Polly's through the terrace doors. Agnes fleetingly appreciated how nice it was to ignore ceremony now that Dick was gone. Another punch in her ticket to hell.

"Polly!"

"In here!"

Agnes found her in her own den, pacing the length of a telephone receiver cord in front of her TV. She shrugged helplessly and covered the receiver with her hand. *James,* she mouthed. Agnes settled into a side chair and stared at the TV, this one in color. Both towers were hideously on fire. So much black smoke. Theo had told her about eating at Windows on the World on a rainy day when the room was in the clouds. She didn't know which tower that had been. No one would be up there this early, surely. The offices, though—would people be at work? She wasn't sure what time things got going in New York. There had to be some people in the building. She shuddered, imagining their fear.

The tower on the left expanded into a cloud of gray smoke and slowly, very slowly, gave way. It seemed to sit down. A gray puff, a collapse. *Oh my God.* She pointed speechlessly.

Polly glanced at the screen. "James! Are you all right? Yes, yes, okay. Yes. I see. Good, thank God. No no, please don't hang up—"

She put the receiver back on its hook. "He has to keep calling everyone." She went to Agnes and hugged her. "It's unbelievable. Jillian is the only one who works in the towers, but she's not there. She was there, but Knox spoke to her and told her to go home immediately. He told her to get out. She was still in her sneakers, so she left. You know what I'm talking about, don't you?"

"That's why I'm here. Oh my God!"

Polly spun around. People were running wildly in the street. A brown cloud rushed up the avenue, chasing them. People were covered in gray dust, choking. Running from a tsunami. Or a volcanic eruption.

"Oh my God," Polly whispered. "Oh Jesus."

"What about the children?"

"Children?"

"Your children."

"James is calling around."

As Polly paced back and forth, muttering "Call me back, call me back," Agnes watched her with a growing irritation. It was typical of her to fidget, as if that might change the course of history. It was on her nerves.

"Should I call him back?" Polly asked. "I wish he hadn't hung up."

"No. He told you, he's checking on everyone. He checked on you, you're safe."

"But I want to know what's going on."

"So sit down and watch the TV. James doesn't have a newsroom at his disposal."

Polly frowned. "That was unnecessary."

"You are wearing a hole in the rug. Stop it!"

Polly looked down, then up again, perplexed.

"Sit down," Agnes said forcefully. "I can't concentrate with you moving around like that."

"Aren't you upset?"

The reporter on the TV said the words "terrorist attack."

"Oh my God," Polly said, and sank down into the sofa.

"Yes, I'm upset. But I'm not entirely surprised. We've been bullying the world long enough."

"How can you say that?"

Agnes wasn't sure. But it made her feel better to be out ahead of things. "I'm just speaking the reality."

Polly pressed her lips together and looked down at her lap. "You can be quite the monster, you know."

"I'm not the monster, I'm the messenger. I didn't do this thing." She gestured at the TV.

"Maybe you can be so cold because you don't have a family."

"I'm going to ignore that idiotic remark." Agnes's blood thrummed wildly. Breathe, breathe, get a grip. This wouldn't help anyone.

The phone rang. Polly dove for it. "James?" Polly listened, nodding frantically. "Everyone? You're sure? All right. No. Why not—come up here! Tell them all to come. No wait, don't go— I can't hear him." She looked bewildered.

"Come sit back down and stop fretting. He said everyone was okay, didn't he?"

Polly responded to the command and came over. They watched in near silence. The TV reporters were in shock, and in tears.

"Where was James?" Agnes asked.

"In Philadelphia. At the office."

"Oh. I'm sure Philadelphia is safe," Agnes said firmly. Though if national sites were targets . . .

"What about Independence Hall, though? That would be a good target. I mean, as a symbol." Polly had had the same thought.

"Philadelphia will be fine," Agnes said. She'd gotten her strength back in light of Polly's distress. It was automatic to balance the scales with Polly.

The phone rang again. "Oh, thank you, Shirley. No, that's fine. I'm fine. Agnes is here."

"I'm here," Agnes called out.

Polly hung up again. "That was Shirley. She's watching TV with her husband."

"Fun."

"Agnes!"

"Sorry." She thought of something. "What about Robert?"

"He must be safe up there," Polly said.

"But does he even know what's going on? Do they tell them? He may not know." The thought of that horrified her.

"Those poor people," Polly said. "Do you think everyone escaped?" She put her face in her hands.

"Polly—no. I don't."

"But a lot of people must have gotten out."

"Probably. That's not the point right now."

"For them it is." Polly lifted her chin, reaching for a higher truth.

"All right. I am in no mood to argue. *You* are fine, by the way."

"I don't care. Who cares about an old lady? I wish I could trade my life—"

The other tower fell. They moaned and covered their eyes and watched and moaned more and pushed their hands deep into their stomachs and pinched their own arms. Polly slumped down to the floor. Agnes got glasses of water from the kitchen.

"Sit up," she said. She made Polly drink. "Now, let's go outside. I can't sit here anymore."

"I have to be near the phone."

"Just to the terrace. A breath of air. We'll hear the phone."

Agnes helped Polly up, an awkward jerking operation. "Good Lord," Agnes said. "Good thing we're not running for our lives."

Polly stiffened. "How can you make jokes, Agnes? People are dying. Real people."

"I don't see how anything I say can make a difference," Agnes said defensively, though she was stung.

"Just be decent!"

They stepped outside and Agnes looked for Sylvie. She hadn't mentioned Maud to Polly—she was too frightened now. "You're right," Agnes said, steadied, as always, by the sight of the sea. "It's so horrible I don't know what to say."

"Yes. We don't have to talk."

They both ambled around the terrace. Polly did some dead-heading.

"Oh Lord—I hope Maud's all right," Agnes said. She looked over at Polly.

"She is," Polly said quickly. "I'm sure she is."

Agnes's heart pounded. "You really think so?"

"Yes. Wouldn't we sense it if she weren't?"

They looked at each other and their eyes widened. They hadn't sensed it years ago, when Lydia died, and then Nan. They were surprised. They looked away.

"I wish James would call again, though I don't know what more he can say at this point. I wish I were home."

This stung. "What's this place, then? Not your home?"

"Oh Agnes. Not now."

"I mean it. This is my home. I thought it was yours, too."

"It is. And Philadelphia is your home, too. Don't pick a fight."

"I'm not picking a fight. You're the one who wishes you weren't here right now."

"Agnes, my husband is dead. I should be with my children and grandchildren, if we are in a war. Don't you think that's reasonable?"

It was. Of course it was. Yet Agnes wanted Polly on Fellowship Point, within walking distance. Agnes wanted to be the most important to her. "I heard thee tell them to come here."

"I don't know what's going to happen."

"No. You're right," though what Agnes was conceding to wasn't clear. Something about uncertainty, something painful that made Agnes feel left behind.

"Forgive me, Nessie, I just want to hold them. This is so awful."

"It is. Maybe we should pull ourselves together. I think I'll go home."

Polly nodded. "I'll come later? For our drink? Or earlier. I could come for lunch. Would Sylvie mind?" Polly rambled, turning in circles again and wringing her hands.

"Of course not." Agnes was tense, and wanted . . . something. Like . . . resolution. Definition. Truth. But in what form? How was that even possible under the circumstances? Truth: she wanted to hit something. Or someone. A small hurt to distract from the enormous one. She flexed her hands, making fists, opening, making fists again.

"Polly—how does James feel about leaving the Sank to the land trust?"

Polly wobbled her head around, looking everywhere but at Agnes. She got her vague look. Her fingers fidgeted. Agnes smelled blood.

"Sylvie told me she saw him coming off the golf course with Archie and Hamm Loose the younger. Teeter, his name is, I think."

"They all grew up together and are friends," Polly said. "You know that."

"Are they? Were they? I think maybe James wants to wait me out. Wait until I die. My shares will go to you and Archie, and then to James. They have some scheme in the works. You might have told me yourself, Polly."

"Agnes, how can you even be thinking about this right now? The world is blowing up!"

"We put it off last year, because of Robert and Dick. We didn't get it done this year, either. Archie is a problem, yes, but I'm suddenly realizing how reticent you've been about the plan."

"I've had other things to think about. Dick died! And I *have* met with the land trust people. I've gone to every luncheon you have set up. I told the boys about it in no uncertain terms."

Agnes registered that she needed to use the bathroom—in fact she was desperate. But she was locked into combat. "Did you even talk to Dick about the land? As you said you would?"

"Don't speak of Dick." Polly's voice was low.

"Why not? I miss him, too." Agnes was well aware that she was behaving like a teenager, but she couldn't help it.

"Really? You always thought Dick was such a lightweight. And why? Dick didn't do anything to you. He only wanted to be taken seriously. You could never give him that. You couldn't be nice." She tossed her handful of faded flowerheads over the terrace wall.

"I wasn't going to perjure myself for his ego, no. So for that, you'd let this land be developed? You must really resent me." Agnes squeezed her muscles down there. She didn't want to break the momentum.

"No. Oh no, Agnes. Don't put that on me. This is none of my doing, none at all. You have always been welcomed in my family, but you go home and sneer, don't you? You think I don't know? I have known you for eighty-one years. I know everything about you."

"Great. You can work with Maud on my memoir after I'm dead."

"Oh, I will. I'll tell her everything. I'll tell her about little Nan Reed's accident! And how you wrote all those books and got rich to make up for it! But you can't, can you?"

Agnes let go. Vesuvius erupted. Pee ran down her leg and into her shoe. It was pure relief.

Polly put her hands to her face. "Oh Nessie, I'm so sorry, I don't believe that, I've never even thought it before—" She stepped toward Agnes.

A siren began to blare, the declaration of emergency. The first was joined by a second, and then more, sirens wafting across water from small Maine towns.

Agnes stepped backward, away from Polly. "How could you not believe it if you said it? It's what you've been thinking for forty years."

"No. Nessie, I'm sorry. I'm out of my mind today."

"Fuck you, Polly."

There was a pause. "You won't accept my apology?"

"Why should I?"

"You know, I think I'm beginning to understand. It's not so much that you want to preserve the Sank. You want to keep the Point away from my children. I don't know why, but"—and a light came into her face—"but I do. It's the thought I have never allowed myself to have. You're jealous of me, Agnes."

There it was. Polly was just like Grace Lee after all. Agnes felt rinsed, clean, exalted. She stood up straight and towered above the scene. "I came over to make sure you were okay. But you're always okay. Good old true-blue Polly. Seemingly so gentle, but really far tougher than I am. I'm wasting my time." She walked down the steps onto the grass.

"Shut up, Agnes," Polly said behind her back.

"Oh. I'll shut up all right."

Agnes stumbled toward home, chafing from the wet between her legs. Maud, Maud, Maud. Nan. My Nan. My paradise lost.

PART FOUR

Continuing Revelation

CHAPTER 16

Maud, Philadelphia, November 2001

FRIENDS HOSPITAL, IN NORTH PHILADELPHIA, WAS FOUNDED on the impetus of Thomas Scattergood in 1813 under the name the Asylum for the Relief of Persons Deprived of the Use of Their Reason. The Philadelphia Yearly Meeting of Friends had embarked on the project as an alternative to the punitive treatment of mental illness in other hospitals. The Quakers interpreted such disturbances differently, based on the belief that every person was born with an Inner Light which shone with integrity. In the mentally ill, that light flickered, but the mind might heal itself in an environment of rest, good food, fresh air, and general dedication to health. The Meeting bought a fifty-two-acre farm in the west of the city for $7,000 and set out to create a place where people could get better naturally.

The hospital implemented a series of firsts. In the 1830s, they initiated a form of pet therapy. Patients could visit an enclosure for small animals and pet and feed them. The hospital also built a greenhouse, hired women doctors, offered hydrotherapy, and, more recently, opened a long-term care building and a drug rehab program. The philosophy matched Maud's own intuitive ideas about how to help Heidi—it made sense to think that her Inner Light had dimmed. Maud spoke to the doctors at both hospitals and learned that a move could be made without much trouble. Moses agreed easily as well. As long as all he had to do was pay the bills, he didn't really care where his former wife was. In September, Maud took Heidi down and got her settled. Maud felt positive about having her there, though it was more difficult to visit. But she was able to dedicate herself more fully to both Clemmie and to her job, and David gave her a raise and a promise of promotion. She was busy, too much so to examine her degree of happiness, but she got extra satisfaction from her continued correspondence with Agnes Lee. About six weeks after returning from Maine, when her life was relatively calm again, she reread the *Agnes When* manuscript and appreciated and understood it quite differently. That didn't change her goal of convincing Agnes to expand and divulge. The current manuscript wouldn't do what the book should. But she now understood what Agnes had done, and she would keep the version as she kept the tiny old gloves she sought out in thrift stores. Perfect things that didn't cover enough these days.

Maud had made a day trip to the hospital four times now, taking the train to Thirtieth Street Station and a half-hour cab ride to North Philadelphia. Beyond the first time, when Heidi had been terrified of ending up in a strange place, Maud had never dreaded going there. The stately buildings were fair representations of the high-mindedness within their walls—albeit some of the walls could use an upgrade. On the day before Thanksgiving Maud signed in and made her way up in an elevator and down several corridors to Heidi's room. She flicked her hair behind her shoulders, took three deep, centering breaths, touched the gold bangle she'd worn every day since Heidi had to take it off to enter the hospital, and focused on bringing her mother hope and love. She opened the door and immediately smelled the scent Heidi gave off—rotten, sour, brackish. Depression. She fought the impulse to step backward. The shades were lowered most of the way. The atmosphere was brown.

"Hi, Ma." She touched a blanketed foot. The body in the bed

didn't move. "It's me. I'm here to visit you today and tomorrow, too. Clemmie is with Bubbi and Gramp in Livingston. I'll be staying in an apartment on Rittenhouse Square. It's Agnes Lee's apartment, can you believe it?" She pulled up a chair as close to her mother as she could. "Agnes Lee! We're friends now."

Heidi's face was squashed and lined and stained with drool. Her beauty had vanished behind a cloud. She lay on her left side, her legs pulled up, knees to her chest. Her right hand clutched a knot of blanket, and her left thrust up awkwardly behind her head. The hospital was clean and well cared for, but there was no escaping the smell of urine and bleach. Though the urine might be coming from the bed.

Maud kept up her chatter. She washed Heidi's face and brushed as much of her hair as she could. There was a moment when it looked as though Heidi were waking up, or coming to, but she didn't. Maud gave up talking and uncurled her mother's fingers from the blanket and held her hand. She breathed deeply and focused on an image of Heidi skipping in spite of her limp down Charles Street, turning circles and saying hello to everyone. *You are that person*, she repeated in her mind over and over. *You are Heidi Silver, you live in the Village, everyone loves you.* Maud watched for any signs of movement, but though she ached to be the type to fool herself with a twitch or a sigh, she was also intent on knowing the truth. The truth was Heidi showed no response at all.

An orderly entered briskly, his shoes squeaking across the floor. "How are you today, Mrs. Silver?" He put his hand on her bed and gave it a push, enough to be felt. No response. He looked at Maud. "Hi, I'm Tom."

"I'm Maud, her daughter."

"I need to change her sheets, but I can come back."

Maud picked up her bag and stood. "That's okay. I'm going to go talk to Dr. Straight now. Has she been better than this at all?"

"She's on new meds. It takes a while to adjust. I talked to her last week."

"Oh?" Maud's heartbeat sped up. "What did she say?" She knew about the meds.

"She likes that picture." He pointed to a photo of their house on Charles Street.

"It's where we live." As opposed to here. And not for long, either. Moses had made it clear he and family number two were moving in as of June. Six months left.

"The whole house?"

"Yup. Lucky, I know."

Though it felt odd to say so with her unresponsive mother stretched out beneath their conversation. Maud leaned over and embraced her. Heidi stirred and moaned. "I love you, Ma."

"Umm." Heidi pushed out her chin and arched her back. Maud and Tom exchanged a glance. Was it something? They waited for a moment, but she remained curled up.

"Okay, Ma," Maud said. "I'm taking off. I'll be back tomorrow to have Thanksgiving dinner with you."

She and Tom walked into the hall. "Can someone please wash her hair?"

"I'll make a note on the chart."

She walked slowly to Dr. Straight's office, taking the stairs instead of the elevator. The old hallways echoed, and the soles of her shoes clacked against the floors, a sound she always associated with a crisp sense of purpose, though under these circumstances it was annoyingly loud. She wished she were back in the room with Heidi. She wondered what Clemmie was doing. She felt a sudden shiver at the memory of how tense she'd been that morning passing through the large train stations and seeing soldiers everywhere. So much fear, so much hate. She and Clemmie and Heidi had had to move to a short-term sublet uptown for a few weeks after 9/11. The air in the Village had been thick and unsafe for weeks.

She stepped over the threshold into Dr. Straight's office. The scraping and scuffing of the polished corridors gave way to thick carpeting. When she was in a hopeful frame of mind, Maud found this faintly amusing, but now a flash of rage swept through her. Why should he have this? And not the patients! Why should health be a privileged state, and illness akin to poverty? Why should he have on a nice suit, and be so clean-shaven? Resentments crowded out her grief over seeing Heidi so listless, and her energy returned.

He was used to hostility, of course. If he noticed hers, it didn't appear to bother him.

"Hello, Maud. That's a becoming haircut." Dr. Straight was seated behind his massive doctor desk.

"Are you allowed to say that?" she asked.

"It's a compliment." He grinned.

"Thank you," she said without sounding pleased.

His brow furrowed slightly, but she maintained a cooperative expression. She needed him. "Have a seat."

"Oh, okay, thanks."

Another woman entered the room. Again, Dr. Straight didn't stand up. Maud swiftly took her in—short, slender, graying hair, an intelligent down-turned mouth.

"Maud, this is Dr. Goodman. I have asked her to sit in with us to get to know you a bit. She has been working with Heidi."

"Oh. I didn't know."

"I hope it is all right." Dr. Goodman quickly moved to shake Maud's hand with warm, dry fingers. A swift assessment occurred, and through an ineffable, possibly chemical process, the women reached the conclusion that they liked each other. She retreated to a spot behind Dr. Straight.

"I'm afraid the news isn't very good, Maud. We can't seem to lift your mother from her depression. She is on a new medication, but frankly I'm at the point where I think she may need to move into long-term care."

Dr. Straight tapped his pen lightly against the blotter. He was probably sixty, fit, blue-eyed.

"She was fine last spring," Maud said. "She made dinner. She took care of her granddaughter. I don't understand how this could happen."

"I think hormones are playing a role. There are cases of women having severe adverse reactions to menopause. That may be what this is. She has seen an endocrinologist and is on a cocktail of hormones. It is not obviously helping, but she might be worse off without it. Did she have trouble with her periods?" Dr. Straight asked. He opened his folder and flipped through the pages.

"Yes. She had terrible PMS."

He nodded at his papers. "Most likely a severe form of it called premenstrual dysphoric disorder. One of the big clues is that she said the only time she felt truly well was when she was pregnant. Under that circumstance she was being flooded with a different level of hormones. Unfortunately we are only at early stages in understanding the interplay of hormones and mental states. Women usually improve when estrogen levels go down. Heidi isn't following the typical pattern. We aren't giving up, of course."

"So what's the plan?" Maud leaned forward.

"I know you object to ECT. That's up to you. I'd try it if I were you—"

"Really? You first."

Dr. Straight paused and looked down at his notes. "It's not like it used to be, Maud. Not like what you see in the movies. We have come very far with the technique, and I've seen it work wonders."

Maud got a grip. He was trying to help. "I apologize, that was uncalled for. I believe I've read that, too, but I don't want my mother to go through that. She could have had ECT at Payne Whitney." Maud glanced at Dr. Goodman. Was she imagining things, or was she being given a tiny nod? "So what now?"

"Now things become more difficult. Where do we go next? So far we have had her on the ward with many patients who have come and gone and who are coming and going all day, to therapy and activities. Heidi is unable to participate. She is taken outside for fresh air but is not responsive to the stimulation. She is getting physical therapy, but again she is unresponsive to the work."

Maud tucked her hands under her legs and rocked as unnoticeably as possible.

"When we have nothing to measure and she cannot tell us how she feels, we have to go by what we see."

"She might be hearing everything," Maud said.

"She might be. I assume she is hearing some things, and that she has her thoughts and is aware of them. She has had no brain injury or anything to indicate she might be radically different than as you know her. But her depression has her unable to communicate. In my experience this state becomes intractable after a certain amount of time has passed—and it has passed. In my opinion Greystone is better suited to her condition now. It's our long-term care unit."

"I know what it is."

"Maud, I understand that's a hard thing to hear, but I promise you she'll be well cared for there, and comfortable. It's the best long-term unit in the country."

"You mean the best ice floe."

"You don't need to see it that way."

"How would you feel if it were your mother?"

"If it were my mother I'd try ECT."

"You would? You'd make her go through it? With no say?" Heat and anger had risen up in her blood, and she wasn't hiding it very well. Or at all. Though she knew he meant what he said—they'd tried.

"So custodial care."

"We don't look at it that way."

"But not treatment. Not leaving."

"Maud, it would be very difficult for you to care for her at home while she's in this condition."

Maud refused to wipe at her tears. Let him see.

Dr. Straight regarded her carefully. "Maud, I am not the enemy. I promise we will do our best."

"She has gotten worse since she's been here."

"Yes. That can happen, despite our best efforts. It's an illness that can progress."

"Maybe she *needs* to be home."

"If I thought so, I would say so."

Maud's heart stopped. She finally heard him. Heidi was really, seriously ill. Should she consider ECT? She realized she had to. Dr. Straight was being honest with her. "Okay. Okay. Okay." She stood up. "Thank you. I'll think about everything." She touched her bracelet. "Sorry if I was rude, but this is really stressful. I need her back."

"Call me with any questions." Dr. Straight was on his feet, too. Relieved, probably. Or maybe that wasn't fair. Maud had been the tough one, not him.

Dr. Goodman stepped forward. "I'll walk you out."

"Oh! All right."

Dr. Goodman was about the same size as Maud. She smelled of vanilla. Patients were probably disarmed by that. Dr. Goodman gestured for Maud to follow her down the hall. Neither of them spoke as they walked. Maud listened to the echoes, and distant shouts.

"There's an empty room just here," Dr. Goodman said.

She opened the door into a room set up seminar style. "Do you discuss cases here?" Maud asked.

"Yes. Let's sit."

An editor at work had taught Maud the rules of power seating in a meeting room. Never mind. She had no power no matter where she sat here.

Dr. Goodman laid a manila folder on the table. "Maud, I have spent a lot of time with your mother. I have gone through her file carefully. Her history is interesting. May I ask you a couple of questions?"

"Yes, though I can't imagine what I haven't answered already."

Dr. Goodman let this go. "Where are her relatives?"

"She doesn't have any but me and my father—her ex. Her parents died in a car accident—I'm sure that's in there."

"No one else?"

"Not that I know of. Heidi grew up in Florida with an aunt."

"Do you know how to reach her aunt?"

"No," Maud said.

Dr. Goodman opened the folder. "I found a document I want to ask you about." She pulled a paper from the folder and handed it to Maud. On it were handwritten a series of words down the center of the page.

SNOW
COLD
FUR
BOOTS
ASHES

"I have never seen this before."

"It's been sitting in her file, passed from place to place, it seems. I don't know what to make of it."

"But you think it's important."

"I don't know."

"Wait—would you please say that again?"

"I don't know." She glanced up at Maud, who was smiling. The doctor caught on and smiled, too. "I know. Those words are rarely spoken in medical establishments. But I *don't* know. I just wonder. If this is a clue—if there's something specific that happened—I'd like to figure it out. Maybe this is some kind of an exercise? I suspect your mother saw a psychiatrist who asked her to write pages about the car accident that killed her parents. Have you heard of Dr. Pennybacker's work? He came up with the idea of having patients write about a traumatic experience for twenty minutes four days in a row, describing their memory of the experience in as much specific detail as they could, and also their present feelings about the memory. It has become a standard exercise in grief work, because it has positive results."

"I don't recognize anything," Maud said, "except the handwriting. And this isn't detailed, it's just words."

"It may be shorthand for a memory. Your mother seems to be trying to remember a trauma, but she doesn't succeed. My guess—really, this is a guess—is that something severely traumatized her."

"Another trauma? Aside from the accident?"

"Probably details of the accident she hasn't been able to face."

"Poor Ma." Maud registered the possibility as pressure in her chest.

"Her whole early life is a blank. There is nothing in her records before the age of five."

"She doesn't talk about the past."

"And you've asked her."

"I used to, when I was little. But I gave up."

Dr. Goodman nodded. "Maud, I can't know for certain, but there might be a key that hasn't been turned in your mother's psyche, because we haven't found the keyhole yet. These pages could provide an important clue. The person who suggested she do this exercise must have suspected, as I do, that an internal pressure caused her depressive episodes, and that if it were directly confronted or acknowledged she might find relief. This is speculative on my part, but I didn't think it fair not to tell you. And maybe you can help."

What about Greystone?"

"It's not a bad place. I'd make a point of seeing her there as often as I do here. Honestly, I think there is hope."

"What do you think about ECT?"

"It might be effective. As Dr. Straight said, it can really help."

"Does it change people, though? I'm afraid she won't be herself."

Dr. Goodman leaned forward, lacing her hands on the table. "That's a good question, Maud, and it's a hard one to answer. You are accustomed to Heidi having fluctuations in her moods—that's part of who she is. Will she seem different if she doesn't have those moods anymore? She probably will. But the hope is that without that layer of unease she will be more free to be her natural self."

"I see your point," Maud said. "But what about this?" She pointed to the list of words. "Is there a chance that ECT could bury her memory of the meaning of these things forever?"

"That shouldn't be the case, but she hasn't been able to explain this list so far anyway, so it is hard to say. If she isn't as anxious and depressed, she might be able to remember better."

"Okay. I guess I really have to give it some thought. Was I a jerk to Dr. Straight?"

"Not at all. Concerns are natural. Many family members balk at the recommendation of ECT, and other treatments, too."

"Okay good. I do feel protective of her." Maud saw an image of Heidi curled up in her bed in the brown light. It was hard to bear.

"I can assure you, Dr. Straight understands that. Is there anything else I can do?"

"You're doing it. Coming to visit, talking to her, reminding her of her life at home, that's all helpful," Dr. Goodman reassured her.

"The orderly told me she spoke to him last week. I was skeptical." She searched Dr. Goodman's face for the truth.

"She may have. There's nothing physical stopping her from speaking."

"Why won't she speak to me?" Maud heard the note of hurt in her voice.

"Don't take it personally. This illness is tricky." Dr. Goodman widened her eyes—she'd thought of something. "How involved is your father?"

"He's not personally involved. He is financially." At least that, though it came at the cost of Moses expecting Maud to go along with him on other things.

"Could you ask him about this list?"

Maud glanced at the words again. "I'll try." She was slated to have dinner alone with him the following week. He'd ask about Heidi anyway.

Dr. Goodman pushed her chair backward and stood. "Good. I am hopeful, Maud. That isn't a medical opinion, but there is a measure of intuition in medicine."

Maud stood as well. "Thank you. For caring."

Dr. Goodman nodded. "I want to meet the real Heidi, now that I have talked with you."

"All right. I'll think about all of this. Thank you for caring about my mother. May I take this?"

"That copy is for you."

"Happy Thanksgiving," Maud said.

On the half-hour ride back into the city, Maud read the words again and turned them over slowly. She tried to put the puzzle together, but the clues were so scant. She found herself counting the small rowhouses the car passed up to ten, and then starting over. At least she had Agnes to talk to at the other end of the ride.

"All right, then, I'll be off," Mrs. Blundt said. "Don't be shy about calling."

"Thank you," Maud said. "I'll be fine." Though she was not at all certain that was true. She would be alone was the fact of the matter. Agnes was in Maine.

"Happy Thanksgiving."

"You too."

Maud watched Mrs. Blundt walk to the elevator, then closed the apartment door. Now she could figure out how she felt.

She felt angry.

She felt tricked.

She felt elated.

She had the whole night ahead to herself in this beautiful apartment. She could not even remember when she'd been alone with nothing to do. She could lie down on a bed and look up at the ceiling. She could eat and sleep several times in a row. She could read for fun! Mrs. Blundt had given her a tour and showed her the guest bedroom. She headed back there to unpack but stopped to take a spin around Agnes's bedroom. Such sumptuous linens, and a white silk fainting couch to match. Nothing like the stalwart sticks at Leeward Cottage. Maud perused the bookshelf. The only novels were a set by Pauline Schulz. Maud had heard of the *Franklin Square* series but hadn't gotten to it. Too many books, too little time, et cetera. Her decision was made for her here—she'd lost interest in the book she'd brought with her. She pulled out the first volume, *The Franklin Square Girls Make It Do*, to take to her room.

Next she stopped in the living room. Before stepping onto the lush yellow carpet, she removed her shoes; she should have thought of it earlier. Her tired feet sank into the fabric, sending a thrill up her body. She'd never before understood what people meant about the soles being an erogenous zone. She'd have to experiment with that. She gazed out the picture window—a view for the rich—looked at the items on the tables—museum quality—the whiskey in the bar cart—her tongue puckered—and finally arrived at the coffee table and the box Agnes had sent. She opened it, and when she got a first glance at the contents she realized she'd half been hoping it was a present, a fantasy that seemed pathetic next to the pile of notebooks she lifted from the padded interior. She read the typed note on top.

Dear Maud,

I apologize for not being at the apartment to meet you. I had a setback, and I was afraid you wouldn't stay in my apartment while you visited your mother if you knew I wouldn't be there. I want you to stay here. It's convenient, comfortable, and the price is right.

To make up for my absence, here is my written account of the years 1960–1962. I kept a diary of sorts. In these pages you'll find out what you have pressed to know about—how I came to write the *When Nan* books. I think it will be obvious why I want to keep the story private. Don't open them at all if you feel you might be tempted to discuss them with any other living being. No one else knows about these events, and it is my wish that no one ever will.

I hope you'll be satisfied, and will stop bothering me about this.

It will make your mother feel better to have you there, whether or not she can express that.

I'm grateful for another day, for writing, and for the sea. How about you?

CHAPTER 17

Agnes, Leeward Cottage, September 1960

Dear Elspeth,

Polly went back down to Philadelphia on Labor Day, on the conventional schedule. Her departure has had the effect of making our father's death more real. All summer Polly supplied funny anecdotes about him and listened to me talk about him ad infinitum. She wept with me when I needed that. I was able to keep him close, because he existed between us.

Now I am alone with my thoughts of him, and because I cannot arouse a laugh from my own grief-lined innards, I am bereft again. And while I understand that Polly has her own life to live, and children to care for, a stubborn part of me insists that she was mine first, and she should be with me. There is no mourning ritual for the loss of the decades-long exclusive status we enjoyed in each other's lives. Friends must stand aside and understand. I am an adult, so I do, truly. Yet I also recognize that I am left solitary while she is surrounded. True, I wouldn't want to be surrounded in the way she is. I certainly wouldn't want to answer to Dick. Polly is smarter than he by a mile, and the lengths she goes to disguise that fact make me—I was going to say nauseous, but the truth is the spectacle makes me angry. Eve was smarter than Adam. What if God had applauded her curiosity, and ordered the world accordingly? Or was it the Bible's authors who altered the truth to the end of consolidation of male power? Writers!

I'm free. I'll personally make it up to Eve by ordering my world solely according to my intelligence. I have ideas just beginning to form that could take fine shape if I were to develop them with the help of a mind I know and trust. Do you remember my old dream of joining with another soul in love and work? I recall thinking about it from about age twelve, but where did I get such a notion? It certainly wasn't from observing our parents, who couldn't have been less united, and whose work, such as it was, was unknown to each other. It can't have been from anyone else we knew either, could it? Though I believe that Miss Hardy and Miss Wordsworth may have had such a bond, unsung though it was. The Boston marriage, as Henry James called it. Love, hidden in plain sight, under the guise of the practicality of sharing the expenses of a house. We didn't know, did we, El? We knew very little about love at all.

Then, one day, we did know. But how? How does one wake up with an answer on a new day to a question that has seemed hopelessly daunting the day before? What problem-solving elves go to work in the night? I'm sure there is a scientific or psychological explanation for how this happens, but I'm not going to go in search of it. Instead, I'll tell you what the elves did for me last night while I slept.

Early this morning I threw open my window and the ocean air rolled in, and suddenly I saw a way to connect with a sympathetic consciousness. The elves had given me the idea of writing to you. Isn't that brilliant? We have always been so close, the only distance that has ever come between us is the inevitable one that no human can control. You would say you are with God. I, as you well know, don't believe that—and my disbelief affords me the option of thinking that, in some way, you are here with me.

I hope this is all right with you. The interruption may be a lot worse than calling down the hall for you to get up from bed to bring me a glass of water, as I used to horribly do. What a bully I could be! I intend to make this worthwhile for you, however. I am planning to report on a subject neither of us has ever experienced—what it is like to be here after the season is over. I know you're curious! We'll discover it together. I will write about everything important that happens, and the fresh discoveries I make. I promise I won't interrupt heavenly peace too much. You don't mind, do you? But why do I even say that? I already know you don't. You always made me feel as though I was all right just as I was. You even had a way of making room for me to feel beautiful, which I never was nor will be. You were the beautiful sister. If you hadn't been so good that might have been annoying. You were good, though—the best.

I'll tell you a story you haven't heard that makes the point. Shortly before he died, when Daddy was no longer in the present, he sometimes struggled to sit up and look around.

"Where's the angel?" he asked.

"She went ahead," I answered. "You'll see her soon."

"Soon." He always dozed off after that exchange. Soothed.

So, Elspeth, I thank you for being here with me now. This will be fun, I swear.

You already know the lay of the land so I don't have to explain that to you. What's new is a neighbor called Virgil Reed, who comes with a small daughter, name of Nan. He's younger than I, maybe thirty? I haven't been close to him so I can't tell for sure. He and Nan were the subject of dozens of my conversations with Polly this summer—now you will be my confidante. They are living in the Chalet, if you can believe it. In recent years Polly's boys have used it as a playhouse, just as we did. Robert Circumstance has fallen in with them, and before the Reeds' arrival the four boys and their friends swarmed it constantly. They were grumpy this summer that it was occupied and built an alternative fort, but it wasn't as magical and without having an imaginative retreat house, they played differently. They grew up.

The Chalet must be eighty years old. The current Reeds have been there since early spring, surviving with only that small woodstove for heat. I don't know why Ben Reed didn't simply allow them to stay inside Rock Reed. He never comes—he hasn't been here in at least twenty years. Rock Reed is a tomb now. Maybe Virgil Reed doesn't want to stay inside, and I couldn't blame him for that. Maybe in spite of its condition it's too grand for him. He seems terminally anti-materialistic. He has the most ramshackle car I've ever seen, which is saying a lot up here, and no apparent job. He looks like he was just released from a typhus-ridden Confederate hospital—that's how bearded and emaciated he is. Our mother would call him a poor relation, as she called Ben Reed a remittance man. She had no use for the Reeds. Remember when Virgil's parents were killed in a plane crash? I vaguely remember them, and Virgil and his sister, too. What an odd bunch, the Reeds. I say that based on the fact that they rarely came to FP, which I consider to be the oddest thing in the world! Who wouldn't come here, if you could? Uncle Ian said that when Ben dies, Virgil Reed will inherit Rock Reed and be a shareholder in the Fellowship. So I suppose I will get to know him someday. We will have to vote our shares and therefore discuss issues. Little else has been said about him. Polly pegs him as an artist or a composer. I hope so, if only to explain his behavior. His head is in the clouds.

That's him. Back to moi. El, I can't tell you how invigorating it is to no longer wake up in dread. How can the plow horse truly imagine what comes after having the harness removed? The harness limits his imagination. I'm just beginning to see beyond sorrow and hard work.

So picture me now. I'm overlooking the meadow from my perch on the wicker chaise. Hiram Circumstance recently mowed around the house, but as it turns out he never mows anywhere else except the graveyard from the day we leave until right before we return in June. He says it's good for the ground to have a grass coat on under the snow. (He didn't say grass coat—that's my embellishment.) I told him not to change his habits for me, or to change them very little. He said, "I wouldn't know how to do any different."

It's a yellow mid-September day, warm in the sun, the light much softer all around than that glitzy glitter of July that our mother said was nature being tasteless. We had a hurricane a few days ago, but you wouldn't know it now. It wasn't so bad here, though I did hear there was a fire at the Dirigo Hotel in Southwest. I'll drive over there and have a look one of these days. There are a hundred things I could and should do in the house, but one of the new possibilities open to me is that if I decide to shirk the chores, there is no one here to make me feel as though my moral fiber has unraveled. Mrs. Circumstance never chides me or even looks at me sideways. She is out from under a burden, too.

So, with my morality intact but with duty and industry on hold, I'm sitting in the sun, alternately writing you and watching little Nan. She's running through the meadow grass, grasping the stalks, pulling her hands along their full length until, having arrived at the tip, she has to let go, at which point she lurches forward but puts the brakes on with a sturdy leg before she tumbles. She opens her fists and takes inventory of the seed heads she's scraped off, and nods at her successful catch. Now she's rubbing her cache hard between her palms, and when she's somehow satisfied—

with what, the consistency?—she raises her arms, fingers pointed skyward, then bursts her small hands apart, releasing a fine beige powder to its fate on the breeze. What a sight to see she is. What a presence, in all her robust vigor, this gold morning!

Before we knew her name, Polly and I called her Very Very, because she's very very so many qualities—intrepid, solitary, vivid, energetic, darling. And tough. She makes me laugh, but I keep it quiet to avoid interrupting her. I don't think I really need to worry about that, though. She's too occupied to be interrupted by the laughter of a middle-aged lady sitting up on a porch a whole meadow away, miles and miles. A mind away, more than anything, a whole other mind.

Why did we stop running and playing? We loved it so much. Who made the rule that the child's pleasure in the body must come to an end? I blame the Puritans!

Now she leans backward, spins, falls, rises again, hurtles onward, rushes sideways. I lay a scrim over her—like a cellophane page inside a geography book that shows just the mountains or the rivers—and there we are, El, the children of Leeward Cottage and Meadowlea, you, Edmund and I, and Polly and Teddy, running until we can no longer breathe. Our lungs catch fire and we drop into the wildflowers and grass and swallow to squelch the flames. We invent games and argue over rules, but no one ever doesn't want to play, and our angers with each other are brief. Days and years of summers pass this way, marked by our wayward binges and recklessness. We are a small tribe with rituals appended each new year. We swill our freedom and, in our drunkenness, climb trees to their thin, swaying tops, lick blood from our cuts, hold hands, and run in circles until we lose our balance and careen into a heap.

Right now, decades later, I could testify in court that it was Teddy, not Edmund, who just fell on me, yes, I am certain, sight unseen, because I know how each of us felt, our weight, the scent of our hair, the response of my skin to each one's different touch. How simple it was, and how indelible. I see you at every age, El. Today, on the same porch beneath the same sun, hearing the same waves lapping, I can't believe it's gone. Over forever. Yet it is, and I am far from being a child; except for Polly and me, none of those children are alive. Who would have ever predicted that?

Nan grabs two more stalks, one in each hand. I know the feeling of the bladelike stem slicing my palm as I pull along the length of it until the fuzzy plump tips wobble like field mice in my fist. My fingers, like hers, are restless and crave activity, to write in this blank notebook, to paint, to make and do all I haven't had time for since our father got sick. So much time, crushed and scattered in the meadow. So many days spent doing what I never loved. But that is true of many people, to the end of their lives, and I mustn't wallow.

She approaches the graveyard now, a favorite spot of hers. She makes the graves into a slalom course or hides behind stones from imaginary foes. She and Robert Circumstance play here together sometimes, though he is careful not to step on the grassy plots. He's old to be playing with her, eight now, but she's livelier than his siblings and there's no one else. Robert's a thoughtful boy. He especially avoids our father, whose mound is still raised and impressionable. His stone hasn't been set but leans up against a tree, waiting for the day when I ask Hiram Circumstance to dig it in. That will require some degree of ceremony that I don't want to think about right now. Nan has no such scruples. She climbs on top of Daddy and jumps off, all of about six inches. It does me good to see Nan jumping up and down on top of him—remember how we used to walk on his back and he called it a massage?

Now she has headed back up toward the Chalet. Has her father signaled her in some way? I don't see any sign of him. He never seems to pay any attention to her nor tries to know where she

311

is. Polly found his behavior negligent, but perhaps Nan is—in general—better off for it. Not every parent pays attention in a way that is to the child's benefit.

She runs around the back and is out of my sight. Elspeth, can you believe people actually live there? It's as small and plain as it was during our reign. The old shingle roof was replaced a couple of years ago with asphalt tile, but it's thin. The squirrels find it not nearly as hospitable as the shingle was. Polly pressed her father to have the place fixed up for the sake of the little girl, but Uncle Ian said it was Ben Reed's responsibility, not his. We knew the condition the cabin was in at the end of last summer, and presumably it was similar with the addition of winter's wear and tear when they moved in. The woodstove was working, but the wood pile had been utterly depleted. Two little cots, a table, a woodstove. I always loved those sweet rooms. We pretended to be orphan girls there, remember? I have asked Hiram to go talk to Virgil Reed about what he needs and to see what can be done to make the place more habitable. He'll make it sound as though it is routine maintenance, in case Virgil Reed refuses out of pride. I've ordered real beds. I'll have Hiram put them in and see what he can find out about whether or not they plan to stay for the winter. To be honest, I hope so.

Remember I wanted to have five children? Though I got over that by the time I was sixteen. You wanted thirteen, on the theory that out of that many, one of them would be The Second Coming! That's so funny—a combination of a willingness to put in the hard work, and a rather grandiose idea that you'd be the next Mother Mary! Well, you'd have been good at it, and a good saint, too. Between us that's eighteen children wanted, and none created after all. You set such a calm example, El, of the value a woman's life might have without a family to tend to. That helped me enormously, and still does.

I wonder if Virgil Reed even knows we refer to the cabin as the Chalet? Or that piles like Leeward and Meadowlea are called cottages by people like us? I am going to go up to the attic soon to clean it out, and I'll look for our Dictionary of Pretensions and Hypocrisies. You famously said, "A person can feel a lot less guilty about inequality if his servants live in a house, and he only lives in a cottage."

Oh, Elspeth. To say I miss you makes foolish the whole project of words.

The child is running back across the meadow. I wish you could see her, El. She's a stylish mess kitted out in a ragged Fair Isle sweater, brown pants, and scuffed party shoes. Hand-me-down clothes is my guess. She's pink and blonde, with hair down to her waist—very much how you looked as a child. When she falls, she picks herself up and moves along. No tears or crying out for attention. Independent, but naturally so, not for the reason I am—self-preservation.

Polly and I discussed ad infinitum whether or not to approach Virgil Reed. We thought we'd have our chance, but no natural opportunity arose. We prevailed upon Aunt Posy to invite them for tea one afternoon, but Virgil Reed declined. By note. Whatever he is up to requires much solitude. Perhaps he's an outlaw, the less known about him the better. An outlaw hiding in a shack with a child. Such speculations entertained us while I was bruised and exhausted from our father's death in May, and Polly was defending her boys from the judgments of her parents and from the person I still can't believe she married. Polly and I each felt besieged, and Virgil Reed and Nan were our distraction.

Now they are the only people on Fellowship Point aside from the Circumstances and me. They're whom I've got, Elspeth—and you, at the other end of my thoughts and pen.

Nan has reappeared and climbed up onto Daddy again and

is gazing around. What would our mother do if she saw this? Probably nothing, now that I think about it. She walked right over the luminaries in Westminster Abbey, remember? Am I right in picturing her actually grinding her heel? What an American she was! What faith that the world began and ended in Philadelphia! I doubt she'd let the child walk all over Daddy—though she surely did.

Nan jumps, both feet at once. She startles and stoops, runs with her back parallel to the earth. Is this a new game? What's she doing? She looks like a person flailing in bed, having a bad

The sentence broke off abruptly. A cliffhanger. Maud tried to get out of bed to get the next notebook, but the bed held her in place. She hadn't even known such comfort was possible. As Fitzgerald said, the rich were different.

Shadows pooled on the ceiling overhead, and carried her away.

CHAPTER 18

Maud, Philadelphia, Thanksgiving 2001

Maud was woken by the sound of a phone, and she pawed her way up through levels of consciousness to remembering where she was. She was too between worlds to question whether she should answer, so she ran toward the sound in the kitchen and lifted the receiver.

"Hello?"

"Hello?"

"Who's this?"

"Who's this?"

It was Polly calling for Agnes. Maud explained the situation as far as she knew what it was.

"How is your mother?" Polly asked first. Maud flushed at the consideration.

"Not very well. They don't know quite what to do for her. There is a new doctor on her case, though, who seems good." She didn't think it fair to depress Polly with the details.

"So you are alone in Agnes's apartment?"

"Yes, I am."

"Why don't you come have Thanksgiving at mine? Take the train, it's a short ride. One of the horde will pick you up."

"Thank you so much, but I am going to be with my mother."

Polly didn't press. Instead she asked what Maud had heard from Agnes. Funny question.

"And she didn't tell you she wasn't coming down?"

"Nope. I didn't know until I got here and Mrs. Blundt let me in. Agnes sent a note for me along with some old notebooks. That was it. She didn't tell you either?"

Polly described—briefly, in the broadest of quick strokes—their falling out.

"That's not possible. I can't believe it," Maud said. She glanced at the time. It was nine o'clock!

"I called just now to patch things up, if you must know. I can't see that anything is solved by not talking."

Maud thought of Miles. "Sometimes you can't fix things."

"True. But this can't be one of those times."

"No. You have known each other way too long. This is a blip." Maud was the therapist now.

They continued to chat as Maud assembled a breakfast. She opened the refrigerator and took out the quiche. She also found cheese, fruit, a loaf bread—lemon?—and coffee. Mrs. Blundt had shown her the options and she decided on the Bustelo and the French press. She turned on the gas under the kettle.

"Thanks, but I'll be fine. I found an entire set of the *Franklin Square* series and I plan to zip through them."

"I didn't know that she liked those books. In fact I've heard her criticize Pauline Schulz for being too smart for her own good. Which I did point out was the pot calling the kettle black."

Maud laughed. "I'd say so. I started the first one last night. It is a perfect distraction."

"Not everyone in Philadelphia loves those books. They see themselves in the pages. Some of the scenes are so real to life it seemed there was a fly on the wall."

316

"I can see that." Maud poured the boiling water into the glass cylinder of the press. "Sometimes things are too close for comfort. It feels distant enough from me, though, that I find it an escape."

"Good. We all need an escape."

"Speaking of which . . . and stop me if I am overstepping . . . but I'm curious about a man named Virgil Reed. He stayed on Fellowship Point in the early sixties. Do you remember him?" Her breakfast was ready, and she wanted to carry everything to the living room and eat in front of the picture window. But the answer to this question came first.

"I do remember, yes. It was a very sad story. He and his little daughter lived on the Point for two years or so. Agnes knew them well, as they arrived right when she moved up there year-round. There was some sort of an accident in the wintertime, and the man died. The child was sent away to live with relatives, and then she died, too."

"That's awful."

"It was. I was so busy at the time with children and a new baby that I have to say I didn't pay as much attention as I probably should have. Agnes was quite saddened by it all."

"Why, particularly?" Maud regretted this as soon as she asked. It was too straightforward when she really had no standing to know about any of it—not as far as Polly knew. Did she know about the notebooks?

"I'm not sure." Polly indeed retreated.

"But the *When Nan* books were based on the little girl?"

"Maud, you should ask Agnes about that."

"Yes, of course. Thank you again for the invitation. Maybe try calling Agnes in Maine?" She winced after saying this. Polly could do as she wished. Maud felt far more involved than she actually was.

"I will. And maybe *you* can catch a bit of the parade."

ALICE ELLIOTT DARK

"I doubt I'll have time, but from what I've seen Philadelphia is lovely. I'll have to be more of a tourist another time."

"You are always welcome to stay with me. I have plenty of room now."

When she hung up, Maud went to the living room, but her appetite had diminished. Nan died as a child? And—Maud remembered—Polly had had a daughter who died young, too. How terrible would that be? It would change a person, wouldn't it? Possibly more than ECT would.

She got the receiver from the kitchen and dialed her grandmother.

"How's Clemmie? Is she up?" Maud asked.

"Oh yes. She's been up for a while now. She's on a good schedule here," said Gladdy Silver, better known these days as Bubbi. "She ate a good breakfast."

"Okay, great." Maud watched a man in the square berate his dog.

"Yes, I don't know why you have so much trouble getting her to eat. She had a good dinner last night, I already told you that, and now a big breakfast. She eats as if she's been starving."

Maud rolled her eyes. "Thank you for taking care of her."

"She's happy here. She slept through the night."

"Would you tell me if she didn't?" Maud muttered.

"What, dearie?"

"I said is she close by? I'd like to say hello to her."

"She's playing," Gladdy said. "I have her all settled. She hasn't fussed at all."

"Would you put her on, please?"

"I'm afraid it might upset her to hear your voice."

Pick your battles, Maud counseled herself, and carried her plate and coffee back to her bedroom. One more notebook before the hospital.

CHAPTER 19

Agnes, Leeward Cottage, September 1960

Dear Elspeth,

It's night now. I'm writing propped against pillows, in bed. This morning I had to put my pen down in the middle of writing you. A dramatic event disrupted a day I expected to be uneventful. This is all your magic, Elspeth. Contacting you has everything stirred up!

I just reread what I wrote this morning to see where I left off. Now I'll fill you in on what happened next. I am on my porch, remember?

Nan loped along, low to the ground, as though she were about to fall and was extending her stance to try to stay upright. Yet only ponderous adults do that—a child gives way—there's no consequence for falling from her height. What was she up to? She entered the taller grass again, and then, like a bird of prey, she swooped. A sure and deft action. A natural hunter. When she rose up, she was holding a snake, a large garter. She wanted to catch a snake? I couldn't conceive of it. She slid her right hand up to its neck and shook it vigorously. What could she possibly be doing?

"Nan!" I called out. She didn't look around.

The snake's body went limp as a plumb line. She changed her tactics and stroked its face. The sight transfixed and disgusted me. There is nothing in the world that could induce me to be affectionate to a snake.

I willed her to let go, but my will didn't extend across the meadow. The child moved her hand slightly upward. I squinted and I got another shock. There was a chipmunk involved, though only the tail end of it protruded beyond the snake's jaw. Its head had been ingested already. I shuddered. Was she trying to grab the chipmunk back from death? In my experience, death wins, and the snake was far along in its killing. The struggle lasted for several attenuated seconds. Nan's expression was focused and tough. I rooted for her efforts. Was this a kind of surrender, El? It was certainly an inner movement, a broadened loyalty. Her victory went from being a neutral curiosity to crucial—to us both.

She wrapped her fingers tighter around the legs and pulled harder. My hands gripped tight, too, around the arms of the chaise. Come on, come on, come on, I silently cheered, forgoing my commonsense prediction of the snake's success and effectively praying for a miracle. She pulled with one hand and rattled the snake with the other. I watched vigilantly, prepared for a rush to the doctor. The ocean, which had been background music, pounded as if we were in a storm. I lifted my eyes for a moment to glance beyond her, and saw only a placid sea. This momentarily confused me, until I realized I was hearing my blood rushing past my ears. An inner storm.

Suddenly Nan reeled backward. The chipmunk by her effort had become uncorked, and the animals popped apart. She set it on the ground and gestured for it to *wait, do not move.* She still held the furious snake, who was whipping its wiry body against hers, lashing its tail up at her chest. She looked around her and fixed her gaze on the water. She began to run, and finally I unleashed myself and ran, too, across the porch, down the wide side steps, past the graves, to the sea. My pants rasped as I ran faster than I have in years, gasping for air and at the same time screaming those strange croaking sounds of deep terror. I was still far away, too far to prevent her from possibly stepping off the edge of the bank and falling into the cold sea. Would she have the sense to stop short of it? Remember when Teddy Hancock ran over the bank, and Uncle Ian berated him for his ignorance of the laws of science? But he was twelve. Nan is around three, and surely has no idea of science, or any body of knowledge.

I raced, stomach bouncing against my ribs, propelled by the thought that I can't survive another death, I simply cannot. I didn't know that before today, but it was so apparent and true that I felt a literal blow when I realized it. A thump on my back. I called out to her over and over, child child child, but she was oblivious. A great despair rose up through me like a flu. I felt responsible. I'd been watching her, officially or not.

She reached the edge of the bank and stopped. I made a new sound, relief from the depth of my most buried organs. But then she hurled the snake sidearm and teetered from her effort, and the sick terror tuned up again. I stretched my arms out, determined to grab her as soon as I could, but when I'd nearly reached her I was suddenly flat on the ground, the air knocked out of me. I'd tripped. Fled the world. When I came to I saw legs standing close. My senses were playing tricks—I couldn't believe there was another human being in the world beyond the little girl and me. Yet there was Robert Circumstance, age eight, home from school, pointing for the child to retreat, giving me a hand to get to my feet again. A savior.

I hope you don't mind my use of that term. Did you ever meet Robert? Maybe as a young baby? He's a fetching child. Since he was small he has come to talk to me and we have had many good conversations. He is curious, and he puts things together quickly. He's brighter than Polly's boys, who are the only other children I know well. He's handsome, too. I'm determined to help him have a bigger life than the one he was born into.

Once we were squared away, Robert leaped from the bank himself and plunged through the cold water after the snake. Nan tipped her head quizzically, appearing to have no idea what he was doing or why. I stepped behind her and pulled her away from the bank by her shoulders. The snake thrashed violently and even I pitied it. Robert thrashed, too, and made several unsuccessful grabs. I called out for him to be careful, as if that might make a difference. When the creature began to flag, he snatched it up, climbed the bank, and laid it on the ground. I moved a cautious distance away. Nan slipped off, too, to lay down on the ground next to the chipmunk. Her tiny index finger ran down its back and she blew her baby breath into its face. I knew it was dead. She did not.

"Robert, you're a hero. Are you all right?" I asked.

"I am."

I looked down at his sopping outfit. "I'm going to tell your parents how brave you were."

He hung his head, his hair dripping. He's a robust boy who has already absorbed many lessons of good character from his sturdy parents. He brought his feet parallel, so he was standing gracefully locked into a good posture.

"Snakes eat chipmunks," he told Nan. Then he mimicked the action. She watched him and soon sat up. "The chipmunk is dead." He sliced his hand across his throat. She looked at him quizzically.

"What about the snake?" I asked.

"It got a bath it didn't expect."

I laughed. When had he grown up enough to have such a sense of humor?

"It will go off when it warms up."

"Oh." I never like thinking of snakes in the meadow. He deserved a success, though.

He picked up the chipmunk and pointed toward the graveyard. "Shall we bury it?" he said to Nan. "Is it all right?" he asked me.

"Yes, go ahead, Robert. Put it in the pet section." I looked at Nan. "Don't pick up wild animals. They can hurt you."

She nodded.

"Please tell me you understand."

She looked at Robert—for help. He and I looked at each other, and I waited for a response or explanation. He's a handsome boy now with a guileless mouth. His hair has already darkened. I suspect it will be a deep brown, like Hiram's. Scottish hair.

"Miss Lee, she doesn't talk much."

"What do you mean?"

"She understands, but she doesn't talk."

"Is she deaf?"

"I don't think so," he said. He let go of her hand and walked around behind her. "Hello," he said quietly. She turned and smiled at him. Smiled! The murderous little beast was flirting! He moved back beside her again and gave her a squeeze around the shoulders.

"Can she make sounds?" I asked.

"Yes. She knows a few words."

"That's odd. She should have a vocabulary by now. You did, when you were her age. I remember a discussion we had about the tides." I told him the moon controlled them, and he wanted more information. I did what adults do and explained in spite of my ignorance on the subject, when I should have said I don't know. Polly is better about questions, probably as a reaction to Dick's know-it-all attitude. She takes her troop to the library when she doesn't have an answer. That sets a good example. I must try not to feel so much shame when I don't know something.

"I remember that, too, Miss Lee."

"Why doesn't she speak?" I asked. "Does it have to do with her father?" Maybe he had a problem, and that was why they hadn't come to tea.

"He can speak," Robert said.

The child was swinging her toe through the grass, tamping down a half moon.

"Nan." I leaned down closer to her face. I pointed to myself. "I am Miss Lee."

Next, I pointed to Robert and said his name. Then I pointed to her and looked quizzical. "Nan," she said, though the second N was weak so it sounded like Nah. I repeated it. Continuing to point around our small gathering, "Nan. Robert. Miss Lee." She said W for R, Wobert, then she said Miss Lee so beautifully I clapped.

Suddenly I said, "Now try Agnes."

"Agnes," she imitated.

"That's also my name. My Christian name. Agnes Lee, and you are Nan Reed." I turned to Robert. "You may call me Agnes, too."

"Thank you, Miss Lee."

I sighed. It isn't going to be easy to implement a more egalitarian regime around here. I wish you could help me, Elspeth. If there were two of us, we'd be more convincing. Your certainty would disguise my impatience.

"All right," I said, "for now. But I'd like you to consider it. Now tell me what else you know about her father."

Nan reached for the chipmunk, but Robert pulled it away. "It's dead, remember? We're going to bury it now. May we be excused?" he asked me.

"All right, Robert. Your mother will put a snack out for the two of you on the porch. Please come eat when you're finished."

"Thank you, Miss Lee."

"Agnes."

He took the girl's hand and they walked across the meadow toward the graveyard. I went back inside and asked Mrs. Circumstance to make a snack for the children. "Robert's a good boy," I said.

"I'd have picked him," she said, "if I'd a choice. But you don't know who they'll be, and they come as themselves, fully formed."

I headed upstairs and sat at my desk to write letters and pay bills, but my thoughts were jumpy and furious. It was one thing for Virgil Reed to be antisocial, but he should think about his daughter! If she can speak, she should be taught how. I have read about Chomsky's theories of a universal grammar—her innate capability should be brought out. What Robert told me sounded like neglect. Had Polly and I allowed our manners and respect for privacy to blind us?

I looked across the meadow at the children. Robert had Nan kneeling and praying, which would have made me smile another time. Now I was both nervous and furious. I got up from my chair and was propelled up the road by rage. The tiny cabin loomed like a monster's castle. Elspeth, I knocked on his door. It felt odd to do that, when I'd had free passage for so many years. I didn't know what I was going to say to him, but I was ready to say something. No response. His car was parked on the road, so he must be inside. I knocked again. No answer. My thoughts raced and burst. I dug my nails into my palms. I knocked a third time. Silence. It had to be deliberate. I placed my ear against the door and listened for any sound of movement. Still nothing. So I spoke. "Mr. Reed, your daughter nearly fell into the sea. You should be watching her. I can't be responsible." As far as I knew I was talking to myself, but I gave my lecture anyway. I wished I'd brought a piece of paper, and a hammer and nail so, Luther-like, I could nail it to his door.

I finally gave up. When I returned to the house, Robert and Nan were sitting on the porch, eating sandwiches. I asked him to walk her home when they'd finished.

Now, dear sister, I'm too tired to write any longer tonight. I'll leave you with the assurance of how happy I am to be in touch with you, and grateful to whatever good elf came while I was asleep last night to give me the idea of writing to you. You were with me today, racing off the porch. I felt your urgent need to do what is right.

Still September, a week later

Dear Elspeth,

I thought I knew Leeward Cottage completely, every nook and nuance, but now that I am doing an inventory it amazes me how much I stopped seeing or never saw. The house that I believed was a regular lived-in home turns out to also be a museum of the penchants of our ancestors. Nothing has been culled in decades. The drawers in the dining room and pantry are chocked with forks, knives, spoons, dozens of linen napkins, many yellowed and threadbare. Way too many sets of plates sit on the shelves, some chipped, some glued. The rooms and the attic are crammed with furniture—we must have walked an extra mile or two a day just circumventing the obstacles. There are drawers full of prints and photographs, never framed or put into albums, and tennis rackets, golf clubs, badminton and croquet sets, every single item in multiples. And mahogany! I loathe it. Now I can sell it if I like. I must decide how sentimental I am about family heirlooms. Not at all, I think.

I'm beginning to know how I want the place to look. Empty and serene. Beautiful rugs on the floors. Simple furniture in a pale wood. If I never see another ball and claw-foot I will be grateful. Bring on the Shaker life! I'll have the rooms repainted to take the indoors outside, or bring the outdoors in. The number of colors I can see from any window is more than enough to paint each of these rooms differently. The hawkweed alone—wouldn't it make a beautiful room to paint it orange, yellow, green, and black? I am in a grand experiment, El. At the beginning of a new life. Forty years old, forty years spent in waiting, living as a tight bud. It's time, don't you think, for me to become a flower?

I moved into Daddy's bedroom. Every morning the sun shines straight into the windows. Light beams across the room, bouncing off the glass on the pictures. I moved a small writing desk up to the window that faces the sea, and I am writing to you from here. I am both changing and settling in, and it is glorious! Why did I think the fall would be quiet?

Now I have news, and a further report on Mr. Reed. You hoped so, didn't you?

A few days ago I drove to Augusta to do some errands. Art supplies were on the top of the list. I want to try my hand at doing some decorative painting.

On the way home I took a new route. I looked at the map and memorized the gist of it, but as happens with new routes, unfamiliarity magnified its length, and I wondered if I'd taken a wrong turn. The scenery was beautiful, though, and I reminded myself that I couldn't really be lost, and there were houses to stop at if need be. So I tootled along. Then, on a stretch of nothing but woods on both sides, I passed a man holding a small dog and a sign I couldn't quite read. I drove on. Yet a glance in the rearview mirror provoked a clarity I hadn't had when first confronted with the anomalous proposition he created in the middle of nowhere, and I realized what was going on. I think you were behind that illuminating glint in my rearview glass, weren't you, Elspeth? You rubbed the scales from my eyes. I turned around in the driveway of a church and got out of the car a few feet away from the man.

"How old is your dog?" I asked.

"He's just a pup."

The animal was small, his hair scruffy. But a ribbon had been tied around his neck, which made my heart pinch, as it always does in the presence of the innocent efforts of humans to bridge the divide between indifference and a sale.

"Is he going to be big?"

"Nope."

"Does he bite?"

"Nope."

"How much do you want for him?"

"Seventy-five cents."

A sad amount.

"May I hold him?"

He stretched the dog away from his body, and I pulled him close to mine. The animal looked up at me with a mixture of wariness and something like hope, though that would be sentimentalizing the encounter. A silent plea to be unharmed was probably more like it. His fur masked his ribs, but I felt them as soon as I touched him. I thought I'd better buy him and take him to a shelter, if there was such a place around. I didn't know. Shouldn't I know? I feel so saturated with Maine, but am so separate from its people. That will change, now.

Or I'd give him to Robert Circumstance, with an allowance for care.

"Wait," I said nonsensically, as if the man were going somewhere. "I'm going to get my wallet." The dog whimpered as I placed him in the front seat. I looked through my wallet—several bills, including a five, but I pulled out a ten.

"This is all I have."

The man stared at the bill. "I can't make change."

"No? Let me think." I pretended to struggle with this problem, so as not to embarrass him. "All right, look. I want the dog, so I'll just have to give you the ten."

He looked at me carefully. I made my face blank. I am not tooting my own horn here, Elspeth, and I wouldn't describe this bit of charity to anyone but you. It does feel good, though, to give. Why is that?

"So do we have a deal?" I said.

I thought of telling him it was good he made certain of what became of the dog rather than abandoning him to starve. But my opinion seemed superfluous, which is likely true far more often than I care to believe.

"He'll be fine, don't worry."

"He's called Star," the man said. "My girl named him."

Well. My poker face took some doing, knowing a child had lost her dog.

"He'll be okay," I said, nodding my assurance. "Is there somewhere I could call you? I'll let your daughter know where he ended up."

"Nope." He turned away.

"Tell her he'll have a good life!" Possibly better than the girl, I thought. The problem with going out into the world is that the world is not under my control.

I settled Star next to me on the front seat. He was too exhausted to even look around. Driving away, I railed at the unfairness of life. Elspeth, we were at the top of the world's heap. By dumb luck. At least we knew it, and that was lucky, too, for we had a mother who believed that her good fortune was her due.

I got back on Route 3 and rolled down my window, keeping a hand on Star and stroking him gently. The girl must have petted him often, because he accepted touch. I didn't know where the animal shelter was, so I guessed I'd have to go home with him first and make some calls to find it. And I couldn't very well drop him off so dirty and matted, I'd have to bathe him, and what did he eat? Maybe Mrs. Circumstance would have a tidbit. You see where these thoughts are heading, but I was sure I was following a plan. By the time I turned down Point Path, my head was so full of next steps that I didn't see little Nan until I nearly killed her. She was just at the lip of the road before the dip down toward the Point, alone again, in only a T-shirt on an afternoon when I was glad to be wearing a sweater. Oh, for God's sake! I jammed on the brakes in time to avoid her—obviously—otherwise I wouldn't have the equanimity to write this. What choice did I have but to take her home, too? My car had become an ambulance.

"Come on." I beckoned to her. She stared. "Come on, Nan." I got out, walked around, and lifted her in. Her eyes widened when she saw the dog.

"That's Star," I said. "Star." Oh boy. Why was I teaching her his name? I realized my mistake. "He's not mine." As if that meant anything to her. She continued to stare at him, and what could I do but show her how to touch him? Otherwise she might have poked out his eye.

We crunched down the drive. I'd left the house for paints and I returned with a child and a dog—and some paints. I hardly know who I am anymore.

The three of us climbed the back steps and found Mrs. Circumstance in the kitchen. "I'm so sorry," I said to her, "I am arriving with a mess."

She assessed the situation, no questions asked, in much the way Polly does. Mothering nerves of steel.

"I'll boil some water. Hot chocolate and cookies is the ticket." She looked at Nan's thin shirt. "That man," she muttered. "He has a hole in his head."

"You said it. You don't have a small sweater in your house, do you?"

"I'm sure I have a pile of them." She put the kettle on and headed over to get proper clothes. I beckoned Nan to follow me to the pantry. I filled the sink with warm suds, and when I was certain the temperature and depth were right, I lowered Star. He was so floppy I had to hold my hand under his chest to keep his head above water. I worked my other hand through his coat, an inch at a time, removing the mud. Nan strained, tipping her head to either side curiously, and I explained to her how I got Star and what I was doing. Mrs. Circumstance came back just as the kettle began to whistle. She took hold of Nan. "I'm giving this one a bath upstairs." She picked her up and balanced her on one hip.

There's life in the house, Elspeth.

I kept at my work, slowly, and slowly it stopped being work. The dog went from being listless to being . . . on the crest. Wobbling on the curve of the moon. If he tipped one way, he'd be illuminated and face earth; if he tipped the other way, he'd slip into darkness and forever disappear. He was in the balance. What would he choose? The body always wants to live. The spirit is less certain, more susceptible to the heart. You were clear, when it was your turn. You held on as long as you could. I always hoped you didn't overstay for my sake—and I also hoped you did. Selfish.

I continued my slow movements, soaking his fur, rubbing the hairs between my fingers. Every few minutes I drained the sink while still holding him under the warm tap, and then filled it

and began the cleaning again. I heard the water drain from the
upstairs tub. Footsteps circled, the slow and the swift, a reassuring
syncopation. I gave Star a final warm rinse and dried him with a
kitchen towel. He looked like a different creature once I'd fluffed
him up.

Mrs. Circumstance reappeared with a spiffed-up Nan in clean
pants and a little red sweater. Nan's eyes widened at Star's new
look.

"He needs food. I can feel his ribs," I said.

Mrs. C. reached for him. "If he's starving," she said, "he should
have only a little food at a time. He could do with some eggs."

"We don't have any."

"Or maybe we do."

She opened the refrigerator and pulled out a bowl of eggs.
They weren't part of my food plan, but I wasn't going to quibble
with her.

She scrambled them quickly. Nan closed her eyes and inhaled
the buttery scent. Mrs. Circumstance noticed and cracked two
more into the pan. I knelt on the floor and guided Star's head
to a bowl of water. He swung away. I tried again with the same
result, and finally dipped my hand into the bowl and brought up
a palmful. He lay down, and I began to worry. Mrs. C. put a plate
on the floor next to us and sat Nan at the table with a plate of her
own. I tipped my hand and spilled the water back into the bowl and
picked up a little egg. I held him close to my heart, near the beat of
life. Beyond me Nan smacked her lips. No one has ever made such
an uncouth noise in this house before! I looked up at Mrs. C., who
knew exactly what I was thinking. We got a case of the giggles that
I kept trying to quell, but we set each other off, over and over. The
child was too busy with her eating and smacking to notice. The egg
fell from my hand and I kissed the dog on the top of his head.

"Look!" Mrs. C. said.

Star was bent over the plate, wolfing his food. We all watched, transfixed, until he finished and topped off the meal with a big yawn. "I need a cup of chocolate for all my labors. You don't like chocolate, do you, Nan?" I was teasing, but she looked at me quizzically. Poor thing.

I chose the yellow Quimper, hoping it would amuse her. Mrs. C. arranged the tray, the chocolate in a small pitcher, and a plate covered with rings of cookies. Nan watched carefully, and I was aware of giving a performance for her. I don't think anyone has ever watched me with such pure interest—at least not since we were children, El, and you were my openhearted little sister.

I picked up Star again, and we all headed in a procession to the glass room. I created a little nest out of an old cashmere blanket for Star on the sofa. Mrs. C. predictably frowned. "A new broom," I reminded her. Although he'd eaten and was clean, I didn't think he was ready for the child, and thought it best to be between them. Mrs. Circumstance asked if there'd be anything else.

"No, thank you, and I thank you very much for your steadiness today."

"If you need me—"

"I'm fine. I have a guard dog now." And so I discovered I had decided to keep him.

Star stretched at just that moment, and exhaled deeply. Mrs. Circumstance isn't a woman lavish with love, so she surprised me when she said, "I'll bring him a tidbit later. And you be a good girl." She shook her finger at Nan, who reached for that admonishing finger and giggled when it was pulled away before she could grasp it.

Life in the house!

The child lunged across me to get at Star, but I caught her, sat her back down, and told her "No!" This didn't faze her. She gazed around and rubbed her hands on the sofa's soft slipcover. Such an

333

uncivilized thing she is. Unruly. Crazy hair. But Mrs. Circumstance had brushed it out so it looked like a soft, mohair blanket, frizzy in an angelic way. I wanted to touch it, but held back. I barely knew her. I wouldn't touch a strange adult's hair, would I? The best way to teach her how to be civilized was to behave that way toward her.

Yet I also wanted to delight her, and wished I had already painted the glass room, disguised its stark whiteness with tropical glamor. At least the somber family portraits are in Philadelphia, and weren't sneering down at her.

I showed her how to hold the cup and wrap her finger inside the handle. It tipped, of course it tipped, how could I have imagined anything else might happen? I caught it before it spilled, but it was a close call. I shifted strategies and showed her how to hold the cup with both hands from underneath, but she wanted to do it the other way, shrewd creature, knowing it was better, more grown-up. I should have taught her with an empty cup or with water rather than chocolate, but it was too late for that. She watched her fingers and guided them with great effort, poking her index finger through the handle correctly, but balancing the whole cup was beyond her powers. Again, I took her fingers and placed them on the cup. The surface of the chocolate had grown hard, so I broke it with a spoon.

"Open your mouth." I put a spoonful of chocolate in her mouth, and then took one myself. I rolled it around, tasting it with every part of my tongue. The thick rich oily sweetness was an avenue of escape and forgetting, a conduit to an inward journey. I lifted my cup, my finger hooked through the handle, but with the other hand placed beneath. She copied this successfully. She took a sip, then slid off the sofa and placed her cup on the table. She performed an ecstatic modern dance, pressing her mouth with her hands, moaning and more moaning, and swaying side to side. Chocolate!

"You are a hungry baby bird, aren't you? This is surely the best worm you'll ever eat."

She handed me the spoon, and we played the game of moaning after every bite. I was like the pied piper, drugging the child. She spun in circles and rolled around the room as if the floor were pitched like a hill. I put on music for her. Calypso, Harry Belafonte's record that always makes me happy. Could it be that she'd never heard music before? Her reaction was somewhere between terrified and insane. I had to run after her, catch her, hold her and soothe her; keep holding until she understood that it came from a machine and not from some god in the room. I showed her how I lifted the needle on and off the record, but this I wouldn't let her try. She accepted the restriction and settled into the sofa, holding her hands above her head and swaying them to the rhythm. I copied her. We played a game of one making a move, the other imitating, and so on. Star slept through it all. The afternoon passed.

Lances of late sunlight pierced the windows and cluttered the floor like swords laid down after a battle. Nan stretched out on the wicker sofa flat on her back. She didn't require a story, but I so rarely hear my own voice these days that I took the opportunity. I made one up, about a glen in a forest known to only two people. When one person went there alone, it was only a forest glen. When both went together, they could have whatever they wished for, the only limitation being they must stay in the glen. I made them a boy and a girl. They asked for cups of chocolate. They asked for a puppy but wondered what would happen to him if they couldn't take him out of the glen—hunger, predators, and loneliness. Nan breathed deeply, fast asleep, but I kept going, enjoying the invention.

The sun began to set, pink and orange. I observed every nuance of both the change of day, Nan's shifts and murmurs, Star's snuffling surrender to safety.

Then I had a moment of distress. A dark silhouette loomed on the other side of the window, shoulders hunched up like a mad cat. He was face to face with me, on the porch. Virgil Reed. I hoped he hadn't seen me startled. I pointed down the porch toward the French doors at the other end of the room. We walked beside each other toward them, the glass between us. An odd tuneless duet.

I unlatched the door and had some trouble opening it until he pushed from the other side. It angered me that he would do that—push his way into my house.

He raised his eyebrows.

"Yes, she's here. She's asleep on the sofa."

He took a step to pass me. I stepped in front of him.

"No, no, no. Not yet. I have to talk to you. Today is the second time I've rescued your daughter when she could have met with disaster." Yes, I said that. I was furious, and even more so because he was making me nervous. "You don't take care of her. And that is completely unacceptable."

He stared at me.

"You have to start watching her!"

"I am sorry, Miss Lee."

I was shocked. Nonsensically, I'd begun to believe he didn't have a voice. But it was low and—attractive. But that changed nothing.

"You should be. I've nearly had heart attacks."

"She wanders away. I'm so immersed in my work, and I forget—"

He took a step forward. I blocked him. It was my house.

"Listen to me. She is not much more than a baby. She wouldn't last for a minute in this freezing water, she's so light her clothes would pull her under. And she isn't visible from the height of a car seat."

A lecture, a lashing. He looked at me pensively as I spoke. He wears a big beard that hides a great deal of his face, his mouth entirely. It's blond, but a darker shade than his hair. Green eyes. A straight nose. He took his scolding without protest and became less of a monster in those minutes, more—I don't know yet. Something.

"You're right," he said.

My face tingled. "You're mocking me."

"No. You are right. I've been preoccupied. I will do better."

I stepped aside and let him enter. We arrived at the sofa, and he slipped his arms under Nan and carried her back down the length of the room, with me beside him. Star ran, too. I paused to lift him, to prevent him from following Virgil Reed outside.

"I gave her a meal," I said.

"Thank you."

He pulled the door shut behind him.

CHAPTER 20

Maud, Philadelphia, Thanksgiving 2001

A CAB WAS WAITING WHEN MAUD GOT DOWNSTAIRS, AND SHE tipped the doorman as he held the door for her.

"Happy Thanksgiving!" everyone said at once.

She registered on her brief passage between the building and the car that it was a relatively warm day, perfect for standing along a parade route without freezing, but she'd have to save that for another year. If she'd been home the night before she would have taken Clemmie up to the Museum of Natural History to watch the balloons being blown up for the Macy's Thanksgiving parade. Heidi had always taken her when she was a girl, and they'd had the spectacle nearly to themselves. Now, like so many of the things about New York that had seemed like private secrets, it had become an event, and was packed with parents and children and teens out on their own, reminiscing about their childhoods. Her father, Moses, dated this shift to Ed Koch's *I Love New York* campaign. Before then the subways were covered with graffiti and tourists stuck to the greatest hits; the museums, Empire State, the Statue of Liberty. He had liked the dirty, gritty city, so different from Livingston, New Jersey, where he'd grown up. Now the Upper West Side had mall stores, and Central Park was crowded after dark. Upsides and downsides, which seemed to be the reality of adulthood.

As soon as Maud settled into the cab she grew anxious again. She'd managed to push Dr. Straight's recommendations to the back of her mind overnight, having developed a capacity for compartmentalization to endure Heidi's hospital stays and blue periods. It had helped her be away from Clemmie all day at work. When she shifted to focusing on whatever she'd suppressed, though, it was apt to come roaring at her with extra force. She pictured Heidi with a wooden stick between her teeth and a clamp from temple to temple, her body jerking. Then she pictured her in a dead quiet ward where she was checked on only for a few minutes a couple of times a day, never a breath of fresh air. She'd thought she was going to be on a farm! Nurturing plants in a greenhouse and lying on fresh grass with baby goats. That was a vision of the real Heidi, the one Dr. Goodman indicated might be liberated by ECT. Yet Maud hesitated about approving the treatment.

She gave the driver an extra-large tip for working on Thanksgiving and exchanged greetings of the day with everyone she passed inside the hospital. Some visitors were dressed up, likely on their way to happier places. Maud only wanted to go back to the silent apartment and read Agnes's notebooks. To earn that, she'd sit with Heidi for a decent amount of time.

Heidi's room was in shadows, and her body in the bed was still. A hard sob formed in Maud's chest and hurt her, but she couldn't make it budge.

"Hi, Hei," she said cheerily, absurdly. How would cheeriness help matters? "Happy Thanksgiving," she added just as brightly. It was how people talked to the ill.

She pulled the chair up to the side of the bed. "It's Thanksgiving, Mom. I think they have a special lunch for you. I'm going to stay and eat it with you. I hope they have stuffing, the kind we like.

Pepperidge Farm! Do you think that's a real farm? What would they grow, the herbs? Maybe the chickens. I hope not the chickens, though. Just the herbs. Did you tell me that in England they say herbs with the h spoken? Then would you say 'a herb?' I always say 'an herb.' I'd like to go to England . . ."

She rattled on, letting each thought spring from the last according to a convoluted set of turns in her mind. She was like a mouse running a maze for the first time, with no idea where she was going. It didn't matter, either. No one was timing her or watching her. She was on her own, and there was no piece of cheese waiting for her at the finish line. The food came and the orderly helped Heidi to sit up to eat.

"Should she go to the bathroom first?" Maud asked.

"She doesn't go to the bathroom." The woman lifted the lid off the plate of turkey, gravy, and yes, stuffing. She cut the turkey into tiny pieces. Maud considered saying she'd do it, but she felt intimidated and wanted to see how Heidi ate first. She felt the same way she had when she was faced for the first time with giving Clemmie a bath. She'd asked Heidi to do it, afraid she might make a mistake with the tiny creature.

She doesn't go to the bathroom. It was obvious now that she knew. The smell in the room, and her inability to rouse herself. They couldn't take her every hour, like a puppy.

"Has she ever spoken to you?" Maud asked.

The orderly put some food on the fork. Maud vacated the chair for her.

"Thank you, Miss. She's said a couple of words here and there."

"Can you remember them?"

The woman massaged Heidi's cheek until she opened her mouth. She deposited the food carefully, not too far back, and Heidi chewed.

"No, sorry. It's not sentences. Just words."

In a depressed state, Heidi lost sentences, and whole thoughts. She only had words, like the list. If that. It was unbearably sad.

Maud kept up a stream of conversation with the orderly and arranged a shampoo schedule with her. The fact was, she should be living closer so she could be more on top of things. She'd have to come more often, though the thought of making all these arrangements again was disheartening. Her life was so different from those of her friends, many of whom were single and working and out on the town. Maud could barely remember being out. The drink with Miles did not count! Not that she cared all that much, but a choice would be nice. Wasn't that what was always at issue? The freedom to choose.

"I can get you a tray," the orderly offered. "We have extra."

"No thanks," Maud said. "I'll eat later."

"You seeing people?"

"No. You?"

"I'll go to my sister's . . ."

She went on about who'd be there, the food, her relief at not being the cook, keeping up the same kind of patter as Maud had earlier. Maud half listened as she watched her listless mother eat by rote. Sounds made their way in from around the floor, other patients, other families, the metallic ring of a bucket struck by a foot or a broom, the elevator bell. A version of life. This was probably as good as it got, as Agnes Lee had suggested. Maud spent a few minutes lulled by that notion, until she realized she'd begun to acclimate to the situation—realized it when the rhythmic scraping of the plate, the gray meat, the pathetic pudding cup that Heidi couldn't even open on her own suddenly angered her. It wasn't acceptable! Maud had to get her mother better. She chose that she had no choice.

At the end of the meal she asked the orderly to leave Heidi sitting up. Maud went to the bathroom and ran warm water over a washcloth until it was soaked.

"I'm going to wash your face, Mom."

Gently, she ran the cloth over the familiar contours, a well-known and much-loved landscape. Heidi was compliant, and was it possible she enjoyed it? Maud took each of Heidi's hands and washed them, too. She considered doing her feet—surely she needed her nails cut—but that might be too much for one day. Heidi had been traumatized and Maud didn't want to inadvertently poke at a weak spot.

When Heidi was rinsed and relaxed, Maud took her hand again.

"Mom, you have to talk to me now. You can't go on like this. If you do you are going to be moved to a place where no one is expected to get better. That is not what should happen to you! It shouldn't happen to me and Clemmie, either. We need you. So you have to try."

Did she see a flicker of comprehension behind Heidi's eyes?

"The doctor here showed me a list of words you wrote a long time ago. I'm going to read them to you now, and I want you to tell me anything you can about them." She reached into her bag and pulled out the paper. "Here they are." She read them one by one, *snow, cold, fur, boots, ashes*, pausing between each of them to search her mother's face. She gathered all her will into one tough spot next to the hard sob in her chest and aimed a beam out of it straight at Heidi's heart. Speak, she willed. Speak!

But Heidi did not speak. Maud folded the paper and put it away.

"All right. It's a holiday. But I'll be back soon, Mom, and we'll try again. This is not going to be how you end up. It just isn't!"

She helped her mother lie back down and sat for another hour watching over her. She thought she had been taking care of her and in charge of her health, but now she saw she'd been doing it from the vantage point of someone about fifteen years old who still wanted the adults to fix everything. *But I am the adult*, she thought. *It's me and me alone.*

To her surprise, knowing she had to fight harder actually felt good.

She went back up to the apartment and found that an entire Thanksgiving dinner had been left for her on the counter. She began to cry. She wasn't used to being taken care of—she was the carer. Who had done this? Agnes had sent someone, possibly Mrs. Blundt, possibly another helper Maud hadn't heard of, but Agnes had to be behind it. Maud had already half-forgiven Agnes, and this pushed her feeling toward gratitude. Extra stuffing. Extra cranberry sauce. Perfect.

While she ate, she continued her exploration of the lives of the Franklin Square girls, saving the notebooks for a little later purely for the pleasure of anticipation. She opened the third book, *The Franklin Square Girls Know It When They See It.*

Gail entered the Zendo in the wrong spirit. Focus and serenity were about as far from her thoughts as the sun from Pluto. Husband, kids, house, you name it—though when she actually named it, it was called Rosalyn. Her mother. Where other mothers seemed to become softer and more accepting as they aged, Rosalyn was harsher, more cynical, more sharply critical. This morning she had called Gail to say she'd been lying in bed the night before thinking that Gail's bras didn't fit correctly. Too much fat hung over the band in the back, which was a distracting sight. She suggested Gail go to a good fitter, perhaps even in New York, a knowledgeable older woman who'd find styles that were more complimentary. Gail shook with rage, thinking of it. She took a seat on the cushion and leaped right up again. Sorry, she mouthed to the Zen master, and headed for a bar.

So arch! The girls were now women in their forties with children who were caught up in Beatlemania, while they were having affairs and smoking pot and taking tranquilizers and being treated dismissively at work and wishing they were either younger or older but not as they were. Maud carried the book into the tub and then into her bed and read for the rest of the evening. She laughed aloud, often, and wished there were fifty books in the series rather than only six. She'd track down a set when she got home. She decided she'd take one with her to read on the train and mail it back. What harm done?

The next morning, Friday, she packed her bag, unnecessarily checked the train schedule again—she'd take a train in the afternoon—and settled in the living room with coffee and muffins to read the rest of the notebooks.

CHAPTER 21

Agnes, Leeward Cottage, October 1960

Dear Elspeth,

Today I went to the library in Deel Town and asked the young woman behind the desk for help.

She called me by name, yet I didn't recognize her. "Of course, Miss Lee, I'd be glad to help if I can."

"Remind me who you are?"

"I am Karen Concord."

"Karen, of course. I apologize."

"That's all right, Miss Lee. I met you when you came in with Mrs. Wister last summer. I make a point of remembering our patrons."

She was all angles and droopiness. A narrow jaw with an overbite. Brown wispy hair hanging in icicles that poked into her upper chest. Ill-fitting clothes. She smelled of mothballs, to top it off. Honestly, Elspeth, it's not hard to look at a magazine. Or is that harsh?

"I'm sorry I don't know you. Are you from around?" I asked.

"Sort of. My father works at the cannery in Southwest Harbor.

James Concord? But I grew up with my mother in Ohio. I like it here, though."

"And are you working in the library full-time?"

"I am! I'm so excited! To be around books all the time? It was my dream, and it came true."

That can't be too difficult an ambition to fulfill, especially in a small town, where not everyone wants to be a librarian, but I smiled and agreed. "Have you learned the inventory yet?"

"No, not. But I am aware of all the categories. How may I help?"

I described my needs in some detail. She took on my request with the authority of her position, and we headed for the art books and carried a few over to a table. We rifled the pages until we found three good landscape paintings, and then spread the books open and studied the reproductions.

"Daunting," I said. "I have no idea how to paint trees in perspective."

She sympathized. "The last time I tried a tree at all was in second grade, a straight line and a ball of scribbles on top."

I laughed. "Oh, I did that, too."

"I guess everyone goes through that stage. I'll leave you to your work, Miss Lee. Call me if you need me."

"You can stay." That was impulsive, but she had one of your qualities. Your thin fingers.

We looked at the books together, admiring the paintings, talking quietly in a library hush even though no one else was there. We speculated about how leaves were painted. This sparked a memory, and I told her the story. It's not one of my happiest, and I hadn't thought of it in a long time. I told the whole thing to Karen, pent-up speech tumbling out. "There was a girl in my class who knew how to draw trees with far more technique than anyone else. Her work looked like a real tree. I went home that night and practiced how I'd seen her do it until I drew a tree that also was far more artistic and suggestive of real nature than my usual straight line with the scribble on top. During the next art class, I drew my version of what I'd learned from copying her. She looked across the table at what I was doing and ran for the teacher. Look, look, Agnes stole my tree! The teacher looked at her drawing, then at mine. The similarity was undeniable. The teacher said, 'She copied you. She knows you did it first. Don't you, Agnes?' I nodded. The girl wasn't mollified, and made the point, accurately, that we'd been taught we weren't allowed to copy. 'You aren't allowed to copy in some classes,' the teacher said, 'but artists learn by copying. It's a compliment.'"

"Did the girl understand that?" Karen asked.

"No. She only knew she'd been the best until I came along and copied her tree. I only knew that what she made was prettier than what I made, and I wanted to do that, too. The teacher settled it by saying I'd done nothing wrong. It was normal to learn by imitation, and art had always depended for progress on the admiration of one artist for another. She told the other girl to draw a few of her realistic trees and she'd hang an exhibit for Father's Day."

"Did that end it?"

Astute Karen Concord!

"No, she confronted me at lunch and accused me of being jealous."

"You weren't jealous?"

"No! I'm not a jealous person."

"That's good. I don't know if I am or not, I've never really had reason to be."

"Actually, I suppose I haven't either."

"I learned how to draw a horse from a book," Karen said.

"Show me."

She crossed to the desk for supplies. The library was pleasant on a cool afternoon. Out the window, sun-struck leaf dust turned to gold. When she came back, I gave a particularly interested and expectant smile. Poor little mouse.

"It's very easy," she said, "just a series of lines. The nose is a triangle. . . ." She drew slowly, so I could follow. When she pushed the paper and pencil over to me, I realized she was making up for the girl at school. An uncanny empathy. I tried but couldn't replicate her animated creature. I have drawn about thirty horses this evening!

We went back to looking at the art books, and I was faced with no clear solutions. Some trees were drawn meticulously, while others were rendered as dots of color that nevertheless made effective impressions. Karen returned to her post at the desk, and I stayed at the table for quite some time, puzzling out the problem, with no real luck.

I took the books out, and a couple of novels.

"It was nice to talk to you, Miss Lee."

"It was nice for me, too, Karen. Please call me Agnes."

"Thank you."

I turned to go.

"Miss Lee . . . I wonder if . . ."

She hesitated. I was curious.

"I wonder if the next time you come, you might recommend some books for me to read. I want to go to college. But I don't think I know enough to even apply."

"Surely you can go to the campus in Bangor."

"Yes." She nodded thoughtfully, hesitating. She is young, and still equates trust with sharing a confidence. I watched her deciding whether or not to tell me a secret.

"I want to go to Radcliffe," she said.

"Radcliffe!" I showed my own hand with that outburst, but I was too startled to hide my surprise.

"It's the best school for girls, isn't it?"

I recovered rapidly. "Yes, it's considered one of the best. It's very difficult to get in to." Was I protecting her, or dubious of her ability?

She nodded, modest yet intractable. "I've heard that. That's why I need help." She looked at me. "I need a list of books that I should read. Books that girls who go to Radcliffe would have read by the time they get there."

"Of course." Why not? She may as well try. Someone has to go to Radcliffe. Not me—I would never have left Philadelphia for Boston. Penn was fine. You may have done better by going to Bryn Mawr, away from boys. I learned my lesson!

At home, I set the heavy art books on the dining room table, our same old Philadelphia Chippendale, El. I haven't yet jettisoned it, because in size and sturdiness it's useful. Mrs. Circumstance shines it so brightly I can see myself in it, and when I laid the books out next to each other, they threw reflections out to their sides, and the wood swam with color. The sensation of moving light was abetted, as always during the hours of lowering sun, by the rainbows thrown from the crystal pendants dangling from the candlesticks.

Is Nan short for Eleanor?

Dear Elspeth,

Children find a chink and creep in.

This morning, even before I heard her footsteps, I sensed her coming. A vibration in the ether preceded her.

The door opened and shut. I was practicing my drawing at the dining room table, pencils and paper spread out voluptuously. I continued working, but tracked her movements by sound through the rooms. She now has the confidence of the familiar, and walks around the first floor as if she grew up here. I don't warn her, as I was so often admonished, against the possibility of hurting herself or breaking this or that. What does it matter if she breaks something, compared to her feeling as though she belongs?

It was around two in the afternoon. Our routine is drawing or playing a game and then we have tea and cookies while I talk and she listens. I have been telling her about my life—my childhood, that is. School, pets, early books, our parents, you and Edmund, Polly and Teddy, the many rules we lived by in Philadelphia, and the freedom of life on the Point. I could be reading her Tolstoy and the result would be the same. She doesn't understand. Yet I was careful about what I said as if she might, until today. Perhaps it was because she was in a pensive mood, or perhaps I was. In any case, I spilled the beans.

"Come in," I called out.

I kept working. Finally she came into the dining room. I didn't look around. She placed her hand on my arm, a heavy, damp touch, rain falling.

I turned around, feigning great surprise. "There is a frog! Dressed as a girl!" I covered my eyes.

She giggled. Pulled my hands apart. Stared at me, but when I didn't respond, pressed her nose to mine. See me.

"Nan? Is that you?"

She cocked her head and widened her eyes. I love her scent. It's not nice, or pretty. It's the odor of growth, like undergrowth, like dirt.

"What are you doing today? Do you want to do some drawing with me?" I pushed a piece of paper her way, and then went back to my work.

She put her hands on the edge of the seat and climbed up, first one knee and then the other, turned around and sat. I extended a pencil to her. I was trying to draw a campanula flower. Purple cups holding shadows. To my right, a pencil sought a place in a child's hand. I slowed down and grasped my pencil again in the triangular method I was taught. The other pencil got throttled near its tip. I pushed mine across the paper. This was imitated in a line that was slight on the outward foray, but more assured on the return. I went back to my work but was wholly aware of her, her industry, her unquestioning trust in what I was doing, and the simplicity of how she joined me. I doubt it even occurs to her whether or not to like me. I am a given, a fixture. Her companions are the trees, stones, small animals, birds, and Robert. The same companions I have chosen now—but I have chosen them after a lifetime of spending my days with people, and my adult life mainly in sickrooms, working with fervor and purpose during the days of hope, and then dull duty during the hopeless waiting. I'm not certain which is the more enervating, coming sorrow or sorrow itself. When it was going on, I put one foot in front of the next, lived one day at a time, as the dying live. Now I can look into the distance, across the water, past the horizon, with a growing interest in what's there.

Nan worked very hard. We didn't speak, but her breaths are a vocabulary. When she's concentrating, her tongue moves across her bottom lip as if polishing it. The air in the back of her throat laps, tide-like. The quality of her application to the task is impressive, and I believe she has a high intelligence—but I don't know much about children.

We spent another hour drawing, which seemed a long time to me for a child to focus. When Nan lay her pencil down and slid out of her chair, Mrs. Circumstance made grilled cheeses and tomato soup. After we ate, we headed into the glass room for a postprandial stretch on the wicker sofa. Star was with us, as always now. We walked around the room in a parade. Nan stopped to look at various objects, and lingered over the family pictures on the center table. I named everyone for her, and she touched their—your—faces. Then to the sofa, where Star thrust his head forward onto Nan's lap, and she tapped his back. I began to speak without a plan, and found myself back in the realm of the family pictures. As good a subject as any, and all the same to her.

First, Edmund. A car accident. No real surprise to anyone, such was his exuberance, his wildness, too often buoyed by Scotch. He didn't seem like a person who'd grow old, did he? He burned at too high a temperature to last a whole lifetime. He was the light soul in the house, the person who found humor behind every sofa cushion. Only Edmund was undeterred by our mother's austerity. He threw himself at her in every way possible, not so much determined to crack the façade—a mind welded to the society it came from—but to find the place he believed she must have saved for him when she decided to have children, that secret meadow or coveside where his real mother roamed, ready to lie on the ground with him and tickle. We girls kept our silliness confined to our bedrooms, or took it way outside, but he brought it into the living room in the form of jokes, limericks, mimicry, puns, impersonations, dances, and songs. He could imitate the voice and posture of anyone. After a visit from one of Grace's friends, he liked to sit where that person had, and speak exactly as she did. "You must come see my daffodils! I actually fear for their taking over the property! It must be so hard to live in the city in springtime! Please come cut my roses!" He was especially good at imitating Ailish Hancock, Polly's stepmother, the Irish factory girl. "Edmund Lee, it's the Fourth of July, and why aren't you wearing your red, white, and blue? Even the colored don the flag for Independence Day, though it was no independence for them!"

He was ingenious, wasn't he? We laughed until our mirth stopped making sounds and our faces were twisted like dried

apples and we were sure we'd die from lack of air. Edmund
studied our mother's face for signs of amusement—any sign would
do. If her lip twitched or her cheek bunched, he clapped his
hands and threw his arms around her neck. "Mummy, you are a
peach pie!" and she'd throw back her head and laugh!

I don't know what would have become of Edmund had he
grown older. He was getting tight too many evenings, acquiring
an exhausted look in spite of his continued swirling energy. I tried
to talk to him, but he made light of it, hugging me around the
shoulders and assuring me he was finer than fine. I have always
wondered about his accident. A single car accident, they called it.
Instantly dead, or so they told us. Who knows what that means?
What fraction of a second of consciousness might be included in
the word *instant*? If he had that fraction of time, what did he think
of? I'd guess it was his days as a boy, when mischief wasn't deadly,
but brought him love.

Then you. You became sweeter and sweeter as you turned to
Jesus more fervently, believing you understood him better with
every bite taken out of you by your disease. I'd walk in the room
and you'd tell me you were at Station Seven, when Jesus falls for
the second time. "Imagine his pain," you'd whisper. This dramatic
experience of Scripture wasn't part of our upbringing. Lachlan
took us to Meeting, but our mother believed in both the notion
of a Supreme Being and in the social importance of church and
made us go with her. "You are Episcopalians," she'd admonish us,
to correct our manners or wayward thoughts. We weren't, though.
Lachlan put his foot down before we were confirmed in the
Episcopal Church. "Too many worthy people among those ranks,"
he said, worthy being just a shade away from unctuous or holier
than thou. You were sorry, yearning for ritual and ceremony. Once
again I, for the hundredth and thousandth time, was grateful that
he'd protected and saved me.

Elspeth, we were so close, but I never understood your spiritual
life. You secretly wanted to become a priest and were crushed
when you learned that women weren't allowed to. "Doesn't that
prove to you that there's something wrong with the religion?" I
goaded. "It certainly does to me. You'd be a much better minister
than the Right Reverend William Blanchard." He was a snob who
read the prayers and psalms with the wrong words emphasized
and in a singsongy rhythm, robbing them of meaning he might
have communicated if he spoke normally. Instead, he magnified
himself.

Our Father WHO artinheaven HALLOWED beThy name,
Thy KINGDOM COME, Thy will be done on EARTH AS IT isin
heaven . . .

I rolled my eyes every time. "It is unfair," I told you, "and the
church's loss. You'd read normally, and you'd make pastoral
calls without covering your face with a handkerchief." The Right
Reverend, whom we referred to as our own Handkerchief Moody,
had grasped germ theory too well for his role. There were stories
of feverish parishioners shrieking when he entered their rooms,
veiled and dressed in black, appearing as though he'd come not to
comfort but to reap their souls.

You struggled with all the hypocrisies in religion. You were
too smart to embrace passivity, too clearheaded to mistake self-
abnegation for humility. You envied the nuns who started their
own orders and rules as a way to take control of their spiritual
genius. But your good, shrewd mind prevented you from
imagining that you could convince yourself of the sanity of the
church's attenuated stance against women simply by reading all
the centuries of misogynistic literature. Instead you became the
equivalent of a lay nun, devoted to work among the poor. My
parents were pitied, because you were so very beautiful. Beautiful
women are meant to marry. That Jesus tapped you on the

shoulder and asked you to follow him was considered a terrible waste, not to mention tasteless.

Is it awful of me to think that illness suited you? I did think that. You were finally able to simply read and pray all day long. You were on the equivalent of a honeymoon, and besotted. You told me your beliefs if I asked, but you never could speak about your visions. You questioned them fiercely, didn't want to fool yourself or get carried away by what might be a side effect of medication, or cells shooting up like fireworks in your brain, a purely biological phenomenon. You tormented yourself with this question so relentlessly that I had to intervene and ratify your most extreme experiences, against everything I myself believed. I sat by your bed while you were in your ecstasies and asked what you saw, heard, thought, and I wrote it all down. Your insights struck me as being at the highest level of purity and truth. It's a quality of truth that it is recognizable even if it's alien to one's own experience. You said an ant had as much value as a man, that nature was non-hierarchical in value—a truth that God had misunderstood in his early works. There was only one soul that showed itself in different forms, including the oblivion beyond the outer cosmos. Prayer isn't necessary. Prayer can come in between God and the truth. Nothing is necessary. All already happened, all is present, and that is all.

You saw the blazing lights that mystics see, but said you could have done without the pyrotechnics. Based on the dictation I'd taken, you came to accept that you really were a mystic, and I accepted it, too.

You died in summer, with our parents and me present. Your last words were *harvest moon*. After saying that, your face let go into death. I thought you'd have a smile, joining God, but your joy wasn't the stuff of deathbed scenes. We had a box delivered and a grave dug. Mourners dotted both our property and the Hancocks'.

At your memorial service in Philadelphia so many people came that they lined the streets and we walked along as if it were a royal reception.

I began to weep, recounting this. "Nan? Are you awake?" I touched her shoulder. A murmur, a waved hand, meaning—keep going. So imperious. I brushed my cheeks with my fingers and looked, for steadiness, out the window. The leaves have mostly fallen, so the pines are having their glorious reign. It's hard to believe they could be greener, but the cold saturates them gorgeously. She shifted her head back to see my face and pointed at my mouth. The lull had been too long. Keep talking, keep talking. How little she must have heard the sound of the human voice to find mine so desirable. We are a perfect pair, middle-aged woman and tiny girl, neither of us with anything else to do but live through an afternoon together. Neither of us very experienced in the world. Though I remember reading that whoever had lived to age four knew everything about the workings of the human heart. So I must. So must she, or nearly.

"All right, you asked for it. Now comes my mother." I raised my eyebrows portentously. She clutched at poor Star, who arched his back and paddled to be free of her grip. I intervened, worrying for his spine and lungs, by sliding my hand between him and her arms. He hopped across my lap and settled by my leg. She showed no sign that his defection bothered her. "The cow jumps over the moon," I said, and looked to her for acknowledgment.

"The lil dog waf!" she said.

I finished the verse, and she said the words as best she could. Making up for lost time. When her eyes closed again, I continued my story.

With Elspeth—you—gone, I was alone as I'd never been. I still lived with our parents, but they did not whisper with me at night. I worked harder, both on a new novel and on learning

Scherenschnitte—paper cutting. I cut black paper into shapes and pasted it on a plain background. Arduous and fine work, as purposeful as placing a foot correctly when descending a mountain. It required a concentration so fierce as to blot out the small thoughts and distractions that make up so much of what qualifies as an individual personality. I sought to be scoured.

Grace had a heart attack. She was at the Cosmopolitan Club for lunch, in the middle of the full-blown moment of cutlery clinking and perfume and powder wafting and ladies gathering information, when she tipped to her side in the chair and went unconscious. She was taken to the University of Pennsylvania Hospital, where they managed to revive her. A mistake. She didn't want to live, and never got well again. A year later she had the stroke that killed her. I wasn't sad when she died, except in a general way. Self-pity, I suppose. Is that not sometimes justified, though?

I kept my supplies in a man's briefcase I bought for the purpose and sat in different rooms in the house, slowly learning the scissors. I kept at it during Grace's illness. She frowned when she saw the small cuttings fall through my fingers to the floor. I mollified her by asking if she had any requests. I should have known. She wanted me to do Edmund from his various portraits, and then critiqued the result. "But his nose was never quite this long. His jaw was stronger. He had thicker eyebrows." I agreed—I couldn't get him right. She sighed, and left me to keep trying. I cut other shapes for her, but she wasn't interested. Nurses came and went in the room, but I sat with her, read to her, slept close enough to hear her call, helped her dress for visitors and put on her lipstick when Lachlan was about to come into her room. Yet she felt no special gratitude toward me that I was helping her to appear as her old self to the world. She had no will to live, and no affection left in her.

Our mother had a great deal of trouble being handled privately. I tried to interest her in cards, but she was too listless. She didn't even want to go to church. It was a matter of waiting for the last day to come. Lachlan and I both sat with her in the final forty-eight rasping hours. Predictably, she said the name Edmund a number of times, and the words Father and Mother, and Catharine, her long-dead sister. Then at the last, she said, "Put on your gloves!"

Grace Brown Lee. A person of her class. A person whose habits and manners stamped out the development of desire and predilection. A person who'd done exactly as she was meant to every day of her life, with the exception of one episode—the time of her mourning after Edmund's death.

I looked over at my audience. She'd fallen beautifully asleep, with her hands laced on top of her rounded belly. Our chocolate would have to wait a bit. I let her nap and went to speak with Mrs. Circumstance. Star sprang up when I stood, and we walked past windows filled with gold dust motes—ever present in spite of Mrs. Circumstance's best efforts. Every day of this first fall here has been miraculous.

There was only one story left to tell. The hardest one. Daddy has only been dead for five months. I am in the middle of a shift from being pinioned by his illness and its rage, and the beginnings of remembering him as I mainly knew him. He is gone, but coming back to me. Neither a memory yet, nor a presence. Oh, my father. Lachlan Lee, of the sanguine personality, the brightly applied intelligence. A person born into privilege at a time in history when the world changed dramatically. He saw the advent of the automobile, the airplane, the turn of the century. He didn't go to any of the wars as a soldier, but worked hard to offer support to the wounded and the displaced. He never questioned the ideal of pacifism. He practiced mild manners, and deflected conflict when it came his way. His general attitude was one of amusement and curiosity. Over time I understood that those weren't wholly natural traits, but the result of choice and discipline. The stories of him as a boy featured other traits, such as temper and competitiveness. He let those go, to be a light in the world.

He encouraged us to use our minds freely. I knew no other father of any girl at school who took her ideas as seriously as Lachlan took ours. He gave us no sense, at least not when we were children, that he saw limits for us—or that he considered himself smarter than us. We were brilliant as far as he was concerned, and he spent a lot of time with us asking what we thought about this or that. Often he presented us with a business problem he was working on at Lee & Sons, and asked us to tell him what we thought would be the right thing to do. He asked Edmund, too, of course, but that was to be expected, and perhaps because it was expected, Edmund wasn't interested in these sessions, and was apt to drift away to do something else. You and I were enthralled by his attention. He encouraged us to seek commonsense answers. But what was common sense? How did a person develop it? Slowly we refined our understanding of what was possible for the human mind, how elastic it really was, how far we could stretch and how much we needed to know to be sure that what we thought of as common sense wasn't subjective. He was leading us to believe that the best way to reason was to become as well educated as possible. The more we studied and learned, the greater pleasure he took in spending time with us.

I know people wonder if Daddy's attention, the way he treated us as interesting, had something to do with why neither you nor I married. It's a funny speculation, isn't it? That our minds may have been too well respected by a man? The intelligent bluestockings we had as teachers were marvelous, but not meant to set examples for our futures. Grace fully expected us to marry powerful men and be good partners to them. We might well have interests, even work of our own, but the strong message sent to us was that we didn't want to end up as spinsters. Yet both of us did. We each had chances to marry, but one cannot marry simply for the sake of marriage. Or we couldn't. It is true, though, that I liked being Daddy's companion, and chose it over other possibilities. A father-daughter relationship is unique in the kind of delight it brings to both persons, a proprietary pride that also contains an understanding of the boundaries that hold the two apart. I was proud going out with him in the city, having lunch at a restaurant, or in the private dining room at Lee & Sons. Most especially, for drives. Daddy and I both enjoyed nothing better than to get in the car and head out for the day to see what lay beyond. We prided ourselves on our sense of direction and only rarely consulted a map. We had disdain for people who said they were lost. We were only and evermore bushwhacking. We could go a hundred miles and back on a Sunday while Grace went to church and had midday roast beef and Yorkshire pudding in the company of relatives or friends. Daddy never felt the social pressure to be anywhere. Dozens were the evenings when our parents were meant to go out and Lachlan, at the last minute, felt uninterested for one reason or another, and our mother either had to make the call to excuse them or she went alone.

His mind deteriorated after he broke his hip and was stuck with the grinding rehabilitation, the walker, the wheelchair, the bed, death. I was present for every moment of it, and witnessed the gradual winnowing away from his personality those aspects that had served all his life to disguise or mitigate anger and insecurity, until they were all that was left. He needed me to sit with him in the dark, lonely hour before dawn. He spoke of the death of his brother at thirteen when Lachlan was fourteen. He spoke of the feeling he had after that of never really caring what became of him, for who was there for him to share it with? He hadn't cared what he did for a living, or whom he married—the more his wife would leave him alone the better. He wanted to be near his brother's grave here, but I never saw him visit it, did you, El? I'd had no idea of any of this. He often sobbed. Every mistake he'd ever made, every embarrassment, every act of thoughtlessness or perfidy that had been perpetrated against him, or that he'd performed, he relived in detail while I stroked his large smooth forehead and kept my eye on the thin gap at the edges of the curtains where the first gray light showed, and then on good days a rosiness, and finally a yellow that was my release, time to turn him over to the care of the day nurse who'd get him up and bathe him in the shower, or his wheelchair, or his bed.

His brother, his mother, his father, Edmund, Elspeth, and finally his Grace—these were the ghosts who haunted him. "Where is Agnes?" he'd shout at me. "She's deserted me." "I'm Agnes, Daddy," I assured him, but he looked at me with such dark doubt that I didn't try very hard to make him believe it.

He cursed me; he raged at me; sometimes he threw books or pictures or forks or glasses at me. I stood between him and that graveyard outside. I was an abomination, a dried-up old prune of a female, a witch, and a bitch. My father, who'd never once sworn in front of me, now spoke to me so horribly that my stomach turned sour; I could barely eat and had to take medicine to calm it. I knew that it infuriated him to have no control over his legs and body, to need to be diapered like an infant—yet what I knew wasn't a protection, as knowledge often isn't. I did my best to remain calm and detached, to cling to my role and not my affection, but every day, I failed. For him to hate me was unbearable. Yet I had no choice.

We moved up to Maine in the middle of May—he wanted to

die here. Up we came, quite a production, like Lord Marchmain returning to Brideshead to die. We settled him in his bedroom, and he had a couple of days of peace influenced by the sea air, but toward the end he became furtive, and looked at me suspiciously whenever I entered his room. When I heard him whimper at four and went in to him, he pulled one of his pillows to his chest and wouldn't speak to me.

A few nights later I suddenly knew—he was leaving. His skin was pulled tight over the bones of his face. His beard had come in, and I briefly wondered why he hadn't been properly shaved. What difference, I uttered out loud, I think. What does it matter? I watched him, intentionally slowing my breath and making it loud enough to hear. I wanted to calm him.

"Lachlan Lee. Father. It isn't easy to die for a person like you. You devoted your whole life to taking care of other people. You were a great man. Everyone who met you loved you. You ran a company in the best possible way under the current system. You were fair and trustworthy, and you made certain those who worked for the company improved their lot in life. You were a great husband and a beloved father. I love you. You have made it possible for me to live on my own terms and to be an artist. You kept a roof over my head and never once belittled me for not marrying. You treated me as though my thoughts were as valuable as anyone's. You set me free, and now it is my turn to do the same for you. It's time to go."

He struggled for a while longer, then lost consciousness. His breath—that guttural rasp that haunted me in my sleep—grew slower, and less effortful. The gaps between breaths grew so long I was sure he was dead, and was startled whenever he breathed again. Finally no other breath was mustered. His chest was still as a rock. I was glad. I don't know what disease changed him from being the most courteous and high-minded of men into a bitter raving roil of bad behavior. A dementia, certainly, but what and how no one was ever able to say.

I have often wondered why I've survived. Yet I know the answer. It's luck. Luck is a greater factor than anyone who succeeds ever wants to believe. The idea that one is destined to be the person who remains standing, the person smart enough to make all the money, to retain the beauty, is far more seductive. If there is good luck, there is bad luck. That is a reality no one wants to contemplate.

But it is reality. I am merely lucky to be alive.

Mrs. C. came in with cups of chocolate and I jiggled Nan. She rubbed her eyes with circled fists. When she saw me, she smiled. The thrill is astounding. Is this how our mother felt about Edmund?

"You were asleep," I told her. "You were sound asleep. A long winter's nap." She looked around, drawing herself back into the world. "It's time for us to have our chocolate and then I'll take you home."

She nodded. I ran my hand brusquely over her hair and smoothed it down. No matter that her father let her dress and groom like a wild animal. That wouldn't happen in my house.

"A long winter's nap, like a little bear. Shall we?"

I pointed to the cups, but she got up and trotted to the middle of the room, to the table where the family pictures sat. She pointed to Edmund, Elspeth, Mother, and Daddy. Dutifully, I looked at each of them. Then she began again.

Pointing to Edmund. "Edmund," she said.

Pointing to Elspeth. "Elthpith."

Pointing to Mother. "Muther."

Pointing to Daddy. "Daddy."

Yes, yes, yes, yes, I said, and she went through the game again. After the second time, she looked at me. "Aness."

"Ag-nes."

She struggled with her tongue, and we repeated the name until she could say it. My name. Agnes. Ag-nes.

"Agnes," she said. I wished I had a better name for her to learn, but she didn't know the difference.

I wanted to point to everything, tell her the word for each item in the room, in the world, more, more, emotions, ideas, all. All the whole language could offer. But I limited myself to the cups and the spoons. Enough for one day.

"Come on, Little Nan. Let's get you home."

We left the house. The last of the gold sun gave the impression of warmth, and I didn't feel the October chill until we were halfway across the meadow. I had the same sense of purpose as I had when caring for the family—a straight, strong bearing, loose-limbed and capable. A pioneer woman with substantial skills. A lamp shone from a window of the cabin, a compass point, and it was a moment before I realized I'd lost her. I turned around and there she stood, fixed to the ground like a tree, waving rhythmically. "Robert," she called, no lisp, no hesitation. "Robert."

He stood a few dozen feet away and waved at us.

Does love begin at three? It has for Nan. I saw it in the way she turned entirely toward him, body and soul.

So, sister, a child has spoken the names of the dead. Tonight they are all back with me—perhaps you are with them often. I hear their night sounds, their footfalls, their doors closing, and the creak of their mattress springs. I am closing my notebook, turning out my light, falling asleep among them.

Why am I seeing Virgil Reed's face?

Maud stretched. Went to the bathroom, combed out her hair. Called Clemmie, who once again was proclaimed to be too busy to talk. Paced around the apartment. Nan in the notebooks was the same age as Clemmie, which was only a coincidence but nevertheless made her story feel personal to Maud. She supposed she should have seen it coming that Virgil was going to gain in appeal, though she wasn't yet convinced of his reliability and felt protective of Agnes, who knew nothing of men. Reading about Virgil raised the question of what Agnes had really thought last summer when Maud told her about Miles. Did the sound of him remind her of Virgil? Surely Agnes was worldly about such things by now—she acted as though she was. Maud couldn't bear the idea of all this drama being a secret. It was a clever try on Agnes's part to head Maud off at the pass by sharing these notebooks with her, dangling intimacy in exchange for a cessation of the campaign for more revelations in *Agnes When*. Don't kid a kidder, Maud thought.

As she looked out at Rittenhouse Square, she remembered Heidi stopping to watch the chess games and musical performances and break-dancing in Washington Square Park. Often she watched for hours. Maud went home, did her homework, and came back to find Heidi still watching. Maud considered pulling her away, but she saw that the people Heidi watched looked over at her to see her reactions. Maud realized people liked to be appreciatively observed even more than they liked being given money. Perhaps that was what Agnes was after—simply to be seen.

Like Goldilocks, Maud tested out the chairs and sofas before deciding where she'd settle in for her next stretch of reading. She ended up in a chair she moved to face Rittenhouse Square, but she didn't have Heidi's patience or her interest in people. She liked words and how they worked. Maud bore into Agnes's notebooks, searching for an argument for sharing these stories that would work.

CHAPTER 22

Agnes, Philadelphia, December 1960

Dear El,

I have read about cataclysmic changes, in the Bible, in novels. I
like such stories. Jesus speaking to Saul on the road to Damascus,
striking him blind, changing him from being an anti-Christian
murderer into the definer of the religion; Ebenezer Scrooge, the
beneficiary of visits from three concerned ghosts, changing from
miserly to generous; the Archangel Zadkiel staying Abraham's
hand before he sacrificed his child Isaac and made of him a
burnt offering. Visits from supernatural agents of change that are
externalized metaphors, surely, for sudden, swift insights. They
give the lie to the idea that change is always incremental.

It happens—I now know that for sure. How can I explain? Let
me steady myself, El. I must orient myself in order to describe how
disoriented I have been.

First, I should tell you that I am back in Philadelphia, in our
house, here for only a brief holiday visit and a few doctor and
lawyer appointments. Star and I took the train down and arrived
to frost and colored lights in people's windows and strung across
the streets. Pat O'Hara had everything set up when I arrived—

rooms cleaned, fires laid, food ready to be heated—but I was, as I'd requested, alone for the evening. I took a bath, ate by the fire, and wrote out a daily schedule to keep me on my toes. I slept deeply in my old bed and the next morning hopped right to it.

I worked my way through a tray of Christmas cards, answering and posting, and over the next few days made the rounds, including Christmas Eve with Uncle William et co. and Christmas Day at Polly's. Archie Lee was the most amusing of everyone, a very free laugh and a dry wit. I think he's headed for Lee & Sons, as he seems too sybaritic to claw his way up in another business. He pays lots of attention to me, which I'm not against, and is adored by both his parents. When I tried to tell him about FP in the fall, though, he glazed over. He saw me notice and took my hands in his. "It's too quiet for me, Cousin, and too dry. You understand, don't you?" I don't, but I was charmed, as he knew I would be, in spite of my being against charm in principle. Polly's group was fine, too. I hoped to have a moment alone with her, which I haven't yet. I want to tell her about what happened to me, and I must find a moment for a private visit during this short trip. Or she must. Her house is mayhem. Anyway, I have been wanting to tell you first—to write it all down—but I have been too busy and too preoccupied. Now here I am, wide awake from days of sugar and in a heightened state of mind because of all the ghosts of Christmases past thronging the streets of this old city. It is time.

The cataclysm began six weeks ago, one afternoon when I was working at my desk in my bedroom and got up for a stretch. I walked to the window. That day, as was often the case, Nan was walking across the frosted meadow, moving purposefully, pursuing a plan. My heart filled from watching her. Such a free creature, so game. I vowed to paint in the same spirit, yet my heady resolve was interrupted by a more practical consideration. Was Nan dressed warmly enough for such a chilly day? I had been judicious in my warnings and instructions, phrasing them so as not to scare her or inhibit her. I'm determined not to teach her to fear everything, as we were taught, or that manners are preferable to feelings. I honestly don't yet know what *free* is, but I know what it isn't. I decided to trust that if she were cold, she'd seek warmth.

I took Star downstairs and let him out to join Nan. She squealed as he ran to her, and they fell immediately into a game of chase in the graveyard. Then Nan walked among the stones, sometimes banging on them with a stick as if they were drums, sometimes lying on the ground with her head by a stone in the exact position she'd be if she were beneath the earth. Eerie and natural, both. She sang, too. I couldn't hear her, but I saw her sway as she does when she sings. I thought I must teach her more songs—her voice is sweet.

"Bring Star back in when you get cold," I called out. She waved, and I climbed up to the third floor to fiddle with my painting. I'd graduated from practicing on paper or cardboard to a wall. I was painting a mural of a shoreline, pines, water. It wasn't very good—not good at all—but I was pleased by it anyway. One section, perhaps two square feet, came out well; that was encouraging. No one would ever see it but me and Nan and Mrs. Circumstance. Nan criticized my work quite fairly in her limited but growing vocabulary. She suggested adding a dog—a good idea.

I'd absorbed a great deal from the borrowed library books, and was on the way to inventing a style of my own to depict the local landscapes, the flora and fauna of the island. I wasn't interested—luckily!—in making realistic reproductions. I only hoped to capture my feeling for all I love here. This first fall on my own.

Twenty minutes passed, and I felt every one of them tick by. I left the room and went to the window on the landing to check on Nan. She'd climbed up on one of the graves and was waving her arms, pretending to be a bird. Star looked up attentively, a good audience. Nan jumped to the ground, and Star put his paws on Nan's pants and waited for a pat or a kiss. Nan, predictably, offered neither but climbed up again. This was a game that would tire her out. Mrs. Circumstance had a stew on the stove, and Nan would certainly be ready for it by lunchtime.

Satisfied that child and dog were safely within range and well occupied, I went back to my wall and tried to paint a fir tree. I'd worked for perhaps ten minutes when I heard Star barking. The tone instantly terrified me, and I began to run, dropping my paintbrush somewhere and grabbing at the finials on the bannister to swing from one floor down the stairs to the next, skipping steps recklessly, pounding against the risers at such a gallop I sounded like more than one person. I only slowed once, at one window, to look for the trouble. I had no doubt there was trouble, my flesh had risen into a hard carapace, and blood rushed past my ears. A glance showed Nan on the ground and I kept going, running, registering as I ran what else I'd seen in that brief second—a stone lying across her torso. I huffed the harsh grunts that come only from the worst fear.

Mrs. Circumstance came out of the kitchen. "Get Hiram!" I shouted, and we ran out of the house in opposite directions, she to find her husband, I straight to the child. Robert appeared at my side and our footfalls landed out of rhythm, a herd in panic. We arrived in the graveyard and got on either side of the stone—it was Daddy's stone that I'd yet to have Hiram put into the ground, it had been leaning against a rock in the field—and tried to lift it. "Get it off!" My voice came out in a gruff rasp. I summoned all my strength, but the shock of the stone's weight circumvented it, and my fingers were useless as pencils to perform the feat. We groaned. My muscles tore and shredded. After a few seconds we lifted the stone a little, reducing the full pressure on her but no more. Then—we were stuck. If we admitted defeat and let the stone back down onto her, it would crush her further. We stared at each other. The stone was freezing, and because I couldn't feel my fingers anymore I imagined I felt the stone sliding incrementally out of my grasp. I'd planted my feet wrongly to begin with and now couldn't alter my posture. There was nothing to do but wait. Wait and hold on, hold on. I didn't pray—why would I? Instead Robert and I held fast to each other's gaze, sending telepathic messages that we could do this. Not wasting our breath.

I don't know how long that aspect of the ordeal went on— probably not much more than a minute. My hands were dumb, numb stubs. Time stretched long and wide until Hiram appeared and he and Mrs. Circumstance lifted, too, and we got the stone off Nan and lay it flat on the grass. Nan looked intact at first glance, and I very nearly smiled, but when Robert tried to put his arms under her blood rushed from her mouth and nose, and I saw her legs had broken.

"Go call the ambulance!" Hiram told Mrs. Circumstance.

"Bring a blanket and water back," I said. "Please."

Mrs. Circumstance windmilled her arms, pounding across the meadow. Robert's hand hovered over Nan's forehead, but he didn't touch her, only whispered. Oh, the long minutes! We wanted to take her to the hospital ourselves, but decided we must wait, we didn't know how to lift her safely. My legs dampened from the chilly ground. Star licked Nan's hand. Every moment extended into ages. I began to think more clearly about the hours ahead, whom to call, what to do. Mrs. Circumstance prayed. Robert whispered to Nan words I couldn't hear.

All of us had forgotten about Virgil. None of us even thought to go fetch him; he really wasn't a part of our world. So when he loomed over us casting a shadow, he startled and confused us. "No!" he cried out, and the word went through me like a knife. He knelt next to her, his legs bent like clothespins beneath him,

and took her hand. I felt a stab of hatred. He was the one meant
to be watching her, he was the parent! Good Lord, I finally had
my own life and though I loved her and wanted to do everything
for her, I couldn't be her babysitter! I had the mad thought that
he shouldn't even be among us, worrying about her—he'd lost his
privileges for doing so. But that meant I was responsible, which I
wasn't. This was his fault.

Nan was conscious when the ambulance arrived. The team
examined her, and stepped a few feet away from us to confer out
of our hearing. If I'd been frightened before, I now felt useless,
too. The seconds of waiting for them to come back were agony.
Morbidity had become my habit, and I couldn't be like Robert,
who continued to urge her on, but instead I prepared myself for
the worst by rehearsing it. The joy I'd had for a couple of months
had always felt borrowed. My real life was death-drenched.

"We'll need your help," said a voice above me. "Do as we tell
you."

We all painstakingly slipped a pallet beneath her, disturbing
her as little as possible. She moaned. "She's shocky," I heard one
of them say, and they repeatedly took her pulse. She turned gray.
We were dull with fear by then. The ambulance drivers loaded her
into the truck, and Hiram told them that Virgil was the father. I
have to admit, I didn't even think of doing so.

"We can't take him with us, we're going to have to be back there
with her."

"I'll drive," I said. I asked the Circumstances to man the
fort, including Star, and I set off with Virgil Reed next to me, a
theretofore unimaginable occurrence. He was silent during the
drive. A palpable, suffering silence. I rode as if alone, in my own
thoughts. It was a dreadful ride, endless, as we got behind a slow
truck. The land's beauty, as always, provided ballast for my wild
emotions, but not much. The distant mountains' rocks showed

through the bare trees, like a bald scalp. The ocean appeared in flashy, frothy brilliance. Yet I was not at one with them, not under pressure. I was human, and I pressed my stomach to keep from wailing.

Leaving the close atmosphere of the car and striding into the hospital provided relief; it was so familiar to me from all the time I'd spent there with everyone in the family that I felt, for the first time, that everything would be all right. The layout was part of me, and I took myself down the corridor to the nurses' station. Nan had been taken straight to the operating room.

Sandy, one of our father's nurses, stopped to greet me. She led me to the waiting room and told me a doctor would come talk to me as soon as there was any news. The only two there were Virgil and I. We took turns in uncoordinated spasms of sitting and pacing. Occasionally I glanced at him—the father—but I couldn't discern the difference on his face between numbness, boredom, anxiety, fear, or whatever else. In spite of literal movement, he was deadly still. Masked beyond recognition. As with most people in stillness, he became younger in appearance. I had never spent this much time with him, or so close to him. He was really only a youth. I had the thought that I should help him more than judge him, and realized that I was falling apart. Judgment is my home base.

Hours passed before anyone came but Sandy, who poked her head in every so often. When a doctor appeared, he asked for the relative, but Virgil looked as dumb as a fish. I stepped in to do the talking.

"I'm Agnes Lee. My father was a board member of this hospital." Can you believe I said that? Putting myself forward!

"I'm Dr. Mercer. She's alive. But her injuries were massive. Her pelvis is broken and her legs are like soup."

"I see." I behaved as though I were tough, and could handle anything, but I felt undone.

"The leg bone is in pieces. She had vast internal bleeding. We can't work on her anymore for now, her body can't take it. She'll be moving to a room in the ICU soon."

"When can I talk to her?" I asked, as if it were my right.

"We have an Engstrom respirator here and I think it best that she be on it for a while. We have to wait to see how things go forward. It may end up being best to move her down to Boston. The next day or two will make matters more clear."

Days! I wanted her to be home in days. I wanted her in my house, to nurse her myself. I wasn't going to leave that to him.

"I want to see her," Virgil asked.

The doctor looked at me. The rule—only relatives. The reality—I was in charge.

"That's her father."

The doctor remained cool. He'd seen a lot. He turned to Virgil. "You can't go in but may look through the window. A nurse will come get you when she has been moved."

Another wait. It irritated me to have to sit in a room with such a morose and taciturn person. What did he even have to do with any of this? My interpretation of their situation was that Nan's mother had died or had been somehow swept away, that Nan ended up with him out of custom and legality but that result had never made any sense. I berated myself for not stepping in more completely. My manners had made a muddle of things.

A different nurse appeared and led us down corridors and through doors to a glass window in a door. We couldn't see much. Little Nan looked like the subject of an experiment, jammed with tubes and lines, the respirator mask obscuring her face. I watched her for some time, until we were told we may as well go home, there'd be nothing different to see or do that day. "I'll stay," Virgil said. He pointed to the ground, indicating where he might sleep. I asked the nurse to arrange beds for both of us, but then I glanced at Virgil. It is hard to describe what I saw. A mix of grief and some other emotion I couldn't interpret. It seemed his inner being had come to a point, a place of determination. If I didn't entirely understand, I was nevertheless set straight about his attachment.

"I've changed my mind. Just find a bed for this man. He is the child's father. I must go home, but I'll be back tomorrow."

I made the long, quiet drive back to the house in the dark. Star was subdued, as if he knew. I had a bowl of soup and slept in spite of the fact that I was sure I wouldn't be able to.

Nothing changed in the next several days. I went back and forth to the hospital and sat in Nan's room with Virgil, both of them silent. He appeared to be asleep most of the time, but every so often he'd stand by her bed and hold her hand. I spoke to her, though it was a job to overcome self-consciousness in front of him. I encouraged her to come back to us. She showed no sign of hearing me.

One cold morning, when Star and I were out for a walk, I again practiced the mental discipline I'd learned through all my other nursings—the skill of keeping my mind in the cold, bright moment. This was tough, and especially hard with Nan, but it was best I preserve my strength and concentration for all the tasks ahead.

So I looked around me at the day. Winter had come in with great dignity and beauty. No heavy snow yet, but the light was of a different hue than I'd ever seen, gold-toned unless it was rainy, white gold, yellow gold, pink gold, tipping the bleached meadow with an auric veneer. The leaves had bowed out for the year, and the firs had filled with sap for their dominant moment, which they took on with military bearing and notably good posture. The cold road pushed my feet away, but when I walked across the earth, my footsteps melted the frost, and I left a trail of dark marks in my wake. Star too. The small animals he enjoyed chasing in

the warmer gathering seasons had burrowed in, so he pushed
his snout into their holes and sometimes gave a bark to remind
them that he hadn't gone anywhere. He turned around to see my
reaction, and I offered him a believable amount of praise.

We walked down to the end of the road, and then home across
the Sank and through the yards of WesterLee and Meadowlea. I
peered into the houses, at rooms of fantastical white creatures,
oddly shaped, nothing like either real furniture or real animals.
Some of the configurations made me smile, as did the lengths
people went to—or told their servants to go to—to protect
valuable surfaces from the fearsome ravages of dust. Things were
packed up as carefully as they'd be in English country houses,
though there wasn't much here worth protecting. It occurred to
me that a children's book might be written about these creatures.
It could be from the point of view of animals in winter, a squirrel
hanging upside down from the roof and peering in, or a herd
of deer or moose quietly walking by. They'd wonder if these
sheet creatures were a new species come to town. Each of them
would greet the newcomers and ask them to come out to play,
but the creatures wouldn't respond. This would happen over
and over until one day they'd walk by and the creatures would be
gone; people would have returned; and in the houses there'd be
nothing to see but furniture. The animals would move away into
the woods for the summer, but when fall came again they'd creep
back up to the houses and look in at their silent friends.

I took it as a good omen for Nan that I had had an idea that
she'd enjoy hearing.

At the hospital I headed straight to the ICU, only peripherally
aware of the corridors, the nursing station, the beeps and clatters
of the place. Before I went to the waiting room to greet Virgil—
manners, again—I stopped at Nan's room. The heap on the floor I
became was only a vague sensation, and still is. The pain of hitting

the tile, being picked up, spoken to, and told that no, she wasn't dead—she hadn't passed, was how the nurse put it; she'd only been moved out of the ICU into a real room, isn't that good news—all happened as far from me as fear can exile a person from herself. I was numb and didn't feel the mercurochrome or the stitches. I rested on a cot until a nurse came and spoke to me and then a doctor did the same and I was told I was all right and could get up.

I wasn't all right. I'd received a deep shock, worse even than the accident. My mind assumed an empty room meant death.

A nurse led me to Nan's new room in the children's ward. Bright pictures and children's drawings hung along the walls in the halls. Gingerly, I entered her room, for fear of scaring or waking her. The lights had been turned off, and the atmosphere was warm and gray. I made out the shape of a bed jutting out from the center of the far wall. Far fewer machines and fewer lines worked in and around her, and no ventilator loomed behind her. She alone made her small chest rise and fall. I crossed to her and bent over to hold her—not an embrace, but just a light touch on her arms. Her body was thick with castings, but the swelling in her face had lessened. Over the past days I'd often compared her utter stillness to the cabinet cards we had in our house from decades past of small children who hadn't survived—children who at first glance appeared to be asleep, yet on a closer look, could be seen to lack the vitality that inhabits a face even in the depths of sleep. Nan looked alive. Her hair lay smooth on the pillow. Someone had brushed it.

I spoke quietly to her, on the assumption that at some level she could hear. I have no idea what I said. Sweet nothings. Encouragements. I held her hands in mine, lay my head on her heart, murmured and reassured, while gradually becoming aware of a sound behind me, throaty and low. A cough. I whirled around. There was Virgil, sitting mutely against the far wall, watching me.

Had he been there the whole time? I felt angry and vulnerable. Yet I didn't want him to know even that much about me.

I glanced at him, and he slid his eyes to the side.

"You must be very pleased. Look how much better she is. Aren't you happy for that?" I was closer to him than I'd ever been, so close I smelled him, his ragged clothes, his unwashed hair and beard. Who was he to designate himself such an exception to the norms of civility?

He nodded without meeting my eye.

"I fainted earlier when I didn't see her in the ICU. I was afraid . . ." I stopped, and considered how harsh it would sound. "I was afraid she'd died overnight." I stared at him, but he didn't look up. "But here we are, in life as we've known it lately. I've brought soup and bread today." Did I mention I have been feeding him? Or I should say Mrs. Circumstance has.

"Thank you."

His muted acknowledgment, his labored nod, brought up through my veins a boiling anger, the accumulation of a lifetime of caretaking and doing for others tasks no one wanted, whether paid for or obliged to perform, of being thanked in words that can't even touch on what it means to be a living person stuck in the yawning time register of impending death. How was it that he could see me arrive day after day and show a parental level of devotion to his child, and a neighborly sense of consideration toward him, and not even—what? Write me a thank-you note? What did I expect?

I wanted to kick him. His smell nauseated me. How dare he impose his unwashed body on me and everyone else around? There were showers in the hospital. It was unfair to the nurses that he didn't clean himself, and Nan—I could hold this in no more. "I am here now, Virgil. I plan to sit here all day. I've been here every day since the accident. Do you realize that? I have been here every day. I come, stay, go home, take care of Star, help get food for you, and come back. That is what I do. Now I'll tell you what you must do. You must get up now and take a shower."

He laced his fingers. His jaw, a structure hidden beneath the great wave of tawny beard that drowned his face and neck, clenched hard, stubbornly, compressing the skin under his eyes. Two could play at that game. I was our mother's daughter—I clenched my jaw right back at him.

"Virgil—do you hear me?"

He swung his head to me with a bovine torpor. The stench that came of his smallest movements was medieval.

"Right now. I am going to get an orderly to show you where. You are showering, and you are wearing hospital scrubs until I bring you clean clothes tomorrow. If you don't do this, I am going to ask that you be evicted. Do you even have clean clothes?"

Nan's clothes always seemed clean enough. I saw clothes drying on the grass outside the Chalet sometimes.

He nodded.

"May I go in the Chalet and get them?"

He looked at me quizzically.

"Your house. The cabin. We call it the Chalet. May I retrieve your clothes?"

He nodded minimally, but enough. At the nurses' station I made arrangements for his defrocking and ablutions. Two orderlies went to get him, and we passed in the doorway as I reentered to be with Nan. His head was bent, and as he brushed by me, the degree of his exhaustion snapped at my chest. Though I wanted to wring his neck I pitied him and was grateful to him for staying with Nan all the time, though why I should have felt grateful to him, her own father doing his duty, made no sense.

Everything was so mixed up.

After Virgil went to the shower, a nurse skirted Nan's bed, adjusting lines and checking heartbeat and temperatures.

"She's better," I claimed.

She looked up at me and nodded. I kept my expression calm, neutral. I'd learned to manage alarm around medical workers, so they told me more.

"She's improving. She has a long way to go," the nurse said.

"Is she out of danger?"

She checked my face again. "She most likely is."

We seemed to be yelling in the quiet room.

"What can be done?"

"Watch and wait. She's young. Her body wants to heal."

She checked the catheter bag, the dressings, all without asking me to step outside. I'd become part of the furniture. When the nurse had gone, I spoke to Nan quietly and held her hand. She was so large when she was in my house, her spirit filling the space, but in the bed, she was only a small girl, a berry. The thought of Lachlan's gravestone falling onto her made me sick over and over again. I felt it in my own bones.

An orderly stopped in the doorway. I barely looked up, only noticed the uniform. She came in and touched Nan's leg. It seemed too personal a touch, and I bristled.

"Excuse me," I said, which I never say. *Who the hell are you?* would have been more representative of my feelings.

She turned toward me and her hair swung around, flinging droplets. Wet hair, and not a woman at all.

He'd shaved. I'd never seen him without a beard big as a mountain man's, but it was gone now. Without all that hair, his skin showed clear and clean, pale from nonexposure. I stepped away from the bed, making room for him. He passed by me, all soap and shampoo, and he laid his hand on Nan's brow, as he had in the cemetery after the accident. He brushed her hair tenderly

with his fingers. I probably should have looked away to afford
them privacy, but I was transfixed.

After a while he went back over to the two chairs in the room.
I was tired by then and sat down next to him. He looked very thin
without his hair, like a dog freed from a coat of neglected mats.
And he smelled good. That was a first.

"You look a lot better," I said.

He gave a small shrug.

"I'm so glad Nan is better. I can't help picturing her over and
over with the stone on her legs."

Why did I say that? What did I want, what did I expect? It was a
reference to horror—and Virgil was clearly sufficiently horrified.

He let go, of all his muscles, all his strength, his wherewithal
to endure, and collapsed to the side, down and down and down,
until his head and shoulders were stopped by my lap. If my lap
hadn't been there he'd have hit the floor.

And then, Elspeth, the strangest thing happened. I had a vision.
I saw something I can only call his soul. It was an orb, a glowing
sphere with no edges, though wisps sprouted from its vaporous
caul, and searched by sensation for pathways outward in a casual
but also purposeful desire to connect with what existed outside. I
saw a tentacle come for me, and I hoped I had a soul of my own
open enough to receive the gesture—

No. That's abstract. Let me try again.

He was light. A dead branch. I could feel the whole of him.
He sobbed hard and noiselessly and I had no idea what to do.
Awkwardly, I put my arm over him to prevent a fall. His breath
was uneven and tears ran from his eyes. I was afraid to move,
and embarrassed in advance for the coming moment when
he'd realize it was me he'd reached for—someone he didn't
know. Seconds passed. His heart beat against my arm and I felt a
crackling inside my chest, an eggshell breaking. My stony heart.

He still didn't move. All the conventions of comfort were being violated, and I was surprised and undone by it. I lost my bearings, my heart seemed to stop—but instead, it received him. I don't know how else to put it. My mind got out of the way and a door opened. Pictures came to me—Virgil running down a playing field, Virgil walking down a path at a college with his head down, Virgil as a baby working out how to stack blocks, snapshots of his past, maybe twenty in all. I still see them clearly.

He stayed in my lap for a long time. There was no clock in the room to measure by, no nurse came in. We stayed attached, and when he finally sat up and pulled away, it was from a different person than who I'd been when he fell. For many days afterward all I could think was: something has happened to me.

It happened. I feel no skepticism about it. That's because of you. Remember how you always said there is a parallel universe to ours where everything is as it should be? Virgil's naked grief put me in touch with that parallel place, and I saw him at his core. He may have seen me at mine as well. I wonder if we will ever talk about it.

The next morning I set out to get his clothes. It snowed a little overnight, and my footsteps showed on the way to the cabin. A song played in the cold air, each note hardening like cooling candy rather than floating off on a breeze. I listened with a passive curiosity, and slowly it came to me it was my voice I heard. I was singing! "O come, O come, Emmanuel." I thought of you, El, and how delighted you were when we had the opportunity to hear or even belt out this hymn with its dour and solemn duty outlined for the new baby Jesus. Ransom captive Israel. Tall marching orders.

No one had been in the Chalet for weeks, so it was very cold. I got a shiver of nostalgia at the sounds of the boards under my feet, mimicking a downward slide on a scale as I pressed on them, and rising up again as I lifted my foot. Wouldn't it be a pleasure to have recordings of favorite sounds to listen to when one was far away?

In the main room Virgil had moved the furniture to suit his purposes. The small dining table was now a desk on which lay a stack of notebooks and a pottery mug full of pencils. I stared at the tableau, feeling a sense of déjà vu. I opened a notebook and stood by the window and read a few pages courtesy of the morning light. A love story, it seemed. Polly was right—he was an artist. A writer. In a past stage of life I would have been horrified by my invasion of someone else's privacy, but in my grief I'd become more feral, and the niceties of conscientious behavior seemed a bit quaint. Now that I knew he had a project, the contradictory behavior he practiced toward the little girl, ignoring her all day at home but not once leaving her side in the hospital, made better sense. He was working and what is a worse disturbance than a child? Didn't someone say that the pram in the hallway is the enemy of art?

I went to Nan's room. One of Polly's old quilted spreads was pulled up under the pillow—the one with the white background and tiny pink and green flowers strewn everywhere. If I remembered, the other side was green-and-pink stripes; I lifted the corner—yes. A stuffed bear rested against the pillow, and a collection of lucky stones, black with a white line in circumference, walked across the sills. A white wooden chair in the corner, and a small chest of drawers, also painted white, against the far wall—furniture that had belonged to the Hancocks since the age of the dinosaurs. On top of the chest sat the paper, pencils, and crayons I'd given Nan. Her clothes barely took up one layer per each drawer.

At the hospital I handed him a paper bag of clothes, his toothbrush, a notebook, and some pencils. The two chairs were still next to each other, but I felt shy about sitting beside him again. I also felt shy about moving the second chair, but that seemed the less fraught alternative. I carried it to the far wall and opened my book. It was peaceful, really, sitting in the room, reading and waiting. The quiet concentration of thought might be good for Nan, as if we were nuns in the room praying for her. Every so often I looked up and glanced at Virgil. Strands of hair obscured his face. The fifth time I looked up he was already looking my way, but not exactly at me. Looking into space in my direction. I made an expression of compassion, for Nan, and for the long hours we spent sitting here. He blinked. We looked back down.

I brought several tuna sandwiches and Star the next day. He gave a series of sympathetic squeaks when he came near Nan. Virgil and I watched with fantastical hope, but there was no miracle response. Star lay by her for an hour and then I took him home and didn't return for the rest of the day; the drive was simply too long.

So the days went.

Virgil and I didn't say more than a few words to each other over the course of hours every day. Yet much feeling and empathy developed between us in our shared concentration and purpose. I had all the gravestones removed from the yard and taken away. A local stonemason is making flat markers for me, and when spring comes I'll have them dug in at ground level so they'll be safe as a floor.

Finally we were allowed to bring her back to Leeward Cottage, and that is where she is right now, Elspeth, in your room. Presumably she has opened the presents I left for her. I left him one, too—an old fountain pen I found in a desk. I have considered writing to him, but what would I say? I have reports of Nan from Mrs. Circumstance, so I can't use that as an excuse. He hasn't written to me either, but does that mean anything? I am thinking of him, though, all the time. Yes, I know what that means! I am familiar with the literature. I know it's bad. But it feels just the opposite.

CHAPTER 23

Agnes, Philadelphia, January 1961

Dear Elspeth,

I am going back to Maine tomorrow. I can barely wait. I have had that stereotypical yet nevertheless confusing experience of feeling lonely among people—and I have been among a lot of people. My quiet life on FP is richer now. Always has been, in a sense, but my conclusion about the difference between the two is now final.

Anyway, it hasn't been quiet, as you know. That's only what people think. Fine with me.

Two things have happened of note. The first is big, though I am trying not to be too concerned. I went to see my lawyer yesterday—at his request. He told me that because of certain purchases and financial decisions Lee & Sons have made, I will not be able to count on a specific income for the future. I don't know exactly what that means, and nor did he. I do know that I lived like a child under my father's roof, and he paid my way. If there were money worries, I was not responsible for solving them. That may no longer be the case. The implication was that my relatives had made poor business decisions, or that business has become less profitable for whatever reason, and that I was being warned. My immediate thought and concern was for Leeward Cottage. Was there enough money for me to cover expenses there? The answer was that it really depends on the future! It was a cat-and-mouse conversation, maddeningly so, with my lawyer not being as explicit as I would like or need, and me trying to scaffold his crumbly answers into a solid structure. My conclusions are that I need to read through all our bank statements and I need to make money. What can I do? Send me inspiration, El. Honestly, I'd sell myself on the streets before I'd lose Leeward.

My other news is that I finally saw Polly alone, and it was an eventful visit.

She came at noon. I spent all morning getting ready. Knowing I was soon to sit with her was a huge relief. Relief . . . then nothing, nothing at all. The whole of the self that has been focused on one object, one need, one occupation, when suddenly, sharply freed, can't immediately resume its former shape. The cessation of pain bares the soul, and the soul is no person. It has no creaturehood. The frozen emotions and limbs must be thawed after a period of suspended animation, the body revived.

The lull doesn't last long before it is filled with a feeling. Emily Dickinson called it a formal feeling. What a beautiful phrase of double meaning; formal as opposed to wild; and also something formed, deliberately, from out of a void.

I went through the cycle this morning; the cessation of pain; the moment of stupor; the formal feeling. Then I let go. Thank you, Emily, for the rubric.

Polly arrived on the dot, entering in her stalwart way and, as I hoped, noticing everything I'd done to brighten the house for her visit. She knows these rooms as well as I do. I'd brought downstairs a few of our old dolls. She swooped for them, as I'd known she would.

"Well isn't this the living end! Let's see—that's Arantha, Gabardine, Stella, Muncie, Jamaica, Iceland, Therese. I bet you couldn't have named them."

"Not all."

"One?"

I laughed. She shook her head, and we sighed, remembering us, remembering you. You had an elaborate life with the dolls, including naming them so unexpectedly. What other girl had a doll called Iceland? But it did suit her, with her sweater and white hair.

She sighed. "So many happy hours." She picked up Gabardine and straightened her collar.

"You may have your pick, or take them all. If you don't, I'll save a few for Nan."

"I may take one, I do feel sentimental about them." She looked them over. "Remember how protective Elspeth was of Muncie? She thought no other girl would ever want her. The ugliest doll ever made."

"Yes, I remember."

"You didn't differentiate. No interest in dolls at all."

"No. Never."

"Would you mind if I choose Muncie, or do you want to keep her because of Elspeth?"

"That's up to you."

She lifted Muncie, like a baby. "How about it, Muncie? Do you want to come home with me?"

Her eyes welled up, and her face filled with distress. She crumpled to the floor, shoving the doll aside. Mrs. O'Hara appeared to announce lunch and we widened our eyes at each other. I waved for her to go and she whisked off. I knelt down beside Polly and put my arm around her shoulders.

"Polly, Polly, what is it?"

She reached for one of my hands and squeezed my fingers tightly, so tightly I had to grit my teeth to bear it. Her weeping was forlorn and bitter, and it frightened me. I'd never seen her in anything close to this state. We were, are, relentlessly, pridefully, stoical. We admire fortitude. We were raised to think a person has a right to be upset, in the event of loss or disappointment, but there are ways to acknowledge it without plodding through the embarrassment of a scene. Stop crying. Pull yourself together. Be brave.

Selfishly, I wanted and needed her to buck up. It was my turn, wasn't it? What could possibly be so upsetting to her? I felt pressure to talk, to tell at least some of what had happened to me. I shifted back and forth between these extremes, and I wondered about the lunch . . . would it stay warm? The mind is so unruly. The tears lasted probably three minutes, an eon for people like us. Star looked at my face for clues as to the level of danger this posed, so I stroked him and he lay down between us, touching Polly's skirt.

When she sobered, she rubbed her face, and we held hands and leaned back to pull each other up, the way we'd done as children. I leaned down and picked up Muncie and placed her with the other dolls. Polly and I sat on the sofa.

"I'm so sorry, Ness. I didn't think that was going to happen." Her voice was low and thin with exhaustion.

"Please tell me what's wrong?" I feared one of her boys had a disease.

"Oh, Ness, I know how badly you've wanted to talk to me. I've wanted it, too, just as much. But I couldn't bear to. That's terrible, I realize. You want to share your excitement with me, and I couldn't bear to hear it. I'm so sorry. I'm ready, though, now, and I really want you to tell me everything."

"But why didn't you tell me you were having a problem?"

"It seems obvious now that I should have, because I'm thinking clearly. But I wasn't."

I nodded. She wasn't pressing me to forgive her—I appreciated that. I had the choice to forgive her, and I did. Of course I did. I know what it is to be caught in a soundless cage when in the confusion of great pain, during the days when the feet are going mechanically round and round. Emily again.

"Tell me. I can't possibly tell you my news until you do." Star put his paws up on the sofa and I pulled him up.

Polly took a deep breath through her nose, composing courage. She kept her eyes on her knees. "I was pregnant, and I lost it."

"What? You didn't write me about it."

"I didn't even tell Dick. I still haven't, and honestly, I never will. I wanted this child to be mine—a girl. Living with four males . . . I have no one to share my interests with . . . The boys will all get married, and my futures with them will depend wholly on whether or not their wives like me. I wanted my own child, who'd be with me always, beyond marriage, children, everything, as I am with my mother. I've thought of it so often, Nessie, when I arrange flowers or set a table or choose a dress, or do all I do for Dick that he doesn't even know about. My private life—I have dreamed of sharing it with a daughter. When I got pregnant again, I think I went a little crazy. I believed I could make her a girl if I kept her a secret. Insane, I know. But that's what happened."

"When was this?"

"It ended December 4, at sixteen weeks."

"Sixteen weeks?" I tried to do the math.

"I was pregnant in August, though I didn't know it. When I found out, it occurred to me that, because I'd concentrated on her so much, Nan had brought me a girl of my own. Isn't that nutty?"

She was calmer now. She let go of me and leaned against the

sofa back. "I was so happy. Dr. Webber told me not to be, because I'm old to have a baby, but I couldn't help it. I can't remember ever being as happy in my whole life."

I understood. I'd had a happy fall, too, and as nonsensically.

"Did Dr. Webber say why it happened?"

"He couldn't tell. He said it wasn't unusual, and offered his philosophy that lost pregnancies are a part of a natural plan that exists beyond us, and aren't meant to result in birth. I am trying to believe that, so please don't say it's ridiculous."

"All right."

"It was a girl." Polly's face went slack. Pain so great she couldn't muster an expression. It hurt me to the core.

"I'm so sorry you lived through this by yourself."

"Thank you. I feel better now, having told you. It's a peculiar grief to lose an early pregnancy. People don't think it amounts to much. It's not a baby. But it is an event, and an act. I was doing something. I was making my daughter."

"I never thought of it that way."

I'd never imagined it at all, truth be told.

"That's how it feels to me." Polly touched her chest. She was strong again, and regal. Sometimes she astonishes me.

"How soon can you try again?" I asked.

She gave me a sudden quick look. It was as if I'd caught her doing something she shouldn't—or something she should. "Nessie—until I'm here without you, I forget what it's like to be known."

"I understand that very well."

"We're lucky in each other."

"Yes."

"I'm sorry I haven't had more time this week."

"And I'm leaving tomorrow."

"I know." We looked at each other helplessly.

"It's not as if we won't spend the whole summer together. We'll catch up. Meanwhile, my question—when are you going to try again?"

"As soon as it's safe. For now I have to pretend to headaches and backaches." She raised her eyebrows mischievously.

"Polly, please spare me."

"Oh, grow up! How do you think I have all those boys?"

"I know, but—"

She looked at me. "Are you at all curious?"

"No. Maybe I was once, but I'm old now. I can't imagine."

But I have imagined, at least a little.

She shrugged. "You haven't missed much." She walked across the room and came back with Muncie. "I do want her." She took my hand. I don't know which of us had the more careworn hands—and we were rich women. Yet we dug into our lives, and it showed. "Now I want to hear your story. I'm not in a hurry—I've made sure I could stay all afternoon."

We had lunch, and afterward, back in the living room, I recited the events of Nan's accident, except for the part about Virgil in the hospital. I didn't want to hold anything back, but I also wasn't ready to let it be more than private. Polly wept at the image of Nan in the hospital, stuck with needles. "Poor little girl," she muttered over and over.

"She's safe at Leeward now. Mrs. C. is managing her recovery. Her father stays overnight, but that will end when I get back, and I'll be there to get up with her if need be."

"You sound as though you want to."

I blushed. I felt caught, though my desire was innocent. "It will be a pleasure to nurse someone back to health rather than—"

"Yes." Polly rescued me from having to explain. "It will be uniquely gratifying. As will your Christmas present. Be right back."

She got up and went to the hallway, where she'd left her handbag. She came back with a wrapped book.

"You already gave me a Christmas present, the necklace." I touched it at my throat. I'd worn it for her visit, of course.

"Open it."

I slid my thumb under the tape and removed the wrapping. *The Flashing Sea* by—Virgil Reed.

I think I actually gasped. "How did you get this?"

"I asked a man I know in Leary's to find it for me."

I opened it and looked through the pages. "For Otto," it said. Not a woman, I thought. "I didn't even know he'd published a book. He never said." Why hadn't he? "How did you even guess?"

"It wasn't a guess. I asked around about him. I didn't find out much more than we already knew, but I did learn that he published a book. I was going to write to you about it, but then I hatched this plan instead."

"It's a good surprise. Thank you so much." I opened it, but purposely didn't take anything in. I wanted to be alone to read it.

Polly looked at me shrewdly. "You haven't said much about him."

"Oh, he's not so bad after all."

"And?"

"That's it. We spent a lot of hours sitting close to each other in the hospital. I got used to him."

"Did he get used to you is the bigger question."

She laughed. I saw in her friendly, open face that she really didn't imagine the extent of my feelings for Virgil, or that I might be serious. He was our project, our curiosity, our game. In consideration of the sorrow she'd arrived with, I decided to let the whole truth remain unclaimed for the moment.

"It's fun to have new friends," I said, "especially within walking distance."

"Speaking of which, walk me home? Then you can say goodbye to the scoundrels."

She placed your Muncie carefully in her bag. And I have Virgil's book.

Maud got up for another cup of tea. So Virgil Reed had written a novel? And published it? That explained his writing that Agnes had found in the Chalet. It also might be an explanation for why he'd come to stay in the Chalet in the first place. He must have been writing another book. Maud wished she could have seen the Chalet, but it had been torn down decades ago. She was beginning to understand why. Virgil and Nan were indelibly associated with the place.

Poor Polly! And she took the ugly doll home with her.

CHAPTER 24

Agnes, Leeward Cottage, February 1961

Dear Elspeth,

This afternoon I was sitting with Nan and Star, who is very
good at never jumping on Nan's legs. Nan is staying in the
parlor downstairs because it's too cold upstairs without the
fireplace going all day and night and we can't leave a four-year-
old alone with a fireplace. I didn't even think about heat in
winter, meaning the need of more of it. Next summer I'll have
something done.

We played Go Fish and read a book. Then she wanted to draw,
and I sat and watched. I drifted off until I was woken by a bang
and a shout.

"Robber!"

Robert was in the hallway talking to his mother. Nan tossed me
aside without a thought when he was around. Females!

He's been taught to leave his boots by the door, so he came in
in stockinged feet. The cold wafted off of him.

"How was school?" I asked.

"Good! We learned how to divide." He was cheerful, as always.

"And conquer?" I quipped. Couldn't help myself. "Never mind," I said quickly. "That's quite difficult, or it was for me."

He had no response to that. He's sensitive enough that if division was easy for him, he wouldn't want to embarrass me with that fact.

"We were just about to do Nan's exercises with her. Would you like to wait in the kitchen with your mother?"

"I'll stay." He smiled at Nan.

"I don't think that's a good idea." The fact that it was even a possibility was my fault for postponing the exercises until it was already the time he usually came by. I'd procrastinated because I didn't want to do the exercises at all. Nan resisted them with great ferocity. She yelled and thrashed and cried, and I hated hurting her. Only the prospect of seeing her run in the field again induced me to stick with the program. "I'll call you when we're finished."

"Robber stay!" Nan said. She could say his name perfectly well, but now that she could speak better she enjoyed reverting to baby talk.

"I can distract her," Robert claimed.

Why not try? It would be an immeasurable help if he could.

I reached my hands underneath the blanket and took hold of her feet. I nodded at him.

"Nan! Knock, knock!"

"Push my hands away," I instructed her.

"Who dare?" she said to Robert. No movement of her legs, though.

"Come on, Nan, push my hands away."

"Orange," said Robert. "Knock, knock!"

Again, she answered him without doing the exercise. I stood up. "This isn't working. You're distracting her, all right, but too much. She isn't focusing."

His brow furrowed. "What kind of exercises does she need to do?"

"She has to build up strength in her legs. She can't put weight on them yet, but the bones will knit better if the muscles are strong."

He nodded. I often feel with him as though I'm with a peer, not a child. I waited, open to what he'd say. His eyes widened—he had an idea.

"Nan—chase me. When you tag me, it will be my turn to chase you."

She grinned uncertainly and glanced at me.

"You mean she'll chase you where she is?"

"Yes." He looked at her. "Chase me! I'll know if you've caught up with me."

She looked at me again. I was moved that she trusted me on this. I don't always know where I stand with her; I'm the source of a lot of pain and pressure. "It's all right. You'll be fine." I hoped.

"Ready or not, here I go!" Robert called out. He looped his arm in an encouraging wave, as if she might literally follow him. He loped around the room. She watched. "I'm going to get away!" he goaded. "I'll run all the way home."

Her legs moved under the covers.

"I don't think you're fast enough to catch me," he said.

Her legs pumped. She groaned but she kept going. I began to run, too, and soon we were all panting and laughing. Nan's hairline dampened from the exertion, and she wiped the curls from her eyes. Robert noticed, too, and called out, "Aw, you got me." He hurled himself on the ground as if he'd been pushed.

Nan said, "I got you, Robber."

"Should I get you now?" he asked.

"Tomorrow," she said.

How about that, El? Two children under ten working out a complex set of needs and meeting them. I was quite amazed.

I left them alone to play, let Star out and then took him to the kitchen to feed him. Mrs. C. was stirring a pot. I saw her from the back and noticed the careful way she'd tied the bow of her apron. I usually conceive of her as a blur. To notice vulnerable aspects moved me. I'm certain I never move her. She misses our father and was loyal to our mother.

"Robert's clever," I said, and told her about his game with Nan. I thought she'd be pleased. She appreciates him as much as I do. He jollies the other children through their days and helps his father with the caretaking and garden work.

"He'll follow in his father's footsteps," Mrs. Circumstance replied.

"But he's so smart! He could go to college and have a career," I said.

"Not everyone's a good gardener," she crisply informed me. "Or caretaker."

I cursed my impetuous mouth. "I know that," I said quickly. "I only meant he enjoys reading and learning."

"He reads now, and he learns always," Mrs. Circumstance replied, further flustering me. I had trod into her territory and didn't know how to escape.

"Of course. He's headed for a good future."

Mrs. C. frowned. I jollied her until we recovered, but I learned my lesson.

Next, Karen came by after her work day at the library. I have hired her to read with Nan and to teach her the alphabet and numbers. The more people in her life, the better. The idea is to prepare Nan for school in the fall. She'll be in the kindergarten room, and she and Robert can, the hope is, walk to the bus stop together, along with his brothers and sister. I can't wait to see her as part of a group of children leading a regular day. Meanwhile Karen imagines becoming a Somebody, Somewhere Else. She wants a larger life. Who can blame her? I'm teaching her how to think critically about literature. Her education was apparently dull and rote, but she's sharp, and it's fun to talk with her.

As I was walking her to the door, she said she was starting on Forster.

"And?"

"It's wonderful, but I may be missing a lot. I'd like to read the books with you, if you have the time."

"All right. Why don't we start with—"

"*Howards End*," she said. "I already started. *Howards End* reminds me of Leeward Cottage."

"I can see that. Except for the conflict about who will inherit it."

"You can't have a novel without a conflict," she said, thoughtfully.

"People have tried," I said, "but one of the fascinations is to see how others solve problems."

We made a plan to read and discuss piecemeal in the late afternoons after she worked with Nan. We could talk in the room with her; Nan would be happy to listen to our voices.

Shortly after she left—my days are busy!—Virgil arrived. Stomp, stomp, stomp went his boots on the doormat. Fur, Nan informed me. She calls him Fur, Robert Robber, and me Aggie. She straightened up and smoothed the covers over her lap. Is it just in women to want to do a little extra in front of a man? I can feel the impulse rise up in me, too.

He let himself in. Nan and I listened together to his movements as he took off his coat and walked around. He sighed, and we smiled at each other triumphantly, because he sounded relieved to be here. His sigh was one of a heart at rest. I supposed he wrote all day, or performed activities that readied him for writing, but

I didn't know that. We had yet to speak of the pages I saw in the Chalet, or the novel Polly gave me for Christmas. I kept hoping I'd have a minute with him to discuss it, but I had plenty of minutes with him and found myself uncharacteristically reticent. To say something would be to cross a line.

Once he knew I'd read his book, he'd realize I knew a lot about him, and possibly he'd be aggrieved by that. He was here for privacy, it seemed. Or maybe not everyone sees through the words on the page to the author writing them. I love feeling connected with the person holding the pen and sensing whether they are laughing or moaning or chiding themselves or overcorrecting what was fine in the first place. Most of all I love picturing their handwriting, which I believe I can, though as I never check, I could be wrong. Though I doubt it.

Maud smiled at this self-assurance. Agnes had told her that she read this way. She tried to demonstrate a few of her imagined hand-writings but became frustrated when her arthritis prevented her from re-creating what she saw in her head. Maud informed her that most people didn't read that way at all, and that there were schools of criticism that expressed horror at the notion that an author might be connected with a text.

"I'm so glad I missed that development," Agnes had said.

Maud missed Agnes. But Agnes wanted her to know her in this other way. She could have just said so rather than making a pretense of not being able to come at the last minute. But Maud's irritation had lessened. She read on.

Virgil often ate dinner with Nan in the parlor. Sometimes I joined them, but I usually ate by myself in the kitchen and then went upstairs. We'd set up a daybed for him near her so he could watch over her during the night. I would have liked to do it, but I have to let him do something!

So we ate in our separate spots. When I was approaching the stairs to go up with Star, he appeared with the dinner plates, carrying them to the kitchen. Our paths intersected and we stopped.

"Hello," he said.

"Hello."

"She seems well."

He smelled of soap, and his hair had been combed. Did he want to look nice?

"She's doing very well." I told him Robert's innovation of the afternoon.

"That was smart of him."

"That's what I thought."

We stood awkwardly, speechlessly, foolishly.

"Would you like a cup of tea? Or a whiskey?"

"Whiskey!" he said. "That would be a treat."

"I think we have some. Let's have a look." I led the way to the kitchen, and while he cleaned the plates I looked in the pantry lower cupboard where extra spirits had always been kept. There it was, a trove of Scotches and whiskeys and bourbons. I pulled out a bottle based on the typeface.

"How about a snort of this?" I showed him the bottle.

"Why not?"

I looked around for glasses and found a shape I liked. I handed him one.

"This is a champagne glass," he said.

That was funny, coming from him, but of course he knew. He wasn't a real mountain man, he was a Reed.

"I swear it will taste the same." I pulled out a chair at the kitchen table and sat. It was a more neutral spot than the glass room, which might seem—too suggestive. We toasted to Nan's recovery.

"Whoa, Nelly," I managed, after I recovered from the heat running down my gullet.

"Not a tippler, I take it," he said.

"I'm thinking I have been missing out."

"This is a good Scotch. Very smooth. There's a style that's peaty."

"What does that taste like?"

He has long, thin fingers.

"It tastes like death warmed over." He smiled. "An acquired taste." He looked at me and I looked back. A direct, appraising, acknowledging look. We'd never shared even a second of intimacy after that day in the hospital.

"I read your novel," I blurted.

"Oh?" He hunkered down and looked up at me from beneath his brow.

"Polly gave it to me for Christmas." So he wouldn't think I'd gone hunting. I could hardly believe I'd brought it up.

"What did you think of it?"

I wasn't prepared for the question, though it was the obvious one.

"It's wonderful. Truly. Beautifully written and intelligent."

"Is it?"

"If you didn't think so yourself, why would you publish it?"

He shrugged. "I couldn't work on it anymore."

"Maybe being good and being finished are one and the same," I said.

"I don't think so."

"I don't either." I was—interested. The space between his breaths was long. I stole glances at his chest and stomach rising and falling. "You want to hear more, don't you?"

He blushed, grinned, nodded. This flustered me. I knew what was happening but—what was happening?

"Well—the structure had a natural form, like a tree, a trunk and its branches and leaves. The sentences were marvelously various, the words layered with meanings. The story is only a sleight of hand, a disguise for how the book is shaped, which is the real subject. You ask readers to follow a logic, a way of thinking, by giving them—me—a plot to wonder about. Yet it isn't about the plot. Like all the best books and works of art, it's about form, ultimately."

"I agree." He frowned. A mixed message. "How do you know so much about books?"

I wasn't about to tell him the truth. "I read a lot. And I studied literature at college."

Maud paused. What did Agnes mean by the truth here? There was a subtext she wasn't getting.

He still frowned, but in a pleased way. "No one has ever understood my work as well."

"I repeat—I love the book." I pinched myself to keep from telling him it was on my bedside table, and I'd very nearly memorized it. I also pinched myself to keep from rolling my eyes. His book wasn't hard to understand.

He was silent. I waited awkwardly, wondering what I should do. I had invaded his privacy, in a sense. But a novel isn't private. He'd published it. He was hiding away here, but I had been caring for his child for weeks now. His reticence was irritating, really. I wanted to sock him! I was flustered!

"Thank you."

"It was nothing."

Yet it was. I am no doubt his deepest and most careful reader.

I have probably made connections in the book and had insights he hasn't had himself. Or am I deluding myself? I suppose people who love a book always think they understand it best, when the whole point is that the author clamps a ring through the reader's nose and leads him by a rope exactly where he wants to go. All those papers on his table, with their heavy cross-outs, the ink so thick on the pages it weighed them down—he was figuring out now what everything meant and where it should go. All right. I am his good reader.

"Are you writing another?" I asked.

"I'm making an attempt. I'm having a lot of trouble with it, Agnes."

Why is the repetition of one's name by a favored person so powerful? Why does the sound ring true, like the music of the spheres? Agnes. Agnes. The name I'd always rued now sounded just right.

"Agnes was the Roman girl who fought off assault and was killed for her Christian beliefs and her refusal to be raped. She was made a saint," I instructed.

"Oh," he said. "I had no idea."

"Do you know the saints?"

"Not at all."

"My sister taught me them. She was utterly Quaker but also fascinated by the lives of the committed religious. And she was a saint herself."

"I remember her a little."

"What do you remember?"

"She and your brother—"

"Edmund."

"—played hide-and-seek with me and my sister. It was always easy to find her."

"Hiding wasn't in her nature," I said, and held back sudden

tears. "But I didn't finish about Agnes. If a girl wants to know who her future husband will be, she must not eat dinner on St. Agnes Eve, and must sleep without clothes on. He will come to her and kiss her." I was in way over my head. What was I doing? My gaze went to his hands and forearms, and I couldn't swallow. I was paralyzed. I, who'd been so flagrant with John Manning that he'd thought poorly of me, had no wherewithal around Virgil Reed. I looked over at the breadbasket and went on. "Agnes sweet and Agnes fair, hither, hither now repair, bonny Agnes let me see the lad who is to marry me." A yearning swelled in my chest, repeating those words, and my eyes pricked. Sweet hope, not mine.

"Did you do that when you were young?"

"Good Lord no! It's an old wives' tale." How old do I seem to him, I wonder?

"If I were a girl, I'd have tried it. When is it?"

"January 20."

"Darn, we missed it."

We.

"What's the name of your new book?"

"*Scalene.*"

"That word takes me back. A triangle with unequal sides?"

"The very one."

"What's it about?"

"Three people."

I smiled. "Does anything happen?"

"Not yet."

"How far along with it are you?"

"I don't know." He looked sheepish. "I don't know what I've got, to be honest."

"I've read a lot of biographies of writers, and the stage you're describing seems par for the course."

"I hope so. I've been completely preoccupied with figuring it out. Escaping into it, really."

"Escaping from what?"

It was as if I'd hit him. He jumped up. Star began to yap and circle around him.

I stood too. "I'm sorry." Though I didn't know what I was apologizing for.

"No, no," he said. "I just thought of something. Excuse me—I better go write it down."

"Take your whiskey with you."

He was out the door.

CHAPTER 25

Agnes, Leeward Cottage, February 1961

Dear Elspeth,

When I came down to breakfast this morning, I found a sheaf of paper on the third stair from the bottom. It was a letter, from Virgil to me. I'm copying out the opening:

Agnes,

I owe you an explanation, you who befriend me, you who open your house to me to come and go without knocking, you who feed me and quietly care for my needs; you who care for my daughter as well as any mother might and are her healer and teacher; you who have spoken to me openly and honestly while I have stayed to myself. I owe you a lot more than an explanation; but it will have to do for now.

I have been so self-absorbed. I'm embarrassed to say I may have postponed this if you hadn't offered to read my book. I decided I want to show it to you. But first, you should know me better—specifically, the incidents behind Scalene.

I could barely breathe; it was so unexpected. I looked in on Nan, who was still asleep, made a pot of coffee, and went to read the rest in the glass room.

It was an outpouring, that was for certain. Forty-two handwritten pages to be exact. In spots he sounded young, in spots self-pitying, in spots preening, but overall—intelligent, and full of a yearning that I myself feel. For something more. He wrote about his own development as a writer, which made me jealous, to be honest. He attended something called the Iowa Writing workshops, and had the kind of literary conversations and friendships and guidance that are available to men. Of course, the lack gives women the opportunity to be subversive in ways men can't, because they are too busy seeking a spot on the team and each other's admiration. But the opportunities and the possibilities and the unloneliness of it all are taken for granted by a young man like Virgil Reed, whereas they seem like a foreign country to me. Normally I don't think about it— it is ingrained in me not to stew about things I can't change—but reading of his woes illuminated my own very different and dimly lit path, and I wondered how I'd have done if I'd been him.

He took a girlfriend named Ro with him to Iowa. Ro was from somewhere in the West, and had grown up in foster homes that varied widely in kindness and help. She was beautiful and that seemed to be enough to hold his attention. (I rolled my eyes at that.) She took a clerical job at the university and made their student digs into a home. They made love all the time and were happy. Good for them.

Otto Zef, the South African novelist—I've heard of him but haven't read him—took on Virgil as his teacher's pet. Virgil craved recognition for his writing from someone whose opinion counted—like Otto. Otto dangled tales of riches and glamour in front of him and convinced him to move to New York, where Virgil and Ro joined Otto's set and met lots of writers, painters, dancers, and intellectuals in the Village. Ro got a job in a gallery and tentatively began to paint. She was gifted at it, as it happened, and Otto encouraged her. Virgil meanwhile was becoming frustrated at being around the well-known without having his own reputation. Men can say this without demurral as boldly as he wrote it to me. I have made a practice of declining to envy a lot of what men take for granted, but as I read his letter I suddenly wished I could be as frank. As it is, I'd never write such thoughts, much less nurture them in myself to the point of expression. I'd make myself sick. But Virgil confessed all this with the intention of making himself well.

He stopped going out to parties or doing anything but his job at a nearby café and writing. Ro got pregnant, which was a surprise but not an unhappy one. Baby Nan was born without complication, Ro fitted her on a hip, and life went on. She was able to take her to the gallery a lot of the time, and her friends helped her out, delighted to play with a baby. Ro afforded Virgil the freedom to work as much as he wanted to, which he took as his due. He loved her and the baby, but he was preoccupied, much to his present regret. He finished *The Flashing Sea* and it was accepted by a publisher. He did what he could to promote it, but it was bad timing. He wanted to be the new big thing, but Truman Capote and Jack Kerouac beat him out. He moped around on the periphery and tried to write a new book, but nothing really kept him in the chair as the first book had. He went out with Otto and drank too much. It was a crummy period, full of frustration and a sense of failure. Everything he did was halfhearted at best.

One day Ro came in from work without Nan, who was still with one of her friends. She'd gotten knocked down by a car sideswiping her and had hit her head and scraped her knees. She wanted to lie down for a little while—would Virgil go get Nan? She settled on the sofa and he lay a blanket over her. The afternoon was cold and glittery, the sun setting after a bright New York January day. Nan was surprised to see him rather than Ro. He stayed for a drink with Ro's friend and they gossiped about the neighborhood. When Nan got cranky, he took his leave, and walked home holding her hand. She pointed in windows and at dogs and he thought about his work. When he got home, Ro was still asleep. Nan pulled at her arm to wake her, but she showed no response. Virgil asked what he should feed Nan for dinner; still no response. He walked over to look at her, and he was seized with a terror he'd never before known. He knew immediately that she was dead, but he shook her anyway, helplessly.

Eventually he thought to call an ambulance. He was told that when she'd hit her head her brain began to bleed and it had bled so much that she had a fatal stroke. He asked if she'd have lived if he'd taken her to the hospital. I winced when I read that, even before I got to the answer, which was—maybe. It was the kind of question that makes for a future of guilt. No wonder he'd seemed like a madman from a distance. He wrote as much—he lost his mind with regret and grief. He knew he wasn't paying attention to Nan, but he simply couldn't. He hated being in the apartment and even in New York without Ro. He remembered about Fellowship Point and asked his uncle if he could stay there. The rest I knew. He wrote about how terrified he was after Nan's accident that he was going to lose her, too. He's grateful to me for so much. I honestly feel that gratitude isn't necessary or called for, but I suppose among the choices of emotion under the circumstances it fits the bill.

I'm copying the end of the letter here.

The other night when I thought Nan was already asleep, she called to me.
"Fur, will you read to me?"
I went over to the bed and sat by her. I read a line. She nodded solemnly, touched a word, and said, "Tooth."

She pointed to another. "Boat."

And another. "Sal."

"Are you reading?" I asked.

She shrugged. I believe she honestly didn't know.

I read another page and stopped. "Your turn," I said casually.

She put her head forward and peered at the page with great concentration. I pointed to a word. "Clams," she said. Now I was certain she recognized it. I taught her the word "the." You can go far in life if you know about "the." I don't know how Karen is teaching her and I don't want to interfere with that, but maybe it doesn't hurt to take several approaches to the same place. I read for as long as she wanted me to, and accepted the pleasure of having her pressed against my arm, leaning on me, trusting me.

How was is it possible that I didn't understand how to be with her? What I owe her?

How was it possible that I believed I needed to conserve my words to the degree that I withheld myself from her?

And you, Agnes. How can it be that I have held myself back and apart, as if the greatest privilege in life might not be to speak to you?

I hear the sheets clanging against the masts. The buoy bells, the foghorn, the waves lapping. I want to know you, Agnes. May I?

I sat with the letter in my lap for a while and let it sink in. No wonder he seemed like such a wild man, so out of sorts, so antisocial and irresponsible. He was bereft and grieving. What happened to Ro was awful, a shock like Edmund's car accident. I pictured her coming home and talking to him, saying she just wanted to lie down, and that was the last time they spoke. How could he have known to take her to the hospital? They were young and death wasn't yet real—not their own, at least.

I thought about his request. Why is it that when a person moves toward you in a real and considered way the gesture creates an expanse of time unlike any other? His question gave me leeway to dally with my feelings. If I wanted, I could weigh the pros and cons and drag the whole process out for weeks. I could flick him looks without speaking and leave him to guess what I'm thinking.

But I see no point in that. And as we know about me, Elspeth, I like things that have a point to them.

CHAPTER 26

Agnes, Leeward Cottage, March 1961

Dear El,

Honestly I do not have a moment to sit down, except when I
am drawing with Nan or making lists of things that need to be
done. We have her up on her feet every day now, and she is as
determined a person as you were—in her case, to be a regular girl
who runs down the road after the school bus drops her off. We all
clap when she takes steps and she preens at the attention.

She is so natural, Elspeth. In ways we never were. Our mother's
anxiety that we not be the object of anyone's disapproval
influenced our actions and even our thoughts. We were trained so
early about how to fit in. Nan is almost feral in this regard. She has
seen and knows so few people. Her world is expanding through
the books Karen reads to her, but I can't know exactly what she
takes from what she hears. Children are both imaginative and
literal, and it's hard to know at any moment which prevails.

I count on her to tell me how she thinks and feels, and to
that end I tell her how I think and feel. We are playing games
such as opening our fists as slowly as possible and describing the
sensations as our fingers unfurl. Then we scrunch up a leaf or

a piece of paper and watch it make a similar effort to expand. I don't know exactly what this is, science or affection, but we are opening, too.

Virgil and Karen and I are eating dinner together nearly every night now, and our conversations are relaxed and lively. Virgil has completely let go of his reticence and formality. He laughs freely and interposes wit among our remarks. I think he is helping Karen to loosen up. She often comes to the table holding a book—my private discussions are not enough to satisfy her appetite for book talk—and she reads a passage aloud to us and asks us what we see in it. Though Virgil and I have never said so, we have a conceit that she is our little sister, and we are preparing her for life. For Radcliffe. Now I am convinced she could do it. Her insights are untutored and reveal the parameters of my own education, as she often says things that wouldn't have come up in a course.

I wonder what you'd think of her, El.

CHAPTER 27

Agnes, Leeward Cottage, April 1961

Dear Sister,

My rate of correspondence has dwindled, I am well aware. Yet it is for a good reason; I am happy. I know. Implausible! But true.

Virgil came over late morning to show me his new pages. We sat in the glass room, and sunny it was. We kept having to move around to avoid the glare. I read the pages to him so he could hear the shape of his sentences, and then we went through them line by line. It's so exhilarating. It's as if our minds fit together like puzzle pieces. There's so much feeling to it, too. We are speaking our hearts as well as our minds . . . if I do say so. I know it is unlike me to be so . . . what? Something vulnerable, I suppose.

I love his writing, I love Nan, I love the lupines, I love Star, I love the Point, every tree and rock and flower and bird. I love the eagles!

And Elspeth—I got my hair cut.

CHAPTER 28

Agnes, Leeward Cottage, June 1961

Dear Elspeth,

Yesterday I saw Virgil for the first time in two weeks. He'd been away on a trip to New York to meet with an editor about *Scalene*. We only said hello briefly, just long enough for him to say he had some news. I wanted to know what it was immediately—I'm not very patient, as it turns out, har har—but I didn't press him more than once to tell me right away. He wanted time alone first. *Time alone* is a phrase I understand well. So be it.

I found out what happened tonight when we had our usual dinner. Nan sits at the table now. Mrs. C. made a shepherd's pie and squash and spinach on the side.

Nan was very happy to have her father back and doted on him. "Water, Fur?" she asked, holding her glass toward him at a breathtaking angle. Adroitly, he took it from her, with not a drop spilled.

"So?" I prompted. Enough stalling.

"So they want the book." He blushed, deeply pleased. Karen clapped and Nan imitated her.

"Of course they do!" I said. "Was there ever any question? Why would they ask you to travel all that way if they didn't want it?"

He ran his hand through his hair, which was still long but groomed now. I was reminded of Greek heroes when he did this. Oh, brother!

"You've been very sure, but I haven't. I was confident last time, and—" He shrugged. What he thought of as his failure still stung.

"The book is good. Very good." I made it so, Elspeth, to the extent he allowed it. He did too, of course—I'm not taking the credit. But I helped him. A lot! "Details please."

"The editor said he's rarely seen a manuscript as finished. He thinks the book will do well."

I smiled inwardly. His combination of wishing to be modest and to be admired—I obliged.

"That's excellent news," I said, and raised my water glass. "Here's to you, Virgil."

"Thank you."

"I'd like to read it," Karen said.

He looked at her as if he'd never noticed her before. Maybe he hadn't. Again, I stifled a knowing smile, this one having to do with the male ego.

"After it's finished?" he asked.

"As soon as possible," she said. "I'm sure I could get the gist even if it's only a typewritten version."

"Maybe," he said. "I only have one copy."

"I'd be careful. I could read it here." She has a child's eagerness.

He shrugged. "Okay. I'll bring it over tomorrow."

Karen clapped her hands as if she'd received a big treat. He dropped his gaze, pleased. Then he regrouped.

"So what's the news here?" he asked.

We told him, stories piling on stories and jumbling over each other. Nan talks well now—I'd say she has caught up and perhaps advanced past what is usual for her age. I don't really know for sure what that is, though.

Karen continued to be lively. "Didn't you tell me there is an Indian burial site in the Sank?"

Had I? I mainly spoke with her about Nan and about books and colleges. She is young and preoccupied with fantasies of her future glory. As it should be.

"It's not a burial site per se. It was a campsite. A dwelling. Why do you ask?"

"We're going to redo the local history section in the library, so I was looking through books. I found a few descriptions of skirmishes between Indians and settlers that happened around here."

"Oh?"

"It all seems kind of small potatoes. A few people fighting in a field. Surprising each other. And oh! Did you know people had slaves up here? I came across an account of Indians taking a family and their slave as prisoners. The Indians told the family to wait by the river until they got their canoes and guess what? The family ran away and told the tale. But the slave disappeared and was never heard from again."

Virgil slapped the table. "Good for him."

"Or her," I said. "Those artifacts in the living room are things we found in the Sank and also items my father collected. Once I had to defend the site against some plundering boys. They had guns." Wretched Hamm Loose killing the eagle. I always cut him when I pass him in town. He's done well, if you can believe it. That type does. Something to do with real estate.

"I can picture that," Virgil said. "You were a girl of principle."

"I was a tomboy. That was fine here, but not as acceptable in

Philadelphia. I wanted to be an Indian, or at least captured by them."

Nan looked at me quizzically.

"The Indians lived here before the Europeans came," I said, which cleared up nothing. She knew none of those words, or anything of life beyond the Point. "You know the things I take out of the cases sometimes? The moccasins and the stones and the clubs?"

She wrinkled her lips, her expression of concentration.

"I'll show you books later," I said. "I mean tomorrow." I didn't want her to think she was going to finagle staying up late.

I turned to Karen. "My great-grandfather William Lee had a respect for the Indians, in the way of the Society of Friends. When he found the campground on the site, he immediately sought to preserve it. He wanted to offer the Indians to come camp here, but when the Fellowship was formed the rest of the founders rejected that notion. William was disappointed. He was Edenic in his thinking, and imagined many people living here in peace—not just Quaker Philadelphians. But his brother was a Quaker and a Philadelphian who believed that his kind were all he wanted to know."

"I'm familiar with the type," Virgil said.

He smiled at me and raised his eyebrows. We gazed at each other, and all the feeling in the world passed quickly between us. I think.

"I read something else interesting," Karen said. "Maine was part of the Missouri Compromise. It entered the Union as a free state so Missouri could be a slave state."

"That's right," I said.

"I forgot about that," Virgil said. "What an awful compromise."

"I hope you'll keep reading these history books as you organize them. We could learn a lot during these dinners. Maybe you'll pursue history in college," I said to Karen.

"Maybe," she said, and looked at her plate. "I haven't decided yet."

"That's fine, it's better not to have. I was told when I went to college to find out who the great professors were and to take their courses no matter what the subject."

"I read a book," Nan said. "I was in the book."

I made a little book for her, about her saving us from an angry moose. She enjoys these stories of her bravery.

"You are a heroine," Virgil said, and met my gaze.

CHAPTER 29

Agnes, Leeward Cottage, July 1961

Dear Elspeth,

Summer is in full swing here. I know—not an original remark. I am settling down, settling in.

First of all—Polly is here! Life is a thousand times better being able to see her every day. Yes, we giggle, because we are both happy. Nan is back on her feet and mingling with the other children, always watched over by Robert Circumstance. It's moving to see the care he takes of her, and how he explains to her that he'll be back when he has to leave her out. One only has to watch the games to see that he is the one who works out higher systems of play. He also knows about the plants beyond their labels and teaches the children to respect them. His intelligence is palpable. He will go beyond this place, no matter what his mother wants, and I must open the door for him.

Oh, you're curious about Virgil? No, I don't mind you asking, not at all! We are together every day, talking about books, especially his, and talking about everything else you can imagine. He is endlessly solicitous toward me, sometimes to the point where I wonder how he sees me. I remind him I am still young by running and being silly. He's very affectionate, always holding my hand and walking with his arm around me. He kisses me on the lips, but it isn't a passionate kiss. It hurts to even write that down, but I have to. I have to tell you the truth, Elspeth. It puzzles me, though. He seems, if I may say so, interested. So what is he waiting for?

The other day Polly and I were sitting out on the lawn, and Virgil walked by in the distance. He looks so free now, and so in his element. His hair is longer but brushed. His shirt untucked but stylish rather than vagrant. I suppose my feelings are hard to hide.

"Look at you smile," Polly said.

"What?" My defensive posture, developed courtesy of our mother's contempt.

Polly knows this. "It's me, Nessie." She poked me with her elbow. "You think I haven't seen every look on your face since you were a baby?"

I blushed. "Is it that obvious?"

"To me it is."

I ran my hands over the meadow grass in search of a particular size and shape of blade. When I'd found it I wet it on my tongue, threaded it between my thumbs, and blew. Polly smiled knowingly.

"Has anything happened?"

I shrugged. "I don't know how to answer that. It feels like everything has happened, but what you mean—no."

I saw how this must look and sound from the outside. But Polly, good old Polly, said, "Tell me about the everything."

I tried, but it's hard to describe the texture of feeling that passes between two people when they are alone and excited and looking into each other's eyes for the deeper meaning of the words they are speaking.

"Give it time, Nessie. He is writing a book about a woman who died. He may need to be loyal to her to stay in the mood."

Her words embarrassed me, because I hadn't thought of anything as simply obvious. Once again Polly's intelligence about everyday life put my brilliance to shame.

"Good point," I managed. Elspeth, it's a sin what a know-it-all I am.

"Be patient, Nessie. It's not your way, we all know that. But do it now."

"I suppose I don't have a choice."

There was a pause. "And be honest with yourself about the extent of his feelings for you." She laid a hand on my arm. Was that meant to rub away the sting of her words?

"You talk like I'm a girl."

"Isn't that the case in this situation? I don't want you to confuse admiration for attraction. I don't want you to get hurt."

"Thank you. Though I don't know that getting hurt is the worst thing." I gripped her hand and changed the subject. "And why are you smiling this morning?" She was. She usually did, but I detected something else, something I hoped for. I was leaving it to her to tell me, though.

"You see? We know each other very well." She placed her right hand over her abdomen. "It's three months now. She's due at Christmas."

"Oh, Polly, that's so wonderful."

She beamed. "It is. It really is. I haven't told anyone, though. I want her to be mine alone until I can't hide her any longer."

"Dick?"

"I haven't told Dick."

"That's not like you."

"I'm forty-one, Nessie, same as you. I think this is a moment when we need to take the opportunity to be unlike who we were as girls and young women. So it is like me now."

"I like that, Pol. And of course I'll keep your secret."

"That's why I told you."

What will my life be by Christmas?

CHAPTER 30

Agnes, Leeward Cottage, September 1961

Sister,

I was already upstairs in my room. The day was over. Nan was asleep down the hallway, Virgil had gone back to the Chalet, Karen was long gone. I was reading and daydreaming, feeling content and drowsy, so it startled me when Star barked. The sound rattled me and I swatted the air in his direction. He gave me his look that meant he wasn't buying into my blame.

I had dropped my book onto my abdomen and I picked it back up. *The Prime of Miss Jean Brodie*, by Muriel Spark. An aside—I have gotten a laugh out of it. What a brilliant way to write about fascism. According to Spark's standards I am in my prime. She doesn't make much of a case for that being a good thing.

I began to read again but was distracted by Star's low growl.

The walls creaked. Such is Leeward Cottage. I was not frightened or worried—I never am here. I probably should be in this old spooky house and no one for miles—but I'm not, in spite of Karen's lurid descriptions of murders and peculiar deaths in Maine that she's been reading about in the old histories in the library. Cabin fever. Skirmishes with Indians. What would it have been like to settle here but know nothing and get very little news?

Did I hear footsteps? Yes, no, yes, no, yes. I lay the book aside and sat up.

I have heard his footfalls for months now. Sometimes light, now very heavy, they always expressed the grace in his body—as if gravity were pulling him upward rather than down.

Should I stay where I was or get up? I had no time to make a decision. He knocked and came in before I had time to worry about how I looked. Oh, I don't really worry, not around him— what can I do anyway? I am who I am. I wear what I wear. I had on a pair of Daddy's flannel pajamas.

Virgil entered, wafting the mineral scent of a cool night. In his right hand he gripped a piece of paper, and as I leaned toward him he brandished it as if he might swing it like a cutlass and whack off my head. His anger was palpable.

"It's a disaster!" he shouted.

I waited, not saying a word.

"I can't get it right! What is wrong with me?"

Ah. He was talking about his revision. No wonder all the drama.

He had fallen into my arms once before. I'd wondered if it would happen again. I longed to comfort him. But he paced and didn't come closer.

"Let me get up, and meet me in the kitchen," I said.

He nodded and left. I put on my robe and combed my hair. I rinsed my mouth and went down, followed by Star, of course.

He had pulled out the Scotch. A glass was waiting for me.

"Your book is good," I told him. "Very. That is not in question."

"How do you know?"

"Because I know about books. Your editor loves it, remember?"

"I don't know why. It's awful."

I must say, I was somewhat impatient with this line. I had already helped him so much. I reminded myself he was still fragile in many ways, and that I should let him rant. How did I know this? From watching Polly all these years with her males. I used to get impatient with her for indulging them, but I have learned that letting Virgil express his misery is the quickest path to peace. I'll have to thank her for demonstrating what to do.

"I see," I said. "So what do you want to do?"

"I don't know."

"You could start over."

He nodded. "I could, but there are a few decent pages. . . ."

And so it went for another hour, until he had regained his confidence. I must say I was gratified by effecting the change in him. I even had him laughing by the time he decided to go. Could I live that way, though? Honestly, I don't know. Would he do the same for me, or would any man? I'd never seen it. Do women not ask, or is the notion of the helpmeet so ingrained that we all believe support travels in one direction only? Why wouldn't women want the same, and why wouldn't men realize that? I would want equality if I were in a relationship. Virgil is more like a project, or a young cousin like Archie Lee. I suspect he'd be flummoxed if he thought I needed him in return.

I walked him to the door and we stepped outside into the dark. It was a clear and starry night, and without consulting each other we walked farther into the darkness to marvel at the heavens. There wasn't need of talk, and we didn't. We stood next to each other, in the bigger night. I could have asked him what he believed in, or how broadly he could imagine, or what era he thought he really belonged in. What could he have said that would have been more eloquent than this sweet silent communion?

What was he thinking?

He put his arm around my shoulders and I slid mine around his waist.

"This is how I always want to feel," he said.

"Me too."

He kissed me. At least I thought so. Yet now that I am back in my room, I cannot say for sure that it was a real kiss.

I will have to do the most annoying thing—wait and see.

CHAPTER 31

Agnes, Philadelphia, Christmas 1961

Dear Elspeth,

The big excitement in my neck of Philadelphia this year is baby Lydia. She is just starting to smile, which apparently is a major development in human growth. Polly is besotted with her. It's lovely to see. I enjoy being with them—it's a light, contained atmosphere, totally focused on the baby's expressions. We try to talk, but we are interrupted by the bizarre contortions of that little face. She is extraterrestrial. I am awestruck by it, but Polly takes it in stride, so I am awestruck by her.

I brought my work with me, a picture book I'm writing for Nan based on the stories I tell her. It's called *When Nan Walked Two Miles*, about the first walk we took together all around the Point. I may do a series, where Nan will do this and that and the books will be about what she does. My drawings are awful, but if I can improve I'll try to sell them. I have to make money—I cannot count on the company to support me. I want to be self-sufficient. I wasn't raised to be, but that was a mistake both our parents made. They trusted their own version of the past too much.

Polly asked me about Virgil, and I gave a brief report. He has behaved toward me as always, with utter respect and a kind of adoration. We haven't spoken about love, though it is everywhere around us and between us. Every day I tell myself to bring it up, be direct about it. But I have wandered into an arena of life I know nothing about, and where my brusque ways don't have a place. And there's this: I don't know if it's because I saw what I saw in the hospital, his turning orb—that sounds ridiculous, but I don't know what better to say—or if I have against my will absorbed ways of behaving around men that I don't approve of but can't help. So we are suspended between silences and uncertainties, though pass through happy days.

Loving someone—loving like this—is the most forgiving lens.

In other news, Star immediately recognized everything about our Walnut Street house, and Mrs. O' Hara had a plate of meat ready for him and has been feeding him fresh-cooked food three times a day, winning him over completely. I am still working on my jettisoning. I want everything to be spare, but it could take a few years to get there. Polly is talking about moving out of the city to Bryn Mawr or Haverford now that she has four children. It makes sense, but what will it be like not to have her close everywhere? She agrees and sighs, but proximity to me isn't her prime consideration. Well—I must be an adult about it.

For New Year's Eve I've accepted an invitation to a dinner dance. I may also wander down to watch the Mummers.

I am looking forward to 1962!

That was the last of the notebooks, but Maud looked in the box anyway, in case she'd missed something. How could the story stop in the middle? Maud wanted more—she had no doubt there was more—but she suspected putting her in this position was part of Agnes's plan.

She placed all the notebooks carefully back in the box and left them on the table in Agnes's study. She had some time before she had to catch the train, so she picked up the next volume of the *Franklin Square* series. Soon she was immersed and amused and feeling more relaxed. Yet something had been tugging at her brain as she read the books, some distant echo that she couldn't place. Something about the style, the sensibility, the sometimes odd configuration of words. Here was a perfect example—the character Gail talking about a mystical experience she had in the Zendo: "It made foolish the whole project of words." Hadn't Maud recently read that same odd phrasing? She stared at the page until her eyes swam, and suddenly the names of the girls—Susan, Nola, Gail, Eve, and Annie—darted around and rearranged themselves into an anagram. AGNES.

PART FIVE

Discernment

CHAPTER 32

Polly, Haverford, March 2002

"JUST BE CAREFUL THAT HE ISN'T TAKING ADVANTAGE OF YOU. Is he paying his own way?" James leaned over his plate to take a bite out of the grilled cheese sandwich Polly had made for him, but he kept his eye on her.

The question felt to Polly like an inflating blood pressure cuff, designed to measure the truth about her inner state. She still felt her childhood compulsion to confess her thoughts, and it tended to override her knowledge that in most instances, she wasn't obliged to. She had settled on a simple method of counting to three before she answered a question that might incriminate her, though often she blurted before she took the time, and often it didn't help. In this case she'd known the question would arise, and she was prepared. More or less.

"Knox is my son, James, as you are. He is in a difficult moment in his life now. He's doing a lot around the house, and he's keeping me company." There. That was the answer she'd planned, and it came out well.

"So you are paying for everything. Don't take this the wrong way, but for the sake of my children I feel obliged to point out that what you give him subtracts from their inheritance. I just want you to think about that, Mother."

Polly put her spoon down and looked at him. He was clean-shaven, and dressed in a navy-blue cashmere sweater over a collared shirt. He wore a wedding ring and Dick's Hamilton watch on an alligator band. He stopped in on Wednesday evenings and at some point on the weekends for a meal if he had nothing more important to do. He was determined to be a good son. Polly, because she loved him, let him believe he was succeeding, but he didn't come close to how Theo listened to her or how Knox, since he'd move in, noticed what would make her life easier and did it without being asked. James fulfilled his schedule and that was that. If she told him what was lacking, he'd defend himself mightily and honestly not understand. She was sure Agnes disliked him, though she'd never say so. Agnes had a code and lived by it; there were things she'd never say. Sometimes Agnes's dislike popped into Polly's mind just at a moment when she was in danger of feeling that way herself. Agnes saved her from herself. It was enough for one of them to look askance at James.

"James, you know perfectly well the trusts are set. I couldn't spend that money if I wanted to. And I don't." She gazed at her sandwich regretfully. She'd been looking forward to it, but it wouldn't taste like anything now.

Skeptically, he raised his eyebrows at the same time as he nodded. He didn't believe her. He would be watching. Polly got all that. She wished he'd just leave. He wore her out when he came, and though she didn't have the capacity to tell him not to visit, she often found herself dreading it. Her worst thought, one she'd buried as swiftly as possible, was that the wrong child had died. It literally took her breath away when that sentence had formed in her mind, and she'd questioned her claim to being a good person ever since. She clung to what Agnes had said decades ago about Jimmy Carter having sinned by lusting in his heart after women other than Rosalynn. "Thoughts are real, but they aren't sins," she'd said with absolute finality. "Only actions qualify as sins. Though there is no such thing as sin." Polly hoped that her thought wasn't a sin, but she'd never felt the same since she'd had it.

"I know Knox," James said. "I'm not at all mystified as to why Jillian left him. That's only the reason she gave. I know she claimed 9/11 had awakened in her a desire for more, a bigger life—but frankly, though she didn't express this explicitly, I know it's also him. He's dull. You know it as well as I do. He's also a moocher. That's what worries me."

"As I said, you do not need to concern yourself. I am happy to have him for as long as he needs to stay. One rarely has the opportunity to spend this much time with a grown child."

James sighed. "You're naive, Mom. Dad would want me to look out for you."

"Dad is looking out for me himself," she said. "I have his voice available at all times."

He looked at her suspiciously. "All right."

"I want to go back up early again this year," Polly said. "Do you have any idea when you'll be coming?"

The front door opened. Knox blew in, wafting chilly air. He slapped the mail on the table next to Polly. "A letter from Robert Circumstance. Again." He looked at James. "They have a heavy correspondence."

"You do?" James asked. "Why?"

"Your father would want me to write to him," Polly said. "And I enjoy it."

"Don't forget you have your own family that needs your attention," James said petulantly.

"I couldn't if I tried," Polly said.

* * *

Sometime in January Polly had realized that she was strengthening, though she didn't think of Dick any less. She missed him differently—missed, now, his constant determination to do things well. She wrote about this to Robert, who wrote back that Dick set a good example for everyone around him.

She hadn't been able to find—yet—any of his new work on pacifism, no argument, just notes. In the meantime she was organizing the rest of his writing with a view toward publication. She used colored markers to indicate categories, not that it was always clear to her. She could only do her best. His letters were already meticulously organized, and she was reading through them. Those she thought of general interest she put into a new folder on the desk. He'd kept copies of his letters to the boys, too, and she had to smile at Dick's awkwardness. He felt compelled to offer wisdom and advice. Polly had a sensation of hearing it fall flat. Thud!

Between this work and writing to Robert and sharing living space with Knox, she was well occupied. She wrote to Robert every day, adding thoughts and observations as they occurred until she'd accumulated enough for a letter. Her correspondence grew and broadened through the winter. She was trying to be more honest with herself about her true feelings rather than doing what she'd always done, explaining them away. "It's an excellent habit to avoid calculating what it is possible to get away with," Robert wrote her. That hadn't been what she meant, but Polly decided to monitor herself for wanting to get away with things, and found the impulse was constant. She confessed this to Robert and asked for help. "Beats me!" he wrote back. "But I think it's not such a problem when a person's impulses are good."

Recently she'd written that she couldn't wait to get back up to

Fellowship Point and that she planned to go early this year, for lu-
pine season. "I've never walked in our meadow when it's pink and
indigo." After she dropped the letter into the slot at the post office,
it occurred to her how insensitive she'd been. Robert couldn't see
flowers at all. It was one thing to write about her garden, which
he'd cared for and augmented, but it was quite another to go on
about the glory of spring, and to use a word like *meadow* that caused
a yearning in everyone. Over the next couple of days she spilled
things and tore a hole in her sweater. She worked on another letter
but crossed out line after line. If she never heard from him again,
she'd deserve it. Kind impulses—right!

But he did reply, and only five days later. He wrote, "You think
you can't wait to see the lupines!" She laughed aloud, a sharp, delighted laugh of a sort she'd forgotten she had in her. Before reading the rest, she made a cup of tea and settled on her back on the
sofa, legs up, shoes off. This was a new posture for her, but it seemed
the sofa had been waiting to be stretched out on all along. When
she'd arranged the pillows—one under her knees—and was thoroughly comfortable, she took a few slow breaths, the kind required
by her childhood piano teacher. Then, in the middle of the letter,
a buried headline.

Now for the big news, which hasn't been made public yet. I'm
telling you first. Are you sitting down? I haven't been able to since
I heard, but you should before you read further. Are you? Okay,
here it comes!

I'm getting out soon. The judge granted time served. So, Polly,
I may see the lupines myself.

Polly gasped. She lay the letter down. This wasn't like his other
letters, those she read over and over. This was not a communication
soul to soul, but a message from reality that she grasped instantly

443

without need for contemplation to fully understand. It was an event, and a shock.

It was hard to know how to react. In movies, the glee of women was often expressed in pictures of a person running down streets or hills to spread good news, or jumping into the air and clicking heels. But her glee, at least for the moment, was sober, or even somber. She'd been so overwhelmed by the specter of time lost, both past and future, that the first thing that came to her was grief for the two years Robert had spent in prison for nothing more than being in the path of a pair of reckless vipers. She closed her eyes to try to change her mood—she must, before she wrote Robert back—but all that happened was that the light left the sky while she wasn't looking, and when she opened her eyes again the windows had changed from being vitrines of trees in varying perspectives into dark gray blots on her walls. It was time to turn on the lamps. Her stockinged steps across the carpet sent up sparks. How was it that the rug was more capable of celebrating than she?

She ate her omelet and told Dick. She knew perfectly well he was nowhere to hear her. But she often talked to herself as if she were speaking with him. Dick would still want a total exoneration, both for Robert and to vindicate Dick's position and crusade. The injustice done to Robert had broken Dick's heart. She wondered how Agnes would react to the news of his freedom. Would she call? Polly hoped so. She'd written so many letters to Agnes but hadn't mailed them. She felt both right and shy, and afraid to make the gesture. She was hoping the proximity of the Point would be the remedy. They were too old not to be friends. Fallings-out were for those who had time to meet new people.

These ideas were simple and clear, but there were others more subtle that she couldn't easily parse or name. If she were versed in complexity, she might have understood that she felt uprooted by the change in her routine that would be generated by this shift in

Robert's status. She might have been able to admit that the central place Robert held in her life was made possible because of his captivity. Now she felt a hollowness that might have signaled abandonment, had she known better how to name her wounds. For the second time in two years she was being tossed into the unknown without her choosing it. *It is good news, wonderful news,* she told herself, and yet she felt loss. She loved their correspondence, and hated the thought of it ending. The quiet hours spent discovering who she was at the tip of a pen, and with him open to learning her, had been like nothing else she'd ever done in her life. This selfish thought pressed at her ribs, hurting her, and she pressed back with her hand. Could she be having a heart attack?

No. She'd seen a heart attack.

She stood up to walk around the room and to think.

What would become of him? She remembered Dick saying he wouldn't be able to get a job. He was a felon, and there were rules for felons that made a normal life difficult to pursue. He'd sold his house. When he was released, he'd be alone without a place to live.

The habit of a lifetime of acquiescence wanted to defer the question to broader shoulders—but—but—in being alone, she'd developed a better understanding of her own intelligence than she'd ever had. She'd always been known for her thoughtful gestures, but they weren't really a manifestation of morality, or idealism—they came of a sense of balance that was innate and simple, the same that made it easy for her to arrange flowers or place furniture in a room. She balanced what went on around her, too—she'd really have to correct Robert on that point, she couldn't have him thinking she was good, not in the way Elspeth Lee had been. But she could be relied on to seek equilibrium.

Suddenly she wished to look in a mirror—to see her whole self as she appeared in the world. Her granddaughter Maddie told her she had a hump like a camel—a remark she knew was true when the

DILs got cross with Maddie. How true, though? The largest mirror in the house—the only one that could offer a full view—was a horizontal piece of glass over the sideboard in the dining room. She could barely see the top of her head in it now. There was no other option, though, so she climbed onto a chair on her knees and then tried to step up onto the table, but that didn't go well, so she got Dick's cane and used it to push herself up on the chair first, and then one step higher onto the table. She stepped to the middle, just to the side of the chandelier and turned sideways. Yes, a hump, there it was, undeniable. She tried to straighten out, and could a little, but soon she was tired from pushing back against the inclination of her tendons and bones. The person she'd been for most of her life had disappeared, never to be seen again. How odd. She was an old, bent woman standing on a table, unsure of what to do. A person who'd spent her life among others, acting as a counterweight to ensure fun and peace, but was now so alone her closest friend was a prison pen pal.

She faced the mirror and closed her eyes. "Take stock," she said aloud. Brother parents friends Dick children grandchildren—her people. The Battle of Hastings occurred in 1066; red and blue make purple; I before E except after C; Let me lift mine eyes to the hills from whence cometh my help; *vous* is formal *tu* is familiar—her learning. School college Philadelphia Maine—her places. What of her loves? Her passions? She'd once worshipped an older girl at school when she was a girl herself, and then a boy when she was a little older. For decades these loves had stayed with her as talismans, and she turned to them when she needed to remind herself of how high a person could reach. But while watching her children go through these stages, she'd realized that early love was more a figuring out of the self than a genuine apprehension of another. She was still figuring herself out.

It seemed to her that except for Dick and the children it was time to clean out her memory. Time for all ideas to go, all religion, politics, philosophy, science, every theory of mankind. What did she need of them now? Nature could remain, and memory. What did she need of anything else? The scent of her grandmother's hallway, lemony and lavender. The poke of pine needles through her blouse. Wind on a mountaintop nearly sweeping her off. Sex with Dick—it had been fun. She'd read somewhere that children come from a man's pleasure, not a woman's. But during her pleasure, the children were made.

When she was so exhausted she was afraid of falling, she climbed down with Dick's cane on the chair and then the floor. Ridiculously—she knew it—she spoke to him aloud. "Dick, what would you think of me asking Robert Circumstance to come live at Meadowlea?" Silence. No voice in her head, no reply. She tried to think how far Dick would go in realizing his ideals, but she simply wasn't sure. He'd hadn't given the children an allowance in college so they'd learn to budget their summer earnings, but he had paid for the tuition of the child of a cleaning woman in his campus building. That was money, though. Not proximity.

She went to bed and asked him again. She reached her hand across the mattress to touch his spot. "Dick, what should I do, tell me."

He made no sign. It was up to her now.

In May, soon after Polly arrived on the Point and with the help of Shirley McQuellan, Polly updated and added touches to one of the houses in the Rookerie. Robert wouldn't live at Meadowlea itself, but the Rookerie made sense; he'd do repairs to pay his way. There was no use in arguing with him about that, and repairs were needed. The house was rarely used anymore, and the neglect showed, as neglect always does. Robert wrote that he was excited to do it. His hands ached with disuse.

The morning he was to be released she got up early and checked

447

the house again. The plan, since she'd made it, had been so important that she'd never considered that she'd be an old woman driving up alone to a prison. *This is crazy*, she thought. *A thousand things could go wrong.* But as she drove the route she relaxed. The roads leading there were like other Maine roads, lined with white clapboard houses and old barns, some fit for use, some rotting and tilted to the side, improbably still standing. What did they look like to other people? Tourists? To Polly's eyes they were beautiful, and no wonder they were subjects of many paintings. She noted the roadside stands, not yet selling but getting ready, and fields of lupines and hay. She drove well if she didn't say so herself. It was preposterous that Dick had thought he might make the drive. That whole last morning he'd been fading in and out. It was clear to her now that he was losing blood to his brain, and his speech and actions reflected that. It had worried her at the time, but for the wrong reasons. Wasn't that often the case?

She'd expected to feel awkward and uncomfortable at the Supermax. What kind of a word was that for a prison? Instead, she wanted to tear the place apart. She wished she were better with words so she could explain even to herself how such an impersonal edifice made her feel. There was cruelty in its conception. It represented exile. It wasn't just one person or one mind that had created this place and all the others like it. It was an entire system. Robert was not the only innocent person here, surely. Not only that—how many of the guilty really belonged in such an environment? What good would it do them or their families? The mistake of an instant being amortized over years. Nonsensical.

She waited a long time. Apparently there was a lot of paperwork that went along with being let go. There was a fair amount of activity around her, but she had no interest in observing it. The thing was to get away and never return. Robert was finally let through and they shook hands and embraced awkwardly. His appearance had changed to thinner and older but not vastly different. She smiled at him warmly, willing him to make the transition back to the kinder world—though it was the kind world that had sent him here. He smelled antiseptic, and his clothes—what clothes were they? They were indignities.

"The house is ready for you."

But he already knew that. Every detail had been discussed through the mail. He'd already let her know that Agnew knew, too. "Thank you," he said. He touched the dashboard, and the seat. He touched the door handle, and rubbed his feet against the mat on the floor. "I'm grateful."

"Please let that be the last time you say so."

Robert dropped his head and nodded. He kept his head down for a long time, and it occurred to Polly he might be weeping. To afford him privacy she turned on the radio. After a decent amount of time had passed, she pulled into a roadside restaurant and parked. "I was too excited to eat breakfast." Not wholly true, but true enough.

Robert gave a shy smile. "Me too."

They settled into a booth and ordered. Robert asked for a tuna melt. "None of those in prison," he teased. Polly looked at the table with an appreciation for everything on it—utensils, ketchup, sugar packets, a small vase with flowers—as if she'd been deprived as well.

"I have a lot for you to do," she said, reeling slightly from all the sensations of color and light.

"Didn't the guys do a good job?" He opened his mouth wide to take a huge bite, then remembered Polly and minimized his attack.

"Yes, but I held off on making changes until you were back."

Robert made a small groan. He loved his sandwich.

"Have another."

"If you have time, I will." He ordered a roast beef on rye and a vanilla milkshake. She wondered if he were going to get sick. Was it better to drive fast or slow under the circumstances?

"Are you still planning on the walkway?" he asked.

"I want to discuss it with you. I have some new ideas, too."

He grinned. "I bet you do."

When they reached Cape Deel, she purposely avoided the route that would go past his old house and he didn't correct her. They would get to that eventually.

"There was another eagle killed last week," Polly said. "Shot and plucked."

"Hmm," Robert said. "I'll work on it."

"I know you will. There's something else I need to tell you. I didn't want to put it in a letter. Agnes and I had a fight. We haven't spoken since September. She may have told you."

"No, she didn't. I'm sorry to hear it."

When they turned down Point Path, he twisted his hands around and around in his lap. "It's so beautiful."

"Yes. Should I drive all the way down before stopping at the Rookerie?"

He nodded. On the way, he took a look at Agnes's beds and bushes.

"You must take care of her as always," Polly said. "You can't let our issue get in the way."

"Thank you. I hope it doesn't last much longer, though."

"You know Agnes. So stubborn."

"I know both of you." He raised his eyebrows.

"Very funny. Well, we'll see. You'll be good luck, I imagine."

"I don't even have a joke for that."

They lingered by the Sank and crawled slowly back up to the Rookerie. She showed him the house and was careful not to point out the little luxuries she'd added, like a TV and a reading chair and bookshelf, and left him to set up. She had to walk off her extra energy from having him back. This was good. This was very, very good.

CHAPTER 33

Agnes, Leeward Cottage, July 2002

AGNES GATHERED THE PAGES SHE'D WRITTEN THAT MORNING and placed them under the pink-and-gray speckled beach rock she used as a paperweight. She made a note in her writing log about what and how much she'd accomplished, and a note about what she wanted to write the following day. It was excellent to be back at work. Bless Maud Silver, girl detective. Agnes had been at it for nearly seven months now, and *The Franklin Square Girls Talk to the Hand* was taking shape.

It wasn't what she'd expected to come of having Maud stay in the Rittenhouse Square apartment alone over Thanksgiving. Agnes wanted to help Maud. Guide her. But she didn't want to write the memoir.

It had been many decades since Agnes had met anyone she liked enough to think about, but Maud had aroused her interest. Agnes had done what she could for her mother—Agnes admired Maud's ferocity about Heidi's care. It was also gratifying to picture Maud luxuriating in her apartment alone, with all food supplied. Agnes tracked the hours of the visit closely. She cared more than she'd known about what Maud would think. She'd been careful to remove pages in the notebooks where she'd written about writing, but she hadn't considered the set of *Franklin Square* books in her guest room bookcase.

Maud had called right after her stay at Agnes's apartment. Agnes had made it clear she didn't like to use the phone, so she figured the call must be important, and took the receiver from Sylvie.

"Hello, Agnes."

"Hello, Maud."

"Or should I say, 'Hello, Pauline.'"

Agnes froze. For a long moment a very loaded silence passed between them. Agnes considered denials and demurrals, but what was the use?

"How?" she asked.

"The anagram of the names. Annie, Gail, Nola, Eve, Susan."

Agnes was truly astonished. "I had no idea."

"You didn't do it on purpose?"

"No. Though I wish I'd thought of it. If you didn't so thoroughly surprise me, I'd have had the wherewithal to pretend I did."

"I'm amazed," Maud said.

"That makes two of us."

"I have so many questions."

"I'm not sure I could answer right now." Agnes was downstairs in the den. She looked at the bookshelves but couldn't read any titles. It was dark out and not even five yet.

"I won't tell anyone," Maud said. "I wouldn't. I want you to know that."

"Thank you." Good Lord, Agnes hadn't even thought of that. She was thinking slowly. It was dizzying news.

"I can't believe you wrote all those books!" Maud said. "I really liked them. In fact I'm obsessed with them, I read them all. Is that what you've been working on?"

"Trying to." It was so odd to talk about it!

"Are you angry?" Maud asked.

"I'm not sure yet."

"I didn't figure it out on purpose. It just came to me. The anagram. That and the fact that those were the only books in your apartment. . . ."

"I understand." Agnes saw it now. She wondered if she'd been waiting for Maud to come along, if she'd planted the clues for someone like her. Or had she subconsciously created the anagram so she could, in a sense, have her name on the book?

"I read your notebooks, too."

"Oh?" Agnes had forgotten about that!

"You know I did. I found them very moving. Nan Reed! She is the perfect muse, and I can see how you got all the books from thinking about her. And she was Clemmie's age. I could picture her so clearly because of that—in fact, they kind of ran together in my mind, and Nan's accident horrified me."

"Oh, I'm so sorry." Agnes hadn't thought of that when she sent the notebooks.

"It's all right. I do think we could find a way for you to write this story without revealing anything you don't want to."

"I'm sure we couldn't, because I don't want to reveal any of it. That was my point. I hoped you'd understand." Back to this?

"There's really nothing in here that is startling. You wouldn't have to write about Virgil except as Nan's father. Was *Scalene* ever published? I haven't had a chance to look it up."

"No."

"That's too bad."

It was. Agnes had tried to salvage the book, but her sensibility was too far distant from his for her to step in with any conviction. Virgil Reed was out of print.

"I guess we have to decide what comes next," Maud said. "Now that the cards are on the table."

"What comes next. The hundred-million-dollar question."

They hung up both agreeing to think about it. Gradually they ironed out a plan for Maud to work with Agnes on *The Franklin Square Girls Talk to the Hand*. If it came together well, Agnes would—anonymously—introduce her to her *Franklin Square* publisher with the stipulation that she wanted Maud to take over as editor. Maud said that from what she knew of how things worked, it would be a real reach for her to get a new position that way, but they may as well try. If it all worked out, Agnes agreed to reconsider the memoir. It was a decent gamble. She'd most likely be dead by then, and wouldn't have to do a thing.

Robert offered to drive her to the doctor in Portland. She didn't have as much time with him as she'd have liked these days. In her magnanimous moments she was glad he'd gotten close to Polly because Polly didn't know how to be without a male referent, not in the way Agnes did. But most of the time it was aggravating.

Halfway to the city Robert said Polly's family was coming.

"When?" Agnes pictured James strolling around, hands in pockets, portraying the attitude of mastery.

Robert frowned. He didn't like being in the middle.

"The beginning of August."

"Is James staying at WesterLee?"

"That's nothing new."

"No. But now it's sinister."

"That's a strong word."

"Oh, I've thought stronger, believe me."

"He loves the Point."

"Not if he wants to develop it, he doesn't."

"Polly says he swears there's no plan for that."

Agnes began to respond but checked herself from saying Polly was credulous when it came to men. How could he hear that objectively?

"I have a friend arriving around then as well." Maud was coming to work with her again. Did Polly know? Did Robert know? Agnes hadn't forbidden Maud to be in contact with Polly. That was beyond her scope. Polly would twist it to both take the high road and be the injured party. Agnes hated that particular configuration of behavior. She hated even more that it had a feminine contour to it, because she didn't think it essentially feminine. It was a perversion of female power, a turning inside out of the anger attendant to hurt. The tight-lipped wife, the woman turning on her heel, sinking to her knees, broken, broken. Agnes did not want to be the one to prompt self-pity, either in Polly or herself.

Robert dropped her off and went to do errands, and Agnes settled in the waiting room with the cancer patients. Was it her imagination, or did they look less ravaged than the similar cohort in her doctor's office at the university hospital in Philadelphia? Her doctor here, William Oswald, was as medically oriented as the next oncologist, but he coupled his knowledge of chemo protocols and surgeries with a deep curiosity about his patients and their lives in order to figure out how best to treat them. In Agnes's case, he'd twice advocated that she forgo chemo in favor of fresh food, fresh air, and sleep—much the same philosophy as at Friends Hospital. He knew she would prefer to risk a statistically higher chance of recurrence in order to feel all right every day, to work and be outside. She'd beaten the statistics for her last cancer. She'd chosen the same course this time: surgery and vegetables.

It didn't always work, he'd been careful to tell her, if by *work* one meant a cure, or maximum longevity. It did afford a swift return to a somewhat regular life. Agnes thought some of the other patients must have made the same choice. They didn't look exactly hale, but they didn't look like they were being poisoned either.

She was called to have blood drawn, her least favorite part of anything medical, but no one would know that from how coolly she watched the blood being removed from her arm. Today it looked nearly black. Good? Bad? Should she ask the phlebotomist? A four-syllable word if she ever heard one. Never mind. She'd find out soon enough.

Then it was time to sit some more. Agnes pulled her recent pages out of her bag and fished for her pencil. No time to waste. She and Maud had an arrangement now, whereby Agnes would send her pages every Monday and Maud would respond by the following Sunday. Rinse and repeat.

She was on Chapter Seven. The girls, at eighty now, were girls again. Her feelings for all of them were mellow and magnanimous. When she was young, she'd been far more judgmental, and had mocked them deliberately and rather cruelly, ignoring the writing advice she'd read that claimed it was paramount to love your characters. What did love have to do with it? They were her talismans against making bad choices herself. She imagined being married, or working at a bank under bosses who saw her as a curiosity at best. At best! The stories she heard from women in her travels around Philadelphia indicated much worse than benign wonder, and she wrote them out, explored, exposed hypocrisy and sexism and racism in the City of Brotherly Love.

She'd always hoped her books were cautionary tales, and that real women would learn from the Franklins' mistakes, many of which were attitudinal. She'd spent a lot of time demonstrating that no woman was ever going to be truly rewarded for quietly going about her work, hoping someday someone would notice. "Dick appreciates me, he just can't show it," Polly had often said. Agnes had seen Dick fawn over people whose approval he desired. He was capable of showing appreciation when doing so held a potential benefit for him. Polly supplied herself with approval of her efforts, letting him off the hook, and eventually leading to his inability to notice. Men were creatures of the culture as much as women were, and performed as expected, including taking the ministrations of women for granted. But they could choose otherwise. So could women. That was where she came in.

Or, had, in her heyday.

She'd put the girls through so much, and still they came back to her, wandering into her study in the mornings, coaxing her to move her pen across the page. They still wanted things. They were old, but they weren't done. She very much wanted to portray their ongoing growth. Now when she sat at her desk every day she asked them what she could do for them. *What would you like to think about today? Where would you like to go, what do you want to remember, who do you miss, what do you want to learn? Tell me your desires. I am at your service, my girls.*

She had to admit, she was glad someone knew she was Pauline Schulz. Not someone: Maud. Maud, as it turned out, was the person she hadn't known she needed. Maud understood. She completely understood. Agnes didn't know how that was possible, but she knew why. Maud was interested in writing, in a deep, serious way. She had a feel for the possibilities, and an intuitive comprehension of the strange alchemy that occurred as imagination got hammered out on the anvil of the subconscious, the personality, the will. Maud had no interest in writing herself, but she was brilliant at seeing what was too much and what not enough. She was helpful. She would keep Agnes's secret. Agnes hoped.

Agnes had never showed her writing to anyone before it was finished, but she was deeply enjoying the process. She'd trained herself to be her own editor, as writers do, but it was incredibly useful and bracing to be able to ask questions in medias res, and to discuss possible plot developments and have another mind seeing different angles. She was teaching Maud how to edit along the way. Maud was aware of this and asked a lot of questions about how to pinpoint what was wrong in a scene or chapter, and how to best communicate her responses. Agnes was touched by her ambition to become like one of the old-style great editors. A desire for intimacy and integrity. To truly understand an author's deepest intentions and capabilities, and to foster them into a manuscript and then fashion that into an aesthetically coherent object—how high-minded that was! A pinnacle of human endeavor. Agnes had all the respect in the world for the intelligence of the other animals, but there were certain areas that separated them from humans, and the writing and editing of books was one of them.

Maud kept her word and dropped the subject of the memoir entirely, with the unsurprising result that Agnes thought about it more, and wondered if she should expand it. So far, the answer had been no, but it wasn't as loud.

The door to the inner sanctum of the office opened. Agnes glanced over in spite of her belief in not staring. A person appeared feetfirst on a wheelchair footrest. He was pushed forward by a woman who looked more like a daughter than an aide. Aides always wore pants. The daughter was dressed in a skirt and stockings and Top-Siders. The father—at the end. Last days. Gaunt and gray, head hanging to the side. The daughter collected coats from the closet.

"All right, Daddy, let's put this on you now. We're about to go outside."

She draped the coat over his shoulders. He moaned at its touch, and from the effort to tip slightly forward so it could be bunched behind him. A nurse stepped out behind them.

"Mrs. Lee?"

"It's Miss, thank you."

Agnes heaved herself up. Not easy anymore, just not so easy. Yet better than that guy.

She exchanged glances with the daughter. Agnes meant to commiserate, but the daughter offered her pity. Yes, of course. She was in his category, though she would always think of herself as the daughter of a father.

The nurse led her into an examining room. "Let's get your weight."

Agnes stepped on the scale with her shoes on. The days of peeling off clothes and even bracelets to weigh a bit less were way behind her.

"One thirty-one," the nurse announced. She looked at the chart. "Down three pounds."

"Bikini season," Agnes said.

No response. She thought of a title for one of her magazine pieces: "The Oncologist's Office: Where Jokes Go to Die."

"Everything off except bra and panties, gown on with the opening to the back."

"I'm not wearing panties, I am wearing underwear."

The nurse suddenly looked at her as though she were a real person. "What's the difference? I never knew."

"Panties are for men. Underwear is for women."

The nurse nodded. "That makes sense. I have both, I guess."

"Thank you for sharing the state of your underwear drawer with me," Agnes said.

The nurse blushed.

"I'm sorry," Agnes said. "I have the British teasing gene."

But it was too late. The nurse grew crisp. "He'll be in soon."

Agnes undressed. She was at the stage of writing her book where all her actions were filters for details she might include. She wasn't herself undressing in a doctor's office, or not only herself. She was also one of her characters. She observed the stiffness in her back as she bent over to retrieve her slacks from around her ankles. She folded her clothes carefully, for the benefit of Dr. Oswald. If she were neat, he'd let her live. Then she looked at the pictures on the walls. Thank God he didn't have diagrams of innards or ads for drugs. Instead, Maine landscapes.

"I love Maine," Agnes said aloud. "I love Fellowship Point. May it live forever."

There was no one to overhear her, but she was pretty sure she'd reached the stage where no one would hear her even if they heard her.

When Dr. Oswald—Bill to her—came in, he looked at her carefully as he shook hands. She'd discussed this with him at an earlier appointment, this old-school way of doctoring by actually studying the patient and partly from experience and partly from intuition getting a sense of what the body was up to.

"I saw that man come out who was in here before," Agnes said. "Does he really want to go on?"

"His body wants to. The body wants to live. It's amazing what it will tolerate in order to keep going."

"Please don't let me live like that."

He began to touch her gently. He always felt for her heartbeat with his fingers on her pulses and over the organ before he laid the cold stethoscope on her skin. He was one of the few men who'd ever communicated that her physical being was worth something. That was an assessment she'd mostly had to make for herself.

"You don't know how he feels from the inside."

"I don't even want to look that bad. His poor daughter."

"Yes. She's not having much fun these days."

"I did that, for about fifteen years. Not my favorite."

"I have been doing it for nearly forty years, and it is my favorite." He examined her scars so unobtrusively that she barely felt violated.

"Somehow it seems different in your case."

"To tell you the truth, professionalizing the role only shifts it. The realm is the same. It's the realm of life that doesn't feature growth."

"Cancer cells grow. Tumors grow."

"You don't say." Bill smiled.

Agnes laughed. More than any other interaction, she loved it when someone wouldn't let her get away with her stuff. "I'm a know-it-all, quite famously so."

"That helps, actually. So how have you been?" he asked. "Actually, why don't you dress and come to my office and we'll talk there."

"Thank you," Agnes said.

He had a surprising office. Minimalist, serene, carefully thought through. It was a place of work, where nothing would interfere with his thoughts. Patients might think it was for their benefit, but he was for their benefit. His office supported him.

Childishly, she liked to believe that not every patient was invited in.

"So. What are you thinking about the future?" he asked.

"I want to finish my work. I want to defeat my enemies."

"So you need energy and all your wits."

"Yes. Perhaps not all my wits, but enough."

"Do you have any pain left from the surgery?"

"A bit. As predicted. I can't lift my right arm above my shoulder."

"Is that bothering you?"

"I'm getting used to it."

"Do you meditate, Agnes?"

"I walk on the land every day. Well—if it's too stormy, I watch the storm. I keep company with a cat. And I write. Or I sit there and wait for words."

"Do you ever think of bringing a love of your body into those thoughts?"

"Nope!"

The doctor smiled. "How did I know that?"

"I am fourteen at heart."

"Did you like your body then?"

"This seems a bit more like therapy than oncology."

"Which brings us back around to the mind-body problem. What would you like to do now?"

"Cancer-wise?"

"For starters."

"I'd like to ignore it completely. What are my odds?"

"Without treatment, you have a chance of it spreading."

"A good chance?"

"If you were young, I'd say yes. But cancer behaves differently in the old, and there aren't as many statistics that I consider definitive."

There was a pause. Agnes felt in her arms her own perennial urge to wage war, to be in combat. He wouldn't meet her in such a spot, so she flopped and floundered until she discovered what lay over the hill.

"I'm inclined to let nature figure out the schedule. But . . . can you help me when the time comes?"

"As I said earlier, the body wants to live. It's very hard to know when the time comes. People miss the moment."

"No feeding tubes. No hospital."

"Make a living will, and make it really clear. You can go into hospice."

"Yes. I'm sure that's just great. But I don't want to lie around dying."

"I understand what you're saying, Agnes. I can only do so much. I can point you to people to discuss all this with and who can help you make decisions."

"Remember *Harold and Maude*? When Maude made a plan to kill herself on her eightieth birthday?"

"One of my favorites."

"You're suggesting I emulate Maude."

"No. I'm suggesting you think it all through. And tell your near ones."

"I see." She did. She had to figure out when her mind would still be in charge of her body. Once the body took over, she wouldn't be in control anymore. "That's very good advice. I think you're gypping yourself out of some money, though, by not pushing treatment."

"Funnily enough, it hasn't worked out that way."

"Hmm. A reversal of expectations. That's my stock in trade."

"You may be fine, you know. It wouldn't be delusional to assume that."

He meant this genuinely. He was the poster boy for male doctors who weren't condescending.

"Thanks. Delusional or not, that's what I'll do."

Robert was in the waiting room when Agnes stepped out. Rarely did she have so much male attention in one season, much less one day. It wasn't really what she wanted or needed. But she was not averse, as it turned out. Not anymore.

"Ready?" Robert said.

She had a starry sense of being watched. She'd always liked that; it made her feel significant. Funny of her to choose a life of being anonymous for her painstaking oeuvre.

On the way out of the building she dropped her handbag near the newsstand. It just slipped from her hand. Both she and Robert leaned over to pick it up, and on her way down her gaze alighted on a copy of the *Cape Deel Gazette*. What it was doing in Portland she couldn't say, but there were papers from all over. The picture on the cover was of a house on Cape Deel.

"I want to buy this," she said, rattling the paper.

She made the transaction and tucked it into her bag. Now she really felt as though she were out in the world. She never bought newspapers!

"So what did you do while I was being examined?" Agnes asked. They walked to the car.

"Errands. This and that."

"Sounds fun."

"Pretty much everything is fun these days."

"I wish you'd tell me more about it." She buckled her seat belt.

"There's nothing to tell," he said. "It's exactly like in the movies."

"I'm sure it's the opposite."

"It is, actually. Prison is all about time. The passage of time. Two hours is no time at all."

"But that is the one aspect of it I might be able to comprehend. The passage of time is my central subject."

He considered this. "The thing is, everyone understands that that's what it's about. The least intelligent guards nevertheless understand that manipulating time is a more successful form of torture than beatings. Solitary confinement ruins people. Partly because it's lonely, but I think more because with the lights on all the time you have no sense of day or night, or how long you've slept, or anything. People try to keep track but it isn't possible. You don't know if the sun's up or the moon's out. You know nothing."

"Were you in solitary confinement?"

"For a while. For infinity, I should say."

"How can it be so beautiful here and all that go on? I feel like a child saying that, but I've never gotten anywhere with the question. I've tried. I've tried seeing it as all a part of one flow, or that I was lucky, or out of touch, or that opposites contained each other, all those ideas . . . but nothing has ever helped me understand. Nothing."

"Our minds are small," he said.

"I was just reminded of that."

"Polly is determined that I feel the luxury of having time to squander."

"You're not going to be able to repair this by reminding me of her gifts. I know her better than anybody. And since when did you ever have time on your hands?"

"She's a strong person."

"Don't try to make me miss her." Agnes's stomach had tied up at the mention of Polly's name.

"Okay. I'll stay out of it."

"That would be best." She pulled the paper out of her bag. "Let's go by this house. Do you know where it is?"

"I do, exactly."

Agnes flipped through the newspaper. There were ads for jewelers and Realtors and restaurants. "Maine has gotten very lively," she said. Then she got to a page that stopped her.

"Hamm Loose, Man with His Eye on the Horizon."

There was his ugly mug, staring straight at her, his big middle, his ham-fisted hands. The article described the properties he'd already transformed from being pristine places of nature or lightly used into flashy resorts—as flashy as it got in Maine, that was. The word *tasteful* was deployed more than once, which made her furious. What was tasteful about destroying so many trees, so much habitat?

> Loose Properties has broken ground at the site of a major
> marina resort northwest of Deel Town. "But Fellowship Point
> is my dream spot for a resort and village." Time will tell if
> Hamm Loose, Junior, is able to fulfill that dream.

"Never mind," Agnes said, "I want to go straight home."

"Are you all right?"

"Would this be happening if I weren't an old woman? Would these men feel so free to disregard all my experience and wisdom and knowledge? James! Archie! I watched them grow up. I helped them grow up!"

Robert pulled over. "May I see?"

She handed him the paper. He read quickly, and sighed.

"I mean, how brazen can you be?" she said. "Now do you understand why I can't pretend with Polly?"

"I have always understood."

"Tell her she's wrong," Agnes said. "Please, Robert."

Then a great wave of rage swept through her, and Agnes brought her fist down on the dashboard. Robert jumped.

After a moment he laid a hand on her shoulder and awkwardly patted her. She pulled herself together.

He folded the paper but stopped halfway. "What? Listen to this."

A seventeen-year-old female, Mary Mitchell, was arrested today for shooting an eagle with a bow and arrow. She was spotted in the act by a local resident near Kim Lake who called the police.

Mary Mitchell was taken to the police station in Deel Town where she claimed she is a member of the Abenaki tribe living off the reservation. She admitted that she has been shooting eagles for years.

"The eagle is sacred to my people. It is the creature that comes closest to the Creator. We have always lived with and understood eagles. But now we are not allowed to have them for our ceremonies except through a repository in Colorado. It can take four years after an application is made for feathers to be received from there. I have been harvesting eagles for use in sacred ceremonies. I seek no profit. I do this according to a vision I had when I was twelve."

"Good grief," Agnes said. "All along it was a child. A child with a vision on a mission. I pictured a big crude brute. Is she in jail?"

"It seems so."

"How can she be an Abenaki?"

"Maybe she is making a political point."

"I should say so. I want to talk to her. I'll call and see if I can." Agnes's arms stirred with vigor. "I have to live, Robert. I'm not done."

The next morning, she called Dr. Oswald.

"Bill, I thought it through," she said. "I want you to go ahead and poison me."

"All right, Agnes. I think it's a good decision. Let's start with an oral chemo. I'll call it into your drugstore. You'll need to know a few things, and do a few things to support yourself while taking it. I'm going to have you make an appointment for a phone call with the nurse, so stay on the line, all right?"

During the wait, listening to medieval choral music, Agnes was wickedly tempted to hang up. As if that would change anything. Instead, she made the appointment, and called her lawyer.

CHAPTER 34

Polly, Cape Deel and Meadowlea, Summer 2002

"P OLLY, HOW'S ROBERT CIRCUMSTANCE?" ASKED ETTA McPherson.

Polly was prepared for this. She had planned to give the answer some spin, as they said. A lot of Robert's clients had dropped away, and she wanted to give him a boost. "Oh! He's doing wonderfully well. His business is picking up. It may be hard to hire him pretty soon—he has a lot of new customers, as well as his old ones. Meanwhile he has made my house into a palace. He's painting the upstairs hall right now."

"You feel safe—leaving him alone in the house?"

Polly stiffened.

"I trust him completely," she said, her voice unfortunately quavering. She wasn't quavering, however. She was prepared to fight if necessary. Since her falling-out with Agnes, she'd toughened up. The weather helped. The day was a hard bright blue, glittering the way only July glittered. The dining room of her friend Rosie Bayer Baines's house overlooked the sparkling sea, with a view for miles. There were five ladies around the table, all old as the hills and cloistered as ever.

Glances were exchanged.

"You should trust him, too," Polly said. She gripped her napkin under the table.

"It's all right, Polly," the hostess, Rosie, said.

"He's innocent. Obviously."

"Seela is still very upset," said Gaga Bunting.

"Well, Robert is, too! He spent over two years in prison for a crime he didn't do."

"Let's change the subject," Rosie said. "Has anyone been to Thuya Garden this summer?"

"I wish someone had told me what you've all been thinking," Polly said.

"It is hard to know what to think," Etta said. "Seela swears she saw him take the necklace."

Polly shook her head. She hadn't been as upset in a long time. "But that isn't true. He pulled the necklace from the toilet. He rescued it for her."

"It's one word against another."

"No, it isn't," Polly said hotly. "Seela's story never made sense. She simply forgot leaving her necklace in the bathroom."

"I don't think she'd go so far as to frame a man. Anyway, he knocked her down. You can't deny that."

"That's not the only way to describe what happened," Polly said. She folded her napkin, in preparation to leave, and stood up from the table.

Rosie stood, too. "Polly, please, don't go—I'm so happy to have you."

Polly pushed past her and walked to the door. On her way out, her gaze went to the Civil War sword that hung above the mantel. *What a waste*, she thought. *Nothing to be proud of, these stupid wars.*

"Polly, Polly," called a chorus behind her, until Gaga—Polly recognized the voice—said, "Oh, let her go."

At home, Robert noticed her agitation, but she was too embarrassed to tell him what happened. She'd looked forward to spending the afternoon with him, but he went into town for supplies. She picked up her needlepoint and immediately stabbed herself. She sopped up her blood with the skeins of wool in her lap. Each color had to be set in a strainer and run over by boiling water from a kettle in hopes of restoration, and all the while she was flooded by wave after wave of shame and anger. She didn't think she'd ever before been the subject of gossip. She felt alone in a new way, not merely personally—a feeling she assumed was familiar to every human being—but as though she were tethered to nothing.

Stop it, she told herself. *Buck up. Buck up.* Things were going well. Very well. What did it matter what people thought? Robert was starting to relax. Those old women—who cared? They were as irrelevant as Polly herself was, and she was shown and told about her diminished status at every juncture.

She liked having Robert on the Point. They hadn't eaten together very often after the first day, when he was getting settled. Usually they met out back and chatted, or had coffee after he fixed something in the house. Occasionally when she saw him puttering around at dawn she asked him inside for breakfast, but there was a tacit agreement between them that they observe the dinner hour separately. She gave him the second set of keys to the car so he could go to town on his own and buy his food, and often she'd leave him a list of what to get for her, too. His crew still had his truck, and he was taking things slowly about asking for it back. He seemed to need time alone.

As easily as she and Robert got along, they couldn't speak as they'd written. Their letters were done, that mode past. Polly had never spoken such naked feelings aloud, and she supposed he hadn't either. She'd traded their intimate written exchange for his presence, and joked more than emoted. They could look at the same thing—for example, a pancake that came out looking like Richard Nixon—and both get the giggles. The days beaded a smooth chain of fine feeling. Polly was aware of a loosening in her shoulders. Her parents' old prohibition against reading in bed in the morning lifted, and sometimes she made coffee and then went back up. Some days she and Robert didn't even see each other except to wave from a distance. Others, they worked closely during most of the hours of light. Their conversations mainly involved the steps in each fix-it job. "I woke up thinking of the lip of the patio," he might say, "and I pictured a low wall."

She would see the picture, too. "Low wall," she repeated. "Sounds like poetry."

"I see it as smooth and carefully joined," he said.

"And the stones are local and hand-cut."

"Granite."

"A few of the pink set oddly—in no pattern." She was sure they were picturing the exact same thing, and building it together in words, first.

"Not spotty, though."

"No."

They walked to the proposed place for the wall and each held their hands parallel to the ground at the height they thought it should be. They differed by about six inches; another discussion then. The project started and they commented on every stone laid. Robert was like a child wanting his drawings praised, and she was a person who'd never gotten to have much of a say.

"You don't mind, do you, Dick?" she asked when she was alone.

She waited for a sign. Silence had always signified disapproval to her, so she waited until she heard a creak, or a car going past, or a birdcall. The sign always came. All the changes Dick had put off, he didn't mind now. Death had mellowed him.

One day she saw Lydia in the field by the new wall and automatically Polly went toward her. The toe of her shoe caught on the bottom step. She lurched forward and loped for a few steps with most of her body nearly parallel to the ground. The width of her steps increased so as not to fall, and her arms stretched forward automatically, in case she did. The speed of the fall was maddeningly slow, affording her time to think of the inconvenience of another broken wrist. The heavy clomping of her footfalls maddened her as well; so graceless and crude. Stand up, she commanded herself. Then she'd landed. Her face hit her arm.

She lay in the limbo and shock of an accident having happened, the odd restfulness of knowing there was nothing more she could do now. She settled into the grass and ran her mind over her body, concluding nothing had broken. *Lydia, did you see that? Are you laughing? Well, it was funny.*

A face appeared. She heard her name. She was lifted up, whirled around. She saw her blue river. She turned to the face. She looked at the mouth. What do you do with a mouth but kiss it?

"Polly, you hit your head."

She heard a voice in the distance, then close again. Dick hadn't picked her up in years. "I'm taking you to the hospital. You might have a concussion."

"I'm fine," she said. "I don't want to go to the hospital. Let's just sit a while."

Robert took her to the hospital anyway. Polly had a mild concussion and was not to drive for a month. On their way back down Point Path they saw Agnes and Maisie heading for the graveyard.

"She looks so normal," Polly said. How could that be, when they were estranged?

"A new look?" Robert teased, making Polly laugh and get a headache.

They decided on another wall farther down the meadow, parallel to the horizon, that would add a subtle note to the view. Robert came and went into and out of the house without knocking, and now they ate together at night without her inviting him. They spoke more freely, too, and once begun, the conversation was as deep and open as when they'd been safely invisible and had pen and paper as their go-between. Every day they revealed themselves more and shifted their habits to accommodate each other. Shirley got the meal ready and then went home. Robert showered and changed before he came over. Sometimes after dinner they took a walk down the road to the Sank. Every time they stood at the tip of the Point, one or the other said it was the most beautiful spot on earth, and it was always the right thing to say.

On some days he rearranged his schedule so he could take her to town.

One Monday they arrived at the time of morning when the windows along Main Street were black daubs one minute and in the next, flashes going off at the passing cars, as if each might contain a movie star. They parked, and Polly saw the two of them reflected, a Mutt and Jeff. People stopped to say hello, and some of them looked sideways at Robert. She wanted to smack them. He noticed, of course, but said nothing.

A couple of kids came muscling down the street, heedless as all boys.

"Natives," Robert said.

Polly looked at him quizzically.

"Native Americans. I don't see them often in Cape Deel."

"How do you know?"

He shrugged. "By the way, Agnes hired a lawyer to defend the girl who shot the eagles." He bumped her with his elbow.

"She would. I mean that in the best way."

They stopped in the library and each chose two books. Robert picked out a new novel and a gardening book. Polly wanted a particular Edith Wharton, though she couldn't remember what it was called, so she took two. No way to miss with Edith.

Next Polly sprang for a pie—a very expensive pie!

By the time they got back to the car, Polly was tired and didn't notice until they were already in the interior that he'd gone the back way. She moaned.

"What? You feel bad?" he asked.

"Oh—I try not to come this way."

"It's faster."

"I feel nervous here."

Immediately she wished she could take this back.

He didn't take offense. "Shall I turn around?"

"No, no. It's fine."

He tapped at the wheel and whistled. Polly sat back. The children were out, as always, and dirty, as always, and stared at the car—if they noticed it—with faces big and blank as basketballs.

"Hey," he said, "remember when you were in a car and you looked straight ahead to see the trees as they are and then turned your head fast to the side to make them blurry?"

She smiled. "Yes. I loved doing all those tricks—like covering one eye and seeing a completely different part of the scene than with both eyes."

"How about staring at a light bulb and then closing your eyes and watching a light show?"

"Going into a completely dark closet and waiting until your eyes adjusted and you saw shapes?"

"I haven't done any of those things in a long time. I guess I've stopped playing." He had a new melancholy note in his voice this summer, and who could blame him. "I can't even remember how."

"It'll come back." She wondered how much he cared that he'd never had children.

He drummed the steering wheel. "I guess it's play for me to build a pond, or design a terrace."

The conversation had pushed the street into the background,

475

and she'd nearly forgotten it. Yet a part of her had kept track, and as they approached *that* yard her muscles tightened. Her grandchildren had had an incantation they repeated when passing a graveyard, but she saw the dog before she could remember it. She saw him from behind, before they pulled parallel. Her heart beat as if the dog were her true love, found again. Nothing about the situation had changed. He still stood on top of the doghouse, listless in every aspect. He'd still hang if he stepped off the box.

"It's him," she said, heart slamming her ribs.

"Who?"

"The dog."

Robert peered at it. "The dog?"

"It's the one we saved. How is he back?"

Robert squinted through the windshield. "Are you sure it's the same dog?"

"Yes!"

He parked the car.

"I have money," she said. She fished out her wallet and handed him a few bills.

He took them and nodded. "Why not wait here?" he said lightly.

She nodded, fighting frustrated tears.

Robert walked past the dog without glancing at it and up to the trailer door. He knocked. After a while the door opened, and Polly saw him turn around and point at the dog. After a minute Robert walked back across the yard, slipped the rope off the dog's neck, and carried it to the car.

Polly got out and opened the back door. Robert repeated "Shh, shh." Its head fell back against Robert's chest, and Polly touched her hand to her own chest. The boys' heavy heads, the scent of sweaty curls, trust imparted. The dog shuddered and paddled its legs. Robert lowered him. He stood stiffly on the backseat, shaking so hard the car seemed to rock.

"Jesus wept," Polly said. She'd never said that before, but it had always stayed with her from a moment in the movie *Lawrence of Arabia*. A scene of carnage, and someone saying *Jesus wept*. The shortest verse in the Bible, she'd learned.

"What are we going to do with him?" she asked.

"Too soon to know," Robert said. "He's not much at the moment."

They emerged from the road. An eagle flew low over an open field, the same sight Polly saw the first day she found the dog. "Dick never allowed the boys to have a dog."

Robert considered this. "Would you rather I take him somewhere else?"

He'd understood her, once again. It was all she needed to find her own feelings. "No. He can come with us."

Back on the Point, Robert dropped her off and took the dog with him to his house in the Rookerie. She didn't see Robert again that day. The next morning he showed up during her breakfast.

"I want to name her Hope," he said.

"He's a girl?"

"As it turns out, yes."

"Hope's a good name," Polly said.

"I'm taking her to the vet."

"I'll pay for that."

"We'll see," Robert said.

Nothing had to be decided today.

Her boys joked about Dick during their visit, telling stories about moments when he'd embarrassed them at restaurants, or came down hard on them for something small, yet they had always had her intervention on their behalf, and their own solidarity, to buffet them, and their recollections weren't bitter. It was she who heard

Dick's voice in how her sons spoke to their own children. "No, and that is final." "No, because I said so." "Do I look like a bank to you?" No one, including her, said it was unnecessary to speak so harshly, but it jarred her, just as it had when Dick did it. Dick had been strict with them—too strict, in her opinion. She had explained to them over and over that he wanted them to do their best, and she explained to him that they were children. She always thought—if only he knew them, and they him. But they had known him, how he was. The less powerful always know the ways of those above them.

They had his good qualities, too: intelligence, focus, high-mindedness in certain areas. They all felt strongly about social justice, and were solicitous toward and inclusive of Robert in their activities. He declined to join in except for two dinners. Asked and answered, decent all around.

She didn't really know them anymore, not even Theo. They had grown away from her, as boys did. It was, apparently, natural. She'd mourned it—the loss of their easy affection, especially, their sweaty bodies in her lap, the spontaneous, completely ecstatic embraces that weren't mere hugs. All that, long gone. Past that, there'd been other distancing. The relationship now was one of people with a shared common past, nostalgic and wistful. They asked her how she was, but didn't really ask; she asked them, and they didn't really tell. Instead, they all turned to the grandchildren, who were inventing their own common past, their summer rituals. *Remember last summer when we . . .* Polly understood—they wanted to repeat that thing rather than try something new; they wanted to know what summer would hold for them at Meadowlea. This made it easy to be together, and made up for the lack of intimacy. If she knew anyone now, it was Robert.

On the second-to-last day they all gathered on the terrace for cocktails as usual, but after a moment everyone left—except her sons. Polly knew to be wary, yet she had the pathetic hope that they had a good surprise for her. No such luck. They spoke to her again about the practicality of signing over the properties to them, reminding her about the cost of nursing homes, medical issues, and so on. They each spoke this time, including Theo, as if this would be more convincing. A united front, with her best interests at heart. She repeated her decision of the summer before.

"Your father would want me to go on as I am."

"I disagree," James said. "Ma, Dad believed men should shoulder the responsibility for things like this."

"But Meadowlea was never his," she said. "He never had responsibility for it. And if it seemed he did, that was because I wanted him to feel respected. As everyone wants." There was a shifting around of bodies and postures. "And to bolster his male ego," she said, grateful for Agnes for pointing this out so many times over the years. She saw it clearly now. "I'm fine as is," Polly assured them.

James leaned forward, hands laced. Such a good jaw. Why was that handsome? A hardwired signal, she guessed, meaning . . . what? A good hunter? Easier to chew raw meat with such a strong jaw?

"Ma," he said. "We don't understand why Robert is here."

She didn't follow. Or didn't want to.

"It made sense in the beginning when he'd just got out of prison. It was nice of you to help him out. But now he's on his feet—so why is he still here? That's what concerns us. There have been cases of nurses and lawyers who swindle old people—"

She raised her hand. "Stop this right now. I don't want to hear another word about this."

"I know this is difficult, but it has to be considered," James said. Theo looked at her with sympathy and concern, but he was a part of this, too. She remembered that he'd explained that he'd live on without her and with his brothers.

"Robert is a good man, but you never know," Knox said.

"*I* know." She stared at him. "I know." This was what they imagined was going on? Robert was priming her for the moment he could slip a paper in front of her that she'd sign to their detriment? It wasn't even possible within the Fellowship agreement. When had they become so suspicious? It physically hurt her; she felt it like a blow. "I am your mother." She pushed herself up. "Robert is your friend. You have known him your whole life."

"Ma, we didn't mean to upset you, we're trying to do what's right."

"*I am* doing what's right. How can you not know that?"

They ringed around her, anxious now. They'd never liked it when she lost her near-perpetual good cheer.

"Move, please." She swam her arms in a breaststroke, clearing them aside.

"Where are you going?" James said. "You're not going to tell Robert, are you?"

Polly gave him a withering look. "Why would I do that? It would hurt him."

As she headed down the terrace steps, she heard Theo say, "I told you you were wrong about that. It's paranoid. And greedy."

And that's with the benefit of the doubt, Polly thought. Which James wouldn't understand.

CHAPTER 35

Agnes, Leeward Cottage, August 2002

AGNES WAS TALKING TO HER FATHER'S GRAVESTONE WHEN SHE heard a voice.

"Nessie, Nessie!"

Who was calling her name? She was too far away to think it through. Wait—was it Polly? Polly!

Polly came huffing up, and when she was close she bent over, hands on thighs. To catch her breath.

"Are you running from the law?" Agnes asked.

Polly straightened. "Scarier. My children. Nessie, they're such beasts!"

"No comment," Agnes replied.

They hadn't spoken in nearly a year. Agnes was ready. She was tired. Her efforts to secure the Point hadn't worked. She had many thoughts about that, ranging from outraged judgments of her enemies to a more philosophical recognition of the differing opinion of others, but mainly she'd been cut down to size by ill health and age.

She had tried and failed. Now she missed having a friend. And she'd even considered the possibility that the friend might have a point, too. Perhaps it was up to the next generation to decide what

ALICE ELLIOTT DARK

to do with the Point. Perhaps when James became a principal, the
responsibility would shift his perspective more toward preservation.
They always said Supreme Court justices grew into the job. Maybe
James and Archie would, too. Perhaps, perhaps. She was done. The
chemo was exhausting her.

"What happened, Pol?"

"They're suspicious of Robert's motives."

"No!"

"They actually used the phrase 'horning in.' Knox did."

"Theo?"

"He was there and silent."

Agnes shook her head. "I'm so sorry."

"Me too. It's so disappointing."

Suddenly they both had tears in their eyes. It had been a long
year. They linked arms, walked slowly around, as they'd done hundreds of times.

"I really am sorry, Pol." She looked over shyly.

Polly shook her head. Her child's wispy haircut blew across her
cheeks. She pulled hair from her mouth.

"Nessie, I'm the one who's sorry. I let you down."

"And I expected too much of you, to ignore your children."

"Well. You may have been right about that. I don't understand
how they could be so bossy."

Agnes's mind screamed, *You don't?* But she had learned a few
things, and just listened.

"They wouldn't do it to Dick."

"No, they wouldn't do it to Dick."

Polly sighed. "Though I wonder how much was me wanting both
the children and myself to believe he was more than he was."

Agnes was shocked. She'd never heard Polly say anything like
this, though it was long overdue. Yet again she hung back with her
opinion.

"I think he betrayed me, truth be told. The dog? Remember Dick was supposed to call the police to pick it up?"

"Yes."

"I don't think he did." Polly shook her head and toed the grass. "I don't think he did. Hope is the same dog."

"I know. Robert told me. I thought about it myself. Listen—there's a possibility that Dick did call but the owner went and got the dog back from the shelter. Or he may have forgotten quite innocently. He was having those little strokes."

"You think so?"

"Yes, I do." She'd never say otherwise. The days of her opinions about Dick were over.

They had wandered to Lydia's grave. In the old custom of the graveyards around, her stone, laid flat in the ground, was etched with a lamb. A dead child.

"She was so lovely," Agnes said.

After a pause, Polly spoke in a quiet voice. "I still see her, you know."

Agnes understood that she'd been entrusted with a great confidence. "I'm glad."

"You believe me?" Polly grabbed at her arm and stared at her.

"I accept it."

"I want you to believe she is real."

"Then I do."

Polly turned in a full circle, as if looking for her. She came back around to Agnes.

"But she isn't, you know. What was that phrase? She's a figment of my imagination. I know that even as I am looking straight at her. I both know and don't know."

"I don't see the harm in it," Agnes said, "if it makes you feel better."

"The harm is—" Polly chewed on a fingernail, a gesture Agnes

483

had never seen before. "The harm is that I am always waiting to see her again. I am waiting instead of living."

"Oh Lord, if that's a crime, the whole human race is guilty! How many people are waiting for Jesus? Or for Judgment Day? Or for a miracle?" She thought, but didn't say, her own version—writing is waiting.

"I've always wanted to ask you," Polly said. "Did you realize Nan in your books is nine and that Lydia died at nine?"

"Yes. But it's a coincidence."

"Why did you make her nine? Older than the real Nan was."

"Nine-year-old girls are perfect humans," Agnes said. "Nan would have been. Lydia was."

Three cars left Meadowlea and headed up Point Path. Agnes waved, and Caroline called out that they were going to a lobster pound for dinner.

The breeze was beginning to die down, as it did at this time of the afternoon. When Agnes and Polly and Elspeth were girls they had imagined an orchestra conductor guiding the whole day, bringing up different sounds at different moments. When the afternoon wind settled, and the air became like a skin, the smaller birds and insects that hadn't been heard from for hours insisted on having their say. The piccolos.

"What do you want on your grave, Pol?"

"You'll read it soon enough."

"If I don't, though. For some odd reason."

"I don't really care. Nothing, probably. Maybe an etching of a tree."

"No name?"

"Who will care? Who will remember before long?"

"That's awfully unconventional of you."

"We didn't used to mark our graves."

"As you wish."

"Watch Archie erect a mausoleum for himself."

They laughed.

"How about you, Nessie? What do you want yours to say?"

"I'm still working on it," Agnes said.

Polly squeezed her arm this time. "Let me know, will you, when you decide? In case I'm not here to see it."

"Don't be ridiculous. You'll waltz on my grave. Though not before—" She broke off. This was not the time to raise the issue of the Fellowship agreement. "I'm having treatments now. In fact I think I'm meant to not embrace anyone. I might be radioactive!"

"What does Dr. Oswald say?"

"He says to have fun and eat healthy food."

"Are you sick from the medicine?"

Agnes appreciated how Polly could shift to being matter-of-fact when a lot was at stake. "So far it's not bad. It will depend how much I want to do."

"Are you allowed to drink?"

"I'm allowed to do anything I allow myself."

"Come back with me. I want to show you something," Polly made a beckoning motion though she was two feet away.

They walked across the meadow and up the porch steps of Meadowlea and Agnes admired the new pink wall. Polly mixed them each up a quick mint julep made with bourbon and maple syrup, and they carried their glasses through the cool rooms, Agnes taking in details and admiring the changes made since she'd last been inside the house. None of the furniture had moved an inch, but there were fresh touches—bright pillows, a sofa reupholstered in a floral, Pollyish things. The windows were open and the curtains filled and rose and fluttered. Flowers were plonked into vases on every table and browning petals littered the wood. Agnes's was a family that enjoyed writing their names on dusty mirrors, but the Hancocks preferred a setting.

They walked into Dick's study. It was a large space, with two desks, a chaise, and beautiful built-in bookcases. "I don't think I've ever been in here. Not since it was Dick's, at any rate," Agnes said.

"He never invited anyone in. He always said it was an extension of his mind, and if people came in they were stepping on his ideas."

"I'm sympathetic to that," Agnes said, privately thinking that she'd never heard a thought of Dick's that was worth so much drama. But there was something to be said for the thinking life of even a small mind. It kept people off the streets. Dick's study looked like a professor's study, or perhaps the landlubber refuge of a sea captain. The wood was all cherry, the rug centrally orange and green, the shelves many and groaning with books. Enviable.

Polly went to the desk and lifted an envelope. "This is what I wanted to show you. See if it rings a bell."

Agnes opened it and began to read. The words were familiar. Yes, she knew this piece. She had the same one in her desk. Polly had sent it to her after the birth of . . . Theo? She thought so. She looked up at Polly, whose expression was cautious.

"I found it in Dick's papers."

"How? I told you not to show it to him. Did you show him anyway?" Agnes shook her head. "Forget I said that. That was your choice. I just couldn't imagine he'd understand."

"I sent it to him anonymously, at his office address. I don't know what I thought would happen. Maybe he'd come home from work brimming with excitement over the brilliant thing he'd read that day. Maybe he'd share it with me, and I'd reveal that I was the author. But he never mentioned it. It's embarrassing that I thought he might."

"That he might be different than he was?"

"That he might think I was smart."

"He kept it. That's something."

"Yes, I suppose. But he was a bit of a packrat. I don't want to embarrass myself again with another stupid fantasy." Polly shrugged.

"But wait, Pol—look at this." Agnes pointed to a few words that had been written in pencil on the back of the letter.

Polly held the page away from her at arm's length. "I can't read it."

"It says, 'Find out who wrote this and invite him for a lecture.' Him! Of course he'd never think it was a woman. They're all so—"

Polly put her hands over her face.

"What is it?"

"He thought it was good."

Agnes felt a flash of her old irritation at Polly for being more moved by Dick's opinion than by hers—Agnes had told Polly perfectly clearly this piece was good, very good. That had gone in one ear and out the other and all this time she'd waited to see if Dick would say anything. Good grief. *Best behavior, Ness,* she coached herself. "Yes, he did. And good for him for knowing it."

"Yes, good for him." Polly sank onto the sofa. "But what would it have been like if he knew it was me? If we could have talked in that way with each other?"

"Do you think he would have?"

"I don't know. He might have read it differently if he knew it was me. In fact, he would have. Look at me, getting sentimental now. Just when I've pulled myself together. Anyway, if you see any books you want, or desk stuff, let me know. I'm clearing the room and making it mine."

"Okay! I'll help," Agnes said.

"Now?"

"No time like."

"Thanks!"

Polly hopped back up and went to the shelves. Open boxes sat on the desk waiting to be filled. She pulled two books off the shelves, lay them both down, picked up one at a time and wiped it, then placed it spine-up in a box. Then the other. Then back to the shelf. It was soothing to observe. "You start over there," Polly directed. "Please. Take anything you like."

Agnes picked up volumes, paged through, and replaced them. She already had enough books and had no reason to take Dick's. It would be absurd. Yet she set aside a copy of *Moby Dick* illustrated with woodcuts, and a volume of *Robinson Crusoe*, and a few books about the Nazis. It was important to let no year go by without thinking more deeply about the Nazis. The dark mind of the species.

"Are these all right?"

Polly glanced over. "Of course. Are you still reading as much? I can't concentrate for it."

"Not as much. I dabble."

"Are you on a book?"

This startled Agnes. How could Polly know—had Maud . . . ? But of course she was referring to a *When Nan* book.

"I'm horsing around with some ideas. I want to have Nan become aware of the passage of time. *When Nan Visited the Royal Conservatory at Greenwich*. But that's a mouthful. Maybe a seed bank. Time is stored in seeds. Anyway, I'm thinking about time, so Nan might as well, too."

"Do you remember that woman Helen I used to know? I saw her last winter. She told me she realized she should get a divorce when it occurred to her that time spent with her husband felt longer than time without her husband. She often watched the clock tick. She tried to tell herself that her life would seem longer because of this, but she thought at the same time that her husband's gift for boring her would cause her to wither up."

"Yes. I'd like Nan to perceive something like that." Good old Polly, much quicker than she was given credit for. Worthy of lecturing the philosophy department at Penn.

"School. Or sitting in Meeting. Or caring for young children."

"Yes. All those things. Time fast and slow." Agnes set aside a copy of Margaret Mead's *Coming of Age in Samoa*.

"I'm going to volunteer at the animal shelter this fall. I think it will have that quality to it," Polly said. "Animals expand time."

"You know you'll be bringing everyone home with you."

"It wouldn't be so bad. I love Hope. I'd ask how Maisie is, but she wanders over."

"And you feed her."

"Maybe a little tuna here and there." Polly grinned.

"Whatever happened with Dick's book?"

"There is no book, Nessie." She tucked two more neatly into the cardboard. "I have found nothing but scribbles and scraps. He hadn't written anything substantive in a long time."

"That's too bad."

"After he died I wrote to Adam, the head of his department, and asked him if anything had happened with Dick. It puzzled me that he wasn't granted emeritus, and that Adam refused to write a foreword to a book that didn't even exist. They could have jollied him along. Adam wrote back and said that there'd been complaints, and they didn't want him on campus anymore." Polly shrugged. "I suppose they can't help themselves, these old men. Too much self-control for too long. It doesn't matter now. None of it does, I'm well past worrying about his reputation with anyone but me."

"It's about time!" Agnes clapped.

"I was so eager to be in love. Why? What made that seem so important to me, when there was so much else I could have been thinking about? I wonder now if I ruined the boys by defending Dick so much."

"Your boys are all fine people," Agnes said.

"I know. You know what I mean."

"Yes. They hurt your feelings, and believe me, I'll wring their necks for it."

"Thanks, Nessie. I'll let you."

Polly mopped along an empty shelf and started on the row just behind Dick's desk. Together they watched as wadded pieces of material sprang from behind the books and tumbled over the lip of the shelf.

"What—"

Polly bent down and picked them up. "Oh my God."

Agnes was perplexed. She bent down to help and felt a sting in her wrist. Polly had slapped her hand.

"No!" Polly shouted. "Stay away!"

But Agnes had picked up a wad. It unfurled and revealed itself to be a pair of men's underwear. She looked at it briefly before realizing it was soiled. "Polly, let's get some rubber gloves and clean this up."

"How could he do this?"

"He was tired."

"I'm so sorry, Agnes."

"It's nothing. It's human."

"I feel ill."

"Stop it. We have a job to do."

"You're right. You're right. Let me just splash my face."

They headed for the kitchen to get supplies. Polly opened the broom closet, releasing a scent of sunbaked wood. She pulled out a bucket and pointed Agnes's attention to the cupboard under the sink.

"Comet?" she asked.

"No. The vinegar."

Agnes pulled out the jug. Polly poured some into the bucket and mixed it with water. "Grab a new sponge, too." Agnes bent down again and studied the open packet of sponges with three left. She chose the purple. They processed back to the study, Polly leading. The evening wind cut ripples through the meadow grass. They went back into the study and tacitly divided up the tasks, Polly dealing with the bundles and Agnes wiping down the shelves with the vinegar solution.

"Poor Dick," Polly said.

"He was an old man who didn't want to be."

"You're right."

"I am. That's all this is. Nothing more or less."

They carried the bucket and trash bag back to the kitchen. Polly straightened up and bent backward and stretched side to side. She heaved a big sigh and dropped her arms.

"I loved him, though," Polly said. "What can you do?"

Agnes could almost see shimmering energy in the space between them. There was a bridge to cross.

"I do know my epitaph, Pol. I want my gravestone to have my name and dates and then three words—*I loved someone.*"

"Who?"

"Wouldn't you like to know! I have to maintain some mystery, don't you think?"

Polly didn't smile. "As a matter of fact, I don't think so, Nessie. I think it's time we be honest. Completely honest."

"We had some honest words last fall and look what happened."

Polly shook her head. "Those weren't honest words. Those were terrified words. I'm saying—from now on, the truth. What's the point of it all if you don't tell someone who you are?" Polly asked. "I want to, Nessie. I don't want to be afraid anymore."

The next morning Agnes walked over to Polly's and handed her an L.L.Bean bag packed with her notebooks, including the final two she hadn't shown to Maud. She would, though. She would. It was time to remove her caul.

CHAPTER 36

Agnes, Leeward Cottage, February 1962

Dear Elspeth,

I woke up thinking of Virgil, as I always do, going over
conversations, thinking of things we said and things I was too shy
to mention. Then I turned onto my back and thought ahead into
the day. I'll write, mainly. When Nan comes over in the afternoon,
I'll mark up the morning's pages while she draws or naps by the
fire. Aside from working on the Nan book, I'm also writing a
sketch from childhood, a description of what Thanksgiving was
like in our house. It's so different, El, to carry the pictures and
feelings around in memory than it is to seek the words to describe
those days so that someone else might feel what it was like for
us. It's hard to make it vivid. It's also hard after only writing
fiction to tell the exact truth. I find myself embellishing, writing
descriptions of my ideal version of what our Thanksgivings could
have been like with a loving mother. In doing so I call up the
tender emotions I wished for—the connection to our ancestors,
the boundless affection of kind parents, the security of a warm
and fortunate house, a safe haven bursting with cosseted children.

I'd like to write about how hungry we were all the time, how little food we were given. Mother wanted us thin.

I'm writing these sketches for Nan, who is curious about our childhood. She believes in the memories more if they are written down. A reader in the making.

Hawkweed landed—thump—on the ground after a leap from his chair. His soar was silent, though surely the molecules of air rattled when he parted them. Next, the second bam of his landing on the mattress, near my feet. Star was under the covers and gave a little growl at Hawkweed's approach. "There's room for all," I said, my first words of the day. He looked at me as though I were stating the obvious. He touched his nose to my leg, a small gesture that magnifies my spirit, as you liked to quote. The lightest touch, the sweetest. Pure trust.

Slowly, in full confidence of a welcoming reception, Hawkweed walked the length of me, the tip of his tail peering around the room like a periscope as he deliberated where exactly to step up onto my chest. He stood for a moment on my breastbone looking into my face, and I closed and opened my eyes, a greeting he returned. Then he lay down, lowering his front legs first. He is as careful as if I were a raft on which he has to find his balance. This is a delicate operation that has developed with an eye to Star, designed so that he doesn't register the cat's movements as the usurpation they actually are. Hawkweed would be the perfect Queen's advisor who pulls all the strings during a reign while going unnoticed by everyone. His aggression is utterly masked, yet within a couple of minutes of my first waking I am covered neck to waist in cat. He's so sure of himself that one orange foot slips past my waist and dangles.

Then we stare into each other's eyes, taking care to look away at regular intervals, respecting each other's need of privacy. I begin my ritual massaging of his face, head, neck, back. If I have a thought that goes beyond the communion of the moment, he reaches forward and presses his paw at the base of my throat. I envy the assurance that demands so much, so directly. I picture him sitting in a slender chair in the Piazza Navona, an arm slung over to another chair, nonchalantly demanding the attention of not only his companion but of all Rome.

Hold on—I'm not sure now I even mentioned Hawkweed before. He came in the late fall, walked right up to me outside the market. He'd had enough of the outdoor life.

Just now I had the thought that he is a bit like Karen. She, too, is focused, her quiet manners obscuring her good mind. A great professor should take her on as a protégée. A brisk bluestocking type who will guide her into a solid mental discipline and a reliable career. I wouldn't count on a man to help a young woman start a career. El, did you once tell me that passivity contains a power as great as an atom that, when opened, explodes the world? Or am I thinking this now myself? Sometimes I don't know the difference between us. But—we did speak of it—you were in your extremis of pain, and perversely ecstatic. You read me a Bible verse—

—I just looked it up. I have your old Bible on my bookshelf. No, dear El, don't get your hopes up for me, I don't plan to make a habit of it. I'm a sinner through and through.

The verse:

"The Lord said to me, My grace is sufficient for you, for my power is made perfect in weakness."

The world through the looking glass, the parallel universe where life is as it should be, so close to us yet impenetrable except when we accept the graces and the love offered to us. What I have learned is that grace and love are offered all the time, in every new moment, at every glimpse of the sky, or dawn of a day that has never before existed, or squirrel skittering along a branch, or conversation with a sister or a friend, or the sense of time suspended when reading a good book. We are free, always, to accept what is offered; it is we who don't recognize this. That is our free will. The result is what we call our experience, which in turn forms our beliefs. There are a lot of bad ideas in the world. I have less and less patience with any ideas at all. Animals, flowers, the sea. Friends. Children. Art. The end.

I lifted Hawkweed off me and went downstairs to discuss the food for the day. Mrs. C.'s children were sick with colds and she was keeping them home, except Robert who was going to school and would escort Nan to the bus stop as usual. Mrs. C. had already made me oatmeal and had started a soup for the lunch, far more work than she needed to do for me, but I've stopped fighting her about her command of the kitchen. My pens sit above my paper. The pencils are sharpened and the eraser is close by. I have copied the last two sentences of what I've written on a new clean sheet.

I want to write to you a little longer, before I begin.

The morning sleet has become fat flakes. The sky's mostly white, but every so often a shaft of sun pushes through, and there's a sudden glistening in the air. I just walked across the hall into Edmund's old bedroom and saw chimney smoke pulsing from the Chalet. Robert appeared in the scene and headed up Point Path, to fetch Nan. I crossed my fingers for a glimpse of Virgil, but he was out of sight. I watched the children head for the top of the road where the bus would pick them up.

All right. Goodbye for now, I'm going to write, with a capital W!

A little later. I wrote as planned, but every half hour or so I got up to stretch and found myself looking out the library window toward the Chalet. It spurs me on to know that Virgil is also writing—it feels fantastically companionable, after so many years alone. I want to—hold on a sec. A car is coming down Point Path and turning into my driveway. Karen's car. How odd. Why didn't she call ahead? She always calls before she comes now that Nan's at school. Why isn't she at work? Still, I'm glad she's here to get me away from this desk!

She steps into the snowy driveway and looks up at the sky, smiling. She's wearing the old wool cape of yours I gave her, and the sheepskin-lined snow boots she found at the church thrift shop. Her hair stops at her scarf, red against green, like a Christmas ornament. She's marching to the door. Later, gator! I'm going down.

Elspeth, I am back. I am at last alone in my bedroom again, after what has felt like a decade of a day. Nan is in your old room with Star, both under a pile of quilts. Hawkweed is with me, sitting at the end of the bed, purring off and on in a pattern I can't entirely parse. It is a peaceful tableaux, one that has become the norm here, for which I am boundlessly grateful. But for once I half wish Nan weren't in the house and that I could be alone to pace and make whatever noise I want or need without inhibition. A noise that expresses that I am ridiculous. Absurd. I made a complete fool of myself, and have no one to blame but me. Who did I think I was, Elspeth?

I am completely embarrassed, even though no one knows. Well—Virgil knows.

I hardly identify with my pathetic, happy pages from this morning, when I was yearning but free. Here, I continue on, into a sober future. I am going to tell it as it happened, without hindsight. It has to be recorded plainly, for me to have as a referent in case I am ever tempted to reinterpret the events. I must never fool myself again.

I went down to find Karen bubbling, so much so that I giggled without knowing why. Even Mrs. C. was smiling. Star barked happily and Karen picked him up and hugged him and let him lick her face.

"Karen! Hand me your cape!"

"No, Agnes, you come out! Put on your coat and come with me over to see Virgil."

"But we can't interrupt him! I'm sure he's working."

"Not today. He's expecting us."

"He is? How do you know?" I was confused.

"Because we made a plan." She grabbed my arm in both her hands and tugged.

"You and Virgil made a plan?"

She laughed. "Put on your coat and boots."

"What about soup? I can bring lunch."

"Virgil is making lunch for us," she said.

"He is?" I kept repeating that. He is? He is? It pricked that she was bringing me the invitation rather than the other way around.

"Yes, he's making lunch, all by himself. He's going to be our host. You can't pass up the opportunity to see that, can you?"

Her excitement was infectious.

"I just need a few minutes to get ready," I said.

She giggled. "Oh, I'm sure you'd do a hundred chores before you put on your coat. But I'm not going to allow it. Come now, right now! You too, Star!"

"The snow isn't too deep for her yet?"

"If it is, we'll take turns carrying her. She'll have fun."

I patted Hawkweed and we stepped outside. For a moment it

was warm. I had the same old thought I always have had in those circumstances—it's not cold out after all, why are we so bundled up? Then after a few steps I walked into the wall of cold. The day was low and close, the air tinged with the scent of woodsmoke and snow. Though the flakes looked light, they covered the branches in heavy sleeves. The trees creaked. Automatically I craned around to look at the graves halfway across the field. I'd had all the stones removed after the accident, so the meadow ran unbroken down to the Sank. I thought as I always do how unfathomable it is that you are there, lying in the ground. Beyond the land the slate water looked like a hole.

Karen spoke about the Christmas just past, how fun it had been to watch Nan open her presents. I said I wished I could have been there, but I got to hold Lydia. Were we competing? Hard to tell in that weather. The snow pulled the day close around us, and made our footsteps and voices loud to our ears. I picked up Star and he snapped at the flakes from the luxurious throne of my arms. I remarked that I felt like a Russian struggling over the steppes. Karen smiled. She looked almost pretty.

At the Chalet Virgil opened the door for us and we stomped our boots and went in. The table had been cleared of papers and surrounded with three chairs. The settings were spotty, but Karen rounded them out swiftly with items she pulled from a satchel, including a loaf of bread and butter wrapped in foil. I kept smiling, but I was perplexed. How had they made a plan without my knowing? Did they speak privately? Sometimes Virgil walked Karen outside to her car after dinner, but I could think of no other time they were together, and Nan was usually with them then. It was all very odd.

Three places were laid, humbly but with a stark glamor. I noticed a pot sitting on top of the woodstove, vapor climbing up its sides. Scent of onion and carrot. My mouth watered.

Virgil poured us glasses of wine. "Scandalous, in the day!" I teased. I was relaxing into the situation.

"Here's to friends," he said.

We drank. I followed the rule of meeting eyes over a toast, but neither of them seemed to know of it, and only looked down shyly into the maroon liquid.

He'd decorated the room with fresh green tree boughs. A bowl of acorns adorned with sprigs of holly acted as a centerpiece. He'd thought this through, and gone to trouble.

"This is such a treat," I said, my manners compelling me to shape the moment. "Are you planning to start entertaining now?"

"Maybe I'll oversee the Point Party this summer."

How I loved teasing with him! His height, his scent, his arms even under his sweater—all were so dear to me.

"You're going to need a lot of practice. I think we'll have to eat here a lot, don't you, Karen?" I continued.

They looked at each other. More than just a look—a conversation passed between them, a swift back-and-forth that I saw very clearly; but it was an exchange in a foreign language, and I didn't know what it meant. I watched and waited, bewildered. I felt like a child.

Finally—or it seemed like finally, but was probably a second later—he nodded.

Karen came close to me and took both my hands. Her plain face glowed. The walk in the cold had brightened her skin and loosened her hair, and the dim light in the room softened her features.

"Agnes, dear Agnes, we have something very happy to tell you."

The look on her face—I'd never seen it before. Yet instinctively

I understood it to be a threat. My whole body tingled with wariness. "Oh?"

"Yes! We are engaged! Isn't it wonderful?"

She beamed. Virgil stepped forward and put his arm around her shoulders. A log in the woodstove, as if on cue, cracked and burst. A roar of fire shot up through my torso, a great flame shooting and huffing and threatening to immolate me from the inside. My arms ached, and I wanted so badly to do something with them, to hit or squeeze. My legs tensed in a desire to run.

Instead, I nodded, jerking up and down. I didn't dare look at Virgil.

Karen held out her hand to show a piece of string around her finger. "A placeholder," she said. "Virgil has asked me to marry him! And I have agreed."

"I'll get something soon," he said to her, as pleased as if he already had.

I thought of all Grace's rings, sitting in a safe deposit box in Philadelphia, useless. But I made no offer.

"So what do you think?" she asked. "We have been wanting to tell you for so long."

"How long?" I asked.

"Oh, we can tell you while we eat. I'm starved! Let's get the food on the table."

"What about college?"

"I still want her to go," Virgil said.

They exchanged a gaze that encompassed their burgeoning domesticity and all its quiet pleasures. I saw it as if it were a shelf full of photo albums. I saw it all ahead. Their life. Would she go? Or have babies instead? I felt as betrayed by this possibility as I did by Virgil not warning me this was coming. As if reading my thoughts, he looked at me sheepishly.

He got a towel and wrapped his hands with it to lift the hot pot. The wind whistled outside and they murmured in appreciation. "I feel a draft, don't you?" Karen asked him in a beseeching feminine manner I'd never seen her employ before.

He nodded as if this were of no concern. He ladled out the soup and passed the bowls while Karen cut the bread. As we ate, they told me their love story. It began last fall . . . or earlier, depending, though they weren't aware . . . hadn't said . . . hadn't spoken to each other. The first thing that was said was in, again depending, October, but the signal had been missed, or had there been one? There were glances, and moments, but neither was certain of the other. Didn't I remember when she'd asked if Virgil would be there for dinner that time? So on and so forth tumbling over each other, excited and thrilled to have an audience, what love doesn't want one, what is better than having love witnessed? The worst irony: I was making them happier by the moment, and sealing them tight.

I smiled. I congratulated. I died.

I died.

October. I'd been so sure his whole mind was on me. I wondered if he'd ever thought about me again after that night under the sky. All along I'd believed that aspect of our love would return. What a fool.

We washed the plates and sat back, feeling safe and fortunate, or they did.

"Have you told Nan?"

Virgil looked at Karen, and Karen touched my arm. I'd never known her to be affectionate, but it seemed that in love her body had gone beyond its bounds and didn't want to stop. "We wanted to tell you first, Agnes. This is all thanks to you. You are the greatest friend of us and our future, you are our true family, and we want you always as a beloved aunt, welcome with us at all times."

Beloved aunt. Ant.

"We plan to tell her tomorrow."

"Oh."

"And—" She removed her hand and laid it with the other in her lap. Demure. "We have a favor to ask."

I was so uneasy, so miserable, that my mind was growing dim. I wanted to be alone with him, to ask him if all this was really true or if he was under some kind of strange spell, and I wanted to go home. I did the closest I could. I picked up Star and held him in my lap, in spite of my prohibition against animals at the table.

"We'd like to ask if Nan could stay with you tonight."

The look on her face—hunger, tension, pressure, pleading— what could I do or say? I was trapped. How many dozens of nights had Nan stayed at my house? More than I could count, she did so all the time. She was always welcome. To call this a favor! To me! Who was essentially her mother! Or had been.

I dared not look at Virgil. What if I saw that he'd forgotten everything?

"Yes, that's fine," I managed to say. Star tipped his head and stared longingly at the bread, so I gave him a piece.

"Thank you so much, Agnes. You have no idea how grateful we are to you. All right, on to the show!" Karen stood and raised her arms, indicating that all of life could start up now. "Agnes, I'm going to ask you to stand up for a moment." What was this about? What show? The two bounced around the tiny room, moving furniture so we were no longer in a dining room setting, but in a classroom or a theater. Two chairs were placed to face the desk, with the third behind it. Karen continued to touch this and that, not that there was much to touch, but she placed the candlesticks in the corners of the desk closest to the seats and made other similar small adjustments. It's amazing how much difference a quarter of an inch here or there makes to the feeling of placidity in a room. It's like beauty, or identical twins—the fraction of difference in the width of an eye, the lift at the corner of a mouth, the one with pleasing proportions owns the world while the other with a variation indiscernible except in the total effect, the other blends into the crowd of the norm. Karen swiftly made the room more attractive than I'd ever seen it. I had never interfered, thinking that was the more appealing way to be.

"You sit here, Agnes," Karen showed me to a chair, "and I'll be just beside you. Are you ready?" she asked him.

He pulled a sheaf of papers from a shelf and walked behind the table, so it stood between him and us.

"Pretend it's a podium," Karen instructed me.

I went along with all of this with no sense of what was happening, or being too dull-witted to want to try. I settled next to Karen and she squeezed my hand quickly. The scent of woodsmoke came off her clothes. I pulled Star up into my lap again.

"Ready?" she said to Virgil.

He nodded.

"I am going to read something new. It's something like the story behind the story of writing *Scalene*."

Karen clapped, and I took her cue. For the next forty-five minutes he read. I heard a story about a man and his young child who move into a cabin on a point of land in Maine. There they meet the most wonderful woman who lives in the big house nearby. She takes them under her wing, nurses the child through an accident, helps the man with his writing. Pure horror. I died and died and died again. Then the stupid woman introduces the man to the town librarian and they fall in love. No, that wasn't what he'd written. It was in my exploding head.

The shadows and the fire's warmth changed him into a wholly tender man—or love did. So very beautiful. *But not for you*, I reminded myself, *not for you. He will never kiss you again. He will never make you feel beautiful. He'll never speak to you in the dark, nor will you ever watch him as he sleeps. You won't make plans with him. You won't be the person sitting in the front row when his work is performed to great crowds. You won't see Paris through his eyes, or hold him when he is in tears. You won't live with him any more than you do now. You'll never again get dressed in the morning in hopes of pleasing him, nor will you hear his expressions of gratitude as a form of lovemaking. There's as much distance between you now as there was before you knew him. You don't know him; he kept a secret from you. A lie of omission. Now you know. He's capable of lying to you. Now you know. Now you know. What of Nan? She'll learn to love Karen more. Karen will have children, and Nan will be part of a happy family. You'll be a visitor.*

He finished and bowed. We clapped again.

Karen turned to me, her cheeks pink with excitement. "How did you like our surprise?"

"Oh—" I fumbled.

"The piece was for you," she said.

"Was it?" I felt weak, defeated. What I would have given if the piece were really for me.

"Your kindness to him. To us."

"Oh." *Kindness.* Terrible word! Kindness equals nothingness in this context. "Thank you." I stood. If I didn't get out of there, I'd begin screaming. "Thank you so much for the lunch and the reading. I must get back to work."

There was no protest. They wanted to be alone. "I'll just get Nan's things," I said. "From her room."

I rushed across the cabin. I didn't need anything, I had a whole room of things for Nan, but I rattled the drawers anyway and took out a shirt and underwear. The window was partly open, clearly the source of the draft we'd felt, so I shut it.

Virgil walked the few steps with me to the door, with Karen behind. I turned to him. This couldn't be helped. Somehow I turned straight into his arms—I think he was ready to embrace me? I don't want to make anything up, not anymore.

When I pulled back I saw he was weeping. He made no sound doing so. But his cheeks were wet and droplets of water fell onto his shirt. On another day I would have felt exalted being in the presence of so much feeling, and I'd have gloried in my effect on him, but not today. He was happy, and not because of me. An instrument can be pleasing and appreciated, but it doesn't arouse happiness. I was an instrument, the rake that had flushed the snake from the grass. The net that had pulled the frozen man from the sea. It was time for me to be shut up in a supply closet.

Karen swooped in and squeezed me goodbye. "Thank you, dear benefactor," she said.

I cannot even describe what these words did to me. I don't think I can ever look at the two of them again. *Please, Lord, let me hate them as I should.*

Star and I dragged home. The snow still came in thick, fat flakes, wet and heavy, and we had to plow our legs ahead. For once I couldn't enjoy the dog being so oblivious to everything but the present, I was beyond enjoyment of anything.

I sat in my room in a daze until Nan came in. Then I dragged myself out of my stupor and made hot chocolate for her and Robert and piled a plate of cookies high. Their eyes widened at the bounty, and they exchanged glances that warned each other not to mention my mistake. We settled in the glass room, a perfect fishbowl in the purple afternoon.

"Is Fur coming for dinner?" Nan asked. She had the whole plate of cookies on her lap. I left it; what difference did it make?

"No. You're going to stay here, with me."

"But I want to see him."

"You will, tomorrow."

"Where is Karen?" Robert asked.

Was he reading my distress? I had no doubt he could. "Why do you ask?"

"Her car is in the driveway."

Of course. "She's visiting Virgil."

Nan shifted the plate to the table and moved to the edge of her seat. "Let's go see them."

"No!" I saw an image of what they might be doing, a brief flash. "No, we can't. They're busy."

She tipped her head, just the way her father did. "Doing what?" She picked up another cookie and bit it, curious, not suspicious.

"They're working on a project."

"What is it?" Robert asked.

"If you must know, they're planning a surprise for you, Nan."

It was the only thing I could think to say. She instantly displayed a huge smile and clapped her hands. "When can we see it?"

She made a gesture toward Robert. She always included him.

"Tomorrow. You'll find out what it is tomorrow."

"We have school," Robert said.

"School might be canceled with this snow. If not, after school. Now, you two eat your cookies."

I was too beleaguered to set limits, and soon they were in a sugar sleep, the shadows of their lashes on their reddened cheeks long as spider legs. Later I sent Robert home and fed Nan a drowsy dinner, read to her, and put her in her—your—bed, with Star.

And here I am. Going insane. I can't believe it. Should I believe it? Maybe it was a dream, and I'm the one who ate too many cookies and fell asleep by the fire. Maybe I was only working all along and this was a fictional invention.

Elspeth, if you could see the way he looks at me with his eyes shining—that can't be anything but love, can it? I see only love on his face, nothing else.

Why come over so often and ask me for so much help if it weren't to secure a future for us? Am I only a handmaiden to his work? Does he believe I gave and gave because I am good and wanted nothing for myself? I wanted everything for myself. I am not you, not selfless. I *want*. I want Nan officially. And maybe another; I still bleed; I'm not too old. I have thought of it. The person he and I might make together. Why shouldn't I? The hundreds of hours I spent by sickbeds—hasn't that earned me a second chance? I saw what he wanted to be, but that he couldn't do it by himself. He needed help. I helped. I helped.

And I ended up with his gratitude. Cold comfort.

CHAPTER 37

Agnes, Leeward Cottage, April 1962

Dear Elspeth,

My correspondence with you began coincidentally with the day I
first made contact with the Reeds. It was the first time I called you
back. I'd considered it before; I missed you so much. But I didn't
want to tell you about our parents' illnesses and deaths. If you'd
been here, you'd have cared for them to the point of your own
exhaustion, and I'd have been furious watching you. I was able to
do it partly because I was grateful you were spared it. I didn't want
to call out to you then for fear I'd disturb your rest—even though
I don't believe in any of that. Yet believing in things and acting on
them aren't the same.

I told you everything I needed to say about the Reeds. I have
felt heard by you, buoyed by you. I have believed the events were
hopeful enough not to disturb you, either, or startle you from your
place of peace. I have showed you who I became in the wake of so
much death. Life without Father—that could be the subtitle of this
whole account.

But now I have to write something so horrible I don't want
you to know it. But I must confess to you, sister, who accepted me

no matter what. I don't expect that now. I have been insane with grief, walking all over the frozen countryside. Now I am so tired I can't move. I want to die. I want to be with you. Maybe after I tell you, you will find a way to come get me.

When I woke up the next morning after that terrible night of sorrow, I looked out the window to see massive drifts of snow and a cold white world. It was early, and the light had not come up, yet as my eyes adjusted I could see that there was no smoke coming from Virgil's chimney. I was used in the mornings to seeing smoke rising there when I got up—he rose even earlier than I did. That had become one of the pleasures of my day, and to think it had been replaced by a morning in bed with Karen.

Well. It was morning, and daylight had come to staunch the sorrows of the night.

Mrs. C. hadn't arrived yet. The snow was deep enough that I was certain it would be a snow day, so I let Nan sleep.

I found Star in the hall and I led him downstairs to go out. The back door opened without much trouble; the wind had blown the snow in the other direction. But he couldn't get down the thick steps, and I put on my boots and went out with a broom to help him. I made tea and came back up. I had an odd feeling when I reached the second floor. As if I were alone. As if no other soul were present in the house. I'd come to know this feeling well, as I was so often alone. My soul expanded into every corner, finding no other to bump against. This often gave me an exalted feeling, and sometimes I got up and danced, the universe as my partner. Such a stupid, spinster thing to do—but I hadn't thought of myself as a spinster before the lunch with Virgil and Karen.

Nan had never slept so late. True, the house was tucked in the flannel pocket of silent snow, but I began to have an odd feeling. I'd noticed before that her bedroom door was closed, but I didn't think about it. Now I remembered that I'd left it open, in case she had a bad dream.

At first in the dim light I thought she was tucked into the bed as I'd left her, but as I went closer I saw the covers were disturbed. I ran my hand over the sheets and all down around the bottom of the mattress, as if she might be playing a prank. But Nan wasn't in her bed. I said her name in a singsong voice, the one for games. Nothing. She could be looking at books downstairs or gone upstairs to paint. She had free run of the house and didn't hesitate about using it. I called her name, and pretended we'd decided to play hide-and-seek, or hot and cold. I called out the words and waited for a giggle or a response. Nothing. I said loudly that French toast would be ready soon, and she better come down or I'd eat hers, too. "Mrs. Circumstance only has two pieces of bread today, and I'm very hungry!"

I went back to the hall and looked out the window.

The day was gray again, the sky still low, the snow diminished to a smattering of tiny flakes. I stared at the ground until I was able to make out faint traces of footsteps, nearly obscured already by fresh snow. My heart stopped cold. I breathed pure fear. As soon as I could move, I ran downstairs and pulled on a coat and boots and plunged outside. Right away my boots filled with cold clumps. Within a short time my nose and hands ached. The snow came down in tinsel lines, and every few moments one found my face or my eye and bored in, while in the distance they drilled into the dark gray sea. I winced at the sound, scratching like crinoline. It was less than twenty-four hours since I'd walked the same route back from the lunch, and this was so much farther, so much longer.

At one point I saw a figure across the meadow. Who could be

up and out at this hour? An arm rose to wave to me and I realized it was Robert. The explanation for what he was doing out was so simple I instantly supplied it. He was a boy and here was big snow.

The snow had piled high enough to block the Chalet door. I tugged on the handle and worked it outward a little, then swung my boot like a broom to clear a patch, an action I repeated several times until I got the door open wide enough to step in. The stove was out, and the oil lamps, too. It's hard to describe the silence. It was more like a nothingness—an absence of all. "Nan?" I whispered—whispered rather than spoke. The atmosphere resisted interruption. "Nan?" I walked in slowly and let my eyes adjust. The lunch dishes were still on the table, though Virgil's pages had been set down on a chair. I went into Nan's room. The window was now wide open. There was a puddle on the floor; she must have come in that way.

I called their names again. A response—was it? A moan from the direction of his room. I didn't want to go there. Not now. How had this happened, all of it? I stood completely still and listened. Then—

"Ness?"

"Yes. Here I am. Where are you?" A useless question. I knew where she was.

"Nessie," she whimpered.

I set aside my scruples and embarrassment and pushed open Virgil's door. The room was so cold I could see my breath. I beckoned to her and she came out from under the covers. "Is Papa there?"

"Yes."

"Virgil?"

I could sense nothing of him, not a single aspect. I discerned Nan in the room, but no one else. Yet there was a lump in the bed.

"Come here, Nanny."

She came into my arms and I carried her into the main room. "Where's your father?"

"In the bed."

"Asleep?"

She nodded.

"Is he alone?"

She nodded again. Absurdly this pleased me. I was utterly mixed up. "It's very cold in here, don't you think? Should we go get some hot chocolate?"

"Is it school?" She pulled a bit of my hair toward her and wrapped it around her hand.

"It's too snowy for school. Are you sure Fur is here?"

She nodded.

"Did you talk to him?"

She shook her head.

"He must be very tired. Go get a fresh shirt. You can come back with me until he wakes up."

"But I want my surprise!"

Her surprise? Then I remembered—I'd been the one to put that idea into her head. She, a child, hadn't been able to wait and walked over in the night to find out what the surprise was. "In a little while," I said unsteadily. "Now go ahead."

She went to her room and I went to his. I whispered his name but got no response, none at all. A bad feeling centered me. I became utterly calm. I pulled down on the covers until I could see his face, and Karen's. They were both pink, but utterly still. There was no sense of life in the room, and no sign of a problem. I reached out and touched him, and he was stiff and cold. Cold beyond the frigidness of the room. The deeper, more permanent cold. Yet I balked at the truth. Had they gotten drunk? Were they passed out completely? Yes, that must be it, I thought, even though I knew otherwise. My mind was split in two. What happened?

I went back to the main room where Nan waited. "He's asleep," I told her—and then I added, by sudden inspiration, "and so are you. We are in a dream. We are going to go back to bed and wake up for breakfast. Then we'll read and play and paint, have more cookies and hot chocolate . . ."

She looked at me quizzically. I picked her up and left the cabin. "You are sleeping peacefully, aren't you? And having a beautiful dream of snow. You are dreaming that I'm carrying you through the snow and that later you'll build a snowman with Robert, and you'll have lots of treats all day and we'll build a fire." I spoke to her in that manner until she dropped asleep on my shoulder.

I called the police. My story was that Nan was asleep in the bedroom at Leeward when I had noticed there was no smoke coming from the Chalet chimney, and I went over to check but there was no answer when I knocked. I had no idea that Karen was there. We'd had lunch together the day before, but I didn't know she'd stayed on. I hadn't noticed her car outside; I hadn't gone out front. It was all simple; there was no reason to doubt me, and everything matched my description. I was the neighbor who'd gone to check on the heat. Who would think I was any more than that? Not Robert. Not anyone. No one but me knew the passion I'd felt for a year and a half, the depths of soul I'd found. No one but you will ever know, Elspeth.

Nan could be coaxed to forget. Robert might, too, if he weren't reminded of me anymore. By the time he sees me again, he'll have forgotten the whole thing.

Now, Elspeth, I come to the end.

Have you ever wondered what happens when a person dies in winter and the ground is frozen too solid to dig a grave? The body is kept in the mortuary until spring. This causes great devastation to the families as they have to go through a death twice, or so I'm told. The funeral director said this to me as a matter of interest, not thinking I might be among the devastated.

Carbon monoxide poisoning. The oxygen in the cabin was completely burned up by the woodstove fire until there was none left. People die every winter from faulty heating. All the windows were closed. That was the case because I closed Nan's window. It had been left open on purpose and I closed it. It's my fault. Even if I didn't know, I still made a choice that wasn't mine to make.

And I don't have Nan.

She was taken away from here, from me, a few days later. I hired a lawyer and fought to adopt her or have her here as a foster child, but Virgil had a family member who agreed to take her, and the law favored that arrangement. I wasn't given her address. I contacted Ben Reed, but he had no idea about any of it and didn't want to. I plan to hire a private detective to locate her if I can't get the information otherwise. I will stay in contact with her until she is old enough to come back here on her own. She belongs here.

I don't understand myself. I'm usually so measured and sane, but every so often an excitement seizes me, and I feel inspired and changed. But it always comes to grief.

My heart broke when you died, El. I hardly survived it. Now it has broken again. I will survive, but I do not know as what person. That is the unknown now.

Death isn't the end of love, of course. We know that from your Jesus. I know that from you, El. But it is the end of growth and of knowledge.

Elspeth. I brought you back to life, but I don't think that was fair to you. I haven't mourned you during this time. Nor have I listened to your opinions and feelings. I don't know what you'd have thought about Virgil, or my love of him, or any of this. I can guess, but that's all it is, a guess. Maybe there is a heaven, and you can see and hear me, but I don't believe it, and I can't hear you. I have been making you up in these notebooks.

And I can love you best by letting you go.

CHAPTER 38

Polly, Meadowlea, August 2002

O NE AFTERNOON AFTER THE FAMILY LEFT, GOOD RIDDANCE, Polly convinced Agnes to go with her to the Deel Club for a swim. She hadn't had time to discuss the notebooks with her yet beyond writing a note thanking Agnes for sharing them with her. She'd been glad to have them as a distraction from James; which was more heartbreaking, she couldn't say.

As she got ready, putting her suit and sunscreen and flip-flops into an old straw bag, Polly hummed happily. She was grateful to be back to her routine. She wanted to be alone in the house to recover from her anger at the boys for making insinuations about Robert. Hadn't she done enough for Knox by essentially ceding the Haverford house to him? Theo had really let her down, but he was meek. He'd figured out long ago how to escape to Italy. Now she understood.

Agnes had diagnosed James as being in a midlife crisis. Midlife! From Polly's present vantage point, that stage seemed long ago, and inconsequential. A manufactured upset. Midlife crises belonged to men, but didn't women have more of a claim on change? Hormonal mayhem. Polly had been drenched for a few years and said nothing about it. Who'd want to hear it? Polly considered telling him to buy a red car and drive off into the sunset. Or off a cliff. Joke.

James wasn't the type to search for himself. He preferred to stomp around, imposing his displeasure. Was his personality her fault? Or Dick's? She supposed both to some degree, but children came out as who they would always be, if they were raised without much harmful interference. James had stomped around in his playpen, too.

She picked Agnes up at the end of her driveway. She had on her usual trousers and Lachlan's straw hat.

"Where's your suit?"

Agnes pulled up the hem of her T-shirt, revealing a swath of black spandex.

"Do you have underwear for after?" Polly strained to see if she'd missed noticing a bag.

"I don't wear bras anymore and I do fine without the other."

"Hippie," Polly said. "I can't believe I convinced you to step away from your desk."

"It's summer, Polly. And you know I adore everyone at the club. Can't wait to hear all the gossip."

"Har har. Just glower as you do and no one will come to our table." She glanced over. Agnes was smiling.

"Am I that bad?"

Polly had reached the top of Point Path and turned right on Shore Road. "Nothing is bad on a day like this," Polly said, feeling robust. "You know what I realized this morning?"

"I'm not a mind reader. Or I am, but I'm not picking this up. What?"

"I realize what you've meant when you've been talking about feminism all these years." Polly glanced over to see the impression this made. It could have gone in many directions. But Agnes looked interested.

"It means I can make choices. That's the short of it."

"Profound, though, Pol. I agree with you. Choice implies self-knowledge, self-acceptance, responsibility . . ."

FELLOWSHIP POINT

"And independence. I never had that. Now I am getting an inkling, and I wish I could go back and be more independent."

"You can, in your mind. That's a choice as well."

Agnes and Polly both had their windows down, and both reached their arms out to feel the wind. The roadway was a moving river of dappled, rippling shade. Polly had the thought that it was too bad about forgoing the Point Party again, but she noticed that she was interfering with the perfect moment, and made the choice not to dwell on it.

"Dwelling isn't feminist," Polly said. She winked.

"I wish people knew your mind," Agnes said. "Honestly, I get exasperated with you, but you don't bore me."

"My greatest achievement. I don't bore Agnes Lee."

They pulled into the parking lot at noon, and after a poolside lunch accompanied by the pock of tennis balls and a long swim that Agnes proclaimed loudly was divine, they left at three o'clock.

Again they rolled down their windows all the way to smell the warm drying grasses and wildflowers.

"You have to admit that was nice," Polly said.

"I don't have to admit anything. But thanks for forcing me. I feel as though I could take a nap, mirabile dictu."

"You never nap?"

"Nope. Who has time?"

Polly smiled, as she was meant to. They had their windows down, but they were driving slowly enough that they could hear each other over the wind. Another beautiful day, softer now heading toward September. Soon the summer people would leave, but Polly would not. She planned to stay until just before Thanksgiving. She and Agnes could really spend time together in the way they had when they were girls.

"You know," Polly said. "You really aren't to blame for Virgil's accident. Not at all."

"That was a non sequitur." Agnes stretched her legs under the dashboard.

"I don't think so. I think we have both been waiting for a moment to discuss it."

Agnes held her tongue, for once. But—actually—she hadn't been as opinionated lately. Was it her treatments, or had she changed?

Polly continued. "It was an accident, pure and simple. You must know that by now. I want to be assured that you don't blame yourself."

Agnes sighed. "Oh, Pol, I don't know if I even think about blame or forgiveness or anything like that anymore. The Reeds—it was all just so sad. That's how I feel now."

"You never really told me how much you loved him."

"It was foolish. I had been alone for a long time, and I was in grief. He was a handsome writer, also in grief, and we clung to each other. I never think of him now. I did love Nan, though."

"Yes. I understood your epitaph when I read the notebooks."

Agnes looked startled—had she forgotten she'd told her what it was? She appeared about to say something, but closed her mouth and looked out to her side.

"We both lost daughters," Polly said, and her eyes stung.

"Pol—" Agnes reached her hand out, and Polly clasped it for a moment. But she needed it to drive, and took it back.

"I know," Polly said. "I can't get—" But her thought was interrupted by the sight of something in the road. Was it a mirage? No—it wasn't. "Hold on—what's that?"

Agnes visored her eyes and squinted. "It's a bicycle."

"And a person?"

"Looks like. Some dope."

"I wish someone else were going to get there ahead of us," Polly said.

"Ha! That's honest."

It became a bicycle and a person, then a woman, and then—
Seela Lee.

"Oh good Lord," Agnes said. "This feels like a prank. Let's turn around and gun it."

"Okay!"

But they knew that would never be the choice they'd make.

Polly slowed down and parked gingerly.

"Must we?" Agnes said, but she was already opening her door.

Don't ask what happened, Polly reminded herself. Dick had always hated when she asked what happened if the answer was clear to anyone with eyes. Seela had fallen off her bike. The details were unimportant.

"Are you all right?" Polly asked.

Seela flailed. "Ouch! Dammit."

Agnes bent over. "Is anything broken?"

"I can't believe it's you. Just my luck." Seela moaned. She looked at her hands. Polly winced.

"Those are nasty cuts. I think we should go to the hospital," Polly said. "Do you feel all right? You didn't hit your head, did you?"

"I don't think so."

"Feel it," Agnes commanded. "Is anything sore?"

Seela put her fingers to her hair and lightly touched it, portraying an ingrained habit of not interfering with what the hairdresser had wrought.

"Seela, put your fingers in your hair! Your appearance is the least of your worries right now," Agnes snapped.

Seela made a face but did as told and felt all around her head. When her fingers parted the lacquered back, Polly saw a bald patch underneath.

"I don't feel a bruise."

"Good. In that case I won't make you go to the hospital. I'll clean out the cuts. Is Archie at the house?" Agnes asked.

"He's playing golf today."

Good. Polly did not want to see him. "You should rest. You have had a shock, you know."

Seela looked up at her lugubriously. "Go away. Someone else will come along." She winced and drew air in over her teeth.

"Don't you mean, *Thank you so much, Agnes and Polly. You are my saviors.*"

"Oh bug off." Seela got on all fours and yelped. Blood seeped through the knees in her slacks.

"All right. Let's go, Agnes," Polly said, irritated, but not meaning it—of course.

"No," Seela said. "I want to get home." She moved one knee upright and shrieked.

"Maybe you should get over to the grass? We're very close." Vain old woman, Polly thought. Not wanting anyone to see her like this.

Agnes moved closer to Seela. "Oh, for God's sake, Seela, suck it up. Polly, you get under that arm, and I'll get under this one."

Polly found a secure grip in Seela's armpit. If Dick could see her now!

"On a count of three," Agnes said. "One, two, three!" Wobbling and grunting and doing some fancy stepping to keep their footing, they got her upright. Seela gritted her teeth. Polly heard bells as if she were the one who'd fallen, but located the source as Seela's charm bracelets. Plural. How did some people not know when to stop?

They got her into the backseat of the car with lots of wincing and whimpering. Polly was drained and perspiring. She started the car.

"What about my bike?" Seela said.

"Someone can come back for it," Polly said.

"It might get stolen."

"It's mangled."

"Couldn't we put it in the back somehow?"

"By 'somehow' do you mean magic?" Agnes said. "No. No bike."

The drive was labored. Polly tried to avoid jostling Seela, but it was a bumpy road—the reason for the accident to begin with. A lot of pained groans came from the backseat. "You'll be fine," Agnes said, not without sympathy.

When they arrived, Agnes went in to announce what had happened. When she came back out, she said Nora was gathering towels and bandages.

They got Seela into the den, shouldering her skinny body under a barrage of instructions and pained gasps.

"Put a towel under me," she commanded. "I don't want to get blood on the upholstery. It's Brunschwig and Fils!"

She pronounced the *l*, like "fills a glass." Polly and Agnes exchanged glances. Some people didn't know French, that was fine. Invoking a brand name was another matter. They'd been raised to notice class distinctions, and the fix was in too deep to be free of that training, even if they found it as tasteless as what they'd been taught was gauche.

Agnes pressed a towel between Seela's hands.

"What should I do?" Polly asked.

"Moral support," Agnes said.

"You've got it."

Polly couldn't bear to watch the antiseptics being applied. It made her own skin shrivel. She began to look around instead. She'd never been in this room before and was both impressed and embarrassed by its sheen. The wood was polished to a mirrored surface. The pictures were by recognizable artists. The sofas were covered with silk—in a beach house! It was a show-offy room dedicated to hobby and play, complete with a card table set up and ready to go. Along one wall ran cases full of collections, much like the ones they had on the Point. Polly walked along them slowly, perusing the items. There were netsukes and snuff bottles, rocks, sea glass and shells, very high/low, all mixed up. Seela must have been advised by one of her decorating gurus; it went beyond her level of chic. *Stop it*, Polly chided herself. *The woman is right here, miserable—*

Then she saw it. The wampum belt. The one that Archie had claimed had been stolen, the one he tried to pin on Robert. Polly recognized it instantly; she had studied the picture carefully when it appeared in the *Gazette*, on the off chance she might spot it somewhere. It was a beadwork rendering of a series of scenes depicting animals and houses. Archie claimed that it had belonged to Joseph Orono, a claim Agnes said was as likely as was the rampant claim in Philadelphia that a house had been a stop on the Underground Railroad. Yet it was old and valuable no matter whose it had been.

As far as Polly knew, and she would, there'd never been any correction to the claim that the belt was stolen. When had Seela and Archie recovered it?

"Agnes, can you come here for a sec?"

"What is it?"

Agnes looked over, and Polly tipped her head toward the case. Agnes pushed herself up and came over to have a look. Polly saw her recognize the belt immediately. Unlike Polly, Agnes had seen it many times before. She opened the case and took it out, dangling it between her pinched fingers.

"Seela?"

They heard footsteps in the hallway. "Hello?"

Agnes looked at Polly. "The plot thickens. In here, cousin," she called out.

He entered, spruce as always, and rushed straight to Seela. She sobbed when she saw him in a way that touched Polly in spite of herself. Marriage was the weirdest thing that people did. Even these two had a marriage.

Agnes noticed the softening of her expression. "Polly!"

"Yes, yes, I'm here."

"What happened?" Archie asked, turning to look at Agnes for an explanation. There she was, dangling the belt. The image of little Nan dangling the garter snake came into Polly's mind.

"You tell me first," Agnes said. "What's this doing here?"

Archie hardened visibly. "It's not the same—"

"Archie!" Agnes stomped her foot. "Don't kid a kidder!"

"Don't yell at him," Seela said. "We found it."

"Where?" Polly asked.

"It slipped behind the case."

Agnes pulled it out horizontally between her hands and held it up to Polly. For a sec they appreciated the fine work. Then Agnes laid it back in the case.

"You mean to tell me that the police and your fancy New York detectives were on a wild goose chase, and it was here all along?" Agnes asked.

"Get out of my house," Seela said.

Archie touched her shoulder; he'd take it from here. "No," he said. "We really did lose it. But we found it again."

"When?"

"Agnes—"

He looked like a boy, Polly thought. Like James when he was a teenager, and trying to get away with something by means of a lie. Why had she put up with it?

"When?" Agnes repeated.

Archie touched his neck, as if to protect it. "Last summer."

"While Robert was still in prison. Good Lord." Polly shook her head. Yet she felt an electric jolt of clarity unlike any she'd ever felt before. It gave her a voice. "Archie Lee, admit that you knew that Robert didn't steal anything."

Agnes buttressed her demand. "You're a Lee," Agnes said. "You know better."

"That's everything to you, isn't it?" Archie said. "Being a Lee.

Your history, your ancestor worship. How did the mighty Lees welcome my wife? You all sneered. Could I change that by helping you dissolve the Fellowship to save your precious birds? No. You wouldn't be any more accepting no matter what we do. I'm better off being tacky myself and building a marina."

"You could go to prison for this, you know."

"I doubt it," Archie said.

"You let Robert go to prison, lose his house and his reputation—for what?" Polly asked.

Archie glanced over at Seela, and Polly instantly understood. Sudden tears pricked at her eyes. "Well, I feel sorry for you," she managed to say, her voice quavering. To understand was not to forgive.

"Are you going to tell?" He was subdued now.

"Well, Pol?" Agnes said. "Are we going to tell?"

"Good question." Polly turned to Archie. "Here's the alternative to us telling, as you put it. You're going to clear Robert's name. Call the judge, and call the papers. Admit publically that you and Seela were wrong. Robert didn't steal the necklace or the belt. And you're going to join in with us in dissolving the Fellowship agreement." Polly spoke with calm authority. She had no doubt in her, none at all.

"Yes," Agnes said. "You're going to do these things, and then we won't report you."

"No," he said. "I'm not. You can't have everything."

"Then we'll go to the police."

"And I'll stick to our story. Robert did knock Seela over, after all. He never denied that."

"It was an accident, and you know it." Agnes shook her fists. "To think I adored you," she said.

Archie ignored her and instead looked over at Seela, who was sprawled across a beige chair, her feet up on an ottoman. She had a washcloth on her forehead and a pained expression in her eyes. "I will tell you what I'll do," Archie said, "so as not to prolong this. I will do one of the things you say. Either I will exonerate Robert or I will go along with your plan to dissolve the Fellowship now. You choose."

"You unmitigated, arrogant ass," Agnes said. "You are completely in the wrong, and you want to make a deal? You've been caught!"

He was back in control. "Maybe so. But I have time on my side. I can wait you out."

Polly stepped between them and faced Archie. "Robert," she said. "We choose Robert."

"Polly—" Agnes tried to interrupt.

"Shh!" Polly held up a forbidding hand. "Archie, you will call whoever you need to call, and you'll do it today. Otherwise I'm calling the police. Who have they been closer to over the years, us or you?"

Agnes took Polly's hand and squeezed it.

"You can call Eleanor Kendall at the Portland paper," Agnes said. "She'll be interested. And John Holmes at the *Gazette*."

"I will," Archie said. "I promise. Now it's time for you to get out of my house."

"Way past time," Agnes said. "Toodaloo, cousins."

They headed for the car. "Do you think he'll call?" Polly asked.

"Yes."

Polly was certain Agnes was also remembering Dick's failure to call the police about Hope. They knew; it didn't have to be mentioned. Now she thought she should have made the call herself, instead of wanting him to save the day. She could have been in charge of her life.

Well. It wasn't over.

"Wait—I need to pee," Agnes said.

"You want to go back in?"

Agnes looked around. "This will do." She pointed at a topiary bush.

CHAPTER 39

Maud, Fellowship Point, August 2002

Maud left the city after dinner, so Clemmie would sleep for a lot of the drive, and six hours later checked into a motel near the Portland airport to sleep herself. They had a fun breakfast in the lobby, then headed back into the car for the remaining hours. Agnes had advised she take Route 3, which was more scenic than the interstate but not as slow as Route 1. Maud chose Route 1. They stopped for ice cream, and to walk around a pretty town. As the hours went by, Maud let go of the tension she carried in the city. It had gotten especially bad since Heidi had become depressed again, and Moses repossessed the house on Charles Street. She and Clemmie were still there but Maud was looking for a place of their own. Work was busy, too, and she always felt torn about leaving at five to go home to Clemmie. There was never enough time for everything; the garden had been sadly neglected this year without Heidi to snip the plants and shrubs in the right spots. Miles had been calling. She never answered, but he had inserted himself back in her thoughts. What did he want? Had he gotten a divorce? Did he want to apologize?

The farther she drove the more all that receded. What would it be like if she never went back? What if she rented an apartment in Deel Town and sent Clemmie to the local school? She could become a freelance editor or do something else entirely. Maybe she could be a librarian or open a used bookstore. She could go around Maine to garage sales and buy books for her shop. It could be specifically dedicated to books for women and girls.

She could continue working with Agnes. She was really looking forward to seeing her again. Their correspondence had become a lifeline. They mainly wrote back and forth about books, and they got into some heated arguments. Agnes had reservations about Mrs. Dalloway, for example, which was as contrary as it got, whereas she extolled Roth, who mostly gave Maud the shivers. It was enjoyable to wait for the latest volley to land in her mailbox. She deeply looked forward to having these conversations over a glass of iced tea or wine.

Maud allowed the reverie to go on for as long as she could tolerate not thinking of Heidi. She couldn't live far from Heidi, and that was that.

Heidi was still at Friend's Hospital. She hadn't had ECT treatments, but she had been moved to the long-term unit. Maud read deeply about depression and established an open and fruitful communication with Dr. Straight, who had not held her uneasiness against her, just as Dr. Goodman said he wouldn't. She had several conversations with her father about what Heidi had been like in the early days of their marriage and even more particularly about their honeymoon in Maine. Why Maine, Maud had wondered, when she grew up in Florida? "It was those books," Moses said, "the ones she used to read to you." When they crossed Piscataqua Bridge and left New Hampshire behind, Heidi said, "finally," as if she'd been waiting to return, though she'd never been there before.

Moses had no understanding of the list of words that Dr. Goodman had passed to Maud, but he did describe Heidi's first serious depression. It had happened during their engagement and he'd hoped it was a one-time thing, or bridal jitters. But the depressions had kept coming and each one carved more away. She'd been in the hospital for a year now, and Maud felt she was racing against the clock to break through to Heidi before she sank under the surface permanently.

She glanced in the rearview mirror and was satisfied that all was well with Clemmie in her car seat. As it turned out, she was a good traveler, content to look out the window and occasionally doze off. Maud hadn't been at all sure about bringing her, but Agnes insisted. They finally settled that Maud would stay in a house in the Rookerie, recently repaired by Robert and spruced up by Polly. Maud was comfortable with that solution. Clemmie wouldn't have to be asked to be quiet all morning while Agnes wrote.

Above all she was relieved that Agnes and Polly were friends again. She'd have never imagined that people their age could have such deep conflict or be so passionate. She wished she could convey the whole situation to Heidi and once again try to convince her how much she had to live for.

She turned off Route 1 on the road that led to Cape Deel. She'd only been here once, and not for a year, but it all looked and felt familiar. She explained the sights to Clemmie with authority. Her instructions were to park at the Rookerie, unpack, eat, rest, bathe—whatever they wanted, and to come over to Leeward Cottage for tea at four.

Maud turned down Point Path and drove downhill through the glade of trees and out into the open vista. She paused. There was the Rookerie where she'd stay on her left, and the five big houses one after the next on her right. Straight ahead stood the tree wall of the Sank. It made no sense how excited she was—not even tired. She turned around to Clemmie.

"We're here!"

"We're here!" Clemmie clapped.

Maud pulled into the Rookerie and identified "their" house by the mussel shell wreath on the front door. She unbuckled Clemmie from her car seat and lifted her onto the grass. A puff of wind came up and blew Clemmie's hair across her face, which made her laugh and laugh harder as she got tangled up trying to pull it back.

"Stop it, wind!" she said, slapping at the air.

Maud would have to try to tame that mane before teatime.

"Oh my God, the ocean!" Clemmie squealed. "I want to swim."

It was no use telling her not to say *oh my God*. She was imitating— her mother. Maud was the one who'd have to change.

"This water is too cold for swimming," Maud said. Clemmie looked at her quizzically. "It's icy! Brr."

Clemmie looked around, "I want to climb on the rocks."

"So do I. But right now let's look at our house, okay?"

Clemmie put her fists on her hips. "This house? Is for me and you?"

"It is. We have a whole week here."

"Amazing." She raised her hands and shrugged, then started up the steps. "What are you waiting for, Mommy? Come on!"

They explored the house from bottom to top, chose bedrooms, and then traded. They both had a view, Maud's of the Sank, Clemmie's of the sea. "We trade every day," Clemmie said, shaking her pointer finger with authority. Maud wondered how she knew what was the more desirable—the water view—at age four. How did such information filter through? She was proud that Clemmie was so fair-minded, but how had *that* filtered through? Fairness wasn't dominant in their lives.

"Are you hungry?" she asked.

"A snack would be nice," Clemmie said.

Agnes had said the refrigerator would be stocked. "While I make something, you pick out what you want to wear this afternoon to meet the people. We might need sweaters later, so choose a sweater, too."

"Okay, Mommy, and I'll pick your clothes."

"Thank you." She knew better than to resist. All she had to do was try the clothes on and Clemmie wouldn't notice if she ended up wearing something else. Though lately she had been noticing. She was developing so quickly that Maud could barely keep up. She made the mistake of treating her as though Clemmie were about four months younger than she was, which aroused much indignation.

Maud noticed the details of the house now that she had a moment alone. Why was it that she felt so comfortable here? Yes, it was simple and thoughtful and clean and serene, and decorated with one-of-a-kind pieces. But it wasn't that. She looked back and forth from ceiling to floor and wall to wall until she had it. It was the proportions. They soothed her brain. The design vision of Agnes's great-grandfather, who prized peace.

Clemmie came down in a purple dress and sandals. She'd remembered the extra layer, though the choice had been interpreted to include sweatshirts.

"Here's your snack." Maud had found sandwiches already made in the refrigerator. She ate half, standing up. "Will you stay here while I go change?"

"Of course, Mommy. Right here."

Still, Maud was quick. She didn't want to overestimate Clemmie either. A small girl slid along a continuum of competencies. Maud changed into a clean pair of trousers and a French-striped long-sleeved shirt, small gold earrings and a locket, both matching well with Heidi's bracelet. She slipped her feet into a pair of espadrilles. She felt like the M girls in these clothes. She headed back down.

"Ready? Oh wait. I have to brush your hair."

"No thanks, Mommy. I like it wild."

Oh boy. What was fourteen going to be like?

* * *

Before she could knock on the front door, she heard her name being called, and there came Polly and Agnes around the side of the house.

"We were waiting on the porch," Polly said, hugging Maud.

"Did you find everything?" Agnes said, taking her turn for an embrace. They both hugged gingerly, and Maud was careful with their thin frames.

"Yes, thank you. Maisie!" Maud said, reaching down. Maisie rubbed her leg with her tail straight up. "Be gentle, Clem."

"Who are you talking to?" Polly asked. She winked at Maud, who instantly got the game.

"I didn't say anything."

"I heard you, too," Agnes said.

"You are mistaken. I'm completely alone."

Clemmie giggled and pressed into the back of Maud's legs.

"Actually, I think Maud should have stayed here," Agnes said, waving her hand at Leeward Cottage. "I thought she was bringing someone with her, but apparently not. Didn't she say she was, Polly?"

"I thought so. Maybe we misunderstood, Nessie. Oh well. We'll have to put all the toys back up in the attic."

Their teasing voices were a balm to Maud, and she listened to the sounds instead of the words as the game went on. The afternoon had grayed, and it was sweater weather, an end-of-August preview of October to come. The briny, mineral scent of the ocean settled her nerves. Now she was sleepy.

Clemmie giggled in her hiding place behind Maud's legs. Maud knew her rhythms, the extent of her ability to concentrate, and it was about time for her to appear. Maud was poised to introduce her when a man came around the cormer with a large droopy dog. Robert. She'd caught a glimpse of him the summer before. She wanted

Agnes to write more about him, too. He could serve as a bridge between the reader and the families of the Point, a person who was and wasn't part of it all. Though Agnes was too fiercely protective to think of him that way, even, Maud guessed, in her private self.

"A dog!" Clemmie exclaimed and ran over to it, hair flying. Maud had to admit, the unruliness had charm, and more so here in a tough landscape. Clemmie had her own sense of style. It was up to Maud to tamp down her own self-consciousness enough to let it be.

Clemmie reached toward the dog, but as she'd been taught to do drew her hand back and looked up at Robert. "Is it okay to pet your dog?"

He stepped back as though he'd been struck, and looked over at Agnes. She immediately took in his distress, and her furrowed forehead asked a question in return.

Clemmie pulled on his hand. "Can I pet your dog?" she repeated.

"Yes, yes, it's all right," he said, recovering. "What's your name?"

Clemmie bopped a small hand up and down against the patient dog's flank. "Clemmie."

"I'm Robert."

Maud heard this, but was watching Agnes and Polly, who were staring at Clemmie.

"It's not possible," Polly said.

"No," Agnes said. "It isn't. It's just a coincidence."

"What's a coincidence?" Maud asked. "What's going on?" She lifted Clemmie up and carried her over to the women. "This is Clemence, but she's called Clemmie."

"How do you do?" Agnes said, and shook Clemmie's hand. "Try again. Grip my hand harder. Good. That's better. Always show your stuff in a handshake."

Clemmie squeezed Agnes's fingers. Polly and Robert shook

hands with her, too. During this introduction the stares never stopped. Maud was becoming uncomfortable. "I'm sorry, but what is going on?"

"Maud—I apologize. You see"—Polly shook her head—"it's just that Clemmie looks exactly like the child who lived here once."

"What child?" Maud asked. Clemmie pushed away and Maud let her slide down.

"She looks like Nan," Agnes said.

"Really?"

"Exactly." Then Agnes asked, "Maud, how old is your mother?"

Maud noticed a bead of sweat rolling down her back and catching in the material at her waist. In the deeper recesses of her mind she was making calculations, too. "She's forty-five. She had me when she was eighteen."

"And you said she grew up in Florida?"

"That's right. With her aunt."

"Does she remember her parents?"

Clemmie was back with the dog, chatting with her.

"No, not really," Maud said. "Her psychiatrist thinks something happened to her to cause her to forget."

"That's sad," Polly said.

"What happened to her? Do you know?" Agnes pressed. She reached for Polly's hand and the two old women clung to each other.

"I wish I did. No one knows. The doctor thinks if she could remember she might begin to heal. I'm sorry, but is Clemmie's appearance too upsetting?"

"Do you know anything more?" Robert asked.

Maud remembered he'd been Nan's friend.

"Not really. She wrote a list of words the doctor thinks might be a clue—let me see—" Maud closed her eyes and pictured the piece of paper. "I think it's SNOW, COLD, BOOTS, ASHES, FUR. I may be wrong, or missing one, but it's something like that."

"What the dog name?" Clemmie asked, reverting to baby talk. She, too, had caught the nervous mood. Maud thought maybe they should leave.

"It's Hope," Robert said.

Suddenly, Maud pointed to Agnes's wrist.

"Your bracelets! They're just like mine!"

Agnes pulled up her sleeve, revealing two bracelets that were perfect matches. "I gave Nan the third bracelet in the set when they took her away."

Maud's whole body throbbed. "Your notebook—Fur— isn't that what Nan Reed called her father?"

Agnes nodded, tears in her eyes.

"But this can't be happening—" Maud said.

Yet she knew it was, and it wasn't logic or facts that convinced her. It was the sense she had that she knew this place somehow— through the *When Nan* books, yes, but even beyond that. To paraphrase Heidi, Maud loved Fellowship Point before she knew she might be here someday. She loved it in her mother, where its beauty still remained.

"Oh my God," Maud said, and began to cry, and laugh. "Uh-oh, I told myself I'd watch my language around Clemmie." She wiped her eyes as Polly and Agnes and Robert crowded around her, and they all talked at once, expressing disbelief and belief, asking and answering questions, sputtering anecdotes, until any doubts were resolved.

Heidi was Nan. The clues had been there all along, but it took all of them together to figure it out. Each of them remarked that the only thing better would be if Heidi were here, now. They looked at each other wistfully.

Agnes said, "To hell with tea. I need a drink. Who'll join me?"

Maud touched her bracelet, her steadying habit. Agnes noticed.

"Your mother will wear that again one day," she said quietly, and Maud knew it was true.

Drinks it was. Agnes reached out for Clemmie's hand. Clemmie took it without hesitation and slid her other hand under the dog's collar.

"I'm bringing Hope."

CHAPTER 40

Maud, Fellowship Point, August 2002

LATER THAT NIGHT, AS MAUD WAS GOING OVER EVERYTHING again in her spare, shadowy room, she hoped that she, too, would live a long life. Agnes had once proclaimed that the most perfected human beings on earth were nine-year-old girls, but Maud now thought old women were serious contenders. She considered words like *resilience* and *curiosity*, but they didn't express what she had now grasped. Maybe when she got old she'd know how to explain it. She thought of Agnes and Polly's bodies, and Heidi's, too, and how these compilations of skin and bones were constantly changing and adapting, even as death moved closer.

Barely thinking about what she was doing, she got out of bed and went downstairs and outside. It was warm for a moment, and then the cold enveloped her. The grass crunched under her bare feet. That was not what she'd come for, though. She wanted to be part of the vast dark night. She'd never seen so many stars. Her neck ached and she shivered, but she didn't want the moment to end. She shifted between her feet, relieving one and then the other, until the pain became so great that she had to go back inside. But she didn't. She waited, and soon it was all right. It wasn't as important to resolve the discomfort as it was to see what came next.

So many stars, and they were always there, whether or not she could see them. Not very profound, but not something to forget, either.

She looked over at Robert's house. A light burned in an upstairs window. Maybe he was reading, or writing. He had asked her dozens of questions about Heidi, more even than Agnes, and told her his memories of their childhood together, including how she'd picked up a snake in the grass, and how rapt she was every day looking out the school bus window in spite of it being the same route. One day he'd asked her what she saw, and she gave him a list: tree, other tree, tree again, house, car, and so on. She was naming the world, and bringing herself into it as she went.

"She taught me to do that," Maud said.

Robert smiled. "I can hear her say my name. Wobber."

By the light of the sky, Maud named the night for the last time. When she finally did go in, it was with a new comprehension of her future. She couldn't describe any specific goal or path, but she knew she'd never again walk home from work calling the world into being by naming its separate parts. That had been Heidi's habit, a way of trying to stay connected to reality. Maud would simply live in it, somewhere between the stars and the cold earth, in a band of time she wouldn't waste.

PART SIX

A Gathered Meeting

CHAPTER 41

August, Fellowship Point, 2003

T HE POINT PARTY WAS SWIMMING ALONG UNTIL HAMM LOOSE Sr. arrived with his sons.

Agnes spotted them first: Father, Son, and Other Son. She was across the meadow near the ocean, chatting with James, which was bad enough as it was, when her skin sprouted gooseflesh. She'd predicted they'd show up. Her stomach flipped.

She wouldn't speak to them. That was already decided. Earlier in the day, when they were going over the to-do list, she'd made it clear to Robert and Polly to come rescue her if the Looses managed to corner her. Yes, they'd get their paws on this sacred place, but they wouldn't have the opportunity to see how she felt about it.

"Look what the cat dragged in," she said, and watched James's face. He turned and spotted the Looses, and Agnes saw him apply effort not to raise his arm in salutation, and not to immediately ditch her and run off to play with his friends. He turned back to her with a flushed red neck.

They'd been discussing the neutral topic of the death of a tourist whose kayak had flipped.

"It's more treacherous around here than people know," Agnes said.

James got the dig and frowned into his G&T. "I'm not a water person," he mumbled.

She was exasperated. She couldn't talk to James, not even for Polly's sake. "I must go," she said abruptly. She'd been taught never to make an excuse, because of the rude burden it imposed on the other person to excuse her. And what excuse was ever really good enough, except dire illness? No one wanted to know what was more important than they were. James had been taught the same, and said, "Pleasure to have spoken."

Agnes fled. The party didn't need her for the moment. The laughter was gay, forks clinked with gusto against her good plates. The arms of the young bartenders from town—college students back for the summer—darted expertly among the bottles and ice buckets arranged along the tableclothed bars, and the music curated by the M girls wove ribbons of lively beats through the groupings of partygoers. Agnes, in khakis and a blue silk shirt and sandals, hair pinned up in a French twist, headed for the Sank.

Robert would be the one to greet the Looses. He had, at the beginning of the party, positioned himself at the top of the grassy way that guided guests from Point Path over to the party proper. He'd spent some time working out where this conduit should begin, walking from Rock Reed past Leeward Cottage several times to discover the natural turnoff where he'd mow a pathway. Hope accompanied him; she stood at Robert's side now, greeting the guests, anxiously accepting the occasional pat on the head, taking quick looks up at Robert. *It's okay*, Robert assured her, in tone and touch. Polly had wanted the party to happen on a spot between her house and Agnes's but on the other side of the Path, and Agnes had wanted the byway to be obvious enough that no moron would end up in the graveyard. They'd always set up the party this way, and every year they'd swear they'd remember where they'd cut the path, but they never did. That was part of the tradition, part of the fun. After he'd done the mowing, Robert had taken pictures, and he'd also paced off the distance from Leeward's driveway to the spot where the mowing began, so he'd know for next year—if there were a next year. But he would duly pretend not to remember, for posterity's sake.

It was only the day before that they'd realized they had no one to greet the guests. Dick had served as the greeter ever since Lachlan died—for forty years. Ian Hancock hadn't been trusted to do it, he was too likely to make a rude remark before people were fortified with drinks. Archie was too young, and his father—he'd done it once or twice, but preferred being the center of a rowdy group rather than a calm welcoming presence set apart from the gaiety. Dick had been good at it; he moved people along with a clap on the back and a compliment. They hadn't had to deal with figuring out an alternative because there hadn't been a Point Party since Dick died. The one that would have occurred in 2000 was canceled because of his death, and in 2001 Polly and Agnes hadn't the heart for it because Robert was in prison and they were also nervous that Seela and Archie might show up. Then in 2002 Polly and Agnes weren't on speaking terms—they laughed about it now, it seemed almost glamorous to have had a falling-out—until it was too late to plan such an event. What would they do? At the same moment Polly and Agnes said "Robert!" There had been many such moments this spring, since Robert had brought Heidi back to Fellowship Point. So it was decided, by mutual spontaneous concord.

Now here they were, finally, having the party again, and compensated for the wait by perfect weather, and good enough health. Heidi was dressed in one of her vintage dresses, this one striped in Fauve colors—she'd match the sunset later. Robert turned frequently between greetings to see where she was and to gauge her anxiety level. He was at the ready to rescue her. Polly and Agnes and Maud were looking out for her, too, but he considered them backup. His vigilance was what counted, as it had when they were children. He'd never believed she was dead. Not really. Now he was helping her come back to life.

When he spotted the Looses lumbering down the hill, he quickly turned and monitored Heidi. She was chatting to people. Fitting in.

The Looses looked like a pack of bulldogs, all three squat and wide and panting. Who had comb marks in their hair in 2003? They wore tan suits and open collars, no ties. Loafers. Robert, knowing they'd be a hot topic later when Agnes and Polly did the postmortem on the afternoon, took care to notice details so he could take part. Their pants were belted below their large, hard bellies. One wore white socks.

The sons stepped behind their father. Robert had lost the habit of holding out his hand to shake, and as it turned out, a lot of people didn't offer theirs either. Hamm Loose did, though, and Robert swiftly raised his own.

"Hamm Loose." Hamm gestured to his sons. "Junior and Teeter." He reached around and clapped Hamm Jr. on the shoulder.

"I'm Robert Circumstance."

They all brightened—his name registered. They'd never called him for any landscaping. They knew him otherwise, probably as a criminal. He dropped his gaze and let them look him over. Then another check on Heidi. This time, she was looking over at him. That set off a chain of activity inside Robert's body. He couldn't yet see her across a distance without that happening. Emboldened, he said, "You're not on the list."

"We're on James Wister's list."

Hamm wasn't about to budge. Agnes had expected this, so Robert let them go in, afterward wiping his hand on his pants.

Maud noticed the Looses, too, but didn't register who they were right away. She was preoccupied with tracking Clemmie's trajectory across the field toward Robert, who was looking at her mother. Maud imagined she could see energy pulsing in the air between Heidi and Robert. Were they in love? No, it wasn't that. Heidi could barely speak. What was it, then? Was friendship a big enough container? Polly said they were soul mates from way back. Maud had never liked that term, mostly because she had never felt it herself— true love. Not yet, at least.

"Robert!" Maud prompted and pointed. He followed the line of her attention and spotted Clemmie in time to hook his hands under her armpits and swing her high. Her father, Moses Silver, had done that. Maud rode up on his shoulders through Washington Square, and sometimes she flew parallel to the floor with his feet pressed into her stomach. An airplane. Clemmie liked to play with Robert's hands, and that interest came back to Maud, too—working hard to undo Moses's alligator watch band, and just as hard to break him with Indian sunburns. Learning by looking into his placid face not to show her own pain when the kids at school gave Indian sunburns to her. Counting the hairs on his wrist, pretending to shave the hairs on his leg with a twig, laying her head on his heart and listening to it lub dub, lub dub, lub dub. The male body like another country. Maud paced over the grass and peeled Clemmie off of Robert so he could go back to greeting his guests. Clemmie wanted to walk Hope around the field, and Maud agreed to that. Once again she showed Clemmie how to hold the leash. Clemmie tucked her chin and focused. They passed by the Looses, who paid no attention to the child or the dog, so Maud had no reason to pay attention to them. They passed by Polly, too, who had a ghastly look on her face.

A phrase came to Polly's mind. *She didn't believe they would try it on.* Edith Wharton. James hadn't said anything about his plans to betray Agnes by collaborating with the Looses, but then he'd never said anything about what he planned for the future of the

Point—they all knew. Still, Polly had hoped he'd change his mind. Hadn't she taught James to love this place for what it was, or had she shared too much of her feeling with Agnes alone? She rubbed her arms and wished she had her sweater, which she'd left at one of the tables. She calculated the route she'd have to take to reach it and whether she could do so without having to encounter the intruders. For that was what the Looses were, even if James or Archie had invited them. Of course they'd come. People had no manners anymore, or even a notion of their utility—how good manners evened out the imbalances between personalities, how they bolstered the shy by making it clear what to do, and how they held the aggressive in check. Polly had lived her life by manners, and over time had boiled her philosophy down to one precept: in every minute make the world beautiful. She'd gotten bolder about saying this aloud. When she told the M girls, she squared her shoulders to absorb the expected laughter, but they'd nodded and said, "Yeah, that's what you do." Which gave her a boost. A person who lived by those intentions should surely be able to handle a conversation with the Looses on her way to get her sweater. But Archie rushed toward them and guided them toward the bar. Polly fetched her sweater and looked around for Agnes. There she was—slipping into the woods. Skipping out on her own party. *That's fine*, Polly decided. *Let her.* She spotted a long-time-no-see friend and went over to chat.

At the end of the official stretch of Point Path, where the gravel gave way to the grass in an uneven line—like the kelp demarcation on the beach showing how far the cold hand of water had reached onto the land—Agnes removed her sandals. As long as she didn't step on a snake, she'd be all right. Lachlan had taught the children to toughen up the soles of their feet as soon as they arrived in Maine every summer. Grace had met that plan with one of her thin-lipped grimaces, and Agnes had laughed along with her father when he said, "Grace, you're pomping!" He'd invented that word for how

Grace filtered her opinions through her snobbery. He was only teasing, but Grace never budged. The children sided with Lachlan and went out to the beach and toughened their feet by numbing them in cold water and then walking over the stones. Agnes still did so, every May.

She picked up her sandals and stuffed them under the waistband at her back. Her arches cupped over the tree roots, and the fallen fir needles pricked. But she was ready for them—her feet were hooves. When she and Maud and Heidi lay on the chaises on the porch after lunch, dozing and dreaming airy grilled cheese dreams, Clemmie played with Agnes's feet, poking at them with her spoon and drawing on them with crayons, and sometimes Agnes played along and emitted a long howl that built in intensity to a high finish, making Clemmie chuckle like a Buddha. They'd all agreed, along with Dr. Goodman at Friends Hospital, not to rush Heidi. If pushed too hard, her memories might come too fast or become permanently lodged below the surface, and either way, she might . . . It was unclear what exactly, but it wasn't good. So they waited. It was hard. If Heidi could grasp that she was a Reed, she could vote her share of the Fellowship, and Agnes could go ahead with her plan to give the Sank to a land trust. But Heidi's health was more important, just as Robert's freedom was more important. Still, the thought of the Point becoming a marina hurt Agnes's heart. But she had to accept it. And no time like the present.

When no one had come down Point Path for a few minutes, Robert left his post and joined the party. Hope, still tethered to Clemmie, looked over at him. He nodded at the dog, who nodded back, a transaction not everyone present would agree was possible. Yet don't the things that happened define what is possible? As Agnes said, humans had no right to believe they were the superior species until they figured out how to understand the languages of animals and plants. Robert thought that made sense.

549

He went over to retrieve Hope, but Clemmie wanted to stay with her longer, so Robert told Maud he'd watch them and she could be a free agent. He walked them over to the bar table and asked for a club soda for himself and a ginger ale for Clemmie. He'd have a drink when the party was over. He turned around and watched Heidi smile and pull her hair back from her face. She was graying now, as was he, adding to the demographic of what Agnes said was the state hair color of Maine. Robert liked looking at Heidi from a distance. No, he'd never believed she was dead. Nor had he given himself much leeway for grieving. He wouldn't have known how. Children weren't thought to take things to heart, and his attachment to Nan was a mystery anyway. No one discussed her disappearance from the Point with him. He pictured her in New York City living a life like Eloise. His family moved off the Point that spring, and it wasn't for many years that he was back there with leisure time enough to walk around. To his shock, he came across a gravestone with Nan's name on it, next to her father's. Virgil Reed and Nan Reed. Recently Agnes had told Robert and Heidi that they'd had hot chocolate and cookies together often when they were small. Robert couldn't remember, much less Heidi, but they were telling her little things like that. Agnes told them how helpful he'd been after Nan's accident, how he figured out ingenious ways of getting her to exercise. He remembered a little of that—Nan in bed in a downstairs room, a situation he found foreign and enviable. He remembered playing with her, and how fun she'd been, and how determined. She still had her limp. He'd have recognized it anywhere. Heidi only said she always wondered why she limped.

Clemmie dropped the leash and held her cup with two hands. Robert handed Hope an ice cube. He supposed he should be hobnobbing. His business had largely come back, but he wanted to build it. He wanted to have money now. For a future. He liked his present company, though.

"Shall we?" he said to Clemmie and took her cup.

"Shall we what?" she said, and giggled.

"Hmm," Polly said. She crept around until her back was to the Looses and linked arms with Heidi. "Yes," she said, hoping she could pick up the thread after the next remark. It embarrassed her that James stood among them, in front of everybody, but he was a grown man, nearly a robust sixty, out from under her roof for over forty years now, and she shouldn't—Agnes often reminded her—blame herself for how his character had developed. Polly often thought of a moment at a birthday party when James was eight. In those days birthday parties were social occasions for the mothers, too, an excuse for daytime cocktails. Polly left Theo and Knox at home with Dick and the housekeeper and took James and Lydia to a party, knowing a baby girl was always welcome. The house was the same as her house but a few blocks away. Same furniture, lamps, books, plants. Colonial taste. Every woman strived for an original touch on top of the respectable. This woman had modern art, which Polly complimented expectedly.

The time came when Lydia needed a change, and Polly located the bathroom. When she came out, she happened to look down the hallway and saw James at the other end. He had his eyes closed and his arms outstretched and he was turning in circles, counting. Every time his fingers brushed the wall, he whispered a number and began again. Polly was so surprised she pretended she hadn't noticed him. She went back to the living room and handed Lydia around. Later in the party the hostess announced a game of pin the tail on the donkey. Polly blushed. So that was what James was doing in the hall. She shuddered. What kind of child practiced to win a game at a birthday party? Who was he that he'd poked around to discover what the game would be?

She asked him about it on the way home, while Lydia slept in her carriage. "Don't you think it's nicest when winning a game is fair and square?"

James shot her a wary look that portrayed his opinion that she'd just betrayed him irrevocably, an attrition made more fraught by the fact that his cheating had betrayed her. But her moral dimension wasn't supposed to supersede her focus on him.

"I won, Mummy." His eyes dim. His tone ice. She'd lost him. She was too much of a girls' school girl to ever be of use to him, and he was too conniving for her to ever feel truly proud.

Polly had seen bits of herself and Dick in James over the years, but that was the day she first recognized her son as someone completely separate from them, too—someone unto himself. Reflecting on it now, the inclinations toward premeditation and victory revealed on that day seemed to directly enable James's current affiliation with the Looses. He wanted to win above all. Polly hadn't understood who James was then and she didn't now. She loved him, though—the imperative of motherhood.

She couldn't watch any longer. Maud had taken a seat at a table across the lawn, and when Polly made eye contact with her, Maud waved, inviting her to join.

"Excuse us," Polly said, and squeezed Heidi's arm. "Let's go sit with Maud."

Heidi looked over at Maud and smiled. She was better now that she was out of the hospital and on the Point, but Polly had thought she might be further along by now. The restoration of Heidi's health was the major project these days. Heidi should have a life, that was the main goal. There was no telling how much further Heidi had to go before she was legally compos mentis. They decided to accept fate as it unspooled. Polly talked to Heidi steadily as they crossed the lawn. She named things as if Heidi were a child, until Heidi finally briefly leaned her head on Polly's shoulder and said, "I know."

Agnes tore her flimsy blouse on a broken tree branch, and Grace loomed up from the grave to scold her for not thinking about her clothes before going into the forest. *She'd pomp if she saw me now, leaving a party and tearing my clothes.* Grace had suspected her daughter of being a lesbian. Why else would Agnes have broken off with a perfect match like John Manning? Squandered opportunities were perverse. Oh, that voice, still in Agnes's head. Lachlan appeared aphoristically, but her mother was right there in front of her, hands on hips. Agnes shuddered and forced her attention to the immediate. The Sank.

Robert kept it up so beautifully, changed nothing, only clearing away the debris and dead branches, making room for the sun to reach the ground. The moss and ground cover yearned toward the spears of light, and the shadows were bubbles of cool. Agnes stepped lightly, like the indigenous people did in the novels she'd read on rainy afternoons. She and Elspeth had practiced for hours when they were children, making no sound, taking care not to break even the most brittle twig. They sat on the site of the old Native summer camp and imagined being Indian girls. What imagination was that? What was it to build such a fantasy? They took scraps of what they heard and read and combined them with the feel of holding the objects collected from the site in their hands, and they came up with versions of themselves who ate different food and wore different clothes. They couldn't imagine being a person like Mary Mitchell, the girl who'd been arrested for shooting the eagles. They would never think of shooting eagles and rejected those who did. Yet Mary Mitchell was a principled girl, just as they'd been.

What could one do with people whose beliefs were opposite your own?

She looked up at the nest. An eagle flapped out and away, miffed at her intrusion. "Sorry, bird," Agnes said. She no longer knew each one by name, but she still loved the sound of eagle wings beating the air. They cleaved the atmosphere and created temporary yet provocative blank spaces that drew the imagination upward to explore their wake. Agnes stared into the blank space and saw—loss. Her family, gone. Virgil, gone. Grace Lee's face, crumpled after Edmund died. The end of her beauty. The end of her interest in life. The memory still had the power to rile Agnes's insides. She shook her head. What were these thoughts? She should be getting back. Just a quick stop by the summer camp on the way. She put her sandals back on for the trek so she could walk more quickly. She'd already shown how tough she was.

Maud was getting hungry. She and Polly made sure Heidi took a seat that faced the view before Maud set off for plates of food. From growing up in the Village, Maud knew how to walk through a group of strangers looking pleasant and unapproachable, but this practice felt cagey and inappropriate on the Point, where there was no cover, nowhere to hide, no horde of commuters to disappear into. *I belong here*, Maud reminded herself, and though it was real and true, she still couldn't believe it. She and Robert had moved Heidi up to Fellowship Point in March, and Maud and Clemmie had recently arrived to stay for a few weeks, staying in what had become their house in the Rookerie. They were putting the finishing touches on Agnes's novel, and Maud was still coaxing Agnes to write a real memoir. They'd taken over a house in the Rookerie as a writing studio. There they were able to leave their books open and their pages spread out knowing no one else would disturb anything—though they had seen Sylvie peering through the windows. Agnes wondered why she'd never thought of working there before. "It ain't over 'til it's over," Maud teased.

She loved working with Agnes, who actually worked, whose formality was deeply relaxing. Why did she have to be eighty-two years old? Maud wished she could collaborate with her forever.

Maud piled two plates with cucumber sandwiches and hummus and peppers and quiche and cookies. Robert was still walking around with Clemmie, otherwise she'd have asked him for help. She managed—story of her life. As she approached the table, she saw a strange man sit down next to Polly. Her heart sank. Even if this was a party, she'd rather have had her people to herself. Agnes was rubbing off on her.

Agnes slipped between the trees, reaching hand over hand from trunk to trunk, absorbing their strength. A branch snapped loudly beneath her foot. Some Indian girl she was. She came to the spot where she and Elspeth had often returned during their childhood sojourns. They loved it because it felt timeless, untouched by any destructive force. They imagined what it was like to live here before, when the earlier residents paddled around the bend into the cove and pulled their canoes onto the rocky beach below, climbed up the bank and were glad to be back here for another summer, just as Agnes and Elspeth always felt.

So many beaver to harvest, and sardines to pull from the sea. So much open land. The Native Americans were long gone before William Lee arrived, and he didn't even find evidence of their habitation for several summers after being on the Point. Then he tugged at something sticking up from the ground and found a carving. He dug more, found more. He kept a notebook where he catalogued everything, drawing illustrations and noting when and where he found the items. He collected monographs about the local peoples and talked to those who knew much more. He never claimed to have a Native American friend—he was fastidious—but he met men who lived on the reservation land on the Penobscot River near Bangor and asked them about items from his collection. It brought him up short, he'd written, when he conceived of other people living in a different relation to time than he did, something both eternal and more finite.

His words seemed ridiculous now, but that was how it was. Even good, charitable William Lee was a pillager, a colonialist in his own pacificist, Quaker way. The pathos of conquest. Again, the tricks played by imagining. You could only get so far. You could get far enough, though. She'd had to believe that to be a writer, and Agnes did believe it, but she did not believe she could really know what it was like to live inside the body of an Indian girl waking up on an August morning at this summer camp. She could only pay attention to this same vista and beauty, these scents and smells, and think of that girl hearing and seeing the same things. She could ask and she could listen. That was the best she could do.

When she'd made arrangements to pay for Mary Mitchell's defense, the girl had asked what she'd have to do in return. Agnes came up with a price. She wanted to know what it was like to be Mary Mitchell, to know the secret places of the Cape, what Mary dreamed about for her future, but most of all she wanted to know if Mary Mitchell had ever hunted on Fellowship Point. Mary Mitchell said no. She came to the Point by boat to put up the rope swing, and she climbed up the bank to the site of the old summer camp. Stories of those days had been passed down, and a great-aunt had told her about it.

"We were told we weren't making use of it, so we had no right to it."

"I was taught that, too, except it had the opposite consequence." Agnes said. "We believed we knew better what to do with the land, so we deserved to own it."

The Looses and Archie and James thought the same thing—Agnes and Polly weren't making use of the Point.

"I don't believe in killing or eating animals," Agnes told Mary Mitchell. "I have protected the eagles all my life."

Mary Mitchell nodded. "The eagle is sacred. I don't kill it either."

"But you do."

"No. That is not what happens. The sacred cannot be killed."

Agnes was predisposed to dismiss this statement based on her allergies to religiosity, but she found herself returning to it now, alone in the Sank. She thought, now, she understood what Mary meant. She wasn't killing the eagles. She was asking them for their help.

She lowered herself down to the ground, careful careful, and pulled herself in different directions until she lay on her back. A stick poked her between the shoulders, exactly where Grace's nails often prodded all those years ago. Why wouldn't Grace leave her alone? Agnes had pretended not to notice, refused to give her the satisfaction. Those thin, pressed lips, that crumpled, wounded face. Her nemesis. Pushing for recognition now. Agnes couldn't remember Grace ever walking out here to this place, not even once. She'd never liked being on Fellowship Point and only perked up in the middle of August when she started packing to go back to Walnut Street. It was a relief to bury her in Philadelphia and not have to see her name every day in the graveyard. Agnes would be under the ground herself soon enough; she'd had Robert only lightly cover the hole where they'd dug out Nan's stone. It was possible that eventually all the bones might be dislodged in the process of digging the foundation for a resort hotel. So be it. She'd tried. "Why don't you try a little?" Grace said when Agnes would appear at parties in pants and no lipstick. "Why don't you?" Agnes would retort childishly. What had she even been referring to?

Agnes rolled onto her side. From that vantage point she could see down to the beach. Look at that! There was the rope swing,

refastened to the sketchy branch. Friends of Mary Mitchell's perhaps had put it up. She'd have to bring Polly to see it.

Agnes tried to get up but tipped over halfway and banged to the
ground.

Polly wanted to scream. How had she gotten stuck with Hamm
Loose?

"This is Heidi Silver," she said.

Hamm stuck out his paw. "Are you visiting?"

Heidi shook her head but didn't explain. Hamm wasn't all that
interested anyway. "It's God's country up here," he said. "I'd never
live anywhere else."

Heidi looked at him. It was difficult to characterize how Heidi
looked at things. She said very little; they didn't know how much
she understood. People tended to raise their voices to her, which
Agnes swiftly punished. "She can hear you, but maybe she doesn't
want to speak with you, ever think of that?" Polly would love to say
that to Hamm Loose, but it wasn't her way.

"Have you traveled?" she asked Hamm, all manners.

"Yes. I liked Rome."

Polly laughed. This pleased him. He looked at her bashfully. "I
guess that's not saying much."

"No, no, everyone has his own Rome."

"I'd still choose this." He looked into her eyes, seeking—what?
Agreement? Approval? She smiled again. "I haven't been here in a
long time. Never felt welcome!" He belly-laughed at this.

"Why do you think that was?" Polly asked, both on guard and
goading.

Hamm's brow tightened. His sons had skulked away to more
private reaches of the party, and Hamm seemed a bit tetherless
because of it, though Polly was sure only she was noticing that. He

was a big man, not fat like his son Teeter, who must weigh three hundred pounds, but heavy boned and broad and boxy, with meaty legs. Yet his eyes, nose, and lips were all close together in a small circle on the front of his large head, like someone had drawn them onto a balloon before inflating it. His hair was wavy and dark, his fingernails buffed—a point of grooming Agnes saw as a bad sign in a man. Vanity was bad enough in a woman, but in men it cloyed. What did they have to be vain about? Why bother with it if you don't need to? Polly's granddaughter Maeve once told Agnes she was sexist for having such opinions. "Thank you!" Agnes said.

"Old Lachlan Lee had no use for me," Hamm said, answering Polly's question. "He ran me off one time."

"Why?" Maud asked.

"I wasn't his kind of people!"

"No," Polly said. "It was because you shot an eagle."

"Did I?" He raised his eyebrows.

"You most certainly did. We saw you do it."

"Uh-oh! Whoops!" He laughed.

"You don't remember?" Polly shifted to acting on Agnes's behalf as well as her own, pressing now beyond the bounds of politeness.

He gave her a shrewd grin. "Maybe I do."

"Why would you do such a thing?" Polly asked.

"You never know what people will do," Hamm said. "Isn't that right? Do you agree?" he asked Heidi.

"Heidi lives here. She's one of the Reeds."

They'd told Heidi, and walked her through Rock Reed. "It's mine?" she'd asked, and they'd explained the shares to her, but she could only repeat the question: "It's mine?" It was too much of a wreck to live in without repairs and renovation, and it was undecided whether or not she ever would. It was such a big old white elephant. Meanwhile she lived with Agnes.

Hamm didn't react to the news that Heidi was a Reed. Maybe he wasn't in on the details of the real estate transaction perpetrated by his son.

"I have a question," Polly said. "May I?" She'd never have risked this in the past. She counted on other people to be confrontational. Now that she was the person who'd bested Archie Lee, her perception of her place in the world had changed.

"Shoot," Hamm said.

"If you love it here so much, why would you want to develop it?"

He did something then that her father had done, a shift in gears he made when she or anyone else had overstepped. He got a smile on his face, but it lacked humor. It mocked. It dismissed. She used to think she'd made it happen, but she'd seen Ian Hancock do it to totally innocent people. Dick had told her, gently—it was her father, after all—that it was a form of bullying.

She prepared to be bullied by fooling with her sweater buttons.

"You people," Hamm said. "You like to believe you know what's best for this land. You think you aren't developers? Look around." He waved his hand at the five large houses: Outer Light, Rock Reed, Leeward Cottage, Meadowlea, WesterLee, and up at the Rookerie. He turned and pointed at the Sank. "You want the world to stop with you. You think your ways are the good ways. What do you know about us, really? We see you, but do you see us?"

Polly could hear Dick saying that the servant knows the master, but the master has no idea about the servant.

"How do you know what's best for this place?"

"I know as much as you do," Polly said. "I've lived on this land for over eighty years."

"I guess we'll see about that," Hamm said.

Maud was approaching with plates. Hamm Loose introduced himself to her, a flicker of masculine evaluation passing through his blue eyes, which made Polly angry. Maud's eyes widened with recognition when Hamm's name was pronounced, and she gave him a curt nod. She's good, Polly thought.

Heidi also noticed how Maud responded to Hamm, though she didn't know why. Heidi was content to sit at the table with everyone and eat a bit of food. She looked around, something she never got tired of—this was a beautiful place. She lived in Leeward Cottage with Agnes Lee, who'd known her when she was small, and no one made her do anything much. She was glad to be out of the hospital. She took a lot of walks and she watched the water. She tried swimming but it was too cold. Robert walked with her and helped her over rocks and things. She felt very relaxed with him. He said they'd known each other when they were children, which she thought was nice. She also read. There were lots of books in the house. She read to Clemmie, books about a girl named Nan. She knew the words that would appear on the next page, and Maud told her that she had read her the same books when she was a girl, and to Clemmie when she was younger. So much was funny that way. She read adult books, too, and understood them, though when she tried to talk her brain felt like syrup. "It's the medicine," Maud explained. "You'll think faster when you're off it completely."

Heidi dropped a piece of bread and bent down to pick it up. She found herself looking into the face of a chipmunk. The chipmunk was after the bread, too, so she pushed it a little way in that direction. The chipmunk hesitated for a moment but then snatched it and scrammed. Heidi sat back up. She was facing the water, her favorite. The people across the inlet might be curious what was going on here, though maybe they were all here already. There were a lot of people, but now they were at her back. Look—there were Robert and Clemmie and Hope, walking by the sea. She watched them until they blurred. She'd lived here when she was Clemmie's age, she was told. Robert, though older and taller, had been her friend.

Suddenly she caught a glimpse of a different dog, a small white dog. Star, she remembered.

Wait—had she held a chipmunk once?

Agnes lay on her back for a while. She wasn't wearing a watch, so she couldn't verify how much time had passed, but by means of her long experience of the light on the Point—on her face, now—she'd put it at nearly five. People would be leaving. Was there even a point to having the Point party anymore? Not one person today had remembered her father to her or evoked the past. Maybe the spell had been broken by canceling the party for the last two summers, or maybe the party had lost its glamour because she was less interested in gossip and more aware of moving toward the next stage—the end.

She wished she had the faith to believe that after death she'd see people she loved again, but she'd never been able to muster that fantasy. Instead she imagined people who had no existence outside her mind and in the minds of the readers who took up her vision and augmented it with their own notion of what the Franklin Square girls looked and sounded like. She'd made up stories. The Fellowship Agreement was also a story, imagined up by her great-grandfather. He'd made up a story that would preserve this land forever, nearly as it was when he first rode his horse down the peninsula. He hadn't even wanted houses built. The land and the birds were enough for him. He'd compromised in the spirit of fellowship—other people wanted other things, and he'd wanted to be in agreement with them. When he'd set the terms for the dissolution of the association—three shareholders had to agree—did he imagine that such a situation might ever come to pass? Or had that seemed so unlikely that he was, in a sense, making up an absurdity. Three people? Har har! Funny joke! But it had come to that. Unfortunately there was no third person of firm mind who could prevent the joke from being told. Even so, Fellowship Point had had a good run. He'd done well by the land.

The cool of the earth seeped through her silk shirt, and the grass tattooed her arms. She'd like to stay and watch night fall, but she supposed she should go back to her party. Possibly Mary had shown up, though Agnes doubted it. Better for Agnes to show Mary the Point on a quiet day when she could be the only guest. Though it was awkward to think of her as a guest here. If it weren't for the happenstances of history, and the success of ideas that Agnes, as a Quaker, had been raised to view as wrongheaded—war and conquest and hierarchy and so on, all the bad ideas that had hurt millions—Mary might be living here now. She and her people. They belonged here as surely as—

They belonged here. Of course. It was obvious. They belonged here and they should be here. Why not? Why on earth not? Why should she and Polly leave the Point to a land trust rather than to the people who had loved it the longest? Her heart pounded. It had taken her her whole life to see it, but now that she did, nothing could be as clear. The simple truths are always hidden in plain sight, only veiled by the complications of the human mind. Mary belonged here.

Agnes struggled to her feet, filled with the excitement of finally understanding the solution to a problem that should have never existed. No wonder the artifacts had always remained on the Point, in spite of entreaties from museums and collectors. As her father had taught her, all those items should remain in this place. It was as if the artifacts had made their wishes known. There were powers beyond what the powerful could conceive.

She couldn't wait to tell Polly. Agnes knew she'd see it right away, probably even before Agnes finished the sentence. How many hundreds of hours had they spent practicing the skills they'd heard were part of native life, walking without making a sound, imitating bird calls, catching fish with their bare hands? They'd been on the path to this idea all their lives. Agnes was fully aware that they had no third person to help enact this vision but knowing what was truly right was a start. The truth had ways of coming true. Meanwhile, perhaps Mary might aim her arrows in the direction of the Looses.

Heidi reached her hand toward the chipmunk. It jumped sideways and an image came into her head of laying a chipmunk in a hole. Polly looked over to see what Heidi was doing, and felt a tug on her arm—Hamm wanted her attention back. Maud helped Clemmie up on the bench, and Robert fed Hope a crust of bread. Agnes took ten long breaths of ocean air, raising and lowering her arms as she inhaled and exhaled. The breath of life. She bent down and touched her forehead to the ground. Soon enough she'd be in this earth, and that would be all right.

By the time she heaved herself upright and left the site of the summer camp, Hamm Loose would have gotten bored at Polly's table, said a booming goodbye, and offered a wave of the hand before lumbering away to rejoin his boys. The air would be cooling. The daily afternoon breeze would be roughing up the water, lifting the boughs, running grooves through the grass; people would be taking their leave and walking in sated pairs and groups back up Point Path, remarking how well the old women were holding up and how surprisingly good the vegetarian food was, though it left room for their suppers back at home; and the women and teenagers from town who'd been hired to help would be unobtrusively beginning to gather plates and glasses and carry them to the kitchen door of Leeward Cottage, where Sylvie had been directing the drama of refreshment all afternoon; and the Looses and James would part ways in full confidence of their future, each envisioning all they would accomplish here; and the boats that had been out all day would sail or chug by on their way back into the harbor; and the woodland animals and birds and night hunters would pace restlessly, their senses attuned to the influx of noise and scents, waiting for their chance to roam unseen.

Agnes would take the cliff path by WesterLee Cottage where the M girls' bikinis hung over the old gray clothesline by the defunct kitchen garden, and she'd startle when a dog face suddenly loomed in a window. "Sorry, boy," she'd say soothingly, and the dog would tip his head and the gravestone would fall on Nan's legs and Grace Lee would forever lie beneath the ground in Christ Church graveyard, Agnes would forever have not cut her mother any slack, and she'd regret it now.

There wasn't time for withholding, not in this short life when you were only given to know a few people, and to have a true exchange with one or two. Agnes would pass through the graveyard and greet her family, Edmund, Elspeth, Lachlan, and all the other Lees who'd gone before, and Polly's family, who may as well have been her own, and Virgil Reed, who had dangled love in front of her and then taken it back and then died before she'd taken her love back from him, leaving in her a hole like the one open in the ground now where Nan Reed's false grave had been, a death that had sentenced Agnes to write and rewrite the story of a capable girl.

She'd arrive at Point Path and scan the field and spot her group sitting together, Polly, Maud, Heidi, Clemmie, and Robert, and she'd head toward them, knowing that she'd let go of everything except her desire to spend as much time as possible with these people—and writing, naturally—and she'd tell them about her walk; and Polly would lament the ruining of Agnes's blouse and Clemmie would find her lap and Maud and Robert would reenact their conversations with Hamm Loose, and in the middle of their performance Heidi would stand up from the table and take a deep breath, and they'd all watch as she shed decades of confusion and depression. They'd ask her much more about this later when she could express everything, but for now there was this one marvelous shift.

"I was Nan Reed," Heidi announced. "I remember now."

PART SEVEN

Inner Light

CHAPTER 42

Agnes, Philadelphia, November 2008

Greetings and Salutations!

Remember how Lachlan used to say that to us? We imitated it, and felt so exalted.

Last night, elves came to me in my sleep, and informed me you are at the ready to hear from me. I don't know why it takes dreams to inform me of simple realities. I suppose because I never had full faith that anything can be simple. I have changed my mind about that.

So here I am, writing to you. It is a cold afternoon, the sky gray and yellow. I remember at this time of year going over to play with girls from school who lived out on farms in Devon or Paoli and how I loved crunching across the stiff brown meadow grass under a buttery sun. I make so many visits in memory these days. In some ways I like it more, as I can embellish.

But I plan to stick to the facts now. I want to take stock.

The big news is that we have a new president. He is Black, a first. I have always said I'd never see a woman president in my lifetime, and I won't. For a moment there seemed a chance, but this nation is built on race, and this world is built on sexism. I have been aware of it every minute of every day; like a dog I could smell it on the breeze. But all right. This new president seems promising.

I remember reading about a spiritual master who was asked by a disciple how to achieve enlightenment. The master said, "Drink when you are thirsty and eat when you are hungry." Know yourself. Don't overstep. Reach your arms out to the sides and as far as they can go. Make contact at that point. Go no further.

Boundaries. A three-syllable word that I finally understand. Boundaries are not property lines, after all.

Guess what? Maud convinced me it was time for Pauline Schulz to retire. My last novel in the series, *The Franklin Square Girls Talk to the Hand*, was published under the name Agnes Lee, and there was a stir of sorts about my real identity. Soon I will at long last be the subject of a *Paris Review* interview. I have no pearls to offer at this point, or opinions. Writing is waiting. That's the whole of it. If you sit in your chair not doing anything else for long enough, the answer will come. You do have to be in your chair, though, ready to write it down.

I am in my apartment on Rittenhouse Square. I rarely leave here anymore, except for long, slow walks. Thank God I am tall and still relatively upright, so people don't ask me if I need help. I carry a stick, to bop them with, in case they do. My schedule is as ever: rise, stretch, write, eat, write, eat, read, putter around, eat, read, bed. I save reading the paper for before dinner when I am drained and incapable of invention. Then the world is allowed in. Mrs. Blundt comes a few hours a day, and there's the extra room where she could stay over if need be, but I don't want that. I want to remember. I spend hours listening to lapping water and smelling mowed grass and watching the Perseid toss stars straight at Fellowship Point. I curl my hand into a fist and let Nan pull my fingers out straight again. I lie on the sofa with Star and look into his brown eyes and count his eyelashes. Maisie is here with me. I got her a harness so she can walk outside, but she's old now and content to lie on a cushion in the sun. I spend a great deal of time keeping her comfortable—the sun moves, and so must her cushion.

My family appears in my memories and I spend time with them. My puny brain can—finally—conceive of an afterlife. I imagine it as a swirling river of energy. Atoms split in the big bang wandering the universe seeking forever their other half to repair the split. A good idea I read once, and never forgot! I didn't have the opportunity to contribute a repair in this lifetime. I didn't couple with another. Though when I have gone over scenes of the past, I have found a moment with Virgil Reed that was the cusp of love. We were standing outside in the meadow looking up at the stars and he said my name. I heard him, but there was such a great distance between us, so many years and griefs, that I didn't answer in kind. Instead, I took it as a signal to seek the rudimentary kind of shelter—not the sublime. I feel regret about that. Things might have been different. The point, the real point is, there was that moment. I have come to see such chances, or graces as some might call them, as the complement to trying. Combine the two in the right proportions and you have a creation.

In the end I cannot know if Virgil Reed was my cosmic other half, or if he was a medicine that made me a bit healthier, or if he was as he seemed at first, a vagrant passing through. I never made love, or even had sex. I'm rather proud of that, to be honest. I am a woman uninterfered with. Or perhaps I don't fully understand myself.

I did have the singular experience and fulfillment of being wholly responsible for the well-being of other creatures. I was a steward, most ardently of Fellowship Point. All my life I thought about how to care for it, what Quaker values could be upheld there, how to maintain William Lee's vision. What would become of it after my death? The dilemma obsessed me. It must be preserved, which led to several years of meeting with land trusts and sorting through proposals. Then I was stymied by circumstances, mainly not being able to make the decision on my own. Finally, a grace—Nan came back to me, in the guise of Heidi Silver. Heidi was the third vote needed to break the Fellowship agreement, that ancient pact, and we did so.

The right thing to do had been staring at me all along. I looked at the clues every time I passed by the cases of artifacts in the glass room, or when I lay on the grass of the summer camp itself. I stared at it when I read the history of Maine, and when I practiced my personal religion of sisterhood with trees, flowers, birds, squirrels, rocks, and even snakes. I saw it when I disagreed with the Looses and their exploitative style of development. The final piece of the puzzle locked into place in my talks with Mary Mitchell, when we exchanged what it meant to us to live on Cape Deel. Mary's ancestors had come there for their summers, and the Sank was part of their world. They never considered that it was theirs in the sense that we think of property, as something we can take and leave. The land was a part of them.

I could say I felt the same way, and at some level I believe that to be true, but I can't separate myself entirely from my culture, my upbringing, my pride in being a Quaker and a Philadelphian, my childhood a few blocks away from Independence Hall and the Liberty Bell and my early familiarity with what had happened there.

We learned about Massasoit, the Wampanoag sachem (we loved that word), and his friendly dealings with the Pilgrims while he was at war with the Narragansett tribe. We learned about William Penn's fair dealings with the Lenape and other tribes in Pennsylvania, his insistence that they be paid fairly for land and his direction that in any dispute between Natives and "us" that

there be six representatives from each group to weigh justice in
the issue. We learned that Quakers aimed to live peaceably and
were opposed to slavery. Of course, information came my way
later about horrible methods used to acquire land in other parts
of the country, but I went on believing in equality and did my
best to be fair. Now I have been doing the reading and learning
more about the complexity of this country, the terrible events
that occurred and their present consequences, and as always that
a certain number of good people worked to defend or protect or
remonstrate or make peace along the way. In detailing the crimes
of history, we must never lose sight of the good people. The fact of
their existence is a reason to go on. But we must not let our faith
in them obscure what needs to be done to counter those who do
harm.

We did what we could to right the wrongs and to live lightly
and cause no harm. But that was all within the context of my
principles. I interpreted the rest of the world through the lens
of my belief in peace and respect. Only through Mary did I learn
that I had fallen short of my own values. Only when she told
me what an eagle was to her and her people did I feel my mind
expand enough to truly accept ways of life and practices I didn't
understand in my own logic. Above all, I grasped that Fellowship
Point *belonged* to Mary and the first peoples of Maine. They and the
land are one. A land trust was only a metaphor for a deeper truth.

All my life until then I had thought of myself as a steward
of Fellowship Point. In spite of my opinion that the concept of
private property had historically done a lot of damage, I loved
knowing it was mine. I have let that feeling go.

On October 10, 2006, all of Fellowship Point was quietly
transferred to a group of Wabanaki. I have since heard that they
plan to invite those interested in the languages, arts, and skills of
the all the indigenous peoples of Maine to come to the Point and

share knowledge with one another. Such a simple solution, and so obvious, but like all simplicity, it hid in plain sight.

Robert and Heidi moved to Deel Town but go down often to the Point, where Robert shares his knowledge of the plants and the nests and Heidi watches the children while their parents meet and study. Mary Mitchell is full of plans, including college. The graveyard will remain there and is open to relatives for visits. The bones belonged to the land, no matter who lives on its surface. Not my bones, though. I have decided to be cremated and have a handful of my ashes scattered in Franklin Square and in the water off Cape Deel. It was that or wedging myself next to Grace Lee at Christ Church. I have made peace with her, but enough is enough.

Robert will take care of that for me. It's not legal, but he'll manage.

Archie and Seela decamped to Monte Carlo. Yes, Monte Carlo, where they live among tax refugees from all over the world. Poetic justice, of the kind that will be settled in the beyond. Archie wrote me a letter of apology, which I accepted—easier with an ocean between us—so we are mildly in touch. Seela loves Monte Carlo. Can't say I'm shocked. I'm sure her diamonds are exercised regularly there. Is that too unforgiving of me? It can't be helped. I'd need twenty more years of wisdom and maturity to forgive Seela.

The Looses—who cares? But in the interest of sharing the news, they're fine. A new hotel off Cape Deel is under development.

I care about Maud. She and Clemmie are still in the Village, in an apartment now. We went through with the plan of me introducing her to my editor, but she didn't get a new job out of the connection. Maud had said all along that that was not how publishing worked. In the end David introduced her to a friend at another publisher and she is there now, aquiring and editing novels. I have been working on that memoir she wanted so badly, sending it back and forth to her for comments. We still wrangle over how much I should reveal, but I have come around to the idea that what I find shameful and devastating won't seem so to others. Who knows? Maybe it will be a book, or maybe it's my transitional object into the grave. Either way, it's a pleasure.

Sylvie moved to an apartment at Parker Ridge in Blue Hill. She seems content, despite there being "too many old people around."

I have no information about who is living in Leeward Cottage. True visions form in the depths of our souls in the locus of humility. I stepped aside, and that was that. It's not my business anymore. We put no stipulations on the transfer. My father always disdained wills that controlled descendants from beyond the grave, and I agree with him about that. It wasn't easy for me to give up control, but I wasn't alone in doing it, which helped. Now I am completely at peace with our decision. I have an open invitation to stay there, but I never will. Yes, it's too painful, for one thing. For another, I don't belong there, which is the exact opposite belief as I held all my life. Once seen, such a truth cannot be forgotten. Saul on the road to Damascus. I didn't see Jesus, but I got the message. Robert teases me about this apartment, which is also on Native American soil. It will be sold at my death and the money donated to a legal fund for poor Philadelphians. The city doesn't yet make enough brotherly love to be without need of aid.

I have continued to correspond and talk with Heidi, learning her past story a bit at a time. Her aunt renamed her after the main character in *Heidi*, the children's book, and secured her unruly hair in braids. I so regret that I took the report of her death at face value and didn't pursue it further.

I have also talked openly with Robert. For forty years I have feared what he thought after seeing me walk out of the Chalet in the dawn hour of that horrible morning. He must have figured out that Nan had been inside after the deaths. I was always worried that he thought I was helping him in life to secure his silence about those deaths. You know what he said when I brought it up? That he was grateful to me for saving Nan, and he always believed he'd be close with her again. He didn't even know that no one else knew I'd gone over there that morning. He was a child, with a child's interpretation of the events. It's awful what we do to ourselves by not talking openly.

So now I have filled you in, though perhaps you already know all of this and far more from where you are, which I'm sure is the best place if it is any place. Theo wrote me a full description of your last days at his house in Umbria. It was good that you finally went to visit him, and had that time with him and the M girls, who adored you. He wrote that when you saw the Giotto frescoes in the Basillica di San Francesco in Assissi you had a vision of your own. You saw a great white light enveloping all the people who'd gazed at the images over all the centuries and how they were kinder for at least a few minutes after leaving that place. "How Polly is that?" Theo wrote. Yes, it is you, always seeing the best. You saw me in that light, and I cannot begin to quantify the difference that made in my life. And I saw the same in you. Through you, I saw the best in Dick. He was high-minded and stuck by his principles even when that did him no good. I wish I had told you I had a better opinion of him than the one I routinely expressed, but I imagined I'd get to that on my deathbed, when you'd be holding my hand. But you died first, as you thought you would. "Peacefully in her sleep," Theo wrote, "during an afternoon nap in the hammock, after a plate of pasta." Good for you. A simple death. You earned it.

"She was speaking of you just before she drifted off," Theo wrote.

Was that Theo, being kind?

Or were you remembering my epitaph?

I loved someone.

Did you—dear friend—finally realize who it was?

Acknowledgments

My agent, Henry Dunow, read this manuscript in various forms and parts many times and offered excellent editorial advice. He believed in the book and remembered the characters over years of changes. It is a great solace to know another person is also keeping in mind a growing world and story.

Marysue Rucci, my editor at Scribner/Marysue Rucci Books, offered an enthusiastic response that was a monumental relief and inspiration. I had my doubts about the appeal of two old ladies in Maine, but she dispelled them in the most heartening possible way and gave me great notes through several drafts.

Jonathan Karp, Simon & Schuster CEO, offered crucial encouragement, first in the form of an extended contract and then with his enthusiasm for these pages and sage suggestions. His insights made the book better.

My family, Larry Dark and Asher Dark, both novelists themselves, support me in many ways, including making vegan dinners and reading and discussing sections of this manuscript and books in general. That they understand what I do is an extraordinary bonus to their being my favorite and most admired people.

Diane Goodman and Heather Upjohn were the earliest enthusiastic believers in this book and gave me confidence to keep going. I am grateful for the attention to part or all of these pages from Jo Ann Beard,

Wendy Owen, Lisa Gornick, Heidi Holst-Knudsen, Lee Phillips, Bonnie Friedman, Jessica Greenbaum, and Christina Baker Kline. Christina deserves further thanks for being good counsel and ever generous. Nancy Star and I meet regularly to discuss our progress and laugh at how lost we can feel along the way. All of this support means so much to me.

Rigoberto Gonzalez published an excerpt called "A Private River" in Ploughshares when he was a guest editor. That chapter doesn't appear in this book, and I am grateful it made it into the world on its own.

The Grove Street Gang, The Coven, and A.B.L.E. offer friendship and ongoing writing chat.

I have work I value deeply at Rutgers-Newark teaching in the MFA and the English department. Figuring out how to be helpful to my MFA students and discussing books and stories with them has taught me a great deal about fiction. My excellent colleagues are paragons of creativity, scholarship, and dedication.

I'd like to thank the following people who worked hard for this book to come into the world:

At Scribner, Nan Graham, Stuart Smith, Brian Belfiglio, Jaya Micelli, Katherine Monaghan, Brianna Yamashita, Zoey Cole, and Sasha Kobylinski.

At Simon & Schuster, Jackie Seow, Carly Loman, Samantha Hoback, Julia Prosser, Elizabeth Breeden, Zack Knoll, Brittany Adames, and Hana Park.

Thank you to Kate Lloyd at Kate Lloyd Literary.

Thank you to Jeffrey C. Ward for creating a map of a place that existed in my imagination.

VCCA, Yaddo, and Macdowell gave me support so valuable that it can't be measured. I always wish I were there.

I wrote this book over a number of years during summer breaks from teaching and did research as necessary along the way. The following books were of great help: *Changes in the Land* by William Cronon, *Women of the*

Dawn by Bunny McBride, *The Penobscot Dance of Resistance* by Pauleena Mac-Dougall, *Notes on a Lost Flute* by Kerry Hardy, *Maine's Visible Black History* by H. H. Price and Gerald E. Talbot, *A Quaker Book of Wisdom* by Robert Lawrence Smith, and *Birds of Maine* by Peter D. Vickery. Much of what I learned isn't explicitly reflected in the book, but I hope the story embodies the knowledge I gained from these readings and from other sources.

My animal and bird friends, indoors and out, sat with me through all the many hours it took to call my imaginings down to the page.

As a child I learned that I lived on land where indigenous peoples had lived for hundreds of years. I never stopped thinking about this and wondering what to do about it. The question found its way into this novel. I hope we all find a just answer.

About the Author

Alice Elliott Dark is the author of three earlier books of fiction, the novel *Think of England* and two collections of short stories, *In the Gloaming* and *Naked to the Waist*. Her work has appeared in, among others, *The New Yorker, Harper's, DoubleTake, The Literarian, The Best American Short Stories, The O. Henry Prize Stories, Ploughshares,* and *A Public Space.* "In the Gloaming," a short story, was chosen by John Updike for inclusion in *The Best American Stories of the Century* and was made into films by HBO and Trinity Playhouse. Her nonfiction reviews and essays have appeared in the *New York Times,* the *Washington Post,* and many anthologies. She is an associate professor at Rutgers-Newark in the MFA program and English department. Visit aliceelliottdark.com.